Unlawful Deeds

Unlawful Deeds

David S. Brody

toExcel

New York San Jose Lincoln Shanghai

UNLAWFUL DEEDS

Published by toExcel,
an imprint of iUniverse.com, Inc.

For information address:
iUniverse.com, Inc.
620 North 48th Street
Suite 201
Lincoln, NE 68504-3467
www.iUniverse.com

ISBN: 1-58348-623-2

Printed in the United States of America

To Kimberly,

*in whose hands words
become works of art,
for inspiring this book*

Contents

Prologue

[June, 1983]

An incessant chant: "Slumlord, slumlord, slumlord...."

Bruce bit his lip as the words assaulted Grandpa. He tasted his own blood, spit it onto the carpeted floor. He turned and glared at the activists. A few of them noticed the fire in his eyes and swallowed their taunts.

Grandpa struggled to be heard, his leathery skin flushed and pinkish. "If you'll just let me explain. Please listen. I treat my tenants well. Not one of them has any complaints. Some of them are here to speak on my behalf. Please listen to me. I am not a slumlord."

The hearing officer firmly pounded his gavel. "Quiet, please. Mr. Arrujo has the right to speak in his defense." His tone was matter-of-fact—the activists' job was to heckle the old man, his to make the request that they stop.

Bruce turned back to look at Grandpa, noticed the florescent lights reflecting off his sweaty forehead. He shouldn't have let the old man wear his wool suit.

Grandpa spoke again. "Now, if I may just explain the situation to you, you will see that I have not violated the Cambridge rent control laws. You see, my house has only three apartment units, not six as you claim. And since I live in the building, it is not subject to rent control."

The hearing officer interrupted. "We've been through this already, Mr. Arrujo. You also own the house next door. Under the terms of the rent control law, the two properties are combined and treated as a single six-unit building. And six-unit buildings are subject to rent control, regardless of whether you live there or not."

Grandpa pounded the wooded lectern with his fist. "But that makes no sense! The two homes are separated by a driveway, a yard and a fence. They are two separate buildings. Just look at them, look at these pictures." He stepped away from the podium and offered a stack of photographs to the hearing officer.

The young man held up his gavel to block the advance, while his other hand shielded his eyes. "I'm sorry, sir, but we will not revisit this point. The law is the law."

1

"But the law of Cambridge, Massachusetts can't change the laws of physics, can it? These are two separate buildings. Just open your eyes and look!" Bruce saw pockets of sweat seeping through Grandpa's shirt on either side of his tie. He looked around for some water.

The hearing officer stared past Grandpa at some spot behind him on the wall. "The only issue that remains is whether you have been charging your tenants more than the rent controlled rents for a six-unit apartment building. If you have no evidence on this point, then this hearing is over."

Bruce watched his grandfather's large frame shrink into the podium, then lean against it for support. The activists, too, saw it. Vibrancy evaporating under hot lights. They began their chant again: "Slumlord, slumlord, slumlord...."

Bruce had spent the last hour watching a roomful of pony-tailed leeches suck the blood from his grandfather. Enough. He stood and turned, facing the group of activists that filled the small hearing room around him. His voice cut through their rhythmic chant like a laser beam. "Shut the fuck up. Every one of you."

The room echoed in silence. Instinctively the activists sensed the danger in the room, smelled Bruce's ferocious aggression. They edged away from Bruce. He coiled and watched them, his powerful young body trembling. Daring the group to resume its heckling. Praying that just one of them would catcall or hiss or hoot. Seconds passed. Nothing.

A crash, splintering the silence. Bruce spun his head in time to see the lectern bounce once off the floor, then come to rest near the prone body of his grandfather.

Grandpa's eyes were closed. His tongue protruded from the corner of his mouth. His face was ashen. The wooden lectern lay next to him, box-like, its open side facing the heavens. Waiting for Grandpa.

Bruce kicked a chair aside, slid to his grandfather's side. He cradled the old man's head for a moment, then allowed himself to be pushed aside as a policewoman applied CPR. He held Grandpa's cold hand and sat on the floor, numb.

One of the activists snickered. Or maybe it was a nervous cough, or even a murmur of concern. But to Bruce, it sounded like a snicker. He leapt to his feet, bounded across the room and hurled himself into the group of hecklers.

There was no time to escape his attack.

And no defense against the savage blows thrown in righteous fury by a young man avenging the fact that he had been left alone in the world.

Sailing Into a Storm

1

[August 9, 1989]

Bruce stood tight against the urinal, leaning away from the stale breath of his panting companion. Droplets of urine splattered near his thighs.

"Hey, Lonnie, unless you want to hold it for me, give me some room here."

From behind the closed door of a nearby stall, a voice echoed. "I got a better idea. Beat it, Lonnie. Me and Bruce need to talk alone."

Bruce edged away from the urinal, gulped a fresh breath. He immediately recognized the voice from the stall. Gus, all 140 pounds of him, had finally resurfaced. Using his 240-pound voice.

Lonnie turned, searching for the source of the hostile command. "All right. As soon as I finish talking to Bruce about the criminal procedure question."

"Fuck you, buddy. I said get lost, or you'll be taking the rest of the bar exam with your head up your ass."

Lonnie looked at Bruce. Bruce nodded toward the door, and the young advocate scurried off. "Fine. I have better things to do than argue with a toilet stall." Bruce watched him go. Most lawyers, he had noticed, seemed to react the same way to a threat of physical confrontation: Get in the last word, then run away.

Bruce zipped up his fly and waited until the bathroom door swung closed. He turned toward the voice of his boyhood friend, spoke through clenched teeth. "Couldn't you have waited until I was alone?" He karate-kicked the other stall doors—they crashed open, echoed empty.

"Wait? I've been in here for almost an hour waiting for you, people shitting on either side of me. I almost passed out. What do they feed you guys in law school, anyway? Besides, that kid looked like he was attached to your shoulder. He wasn't leaving without you."

Bruce admitted to himself that Gus was right—Lonnie had been breathing on Bruce during the entire lunch break and was probably going to keep it up right up until the time the bar exam proctor called for silence. "And how are you so sure he wasn't a cop?"

"A cop? Come on, the kid was a pimply little Barney with glasses. Even the cops have more pride than that."

"And you're so sure he won't blab about me having strange meetings in bathrooms? You're an idiot, Gus."

"Hey, I took a calculated risk, you know? Every meeting has some risks. And you know, Bruce, it's not like you're on the Ten Most Wanted list. I don't think the cops stay awake at night trying to figure out ways to catch Bruce Arrujo, two-bit art thief."

Bruce looked at his watch. Only a few minutes before the afternoon test session began. He hated to let Gus think he was willing to accept such recklessness, but he was anxious to learn why Gus wanted to meet. He was never happy to see Gus, but at least this time Gus might be carrying a wadded-up solution to Bruce's money problems. The thing about dealing with Gus was that it was always like grabbing a rattler by the neck in hopes of extracting some venom for an antidote. "Well, stay in there in case somebody else walks in. You should feel right at home."

"Consider me attached to the seat. It's not so bad in here. Sort of like a jail cell, you know? By the way, how did that Lonnie kid know you were such an expert on criminal law?"

Bruce looked around again to make sure they were still alone. "Fuck you, Gus. You never did learn when to keep your mouth shut. But it's funny that it reminds you of a jail cell. To me, you stuck in there makes me think of a six-foot wooden box. So you better hope I don't end up in any jail cell, know what I mean? Now what do you want?"

"I wanted to talk about the bar exam. What about that tricky contracts question, huh? No way the hospital should have to pay for the x-ray machine."

Bruce tried not to let Gus surprise him, but even his own superior intellect could not anticipate Gus' bursts of offbeat behavior. "You were in there taking the fucking exam with us?"

Bruce could picture the grin on Gus' freckled face as he answered. Sort of like the time he told Bruce he had hidden a movie camera in the girls' locker room. "All morning. How else do you think I got in here? They've got security guards at the door. What is that, to keep you geeks from fleeing in fear halfway through? 'Oh, no. It's too hard. I'm not going to be a lawyer.' But I figured the crap room during the lunch break of the bar exam would be a pretty safe place to talk to you. I mean, it's like setting up a meeting in a shark tank, all you little lawyers running around. I'll tell you one thing, though, counselor. I'm not sticking around for the afternoon session. Even though the test didn't seem that tough, it sure is boring shit."

Bruce walked over to the sink, cleaned himself up. Only Gus would think to sign up for the bar exam as a cover for a meeting. There were a hundred easier ways to set up a safe—or safer—meeting. But for Gus life was one never-ending opportunity to re-invent himself, and if he could both meet secretly with Bruce and play lawyer for a day, well, so much the better. It was what made Gus so successful. And so dangerous. "You're right, the test's pretty easy. Now what do you want?"

"First of all, I'm glad you're handling the test all right. I was going to pull the fire alarm for you on my way out if you were having too much trouble—they probably would have canceled the test and made you come back next week or something. Give you more time to study."

Bruce braced for bad news—he knew Gus liked to shield himself from Bruce's anger by reminding him that he knew where Bruce's skeletons were buried. And Gus had been there when Bruce pulled the fire alarm during a college exam because he was too hung over to write coherently. "Get to the point, Gus."

"Bad news. I can't unload the Manet. They're watching me, and I'm not going to risk flying to Hong Kong right now just to save your ass."

"Shit, Gus, you know I need cash. And our deal is that it's your job to move the paintings." Bruce moved his athletic frame a step closer to Gus' stall and clenched his fists, hoping that Gus would see the menacing movement through a crack in the door. He was counting on that money. He didn't start work for another month, and his first paycheck wouldn't be until two weeks after that. Before then he needed to catch up on his rent, get current on his credit cards, and buy a couple of suits. He knew that the firm ran credit checks on incoming employees—the last thing he needed was for the firm's partners to view him as a spendthrift. He remembered one of the senior partners lecturing him during his final interview, speaking slowly so Gus would be sure not to miss the word play: "We tolerate neither loose cannons nor loose canons, young man." If the old geezer only knew.

But even more crucial was the $5,000 he owed to a loan shark. If his landlord evicted him, he could live in his car for a few weeks and shower at the firm, or even move back home with his parents. But the loan shark would break his thumbs. Or worse. Bruce was only a week late, and he was already sporting a couple of cracked ribs, courtesy of some brass knuckles, as a gentle reminder that payment was not discretionary.

From inside the stall, Gus flinched involuntarily as Bruce moved closer. He knew what Bruce's fists could do to a man's face, even though he doubted Bruce would risk a scene with the exam set to re-start. "Sorry, Bruce. I really am. But it doesn't do either of us any good if I get nabbed. You may be broke now, but at least you're not in jail."

Again a reference to jail, and again Bruce heard Gus' implicit threat to squeal if he got caught. Bruce had long ago begun the process of divorcing himself from Gus, but he was stuck with him as a partner—for better or worse, as it were—until the Manet was sold. And probably for a while after. "So where's the painting?" He knew that the fact that he was asking the question was a tacit acknowledgment that he had lost this particular battle with Gus—he had no need to know the painting's location unless he was planning on retrieving it himself.

"Same place it's been for the past five years. What I was thinking was that you could fly to Hong Kong yourself."

"You're an asshole, Gus. You know that's your job. In fact, other than buying coffee and donuts, that's your only job."

Gus ignored the jab. He was just happy Bruce hadn't kicked in the stall door. "And I'll do it, I told you, just not right now. If you want the money right away, you go to Hong Kong. I can set it up with my guy there, he's ready to buy. Otherwise, just wait a few months. Look, I sold the other paintings like I said I would—they paid for your fancy law school. But I need to lay low right now."

Bruce thought back over the past few months. He couldn't remember a single heist that fit Gus' m.o. So why was Gus trying to keep a low profile? It wasn't like him to be particularly risk-averse. "You're bullshitting me, Gus. You want to lay low because you got something planned, right?"

Gus and Bruce had known each other since the second grade. Bruce had always been the dominant partner—stronger, smarter, better looking, more popular. Almost twenty years later, Gus still craved Bruce's respect, even though he knew Bruce wanted nothing further to do with him. He also knew Bruce would never rat on him, because Gus could simply return the favor. "Yeah, you're right. I got something planned for this winter. Gardner Museum. They got great stuff—Vermeer, Rembrandt, Degas—and shitty security. They use friggin' art students as security guards. But I can't risk a flight to Hong Kong before that. Even if they don't catch me selling the Manet, it'll just get 'em curious about what I've got planned—you know, why fly to Hong Kong unless something's up? But hey, you want to come out of retirement? I could use your help at the Gardner."

"Fuck you, Gus." It came out with a sharp edge.

"Oh, that's right, you're gonna be a lawyer now. Like that's any better than stealing art. And I bet you've got some scam in mind, some kind of inside job at that fancy law firm of yours." Bruce didn't respond. "Am I right? I mean, I can't see you pushing paper for the next forty years. And it's not like you're Mr. Truth-Justice-and-the-American-Way."

It occurred to Bruce that the biggest problem with old friends was that they remembered too much of your past to be fooled by your present. Gus knew Bruce first and last as a thief, law degree or not, and there wasn't much sense in pretending otherwise. "Maybe you are and maybe you aren't, Gus. But you know the difference between you and me? I don't steal for the fun of it like you do. You're addicted to the high, you love the danger. I just want the money. Once I make my million, I'l' stop. That's why I'll never get caught, and someday you will."

"Well, big shot, you better hope you're right. Because my gut says you got no choice but to hop on that plane to Hong Kong." He flipped Bruce a key over the stall door. "Painting's in the same spot. I'll expect my cut when you get back."

2

[August 12, 1989]

Shelby still couldn't believe how many jerks there were in law school. Most of her classmates had been pretty difficult for Shelby to take when they had arrived at Harvard two years earlier—pompous, self-absorbed, narrow-minded. But now that they were on the verge of graduation, they had fully devolved. Into reptiles. What was the definition of a tragedy? A bus full of lawyers going over a cliff with an empty seat.

Worse yet, she had come to the sudden realization that her current boyfriend, Barry, also deserved a seat on that bus. She had fallen for him because, in addition to being caring and intelligent and passionate and fun loving, he had been an idealist. He had honestly believed in that whole Camelot thing from the Kennedy era that was still popular in Boston and, particularly, at Harvard. Instead of just criticizing the legal and political system, Barry wanted to work to fix it.

Barry had written his college thesis on the problems of modern-day democracy. Late one night, after studying constitutional law with two other students, he had offered to let Shelby read it. Shelby had been both amazed at the clarity of his analysis and stunned that he had actually proposed a solution that made sense. Barry's thesis was simple—democracy on a national level had simply become too large to be effective. Democracy still worked on the local level—for example, citizens of a small town debating the need for a new elementary school. However, in a country of over 250 million people, the voice of any one citizen was simply too small to make a difference. Shelby remembered Barry's next sentence verbatim: "When no one citizen can make a difference, all citizens adopt an attitude of indifference."

Barry's proposed solution had been to localize government as much as possible. He believed that government should still take an active role in society, but that it should be government at the local rather than federal level. It was an interesting combination of the Camelot-like "good government" beliefs and the Reagan administration's efforts to downsize the federal bureaucracy.

The clarity of the argument had won Shelby's mind, and the passion and idealism with which it had been written had gone a long way toward winning her heart.

Unfortunately, the bright-eyed Barry who had written that thesis and the bleary-eyed Barry who was now stretched out on Shelby's couch shared nothing in common except shoe size. Barry had spent the summer working at a law firm in Washington, D.C., and Shelby had noticed a dramatic change in his personality. It was as if his values and ideals had become fluid and gaseous, instead of firm and solid. He would now argue any side of any subject, regardless of merit. And he seemed to enjoy it—argument as an intramural sport. In fact, he was half-asleep on Shelby's couch now because he had been up all night composing a letter to the editor on behalf of one of his employer's construction clients— a letter that argued that highway projects should be decided at the federal rather than local level. It was a position completely contrary to the crux of his college thesis.

Shelby had just proofread the letter for Barry. She hoped she wasn't overreacting, and she didn't give a damn about highway projects, but she couldn't stop her eyes from moistening as she read the persuasive words of the man she once thought she loved. She dropped to her knees in front of the couch.

"Barry, listen to me very carefully. Please just listen. I don't know who you are anymore. But I know what you have become—a mouthpiece. You have always had wonderful intellectual and analytical skills, and now law school has molded you into a great advocate. But where is your integrity?" Shelby could sense that Barry's anger was rising, and she laid her hand on his shoulder to quiet him. "Please, just listen. I've been thinking about this a lot. Just because you can win an argument doesn't mean you should win the argument. You're like a man with a gun—just because you have the tools to shoot someone doesn't make it right to pull the trigger. It's the same with advocacy. You have the tools to win any argument—you're brilliant and analytical and well trained. But does that mean you should use those tools indiscriminately? I thought you were different. I thought you'd first decide which arguments were worth winning, and only then would you go off and win them. But, lately, it seems like you'll argue for anything, right or wrong."

Barry was silent for a moment. Shelby could see that her words reached him, but only barely so. "Look, Shelby, that's just the way the system works. Each side hires a lawyer, and each lawyer argues as well as he can for his client. It's not the lawyer's decision whether to make the argument or not; his job is just to be an advocate. It's up to the judge or jury to decide what's right or wrong, not the lawyer."

Shelby rolled away from him and sat with her legs crossed in front of her. "No! That's not right! You can't simply abdicate responsibility like that."

"Look, Shelby, we're only talking about a highway project here. I know you're sensitive about it, but not everything relates back to your family's death." He paused for a split second. "At least it doesn't for me."

Shelby fought the urge to slap him. He knew he was losing the argument, so he hit her with a low blow. The ultimate advocate—win the argument, no matter what the cost. "You know what, Barry? You're right. Everything does relate back to that for me. I happen to think it's wrong that some asshole can polish off a pitcher of martinis, stagger into his BMW, smash into a car full of people at a tollbooth, and get acquitted because he can afford a team of high-priced lawyers who concoct some story about Chinese food and Listerine causing his high breathalyzer test. I happen to think that a system that allows that kind of result needs to be changed, not bought into."

"I don't know why you're being so emotional about this. I'm not the lawyer who got the guy acquitted."

"No, Barry, you're not. But you'll get another scumbag out of trouble some-day, and not lose a minute's sleep over it. Maybe it'll be some corporation that dumped toxic chemicals into a river, or some bank executive who lined his own pockets. But you'll be the mouthpiece, you'll be the hired gun. You've sold out, Barry. You're not the person I fell in love with."

"Come on Shelby, calm down. I really think you're jumping to conclusions. You're not thinking clearly."

Shelby hung her head for a moment, took a deep breath, then stood. "This is not a debate, Barry. Your advocacy skills aren't going to make me fall back in love with you." She walked toward the door, grabbed her keys. "I'll be back in an hour. I think it'd be best if you were gone."

*   *   *

Bruce drove up the coast, the Boston skyline now only a hedge line in his rearview mirror. On his right the Atlantic churned, slowly calming itself after an August storm. To his left, Marblehead—rocky, stable, unyielding in the face of thousands of Atlantic assaults. Where the stormy sea and the cragged coast met, a score of sailing boats frolicked, harnessing the passion of the Atlantic, skimming across the surface of the sea, mocking both the cumbersome continent and the fuming ocean.

Since Bruce was a boy, his grandfather had preached to him that life was no more complicated than this coastline. Many people were the sea—passionate and creative, but temperamental and unfocussed. Many more were content to be the land mass—orderly and stable, but rigid and common. Only a few were the sailboats.

Bruce looked out over the harbor, his eyes resting on a small blue Sunfish gallantly bucking its way over the swells and into the wind. He recalled a time in his childhood when a similar sail had abruptly ended—a renegade blast of wind had smashed into the backside of his sail, sweeping him into the spring sea. He could still taste the sea deep in his lungs, still remember the power of the ocean as it swallowed him up and then spit him out. He had been lucky that day—he had been able to stagger home with only a gashed knee and a mild concussion. And a lifelong respect for how delicately balanced the sailing ship was between the continent and the sea: a bit too much continent, and the boat would run aground; too much ocean, and it would be swamped.

That was Bruce now—swamped by too much ocean, too much emotion. It was as if he had expended all his intellectual energy on the bar exam, and all that was left inside him was emotion.

But he had a decision to make, and it wouldn't wait. Should he fly to Hong Kong?

Bruce parked at a secluded beach, kicked off his shoes and stood ankle-deep in the warm sand. Grandpa had made a decision based solely on emotion once—the decision to fight the Rent Board rather than simply pay a fine and be done with it. His pride had killed him.

Bruce listened to the sea crash ashore and watched the winds scatter the sand—somewhere in that sea and that sand he had scattered Grandpa's ashes. He closed his eyes and the ashes spoke to him, as Grandpa had while he lay dying in his hospital bed with Bruce by his side. *Don't let the ocean control you the way it did me, Brucie. The smart thing would have been just to pay the fine and get on with my life. I've been acting out of anger and pride, but instead of admitting it to myself, I tried to justify my actions with some fancy words like 'justice' and 'principles'—like that somehow makes my behavior rational. Don't lie to yourself, my boy: anger is anger, fear is fear, passion is passion. They're part of you, and they can give you strength, but they're not rational, and they don't make you any smarter. They're part of your ocean side—make sure you understand that, and make sure they stay off the land.*

Bruce reflected. *Make sure they stay off the land.* Maybe that was his problem. Had some of his emotions oozed across the divider in his brain and short-circuited his intellect?

He slipped out of his tennis shirt and jogged toward the foaming surf. He covered the distance quickly, his long strides propelling him faster and faster as the sand hardened and his traction increased. He launched himself headfirst into a crashing wave, knifed through the wall of water with two strong stokes, and stood.

He raised his chin to keep his mouth above the water line, relishing the familiar power and passion of the sea, and braced himself for the next tidal assault. It hit hard, lifting him up, hurling him shoreward. He re-gained his feet and dug his toes into the sand, bracing for the next breaker, his nipples tingling and hardening as a cool breeze stroked them. He closed his eyes and concentrated, imagining his feet as pylons buried deep into the earth, through sand and muck and clay and rock. The Atlantic crashed into him again, lifting his heels, fighting to rip his curled toes off of the ocean floor, finally abandoning the effort in a momentary truce. Bruce dropped back on his heels, whooped in delight, and readied himself for the next caressing attack.

He stood firm that way for another twenty waves, each wave crashing into him with powerful, intoxicating fury, each wave unable to move him. He remembered Grandpa's words: *The sea should empower you, not overpower you.*

Legs quivering, he staggered out of the ocean and dropped to the sand in the faded twilight. He could see inside himself now.

Fear had swamped his intellect. Fear had left his brain unwilling to reach the obvious conclusion: that he had no choice but to try to sell the painting. He pictured himself staggering into the office on his first day of work—homeless, broken-thumbed, Grandpa's old suit stretched tightly across his shoulders. No good.

Bruce admitted to himself that his fear was justified. If he got caught, he ran the risk of going to jail. And his photographic memory wouldn't let him forget the words of a poem he had read once, written by an inmate:

Sneering guards swing big black sticks;
Leering 'mates point to quivering dicks;
Searing pain from unseen kicks;
Fearing that death is part of the mix.

He shook the visions from his head.

And even if he got lucky and avoided jail time, he could kiss his law career good-bye. He thought back over the past three years of law school—a dingy basement apartment, 40-hour workweeks molded around his class and study schedule, condescending law professors, back-stabbing classmates. And finally a job offer from Boston's largest firm. It was a lot to risk, and he was afraid to lose. Simple as that.

But remove the fear and the decision really was an easy one—go sell the painting.

He took a deep breath and exhaled slowly. Some clarity, finally. What else would Grandpa say? He would agree that fear alone was no reason not to go sell the painting, but he would also point out that fear was a warning sign. Its role was to ensure that Bruce moved cautiously: Was there a less risky alternative? Could he sell the painting without flying to Hong Kong? *Think, damn it.*

Could he sell the painting locally? No reputable dealer or collector would buy a painting that was known to be stolen. No, the only market for such a well-known painting was abroad—a wealthy Asian collector or some Soviet bloc or Third World leader. And no foreigner wanted to risk flying to the U.S. to make the purchase because the laws were too strict. Dead end.

Could he put the painting up as collateral for an extension and advance on his loan? Doubtful. The loan shark wouldn't want—or know how—to handle that kind of collateral. Even worse, it exposed Bruce to threats of future black-mail—a single anonymous phone call to the cops could land him in jail. Bruce preferred a one-time risk over the threat of a lifetime of extortion.

Could he force Gus to lend him the money? Not likely. Gus' idea of savings was to leave a roach in the ashtray for tomorrow. And even if Gus had any money, Bruce's increasing hostility toward him made it doubtful that Gus would do him the favor.

That was it, then. He had no choice. Hong Kong or bust. He had to have the money, he had to sell the painting to get it, and Hong Kong was the best place to make the sale. Any risk-reward analysis was therefore merely academic—he had to fly no matter what the risks. Grandpa had said that, sometimes, you just have to sail into the storm and hope for the best. Plot the most careful course, trim your sails, and hope you get lucky.

He walked back to his car and drove to a pay phone. He called a travel agent and, using the last of his assets—frequent flyer miles, a vestige of his jet-setting college years—purchased a round-trip ticket to Hong Kong.

He became calmly reflective. In the past, he had been Bruce Arrujo, art thief. In the future, if all went well, he would be Bruce Arrujo, attorney-at-law in Boston's premier law firm. In the present, he was Bruce Arrujo, one flight with a stolen painting away from bridging that gap. Grandpa, who respected the lawyer the same way the sailor respected the shark, would have called it a journey beginning with the thievery of art and ending with the art of thievery.

3

[August 13, 1989]

Charese stared at the note, stunned. Red ink on cream-colored paper. Soft flesh bloodied by rabid, vicious words.

After 12 years, Roberge was leaving. To marry a woman. A real, biological, no-penis-at-time-of-birth woman.

Charese screamed, a scream that began deep within her and forced its way through her throat and out her mouth. A symphony of neighborhood dogs barked in response. Her neighbor in the apartment below banged on the ceiling. She was totally alone.

The tears flowed down her cheeks, a salty stream of familiar doubts and regrets. It was one thing to change her name from Charles to Charese, to dress in women's clothing, to attend Roberge's family gatherings posing as his girl-friend. But to agree to a sex change operation just to accommodate his inability to resolve his own sexuality confusion? She had always feared that she had gone too far, had become too dependent on a man who fell in love with her when she was a man but then decided he wanted her to become a woman. Now she was stuck—after years of hormone treatments, and only three weeks away from her operation, she was no longer male but not yet female. And for what? For a man who had decided to marry another woman, probably some preppy college girl with freckles and a closet full of tennis sneakers.

What would she do? What could she do? She had no real friends in Boston and hadn't worked in eight years. She looked in the mirror and saw what she saw—a 38-year old fag wearing a dress who had begun to grow breasts and lose facial hair. She had become the cliché dependent housewife, yet she was neither woman nor wife. Roberge had isolated her, her family had long since disowned her and her life-style, and she had neither marketable skills nor money of her own. All she had was Roberge and the ability to use her tongue and mouth and teeth to give a man exquisite pleasure. And now Roberge was gone.

4

[August 21, 1989]

It was late August, and Pierre couldn't understand why the phones weren't ringing. Normally August for him was a sprint—rent an apartment, broker the sale of a condominium, locate an investment property for a wealthy client. The routine had been the same since the early 1980s: College students moved out of the dorms, where they competed for apartments with Boston's burgeoning Yuppie population. This competition drove up the prices of real estate across the city by as much as 30 percent per year, which resulted in even further demand as otherwise risk-averse investors entered the market in search of these "pig profits". And everything was triggered by the school-year return of students on September 1, which was why Pierre usually earned almost half of his yearly sales and rental commissions in August alone.

This price appreciation made perfect sense to Pierre. Boston possessed a thriving economy, leading the nation in areas such as high tech, health care, education, and finance. But housing supply was a limited commodity in Boston, both for geographic and political reasons. The Atlantic Ocean prevented the growth of the city in all but a westerly direction, and the desire of Boston's political leaders to preserve the historic architecture of its old neighborhoods effectively blocked any significant new construction in the residential areas of the city. It was a simple case of demand growing and supply remaining fixed, and Pierre, though without any formal training in economics, was astute enough to understand what happened to prices during this kind of market imbalance.

Just as he was astute enough to recognize the advantages of not Anglosizing his name by changing it to Peter—there was a certain European snob appeal among many Bostonians, so why not take advantage of a name like Pierre Prefontaine? Even if he was a third generation American, and even if his grandfather came not from a boutique in Paris but from a factory in Quebec.

But this year it didn't matter if he called himself Donald Trump—the phones simply weren't ringing. Pierre sensed that there was a fundamental change taking place in the real estate market. Landlords who were accustomed to raising rents by 10 percent each year were finding it difficult to fill the apartments even at last year's rates. Pierre was actually getting calls from tenants he had found apartments for the previous year asking if he knew of anything cheaper—and in many cases, he did. Parents who would normally be desperately calling him looking for a condominium to buy for little Suzy so that she would have a place to live come September 1 were silent this year, presumably off vacationing on the Cape or in Maine while Suzy talked her landlord into paying for a cable hook-up. And investors had largely abandoned the market, leading to the farcical scene Pierre had witnessed earlier in the week. It had bothered Pierre then, and it continued to gnaw on him as he reflected on it during his distressingly inactive day.

*　　　　　*　　　　　*

He had received a call from a well-known player in the real estate market, a man whom the press had proclaimed the "Baron of the Brownstones" because of the huge number of brownstone apartment buildings he had purchased and then converted to condominiums. The Baron had amassed a small fortune—he estimated his net worth at $3 million, most of which he had re-invested in real estate—by purchasing 1920s vintage apartment buildings in working class neighborhoods of Boston and converting them to condominiums. The conversion process itself took about one week—a few buckets of paint, a new intercom system and, voila, instant condominiums. It was a far cry from the genesis of the condominium concept—ritzy oceanfront high rises in southern Florida—but the Baron had had no trouble selling these condominium units to investors speculating in the booming real estate market. In fact, demand was so high for these units that it was not uncommon for the Baron to double his money in a period of a few months.

In any event, the Baron had telephoned Pierre to ask him if he had any clients who might be interested in purchasing any of the Baron's condo units in Brighton, a neighborhood of Boston populated predominantly by college students and recent graduates. The neighborhood bordered Brookline, where Pierre's office was located, and he did much of his business there. "I just closed last week and I'm starting to fix 'em up right away."

"You mean full renovation—new systems, updated kitchens and baths?"

"No, no, none of that fancy stuff. You know, fresh paint to cover up the smell of the cockroaches and cigarette smoke. Maybe a few bucks into the foyer so it looks okay."

Pierre had agreed to go look at the units and meet with the Baron, partly because he had no other appointments scheduled that afternoon, but more because it was so out of character for the Baron to be calling a lowly broker in hopes of making a sale. When Pierre arrived a few minutes early to scout out the building by himself, the Baron was already there, seated in a canvas director's chair in a vacant first-floor apartment, a rectangular folding table separating him from a group of eight or nine other men seated in folding chairs opposite him.

The Baron was a burly middle-aged man with an orange-glow tan and wavy dark hair pulled back into a ponytail. He wore a shimmering Italian-cut silk suit, and Pierre could see that he was acutely aware that the paint dust floating in the air was coating the suit with a white film. Every few seconds, he wiped his pant leg or his lapel with a handkerchief, trying to keep it clean. The men sitting across from him were apparently members of a painting or construction crew, their clothes and hair speckled with spackle and white paint. The men, eating sandwiches and drinking Pepsis, were on their lunch break, and they were listening with varying degrees of attentiveness to the Baron as he gave them a quick lesson in the joyous profitability of owning real estate. Pierre stood in the doorway and listened, careful not to brush up against the still-sticky paint on the door frame.

"Now, this here building you guys are painting, there are 36 units. They're all one-bedrooms. I'm selling 'em for $80,000 each. I've already sold three. Here's how it works, so listen up." The Baron perspired in the August heat, and his delivery lacked much of the passion Pierre would have expected from an aristocratic mouthpiece. Then again, Pierre was surprised to see the wealthy Baron peddling units to his painting crew in a dusty Brighton apartment at all.

"You guys can each buy one, and it won't cost you a penny. Did you hear me? Not a penny. I've got a bank that will give you a mortgage for $60,000. I'll lend you the other twenty grand and pay the closing costs. You'll own the unit, with the tenant already in place, and all you have to do is sit back and collect the rent. In a couple of years, the thing will be worth $120,000 easy and you can sell it and put $40,000 in profit in your pocket." The Baron paused here for effect, knowing that $40,000 was two years' pay for most of these guys, and brushed off his suit. "Of course, it might be worth even more than $120,000—who knows? Also, anybody that refers a buddy to me who buys a unit gets a grand in cash. Any questions?"

A hand went up, attached to a middle-aged man with thick glasses. The Baron nodded to him. He spoke slowly, struggling in a thick Russian accent. "Mr. Napolitano, excuse me. I come to this country only this winter. I have not any money. A bank will lend to me all this sixty thousand dollars?" Pierre had noticed more and more Russian immigrants in the area. Many were engineers or doctors by trade, but were working here in construction or as other laborers. Many he had met were saving, almost obsessively, to buy real estate.

The Baron was nodding impatiently even before the Russian finished asking the question. "I've got it worked out. As long as you haven't gone bankrupt, you're okay. The bank has a special program—it doesn't matter how much money you make. All that matters is that you make a $20,000 down payment— which I'm going to lend to you—and that an appraiser agrees the property is worth the $80,000 purchase price." Pierre smiled to himself—you could get an appraiser to agree to anything these days. It was how the system worked. If the appraiser gave too low an appraisal, it would kill the deal and the loan officer, whose salary was dependent on the number of new loans generated, would be upset. The next time around, the loan officer would hire a different, more "friendly", appraiser. Pierre always thought it a rather incestuous relationship, but that's the way it was.

The Russian man spoke again. "How do we know the rents will be big enough to pay the bank and other costs every month?"

The Baron sighed patiently, as if he understood the difficulty children have with simple arithmetic. He passed out a single piece of paper, heavy bond with three-color graphics. "This here sheet of paper shows the rents for the last three years and the rents projected by my accountants for the next three years. It also shows the mortgage payments, property taxes and condo fees for these units. The interest rate starts out low, because this is an adjustable mortgage. By the time the interest rates go up, the rents will be higher to pay the difference. You'll always make money." Pierre couldn't see the figures, but it didn't take a rocket scientist to see that the Baron—with the help of his accountants, plural—was projecting that future rents would increase at the same 10 to 15 percent yearly pace as they had over the past three years.

Pierre knew better, and he was sure the Baron knew better, too. Did the workers? When the meeting had broken up, Pierre followed one of the crew outside, sat with him on the cement step.

"What did you think of the Baron's sales pitch?"

The man eyed Pierre cautiously, but Pierre had one of those faces that didn't threaten—round and soft, with large brown eyes and an easy smile. "Look, I've been working for the scumbag for three years. But I've seen him make a ton of money, and so have a lot of his people. I'm not saying it's right, you know, but that's the game."

"Are you gonna buy any condos?"

"Probably—I've already got two. And I put six of my buddies into deals, too."

"Making any money?"

"Not yet, other than the six grand for lining up my buddies. But what do I care?" He took a deep drag on his cigarette. "Ever been to Atlantic City?" Pierre nodded. "See, I'm playing with the house's money—the bank gave me the mortgage and the Baron gave me the down payment. I got no money in. If property values go up, I make a nice profit. If not, I collect the rents for a few months until the bank gets around to foreclosing—maybe make five or ten grand per unit in the meantime. Then I'll just walk away. Let 'em chase me if they want—can't get blood from a stone, you know? Same deal for my buddies."

"Sounds like a pretty good deal. Or at least a good bet. What about your credit getting ruined?"

He gave a short laugh. "What do I care? I never had credit before, so what I am losing? Besides, my old lady's got a credit card if we need it."

Pierre had heard enough. He had thanked the man for his time and walked toward his car. He wiped the paint dust and sweat off his face with a handkerchief, started to head back to his office, and instead went home to take a shower.

*   *   *

The scene had amazed Pierre—the sight of the Baron hawking condos to his painting crew during their lunch hour kept replaying in his mind. What had happened to the real estate market as he knew it? He thought back over the sales he had made over the past six years—sales to doctors and professors and engineers and bond traders, deals negotiated in downtown office towers and four-star restaurants. Had the market come to this? Were these guys the only buyers left? He remembered a story he heard once about Joseph Kennedy, patriarch of the famous political family, who had sold all of his stock just days before the 1929 stock market crash. When asked why, Kennedy was said to have told the story of a shoeshine boy complaining to Kennedy that his stock portfolio had been underperforming the rest of the market. Where would additional demand come from, Kennedy had wondered, when even the shoeshine boy owned a stock portfolio? Kennedy reasoned that without new demand to buy in the future, smart money should sell in the present.

Has that happened here? Has this market maxed out on the demand side? Was there anyone left who didn't already own real estate in Boston? And if that was the case, what did it mean?

The sound of the phones not ringing echoed off the walls in Pierre's office.

5

[August 22, 1989]

Pierre tossed and turned all night. By morning, though bleary-eyed, he thought he had a clearer view of things.

He had always been an independent thinker, and had realized after his first year of college that the orthodoxy of the classroom served him poorly. He was far more interested, for example, in driving to Washington to watch Congress in session than he was in reading a political science textbook. Similarly, the years he spent hanging around, then working, in his parents' real estate brokerage office gave him an almost intuitive sense of how the real estate market ebbed and flowed. So while he was the first to admit that the absence of a college degree put him at a professional disadvantage at times, he also had learned that his gut was a far better gauge of the psychology of the market than was the statistical data being put forth in the popular press.

In this case, the press was reporting that the market had slowed and that further price appreciation would be modest or even negligible. But the press was just echoing the words of the real estate industry spokespeople, many of whom, Pierre knew, hadn't even been around for the last recession and wouldn't know what a bust looked like if they fell into one. This theory of flat prices was based on traditional economic models—prices would become stable at the point where supply and demand had reached an equilibrium. Under this theory, the market had appreciated to the present point of equilibrium, and prices would now remain fairly constant.

But Pierre's experience with the boom and bust cycles of the real estate market told him that the market rarely behaved in a predictable fashion. Unlike the decision whether to buy a new television set or even a new car, the decision to buy a new home was largely an emotional one. As a result, Pierre discounted any market analysis based on economic models. Instead, Pierre viewed the market metaphorically. The market had been flying high, but Pierre's gut told him its engine was now stalling. Like an airplane, a market at this altitude would descend once it lost forward momentum. At best, it would glide slowly and steadily downward. At worst, it would spiral to the ground in a fiery mass of destruction.

It was only 5:30, and Pierre tiptoed out of the bedroom. He could hear Valerie beginning to stir, and he scooped her up, brought her into the kitchen, and warmed up a bottle of formula. She drank greedily, pausing only to give her daddy an occasional milky smile. When she finished, he quickly changed her diaper—what an expert he had become in only eight months. Maybe they would make it an Olympic sport. He brought her back to the living room and sat on the couch. She grabbed his nose with her little fingers—poking and pulling and twisting—as he watched the sun rise over the trees across the street from their condominium.

It was almost eight o'clock when Carla finally came shuffling into the living room, wearing only one of Pierre's T-shirts. Pierre was physically fit but not large, and Carla's breasts swelled under the cotton. "Wow. I feel drugged. I haven't slept this late in months, and my body isn't sure how to handle it." She leaned over and kissed Pierre on the mouth, lingering for a second before lifting Valerie off of his lap.

Pierre smiled up at her, gave his daily thanks to the gods of love. Average Joes like him weren't supposed to marry women like Carla. "Are you complaining?"

"No, not at all. Thanks for letting me sleep. It was glorious, but now that I remember what it's like, I want more."

"Actually, I'm glad you're awake. There's something I want to bounce off you. But first, give me back my baby—you can't just come in here like some conquering warrior and grab all the village treasures."

"Tough luck. You had her all morning—I need my huggles. What did you want to talk about?"

He described his encounter with the Baron and his entourage. "And you know that things have been really slow at the office. I'm really convinced that this is more than just a 'pause' in the market. That's what they call it in the newspapers—a 'pause'."

"Why do you think that? Wait, before you answer, can you get me a cup of coffee? I can see this is going to be more than just one of your silly questions like, 'Who'd win a fight between a shark and an alligator?'."

Pierre yelled from the kitchen. "I thought we resolved that. Pound for pound, the alligator is definitely tougher. He can hurt you with both his teeth and his tail."

"Thank you, Jacques Cousteau." Pierre handed her a cup of coffee, which she held away from Valerie's curious fingers as she sipped. "Okay, now why do you think the real estate market's in such trouble?"

"Well, what happens to the guy who buys one of the Baron's units when rents go down next month? There's no way he's gonna be able to pay the mortgage, condo fees and taxes. I mean, he may be a nice guy, but he's still only making six bucks an hour slapping paint on the wall."

"Maybe rents won't go down."

"No, they definitely will. I'm seeing it already. And the Baron's not stupid. He knows how soft the rental market is—that's why he's pushing so hard for sales now. And what scares me is how many of these guys Baron has sold units to. I mean, these guys aren't going to stick with their properties if times got tough. Why should they? They probably hadn't even thought about buying real estate until the Baron dumped a condominium in their lap."

"The banks are lending to these guys?"

"That's the amazing thing. The banks are so anxious to lend, and there are so few buyers right now, that they'll lend to anybody."

"If the Baron figured it out, other people probably did also. I mean, if you were a developer, it sounds like a pretty easy way to sell your units."

"Exactly." Pierre leaned over and gave Carla a quick kiss. As he did so, he snatched Valerie off of her lap. "There are two kissing bandits in this family. Anyway, my theory is that there are hundreds of these owners out there who will walk away from their properties as soon as things start to go bad."

"Okay. So then the banks foreclose, which will flood the market and drag prices down even more."

"Right. But it's even worse than that. What about the psychology of this market? You know, the boom is less than a decade old, and people already seem to have forgotten that real estate is cyclical. How many times have you heard somebody say, 'Real estate always goes up in value'?"

"I heard it just a few days ago at the health club."

"But think about the people who bought homes recently—they're young, successful, smart. And very leveraged. I'm not talking about the guys the Baron is selling to right now. I'm talking about the Yuppie couple who bought a condo in the Back Bay, or maybe the young guy who bought a condo for an investment because his buddy made a big score. They scraped together all their savings, sold stocks, borrowed from parents. Right?"

"Yeah. Sounds like us."

"Don't remind me. But I've been thinking a lot. I wonder if everyone will panic if the market starts to go down."

"Do you think this generation of home buyers has that little tolerance for risk?"

Pierre smiled at Carla. "I like the way you put that—'tolerance for risk'. But no, I don't think they necessarily have a low tolerance for risk. I think the point is that they bought their homes thinking that real estate was risk-free. They thought that real estate was a sure thing. Once the market starts to dip, I'm worried that these owners will feel cheated."

"And angry."

"Yup. And vulnerable. Will they be patient and wait for the next cycle? Or will they panic? My feeling is that the word 'patience' is not one that many people would use to describe the Eighties generation."

"Yeah, I see your point. 'Instant gratification' comes more to mind."

"So you think I might be right?"

"About Armageddon?"

"No, smart-ass, it won't be that bad. But do you think there might be a bit of panic?"

"You know, Pierre, seriously, you could be right. I think a lot of it depends on how many of these scam buyers there are. If you're right and there's a lot of them, and if the banks do foreclose and flood the market with properties, then prices will definitely come down. I could see that being the trigger for a bit of a panic mentality. Because you're right—real estate is just not supposed to go down in value."

Pierre handed Valerie back to Carla. "I'm gonna run with this for a while, see what else I can find out about our Baron friend. I mean, how many units has he sold to his painting crews? If it's just a few, then it's probably no big deal. But if he's been doing this for a while, I'd like to know about it. Because if the market's going to crash, I don't plan on being at the bottom of the pile." He kissed them each twice, then headed for the door.

"Maybe I'll try to come home for lunch."

"Good. Maybe Valerie will be napping."

6

[August 23, 1989]

Bruce stood self-consciously in the departure terminal. He alternately scrunched his six foot frame downward to avoid being conspicuous in the sea of Asian travelers, and stretched upward to scan the crowd for signs of possible police surveillance. He was waiting to board his return flight from Hong Kong to Boston, via Seattle. Nobody seemed to be watching him.

His mind raced through the possibilities. Could they be waiting for him on the plane already? That would make sense if they wanted to arrest him on American territory. But if that was their intention, why hadn't they arrested him on the flight over to Hong Kong when he still had the painting? Maybe they hadn't noticed him leaving the country, but then had alerted the Hong Kong authorities who were planning to arrest him at the airport before he re-boarded.

Given the choice, Bruce figured he'd rather be arrested on the plane and serve his time in an American jail. He bulled his way to the front of the boarding line, handed his ticket to the boarding agent, and jogged quickly down the causeway. He stepped over the threshold and onto the aircraft. One small step for Bruce.

Small step indeed—was he even on American territory? He thought back to his law classes. In the air, he was pretty sure he would be, since Northwest was an American carrier. But at the gate? The plane wasn't an embassy. Even so, could a Hong Kong policeman simply step onto an American plane to arrest an American citizen without being invited by the pilot? Would the police have bothered to get a warrant, just in case they missed Bruce in the terminal? Does Hong Kong even require warrants? Bruce shook his head in frustration—he was fencing with shadows. He should have taken the time to research Hong Kong law.

He walked toward the back of the half-full plane, scanning faces for signs of interest in him, cursing Gus for making him take this risk. He knew the FBI still had him under surveillance because he occasionally saw them parked outside his apartment. But the surveillance had become less frequent. Was Gus right, had they begun to lose interest in him because he'd been clean for five years? Because he lived the lifestyle of a starving student? Or did somebody just oversleep the day he flew out here and now they were waiting for him on the return trip?

Even if he didn't get arrested, Gus' buyer had been willing to pay only $45,000 of the agreed-upon $60,000 price. But that was Gus' problem—Bruce was keeping his half plus another ten grand for delivery risk. Gus could fight with the buyer for the other fifteen, not that Gus would have much leverage. From what Bruce knew, the Hong Kong buyer had connections with high officials in mainland China that allowed him to travel freely to other Communist countries. Since Eastern bloc rulers were the largest buyers of stolen art, and since gaining access to them was so difficult, the Hong Kong dealer was in a strong bargaining position. It was not uncommon for him to pay less than ten percent of the auction value of a painting, then to sell it to some Communist official for six or seven times that amount.

Bruce focused on his immediate problem—not getting caught. He didn't smoke, but had requested a seat deep in the smoking section in the rear of the jet. He knew that few American travelers would choose to sit in the smoky haze of an Asian flight, so it would make spotting any FBI agents who were tracking him that much easier. He couldn't escape from the airplane, of course, but he might have time to see them coming and make a rush for the bathroom. The thought of flushing $45,000 in bank checks down the toilet revolted Bruce, but with no money and no painting, it would be tougher to convict him. Not that he could afford a lawyer to defend himself.

Bruce thought about the bank checks stuffed into the hollowed-out rubber sole of his hiking boots. He wanted to avoid the paper trail that would be left if he wired the money home, and cash was too bulky, so he had purchased five separate $9,000 bank checks from the Chase Manhattan Bank branch in Hong Kong, thereby avoiding the paperwork requirements associated with cashing checks of more than $10,000. Each check was made payable to "Holder". But he felt nervous carrying them—it had been bad enough traveling with the rolled-up canvas into Hong Kong, but at least the Hong Kong customs authorities had no reason to be suspicious of him. What if his name appeared in some U.S. domestic database that would red flag him when he attempted to re-enter the country? Maybe he should have just dropped the checks in an envelope and sent them home by Federal Express.

Bruce took his seat. As he expected, he was one of the few Westerners in the rear of the plane. Nobody had paid much attention to him when he walked to his seat, and he was encouraged to see that an Asian family with two young children was sitting in the middle aisle directly adjacent to his side aisle seat—if the FBI was planning an arrest, they probably would have kept children away from his seat in the event of a scuffle. Or was he giving them too much credit? He shrugged, then fished a couple of hard candies out of his pocket and handed them with a tight smile to the mother of the Asian children.

Fifteen minutes passed, and the flight attendant requested that the passengers be seated. Bruce stood and fiddled with his carry-on bag, then glanced around the plane. Nobody moving toward him. He waited a moment to be sure, then peered out the window before sitting down. The light rain that had been falling had evolved into a heavy, windy downpour. Good. Hopefully it would be a turbulent flight—his ocean-trained stomach might give him an edge over a queasy FBI agent.

The plane took off. Bruce sat back and tried to guess what would happen next, and when. He saw three possible arrest scenarios: arrest him on the plane, arrest him as he disembarked, and arrest him as he passed through customs in Seattle. The last one he discounted—from what little he knew of the FBI, they did not play well with others. They likely viewed customs officials as little more than dog trainers in charge of drug-sniffing canines. And why share credit for the arrest?

What about as he disembarked? But then they would risk losing him in the bustle of the crowd. It was a small risk, especially because they probably did not view Bruce as particularly elusive or dangerous. But police were trained to avoid these types of risks.

That left arresting him while still on the plane, despite the children seated nearby. Bruce saw this as the strongest possibility, most likely occurring near the end of the flight so they wouldn't have to baby-sit him for ten hours. He wasn't going anywhere, and they knew it.

If he was right, it made sense to stash the money someplace, then retrieve it after the plane landed. That way he wouldn't have the money on him when he was arrested.

He motioned for the flight attendant and requested two cups of apple juice, then a cup of coffee. He waited.

There were six bathrooms in the plane, two in the front, two in the middle, and two in the rear. About two hours into the flight—a half hour after drinking the apple juice and coffee—Bruce unfastened his seatbelt and walked the length of the plane to the front right-hand bathroom, opposite the plane's main exit. He locked the door, and took off one of his hiking boots. With a key, he pried off the entire thick rubber sole. Bruce had hollowed out the sole before leaving Boston—it had gone unnoticed when he wore the boot through customs on the way into Hong Kong. Inside the sole were the five bank checks, wrapped tightly together. Bruce placed the checks inside a small plastic bag and rolled the bag inside a thick roll of toilet paper. He then took a stack of paper towels, dropped them into the toilet, and flushed. Water filled the toilet.

Bruce dropped the wrapped bag into the toilet, pulled down his pants, and moved his bowels into the bowl, covering the bag. As he wiped himself, he smeared feces onto the toilet seat and sink area. The small bathroom immediately filled with putrid air. For added effect, he reached his index finger far down his throat and vomited his breakfast into the sink.

He washed his hands thoroughly, stuffed the boot back into his bag, closed the door, and walked back to his seat.

Eight hours until landing time, and nothing to do now but wait. He was too nervous to sleep, so he studied the passengers around him. He concentrated on the Caucasian men seated nearest to him, and observed each continuously for up to fifteen minutes. He wasn't sure what he was looking for, but he was sure that an FBI agent planning an arrest would, in some way, behave differently than a tourist or a businessman.

Three hours passed, and Bruce had seen nothing suspicious. The sixteen men he had observed were either masterful at disguising themselves or simply not FBI agents. Three were traveling with families. Two others worked on laptop computers, the newest toys of the private sector. Six men were drinking alcohol. One had a cast on his arm. Two men wore facial hair. One was wearing shorts. Another had a pony-tail. If there was an agent on board, Bruce was confident he was not seated in the rear section of the plane.

Or he was undercover. Or he was Asian. Or he was a she.

Bruce cursed to himself. This was ridiculous. Even if the agent came up and introduced himself, what difference would it make? Either they were going to arrest him or they weren't. The money was hidden; there wasn't anything else he could do about it.

He pounded his thigh. How did he end up here, in a plane over the Atlantic praying he wouldn't get arrested? Because everyone in his life was either an idiot or an asshole, that's how.

Gus, obviously, was both.

His parents were assholes, for a thousand reasons. His natural mother, for choosing a life alone as an exotic dancer over a life together with her newborn son. His stepmother, for hating him just because he was the product of his father's illicit affair. His father, for not keeping it in his pants, and then for compounding his weakness by allowing his stepmother to treat Bruce like one of the houseplants. Not to mention his father's economic idiocy—even a guidance counselor should have been able to keep enough money out of his wife's hands to lend his son a few thousand bucks.

And the loan shark, he was just plain stupid. Bruce was set to earn $60,000 a year—why not extend the loan? At 50% interest, it should have been a no-brainer.

Bruce swore he would never put himself in this position again. His boyhood friend had failed him, and might yet betray him. His parents were of no use. His grandfather was dead. There was a lesson here, and Bruce thanked his anger for teaching it to him. Trust nobody. Count on nobody.

Bruce tried to compose himself, tried to focus on what was, rather than what should have been. He sat for another hour, then indulged his curiosity and strolled toward the front of the plane. Just getting out of his seat made him feel better. As he approached the bathroom, he noticed that a number of passengers had switched seats to move away from the stench. And there was a long line at the opposite bathroom. At least the money was safe. He turned around and went back to his seat.

Four hours to go. Dinner came and killed another hour.

A half hour later, they flew into a thunderstorm. The seat belt light went on. Bruce stared at the light, hoping it would never go off.

Then, with no warning other than a slight ping, the light disappeared after 83 minutes. Bruce felt like he had lost a friend. One hour to landing, and suddenly the entire plane was swarming with passengers. Was one carrying a badge?

Bruce tried to stay calm, but he could smell his own fear wafting up from his armpits. He had a newfound respect for Gus—this waiting was sheer torture. At least during the actual theft you're moving, rushing, scrambling. In and out in twenty minutes, then it's over. But this was like being a fish in a bucket—either they shoot you or they don't, but there isn't a damn thing you can do about it. Except sweat.

He thought about Gus again. Maybe Gus wasn't so stupid. After all, Gus was probably back in Boston recovering from a wild weekend at the Cape. So who was the idiot? Who was the one who, after years of planning, could let a mere $10,000 ruin everything, when in a few years $10,000 would be pocket change?

Bruce shook his head. He was supposed to be the brilliant one, the master problem-solver. That was how he had planned the art thefts—his creative side had conceptualized them, and his analytical abilities had dissected the various components of the thefts down to the most minute detail. These same problem-solving skills should have been applicable to problem-avoidance. Yet here he was.

The captain's voice interrupted Bruce's self-flagellation: "Ladies and gentlemen, sorry for the turbulence, but the good news is that the storm has given us a bit of a tailwind and saved us twenty minutes. We are now beginning our descent to Seattle. Please be seated."

Bruce shook off his introspection, allowed himself a glimmer of hope . It would be too dangerous to try to arrest him now, during the descent. They were running out of chances.

The plane kissed the runway, then began taxiing toward the gate. Bruce edged his way forward toward the exit, one of a handful ignoring the command of the crew to remain seated. He ducked into an empty seat and turned, searching for a pursuer. If he saw anything suspicious, he would simply get off the plane and leave the money in its watery dungeon. But he saw nothing.

He pushed his way past the other passengers and walked briskly off the plane, then jogged to the end of the gangway. Nobody waiting for him, no sign of anybody following.

Muttering apologies, he doubled back against the crowd and bulled his way back onto the plane. He smiled at a flight attendant—"I forgot something at my seat." She smiled back, nodded, then moved into the first class area. He slipped into the bathroom. He didn't have much time—there were still many passengers making their way toward the exit, but he didn't want to draw undue attention to himself by being the last one off the plane.

He took a wire coat hanger from his carry-on, fished out the plastic bag, and dropped the bag into the sink. He ran hot water over it. The toilet paper quickly dissolved, and Bruce grabbed the plastic bag and dried it off. "Money-laundering," he whispered. He again removed the rubber sole from his boot, placed the plastic bag inside the cavity, and, using a small tube of super glue, re-attached the sole to his boot.

He opened the bathroom door and peeked out. Nobody waiting with handcuffs, and still dozens of passengers waiting to disembark, some with children still in their seats. He left a twenty-dollar bill for the person who would have to clean the bathroom, and stepped out into the front of the queue of passengers waiting to exit the plane. A few seconds later he squeezed through the exit portal for a second time, then walked briskly through the gangway and headed toward the baggage claim area. Still no sign of anyone following.

Now, all he had to do was grab his suitcase and clear customs. He hoped his theory about the FBI not wanting to work with the customs agents was right. But even if it was, he knew that he was a walking poster child for law enforcement's drug courier profile—young, male, and returning alone from a short trip to Asia. If he was searched, how would he explain a wad of bank checks hidden in his boot?

He found his suitcase, winced as he lifted it off the carousel. His cracked ribs still hadn't healed, and he had skipped the pain killers out of fear they would make him foggy-brained. He dragged the suitcase to the customs line.

He tried to study the customs agents, but couldn't stop himself from turning around periodically to make sure he wasn't being observed. Finally he was at the front of the line. Two customs agent stations freed up simultaneously. Bruce took one step toward a young, attractive woman, then stopped and reversed himself and headed toward the station of a stern-looking, middle-aged man. He would normally have chosen differently—the man was hardly likely to succumb to Bruce's boyish charm. But Bruce had just watched the man complete a thorough search of a young couple's bags, and Bruce guessed that the agent wouldn't search two travelers in a row.

Bruce handed the agent his passport and customs form, then gingerly lifted his bag onto the inspection belt. He thought about asking how the Mariners were doing, but decided it would make him look like a nervous man trying to make conversation. He waited patiently while the agent methodically examined the papers.

Finally the agent spoke. He smiled politely, but Bruce could sense the man probing, trying to read him. "Were you traveling for business or pleasure, Mr. Arrujo?"

"Job interview."

The agent nodded. "What do you do?"

"Just got out of law school. I was interviewing with one of the banks in Hong Kong." Bruce hoped that the combination of careers in law and banking made him sound upstanding.

The agent tested the story. "Wasn't the bar exam this week?"

A few weeks ago. Always the last week of July."

The agent nodded and handed Bruce his passport. "Welcome home, Mr. Arrujo."

"Thanks." Bruce smiled, lowered his bag to the floor, and turned to leave.

"One more thing, Mr. Arrujo." The agent's voice froze Bruce. There was a clipped briskness in the voice, as if it were used to giving commands. Probably military training.

Bruce swallowed, set his bag down to buy a second to re-compose himself. He turned back. "Yes?"

"What happened to your ribs?" The agent eyes bore into Bruce's, trying to read Bruce's face as he had read the bandages outlined beneath Bruce's shirt.

Bruce reacted intuitively. "You should see the other guy."

The two men held each other's eye for a split second, then Bruce smiled broadly, scooped up his bag, and walked confidently toward the gate to grab his flight to Boston. After a few steps, he glanced up into a mirror above the doorway. The agent was still watching him, the hint of a smile on his face.

7

[August 24, 1989]

Charese stepped off the subway and onto the escalator. The warm summer wind blew down toward her, billowing her dress up and away from her freshly shaven legs. She smiled as a man on the opposite escalator checked her out as he descended past, happy that she could still both fool and attract men.

Charese had made a tactical decision, electing to attend this meeting in her female persona. Even though the non-profit Lawyers Advocating for the Poor was a liberal group that likely supported gay and lesbian causes, she guessed that most of the LAP lawyers had never actually sat down for a meeting with a transvestite. Simple curiosity, Charese hoped, would ensure that her request for free legal representation would at least be heard.

In fact, Charese was fairly confident of persuading them to take her case. She had always had an intuitive sense of the spice her transvestite status added to people's lives. In this case, she imagined the LAP lawyers getting a charge out of regaling their friends with cocktail party stories. "Yeah, I'm representing some black transvestite suing a white blue blood for refusing to pay for her sex-change operation."

Actually, Charese wasn't even really black. Her hairdressing background had taught her to kink her hair, and, though only olive-skinned, she was rarely challenged for claiming a status most of society saw as disadvantageous. And being black was one more check mark in her favor on the liberal agenda checklist, one more reason for LAP to take her case.

Of course, in front of Roberge's family, she presented herself as a well-tanned and slightly exotic looking preppie. Or used to.

She knew of LAP from a dispute she had had with her landlord when she first came to Boston. Though they seemed more interested in the publicity they received for beating up on the landlord then in winning the case for her, she had received a nice judgment and they had handled the case for free. Which was all she could afford then.

And all she could afford now. Less than two weeks had passed since Roberge had ran out, and she was already worried about her living expenses. Roberge owned the South End condominium she lived in free and clear, but she would still have to pay all the utility bills. She figured she could last four or five months, as long as she could stay in the condo rent-free and didn't get sick and have to pay medical bills. The operation, obviously, would have to wait. Or maybe she didn't even want it anymore.

The receptionist escorted Charese to a large, neat office. A man sat behind a desk, just finishing up a phone call. Charese guessed he was in his mid-forrties. He was decent-looking, in a frat-boy grown up sort of way, though Charese did notice his hair was overdue for a washing.

He hung up, then half-stood "Ah, yes. Nice to meet you. I'm Reese Jeffries. Please call me Reese." He had a slight accent, which made Charese think of nannies and afternoon teas. He reached across the desk, the scent of garlic reaching with him, and shook and then quickly released her hand. Charese guessed he was the type of guy who kissed you in the morning before brushing his teeth, and thought it was your pleasure.

Reese was one of the full-time lawyers at the clinic, and explained that they were currently accepting cases that would be staffed by law students returning to school in September. The law students would work at LAP for the entire academic year in exchange for class credit. If they took her case, a specific student would act as Charese's lawyer, under the supervision of the full-time staff lawyers.

He asked Charese to recount her history with Roberge. He took notes as Charese spoke, rarely interrupting, his face frozen in feigned sympathy. Charese spoke slowly, trying to be articulate and organized, aware that some vestige of her Georgia accent still came through when she was nervous. As she spoke, Reese made periodic slurping noises, sucking the saliva off the floor of his mouth in a manner that reminded Charese of the straw-like instrument dentists used to keep a patient's mouth dry.

In any event, Reese seemed only mildly interested in her narrative. Although he hadn't stopped her in mid-story and showed her out, Charese was beginning to doubt he would agree to take her case.

Suddenly his attitude changed. "Is Roberge Krygier related to the real estate Krygiers?" Charese noticed that Reese had shifted forward in his seat as he asked the question. She knew that Roberge's father owned many apartment buildings in Boston, and was active in local politics.

"Yes. Roberge's father is Wesley Krygier." Charese paused here, but Reese just stared at her expectantly, as if she couldn't possibly have finished answering such an important question with only six words. So Charese continued rambling, not really sure what Reese wanted to hear. "Roberge and his father aren't that close, but I've met him a few times at family functions. But he only knows me as a woman—Roberge never told his family that I was really a man or even that he was gay. The family just knew me as Roberge's girlfriend. At first they didn't like me, but then they sort of got used to me and used to pressure Roberge to get married so we could have kids. I actually became pretty friendly with his little sister before she went off to college in Vermont."

Reese cut her off. "You mean you attended Krygier family functions as Roberge Krygier's girlfriend, dressed as a woman?" Charese nodded. "Do you have pictures?" Reese was now actually leaning forward across the desk waiting for Charese's answer. She could see spittle on his lower lip—apparently he had forgotten to swallow.

Charese understood where Reese was going with this. She hesitated a moment, then realized she had no choice. Distasteful or not, she needed Reese's help. If the price for that help was allowing Reese to publicly humiliate the Krygier family, well, it seemed like a fair exchange. "Pictures? Yes, I've got pictures."

8

[August 25, 1989]

Bruce slept for two days straight. On the third day, he walked down the street to a rental car agency and treated himself to a red Camaro. It had been four years since he had driven anything other than a used Toyota, and the simple act of starting the engine brought him back to his wild college days.

He had pulled off his first art heist with Gus over Thanksgiving break his sophomore year, a few months after his grandfather had died, and had returned to the University of Massachusetts with money in his pocket for the first time in his life. Fast cars, fast girls, fast drugs, another art heist, more cars, more girls, more drugs. By the time he was a senior, he had committed four thefts and, thanks to Gus' fencing abilities, had stashed over $60,000 in Caesar's Palace casino chips in a safe deposit box. But he knew that, as careful as he was, he could not go forever without getting caught, that his behavior had been too much ocean and not enough continent. So, in his senior year, he moved back into the dorm, gave up the cars and drugs and Gus, forgot about the money, applied to law schools, and hoped the FBI would leave him alone.

Bruce sped up the coast toward Marblehead. He parked at the beach, kicked off his shoes and sat in the sand.

He allowed himself a rare moment of satisfaction. The elements of his plan were, finally, in place. Law degree? Check. The job to provide the perfect cover? Check. The necessary seed money? Check. All that remained was to wait for the proper opportunity, and then to execute correctly.

Actually, the word "plan" was too concrete, too definitive. What Bruce really had was a theory based on three seemingly unrelated observations he had made. First, from his art theft experiences, Bruce knew the importance of access to inside information. Second, Bruce knew that every significant transaction in the American economic system required the use of lawyers. And third, while many members of society disdained lawyers, the integrity and trustworthiness of the largest law firms were generally beyond question. Bruce therefore theorized that a lawyer in a large, respected law firm would be in a unique position to build a little nest egg of his own.

Best of all, a lawyer could likely profit in a way that would be impossible to detect. Bruce had laughed recently when he read about an attorney embezzling money from a wealthy widow; did he think that the heirs would not notice that their inheritance was missing? And a recent attempt by a paralegal to buy the stock of a client who was involved in secret merger discussions was as clumsy as it was naive; did she think that the SEC hadn't seen this type of scam before? No, Bruce was looking instead for some sophisticated back door type of manipulation where the victim would not even realize that he or it had been victimized. Sort of like a dentist molesting a patient while the patient was unconscious, but without any semen stains or evidence of penetration. Bottom line: if there was no victim, there would be little chance of getting caught.

Only one decision remained, and it was at the same time both minor and crucial. In which department of the law firm should Bruce choose to work? The firm had offered him positions in both the corporate and the real estate departments, and he had delayed giving them his decision as long as possible. The area of corporate law was booming, as companies were born, grew, merged. But the corporate arena was also heavily regulated and scrutinized—Bruce didn't want the SEC or corporate officers or dissident shareholders snooping around. Real estate, on the other hand, was a private, individual transaction. No governmental oversight. No stockholders expecting periodic reports. No board of directors. No yearly audits. And it was a one-time event—the property was sold and the transaction forgotten, the legal file kept one year and then archived in some climate-controlled warehouse.

The more Bruce thought about it, the more the real estate choice made sense. Not only would there be less regulation and scrutiny, but the booming Boston real estate market eventually would have to succumb to the cyclical nature of every market. Prices of homes had doubled and even tripled in the past five years. While part of the increase was attributable to the hot Massachusetts economy, some of the boom was a result of sheer speculation. Bruce recalled the college reading he had done on the tulip bulb phenomenon in the Netherlands in the 1630's. Speculative frenzy drove tulip bulb prices up to hundreds of times their pre-speculative value, to the point where a single tulip bulb was valued at the equivalent of a laborer's yearly salary. When the speculative bubble burst, panic selling ensued. A tulip bulb could then be purchased for the price of a common onion.

While Bruce was confident that real estate would never be bartered for table vegetables, he did believe that a price correction was inevitable. With that correction would come chaos and confusion. And chaos was a fertile breeding ground for opportunity.

9

[August 29, 1989]

Pierre drove from his condominium to his office on Beacon Street in the Coolidge Corner section of Brookline and parked. He popped into the office, checked his messages—one, from a panicky landlord asking if he had had any luck renting her apartment—snatched a fist-full of quarters, and kicked off his shoes. He grabbed his Roller Blade in-line skates from the closet, stuck his sneakers and a hand towel into his backpack along with a notepad and his appointment book, and stepped out onto the raised stoop of the brownstone. He sat on the bottom step and pulled on his skates. It was only 8:30, but it was already warm and sticky.

The distance from Pierre's office—Premier Properties—to the Registry of Deeds downtown was about three miles. Pierre expected that the traffic would be light due to the usual August outflux of vacationing Boston professionals, but he kept to side roads and sidewalks as much as possible. He could usually make the trip downtown in about twenty minutes. He began at a leisurely pace—he would save his hard skate for the return trip, then grab a quick shower at his office.

Pierre knew he was still an object of curiosity as he zipped around pedestrians and in and out of traffic. During the entire summer, he had never seen another roller blader on the streets, although there was a group of bladers who were fighting with cyclists for space on the bike paths along the Charles River. Still, Pierre found it a convenient and healthy way to move around Boston when doing errands and personal business. And he loved to skate. For his 35th birthday, Carla had given him a T-shirt that read: "People dream they can fly. Birds dream they can skate." Pierre had loved it, though many of his friends didn't even understand it.

In fact, as Pierre got older, he realized that many of his friends didn't really understand him, either. There weren't confused so much because he had changed, but rather because he hadn't. For Pierre, being 35 was not much different than being 25 or even 15. Of course he had responsibilities and a career—or, at least, hoped to still have one—but Pierre still viewed life as a giant playground. Once your homework and chores were done, it was time to go out and play. Ice hockey and skiing in the winter. Softball and more skiing in the spring.

41

Sailing and rafting and biking in the summer. Touch football and hockey again
in the fall. The problem Pierre was having with his friends was that they didn't
want to play with him anymore. They had become adults. Their toys had become
cigars and gas grills and BMW's.

That's what he adored about Carla. She loved to play. She had learned how to
ski at 31, and within two years had almost mastered the sport. Valerie's arrival
the past winter had kept Carla off the slopes, but she was already planning a
December ski trip. "Next kid," she had told Pierre, "I'm getting pregnant in
February and giving birth in November so I don't miss any of the ski season."

"Next kid," Pierre had responded, "we'll have enough for two-on-two touch
football."

Pierre's skate was fairly easy until the last quarter mile, when the incline of
Beacon Hill forced Pierre to skate hard just to maintain any forward momentum.
Near the top of the hill, it took all of his energy just to keep from rolling backwards. Was the real estate market working this hard as well, just to not lose
ground? Momentum should not be underestimated.

He sat on a bench in the Boston Common opposite the State House, pulled
off his skates, wiped his face and neck, and slid into his sneakers. The Old
Courthouse, which housed the Registry of Deeds, sat in the middle of a brick
plaza, and Pierre knew from an earlier nasty fall that a wise roller blader avoided cobbled surfaces. He walked across the plaza to the imposing doors of the
Old Courthouse, and entered. It was just 9:00, and the lobby was full of attorneys and law enforcement personnel. Pierre walked through the crowd, aware of
a few curious glances at the skates slung over his shoulder, and stepped into a
crowded elevator. "Five, please," he said to the elevator operator, and waited
while the antique lift creaked upward. It still amazed Pierre that the political
patronage system in Massachusetts was so strong that the ancient lifts hadn't
been mechanized.

Pierre was surprised to see that the giant hall was mostly empty, especially
since the end of the month was typically a busy time for closings. Pierre began
researching the Baron's recent transactions. Within an hour, he understood the
Baron's game. It was simple, but brilliant.

The Baron would start with a building with, say, 25 condo units, worth
$70,000 each on the open market. He would then "sell" three of the units for
$100,000. But the sales were actually nothing more than transfers to trusts con-
trolled by the Baron. No real money changed hands. Nonetheless, according to
the public records, three sales at the $100,000 figure had occurred.

The Baron would then contract to sell the remaining 22 condos to members of his painting crew at $100,000 price. The painting crew members would each apply for an $80,000 mortgage, the mortgage bank would hire an appraiser to determine the market value of the condos, and the appraiser, in turn, would dutifully examine the public records and find the three apparently legitimate $100,000 sales. It didn't matter that the actual value of the condos was only $70,000—the bank would then approve a series of $80,000 mortgage loans, the parties would proceed to a closing, and the $80,000 would be paid to the Baron as the seller. And the Baron would incur no broker's commissions or marketing costs.

Pierre did some quick arithmetic: the Baron's little ploy would net him $400,000 in extra profit, not to mention selling out the entire building before the market sank even lower. All he needed was one stupid bank and a roomful of painters.

Pierre was beginning to understand why the Baron was pushing so hard to sell the units to the painters and their friends. The Baron had not acquired his noble rank by failing to appreciate a $400,000 profit.

Pierre found that the Baron had sold almost 200 condo units in this way since the first of the year. Pierre knew most of the properties, and estimated that the prices the Baron had paid to buy the properties were equal to or even slightly above the buildings' current market value. Apparently, the Baron had fallen into the trap of assuming the market would continue to climb. But, unlike most buyers, the Baron had a safety net that had allowed him to unload almost 200 units at inflated prices.

And who held this safety net? A bank that was either stupid or willfully ignorant, and a group of buyers who, though not sophisticated, were savvy enough to understand that they were playing with the house's money.

10

[September 6, 1989]

A little less than two weeks after her first meeting with him, just after the Labor Day holiday, Charese got a phone call from Reese Jeffries. "Can you come down to the office tomorrow morning? We've put together a draft complaint for your case, but we need you to fill in a few gaps and to sign an affidavit. If you can stay the whole day, we could finish it tomorrow and have it filed at the court by Friday. And don't forget the pictures."

"Sure, I can come down tomorrow." Charese hung up, then smiled as she pictured the look on Roberge's face when he got served with the papers. He had probably thought she would just roll over, like she always had before. Not this time.

Charese arrived the next morning at the LAP office. Reese introduced her to a young woman seated at a table, surrounded by a stack of law books. "Charese, this is Shelby Baskin. Shelby is the law student who will be helping out on your case."

Shelby stood, smiled politely at Charese and offered her hand. "Nice to meet you, Charese. I was just doing some research on your case. Can you sit down for a while? I have some questions for you." Charese studied the young woman. Shelby wore a tailored, rust-colored suit over a cream-colored silk blouse, the suit cut to reveal just a hint of her shapely, toned figure. Charese admired the effect—it reminded her of the impression made by the light scent of an expensive perfume.

Shelby sifted through her notes, looking for her list of questions for Charese, then changed her mind, as if it was wrong of her to assume that Charese wouldn't be able to take a more active role in the case. After all, her lifestyle choice had nothing to do with her level of intelligence. "Actually, maybe the best way to do this is for you to read what I've drafted so far—it's the factual summary of your case—and give me your comments. Tell me where I've missed things or where I'm off base."

Shelby handed Charese a pen, and Charese sat down across from her and began reading through the document, filling in blanks and making occasional notes in the margins. As the day wore one, Charese took the time to study the law student further. Dazzling blue-green eyes, understated features, bouncy dark hair, cut short but stylish. She had guessed Shelby was a city girl, and the trace of a New York accent confirmed it. But her self-assuredness was tempered by a softness, a grace that Charese guessed would disarm women who normally felt threatened in the presence of a naturally beautiful woman. She looked like the type of woman who fifteen years ago would have graduated from college and become an advertising or retailing executive rather than a lawyer.

Charese also noticed that, although Shelby was polite to Reese, her demeanor toward him was reserved and businesslike. Though Reese was Shelby's supervisor, Charese didn't get the sense that Shelby was inclined to defer to him. Charese wondered if Reese had come on to her; in her mind she pictured a cumbersome, leering Reese shrugged off—almost condescendingly—by the sophisticated law student.

By the end of the day, Shelby had completed a 17-page complaint alleging that Roberge had agreed to pay for Charese's sex change operation, to marry her, and to support her as his wife. Charese was pleased with the result—her position seemed so compelling and justified in the well-reasoned complaint Shelby had drafted. Could any juror doubt that Charese Galloway had been treated shabbily? And she was glad to see the pictures were not attached to the complaint. "What happens next?" she asked. "I mean, how long will this whole process take?"

Reese answered. "Tomorrow, Shelby will file the complaint with the court and have a deputy sheriff serve a copy of the complaint in person on Roberge at his office. Shelby, you got his work address from Charese, right?"

"Yes. He works as a curator at the Museum of Fine Arts."

Reese continued. "After that, we wait to see what their answer is." He put on his extra-serious face, swallowed, and moved closer to Charese. "But I've battled Krygier and his type before, and they won't roll over easily. Are you ready for a fight?"

There was something in his tone that made Charese feel like she was being spoken to like a child. But she nodded nonetheless. Reese continued. "Good. I'm proud of you. Besides, we have those pictures if things get nasty." Reese chuckled softly, his eyes focusing past Charese on some distant point beyond the confines of the room.

Charese glanced over toward Shelby, hoping to see her react in some way to Reese's comment, but Shelby had already turned away to pick up a gum wrapper that had been lying on the floor for the past three hours, and did not make eye contact with Charese.

11

[September 21, 1989]

It had been a month since Pierre had uncovered the Baron's bogus sales operation, and if anything the September real estate market was even worse than the August one. Pierre had spent the time further researching the market in general and the Baron's empire in particular. First, Pierre had obtained a list of buildings converted to condominiums over the past year by the Baron. He took this list and went to the tax assessor's office and obtained the names of the purchasers of these units. He then roller-bladed from building to building and compared the name of the unit owner to the name of the resident listed on the mailbox. What Pierre found was that entire buildings—and in some cases, entire neighborhoods—were owned by individual condominium investors who did not live in their condos.

Pierre had enough experience with condominiums to know this was dangerous. The idea of the condominium form of ownership was that the association of unit owners would work together for the benefit of the entire building. If the building needed a new roof or a new furnace, the owners would get together and proceed accordingly, the cost of the improvement shared by all. However, when few or none of the unit owners actually lived in the building, the collective spirit vanished. A new roof—which seems like a necessity to the owner-occupant who is being dripped on as he sleeps—seems less critical to the investor living twenty miles away who would rather spend his money on a vacation in Florida.

And, of course, the situation would only get worse in a slumping economy. Rents would go down, tenants would move out, and not only would the investor owners not contribute to the new roof, they would likely stop paying their mortgages and condominium fees as well.

If Pierre was right, he knew that it was only a matter of time before the banks would have no choice but to foreclose on the units. It would be a classic house of cards: the banks would flood the market with the condos they foreclosed on, which would drive prices down even further, which in turn would depress the entire real estate market.

Pierre reacted by making a number of decisions. First, with Carla's assent, he immediately placed his Brookline condo on the market for sale. Three months ago, he had guessed the unit—totally modernized and in an upscale neighborhood near the subway line—was worth $230,000. He priced it at $214,000 and admitted to himself they would probably accept any offer that began with a "2". He and Carla could rent for a year or two, then buy a nice house in the suburbs after the prices had fallen and before Valerie had a sibling.

Second, he cut way back on his overhead. He canceled the third phone line in the office, reduced his advertising by 60 percent, and subleased the back part of his office to a young insurance agent looking for a Beacon Street address. He didn't bother to lay off any of the other four brokers in his office, since they worked on a commission basis anyway. He guessed they would soon leave voluntarily.

Finally, Pierre bit off his nose to make it easier to look at his face in the mirror every morning. He had always believed that loyalty and honesty were valuable commodities in the business world that someday would yield high dividends. He hoped he was right. He dialed a phone number in California, realizing that it was only eight in the morning there, but knowing that Howie would already be in his office.

"Thermotics, Howie Plansky speaking."

"Hey, Howie, it's Pierre. Got a minute?"

"Of course. Hey, Betty Jane, get off your knees and clean yourself up, I gotta take this call."

Pierre had never been completely comfortable with Howie's raunchy sense of humor, and after six years still hadn't quite decided whether Howie employed it to shield feelings of insecurity or because he truly was a raunchy person. Forced to choose, Pierre would guess the former—Howie was short and plump and pasty, and probably used the dirty jokes as a way of interacting in the blond, tan, hip world of southern California. Pierre laughed politely, then smiled as a song from one of Valerie's Winnie the Pooh cartoons popped into his head: "I am short, fat, proud of that...."

"Listen, Howie, I want to talk to you about that deal you're doing." Pierre was referring to the purchase of a 28-unit apartment building in Brighton. Howie was paying $1.8 million, and the closing was only eight days away. Howie had actually reached agreement on the deal back in June, but had not scheduled the closing until October 1 to accommodate some tax planning the seller was doing. "Have you got a copy of the Purchase and Sale Agreement in front of you?"

"Hold on, Pierre, I'll get it." Pierre was the broker in the deal, and should have been given a copy of the Purchase and Sale Agreement by the seller's attorney once the parties had signed it. But it was not uncommon for the broker to be treated as little more than a messenger service by the attorneys, and Pierre had never received a copy of the Agreement.

Pierre noticed his hands were getting sweaty, and he wasn't surprised. What he was about to do was highly unusual. Under the archaic rules of real estate brokerage, Pierre technically worked for the seller of the property. Even though Pierre had never actually met the seller. Even though the seller had listed the property with and communicated exclusively through another broker who was also collecting a $45,000 commission. And even though Pierre had a six-year business and personal relationship with Howie. In other words, Pierre was legally required to do whatever he could to advance the interests of the seller in the transaction, and to simply ignore the fact that Howie was a valued client and long-time acquaintance. Pierre was about to violate that legal requirement. Whether that was causing the sweat, or whether it was the imminent loss of a $45,000 commission, Pierre wasn't sure.

"Got it. What do you need?"

"What's the latest date you can back out of the deal?"

Howie flipped through pages. "Well, I can terminate the deal up until September 25 if we don't get our mortgage. I think that's the only reason, though. We've already done our inspections, and everything's fine. September 25 is next Monday."

"Did the bank approve the mortgage yet?"

"No, not yet. But they said everything looks fine and I should get a commitment letter later this week. They just need a few things from me. Why? What's up?"

"Listen, Howie, I've been doing a lot of thinking lately, and I don't think you should buy any real estate right now." Pierre related to Howie his activities over the past month. He also gave Howie objective evidence of the softening sales market and decreasing rents. Howie hadn't interrupted, so he continued: "Bottom line: the market's dead right now. The last time things were this quiet was when Carter was President and interest rates were, like, 18 percent. It just seems to me that the market's going down big time during the next year or so. I think there's going to be some great opportunities to buy stuff cheap—at foreclosure sales, maybe—but it doesn't make sense to be buying stuff at full price right now."

Howie let out a low whistle. "Holy shit, Pierre. You know I've made a lot of money with you in Boston over the years, and I trust your opinion." Pierre nodded to himself. Using a $50,000 inheritance, Howie had purchased and sold—

"flipped" was the word used in the real estate industry—eight or ten properties over the past six years and had made close to $400,000 in profits. Not a bad nest egg for an engineer. It was this $400,000 that he was using as a down payment on the apartment building, taking six years of profits and "letting it ride".

Howie continued. "But are you sure about this? I mean, you're the one who sold me on this property in the first place." Howie stopped suddenly. "Shit. Of course you're sure—you're walking away from your commission. Forty-five grand, right?"

Pierre grunted. It would have been his third largest commission ever, and if he was right about the direction of the real estate market, there wouldn't be many more like it in the future. "Look, Howie, the way I see it is that your $400,000 will still be there, and that you'll trust me next time when I call you and tell you I've found a good deal. Hopefully we can both make a lot of money over the next few years." A triumph of hope over reality? Pierre wondered. "For now, though, how are we going to get you out of this deal without losing your $100,000 deposit?"

"I don't know. I had my family attorney out here review the Purchase and Sale Agreement before I signed it, but I don't think he's going to be able to help me break the contract. He doesn't really do much real estate law. Do you know an attorney I can use in Boston?"

Pierre knew many attorneys, but they were all "deal makers", not "deal breakers". Over the years, the brokerage community had developed an unofficial network of attorneys (as well as building inspectors and mortgage lenders) who received referrals from brokers in exchange for a tacit understanding that they would do everything they could to make sure the transaction closed. None of the attorneys would want to risk their place in this network by working to kill Howie's deal at the last minute, especially in this economy.

Pierre thought back to the foreclosure sale he had attended the day before. The attorney had given Pierre his card. He seemed pleasant and competent, and he worked for one of the fancy downtown firms. The big firms were definitely not part of the referral network; on the contrary, they usually took such a hard-line position in contract negotiations that many of their deals never closed. In fact, some brokers had begun to refuse to represent clients who used the big firms.

Pierre spoke. "I met an attorney at a foreclosure sale yesterday. He works for one of the big firms downtown. I think he might be a little young, but he seemed like a nice guy who knew real estate law. Plus, he might be able to help us down the road if we want to buy foreclosure properties—I told him I was working with some West Coast investors, and he said he had a lot of foreclosure sales coming up and thought there might be some good opportunities out there. Want me to call him for you?"

"Yeah, would you? I've got a crazy day here. And Pierre, I owe you big time."

Saving for a Bigger Boat

12

[September 21, 1989]

Bruce stepped into the elevator, then reached forward to block the door to allow a latecomer to enter. Bruce tried to extend small acts of courtesy whenever possible, under the theory that they sometimes were repaid many-fold. They rode in silence, then the elevator voice spoke. "Floor 57".

Bruce stepped directly into the newly decorated offices of Stoak, Puck & Beal, P.C. Other lawyers referred to the firm as Choke, Suck & Steal, but usually did so in a low whisper. Ruthless lawyers, 263 of them including Bruce and the other new associates. But eminently respectable in the eyes of the business community, the greed hidden behind the green marble and polished mahogany decorating the top five floors of Boston's plushest office tower.

Most young lawyers are resigned to working in a pressured environment, but among the large firms, a few—like Stoak, Puck—have particular reputations as being sweat shops. Many top law students therefore chose other firms. Not Bruce.

Bruce reasoned that an uncongenial, even hostile, working environment would serve as a natural buffer between himself and the potentially curious minds and eyes of the other associates. So far, the hunch had paid off. Bruce had been cordial and friendly, but the other associates seemed to have no desire to socialize with him or with each other. Emboldened by the other associates' reclusiveness, Bruce had made a point of extending occasional lunch invitations, knowing they would be declined. He figured that these overtures of friendship were the best way to keep the others at a safe distance.

Although Stoak, Puck was conservative by nature, the partners saw the dangers of projecting a close-minded and stodgy image in a state that had produced such contemporary liberal national political figures as Ted Kennedy, Tip O'Neil and Michael Dukakis. As a result, the firm was careful not to discriminate against women and minorities, and the current class of first year associates represented a decent cross-section of gender and ethnic backgrounds.

Despite their outward diversity, the associates' personalities were fundamentally identical—competitive, intelligent, tireless, intent on making partner. Bruce knew the type well from his three years at Harvard law school. It wasn't that they were bad people, it was just that their Type A personalities demanded that they attack this latest challenge in their lives with the same intensity as they had the second grade spelling bee. "Success" for them had become an end unto itself, rather than a means for achieving happiness or fulfillment. They each wanted to become partner not because they necessarily needed the money or wanted the power or even enjoyed practicing law, but because it was the next hurdle in a series of academic challenges beginning with that second grade spelling bee and running through the SAT's, college grade point averages, law school entrance exams, law school class rank and finally the number and prestige of law firm job offers.

Bruce laughed at them. They were nothing but brilliant lemmings—able to outthink almost anybody, but incapable of figuring out how unhappy they were as they spent their lives following each other down a career path that held little promise. They had no clue that they really were leading miserable lives, and that the absolute best they could hope for after eight years of 80-hour work weeks was the possibility of being promoted to junior partner. At that point, they could cut back to 75-hour weeks. Unless, of course, they wanted to make senior partner.

And the reality, Bruce knew, was that only two or three of the 22 first year associates would ever even rise to junior partner at Stoak, Puck. The "Queen Bee" structure at the big firms—a few top partners drawing huge salaries, supported by round-the-clock efforts of scores of drone-like associates—made it impossible for it to be otherwise. Ten years from now, the vast majority of these associates would be facing the first academic or professional failure of their lifetime. The words of one of his law professors came to mind: "There is nothing so misguided as an ignorant man with zeal."

Bruce picked up his messages from the reception area and quietly handed a birthday card to the receptionist. She blushed and shyly stammered a thank you, and Bruce realized that he was one of the few people who took the time to read the birthday list in the firm newsletter. For the price of $1.95 and a three minute detour to the drug store, he had made a friend. She would champion him to the other support staff, and maybe someday one of them would help Bruce out in a crunch. And the gesture had put a smile on her face.

On the way to his office, he knocked lightly on the corner office door of Bertram Puck, Jr., the son of the firm's namesake. Five or six seconds passed, then he heard a gruff response. "Enter."

He took two steps into the office and stopped. A mixed aroma greeted him— pipes, wet wool, leather. "I found some good case precedent for the eminent domain matter, sir. I spent four hours researching it at the law library, but I think it'll be worth it for our client." Actually, it had only taken Bruce half an hour to find the cases, but the great thing about legal research was that it was impossible to predict how long it might take, and therefore difficult for the client to question when the bill arrived. On the other hand, in this case Puck probably would have preferred that it had taken Bruce eight hours so that he could have charged the client more. Bruce had settled on four as a happy compromise.

Puck grunted, but never looked up from his desk. "Brief the cases for me and have a memo on my desk by noon tomorrow."

"Thank you," Bruce said, in a tone that he hoped conveyed: "Thank you for allowing me to brief the cases for you, sir."

Bruce settled into his office, closed the door tightly, and began dictating a memo into a microcassette recorder for his secretary to transcribe. The senior associate in charge of the Yankee Bank foreclosures had asked Bruce for a short summary of the foreclosure sale Bruce had conducted the day before in the Fenway neighborhood of Boston:

> *"On September 20, 1989, I conducted a foreclosure sale on behalf of our client, Yankee Bank, on the property known as Unit 50-6, 50 Queensberry Street, Boston, Massachusetts. Other than the auctioneer and myself, there was only one other person in attendance at the sale. That gentleman did not present the necessary deposit to qualify as a registered bidder. On behalf of Yankee Bank, and as per their instructions, I entered a single bid of $124,350, and executed a Memorandum of Sale accordingly."*

He thought about the man at the sale—his name was Pierre, Bruce remembered. He had asked Bruce a number of questions, said that he was interested in buying properties at foreclosure sales. He had also said he had access to a lot of money, which was why Bruce spent twenty minutes with him answering his questions.

Bruce finished dictating the memo and brought the cassette to his secretary. "Just put it in draft form. I'll edit it and put it in final form tonight after you leave." Bruce could tell she was surprised—few attorneys were willing to even put a letter in an envelope by themselves, much less actually do their own word processing. But Bruce wanted to establish a pattern doing some of his own word processing, a pattern that he hoped would allow him to escape scrutiny when on future occasions he needed to prepare a particularly private document.

He returned to his office, closed the door, and pulled out his billing sheet. He spun his chair around and looked out through his office window at the city below. The exposure was to the west, which gave him a clear view of the Massachusetts Turnpike, the firm's client in the eminent domain matter. On his time sheet, he entered 4.5 hours under the Turnpike's client code, and wrote the following description: "Legal research on issue of valuation standards for eminent domain takings. Also, travel to and from law library." Bruce smiled to himself at the travel entry, and gave the firm credit for its business sense. Why pay to maintain an extensive law library when your attorneys can simply walk a few blocks to the public law library? An extra half hour billed to the client, and untold thousands saved on library costs.

On the next line of his time sheet, he entered 1.7 hours under the client code for Yankee Bank and wrote the following: "Review title records at Registry of Deeds for upcoming foreclosures on Campos, Bluras, Parker, Valentine." Bruce had actually spent only twenty minutes at the Registry of Deeds on this matter on his way back from lunch. But he couldn't afford to fall behind on his billing, and lunch and Swan Boat ride in the Public Garden had taken up a good chunk of time.

But time well spent. Marci, the real estate broker who had helped him find his new Beacon Hill apartment, was a fountain of information on Boston real estate. Better yet, she was happy to share this knowledge with a young, single lawyer, especially a tall one with jet-black hair and a shy smile. So he was pleased with himself for making time for the Swan Boat ride, not that Marci—reasonably attractive, but with two younger sisters already married—seemed to need further encouragement. It was a good move, the type of thing that women bragged to their girlfriends about.

Marci had been lively and vivacious, and Bruce—unattached since he ended a college romance out of fear that his girlfriend would discover his hobby of collecting art—had enjoyed the outing. But he didn't lie to himself. It was Marci's knowledge of Boston real estate that he found most attractive.

They had made plans to go out again Friday night. Where should they go? Bruce was convinced that women over the age of 25 generally dated for one reason—they saw dates as an opportunity to interview potential husbands. He believed that most women saw the ideal husband as providing three things: financial security, romance, and good parenting skills. Bruce therefore tailored his dates accordingly. The Swan Boat ride had already illustrated Bruce's romantic side. He decided that their next date would be a trip to the Children's

Museum. He would take off his suit jacket and help the children blow bubbles in the giant bubble display, then stand up and watch Marci read the words "good father" on his forehead. From the Museum, they would go to an expensive restaurant, evidence of Bruce's financial success. Bruce phoned Maison Robert, one of Boston's most elegant restaurants, and made a reservation for a late Friday night dinner.

Social plans set, Bruce pulled out his list of firm clients. On his first day at the firm, Bruce had gone through the firm client list and had highlighted all of the clients that were either large institutions or were plaintiffs being represented by the firm on a contingency basis (that is, the firm received one-third of the client's recovery). These clients' cases were the ones Bruce wanted to work on, not because they were necessarily interesting or challenging, but because they afforded Bruce the most obvious opportunities for creative billing. Large institutions seemed never to question their bills, and plaintiffs being represented on a contingency basis were never billed at all, although associates were fully credited for the time they spent working on contingency cases. These types of clients would allow him to continue billing the quota of hours demanded by the firm, even if his personal business required him to spend large chunks of time outside the office.

Bruce's secretary interrupted his reflections. "There's a Pierre Prefontaine on the line for you. He says he met you at the Queensberry Street foreclosure auction yesterday."

*   *   *

Pierre waited while Bruce's secretary connected the call, then he heard Bruce's friendly, confident voice. "Bruce Arrujo speaking."

"Hi, Mr. Arrujo, my name is Pierre Prefontaine. I met you at the Queensberry Street foreclosure auction yesterday."

"Of course, Pierre. What can I do for you?"

Pierre summarized Howie's situation. "Now Howie has changed his mind and wants to back out. I told him I would try to find an attorney to look at the contract for him. Can you do it?"

"I'd be happy to try. But why doesn't he want to buy the property?"

"To be honest, he's getting nervous about the real estate market. He'd rather save his money for other deals after the prices come down." Pierre left out his own role in Howie's sudden conversion from bull to bear—he saw no need to further publicize his disloyalty to his "client", the property's seller. In fact, he probably shouldn't have agreed even to make this phone call to Bruce.

"All right. Why don't you send me over a copy of the Purchase and Sale Agreement, and I'll take a look at it."

"Howie has a fax machine at work. I'll have him fax it over to you."

Bruce gave Pierre the fax number. "Pierre, should I call you or Howie after I've reviewed the agreement?"

Pierre smiled to himself—Bruce was aware of the fact that Pierre was being disloyal to his 'client', and was being sensitive to it. "You should probably deal directly with Howie from now on. And thanks for asking."

*   *   *

The fax from Howie arrived at 5:30 that evening, and Bruce sat down to review the agreement. Most young associates would have been thrilled at the thought of bringing a new client—and, from the looks of things, a fairly wealthy one—to the firm in their first month on the job. After all, a good client base was often a decisive factor in the promotion of an associate to partnership. But Bruce valued Howie and Pierre not as clients, but as potential resources in the real estate community. Between the two of them, they provided both ready capital and market knowledge, two assets Bruce was lacking. Bruce figured he would win their trust and appreciation if he could help Howie get out of this deal, especially if he did so without charging Howie an exorbitant "big firm" fee. The fee part would be easy—Bruce would simply not record much of the time he spent on the case. The firm would never know the difference, and Bruce's "creative" billing practices would allow him to make up the hours elsewhere.

Getting Howie out of the deal, however, would not be so easy. The seller's attorney had drafted the contract, and it left Howie little wiggle room. All the contingencies in the transaction had either already been satisfied or been deemed waived by Howie because the relevant dates had passed. The only remaining contingency in the deal was the written commitment letter from the mortgage lender. And according to Pierre, the letter was just a formality.

Bruce read the agreement a second time, looking for an escape hatch buried beneath the thirteen pages of legalese. If one existed, Bruce was simply not experienced enough to identify it.

Bruce walked to the men's room, splashed cold water in his face and spoke to his reflection in the mirror. "Stop thinking like a lawyer, you idiot." He had only been at the firm for three weeks, and he was already analyzing problems like a nerdish law student, trying to find shades of meaning in words and the placement of commas. But law was theoretical, it only became real when applied to a set of facts. The solution to most legal problems, Bruce had learned long ago, lay not in the law itself but in the facts. He would leave the technical scrutiny to others.

In Howie's case, the law (as stated in the contract) was clear—if he got a mortgage commitment from the bank, he would have to either close on the property or forfeit his $100,000 deposit. But the facts were still fluid. Would Howie get his mortgage commitment? Pierre had said it was imminent, but could anything be done to change that? Bruce returned to his office and telephoned Howie. It was only 5:00 Pacific time, and Howie was still in the office.

"Hi, Howie. This is Bruce Arrujo calling from Boston."

"Oh, yeah. Hi. Pierre mentioned you might be calling. Thanks for helping out. Did you get the Purchase and Sale Agreement I faxed you?"

"Sure did. That's why I'm calling. The agreement is pretty airtight, assuming you get your mortgage commitment. But you haven't gotten it yet, right?"

"Right. The bank said it looks fine, but they just wanted a couple of more things from me before giving the final approval. I was going to send the stuff to them by overnight mail tonight."

"What kind of things are they looking for? And what bank is it?"

"It's Bank of Boston. Let's see. They want copies of my 1986 and 1987 tax returns—they already have 1988. They want a letter from me explaining why I missed a few student loan payments in 1981. And they want copies of my last six monthly Merrill-Lynch statements to show that the $400,000 I'm using for the down payment is my own money."

Bruce didn't immediately respond; he was studying the notes he had just taken. "The 1986 and '87 tax returns—what do they show for income?"

"High enough to qualify for the loan, if that's what you're thinking. Maybe $120,000 in '86 and $140,000 in '87."

"And the Merrill-Lynch stuff. It'll show the money in your account?"

"Yeah. It's been in a money market account while I wait to close."

"That leaves the student loan. Why didn't you pay?"

"I don't remember, it was my first year out of grad school. I was, like, 26 years old, didn't have a job yet. I probably paid the rent instead. When I got a job, I caught up on the student loans."

"Were you living in San Diego at the time?"

"Yeah. I was teaching Spanish part-time while I looked for a job. Why?"

"I'm just thinking out loud." Was there a way of somehow making Howie's explanation for missing the loan payments so offensive to the bank that they would turn down his otherwise solid loan application? "Howie, will you be there for a while?"

"Yeah. Another hour or so."

"Good. Check the fax machine in about half an hour. Then call me."

Bruce turned on his computer. The combination of the Bank of Boston and Howie teaching Spanish had sparked an idea. He typed the following:

Dear Sir/Madam:

You have asked me for an explanation for why I did not pay my student loans for three months in 1981.

I did not pay these loans because the bank that held these loans was acting as an imperialistic tool of the oppressive United States government. This bank had been making predatory loans to Latin American countries in the hopes that these countries would default on their payments, which would give the U.S. government the excuse it needed to install Fascist dictatorships in these countries in the name of "fiscal responsibility". I could not in good conscience bring myself to support these efforts by sending money to the bank when the bank—as an obvious agent of the Reagan administration—was acting in such an imperialistic manner. By withholding these payments, I considered myself a "conscientious objector" to the illegal U.S. foreign policy in Latin America.

Sincerely,

Howard Plansky, September 21, 1989

Bruce faxed the letter to Howie, and waited for the phone to ring. Five minutes later it did.

Howie was laughing when Bruce answered the phone. "This is brilliant. Absolutely fucking brilliant!"

"I thought you might like it." Bruce couldn't help laughing also.

"Except one thing, Bruce. Who would believe that a left-wing crazy would become a capitalistic landlord?"

"Good point, Howie. But do you think the Bank of Boston will even think it through that much? I mean, they do a ton of business in South America—that's what made me think of it. I bet they get this letter and spit out a denial of your mortgage application in about ten minutes. Who would make a loan to you after reading that letter? To a banker, that letter is blasphemy."

Howie was still chuckling. "You know, it just may work. It's a crazy idea, but it just may work. I'll never get another loan from Bank of Boston, but there are plenty of other banks out there. Besides, it's the only chance I've got, right?"

13

[October 21, 1989]

It was cold, but it was also Saturday night, and Charese knew that if October was cold, November and December would be colder. Not to mention that next weekend was Halloween weekend, and Charese knew from experience that trying to turn tricks with masked johns was just asking for trouble. She pulled her waist-length fake fur around her, and buttoned the bottom two buttons. The top two buttons she left open, revealing what little there was of her breasts covered only by a red silk teddy. Her breasts had been steadily growing, but the hormone pills took time to work and she still considered herself small-busted. Later, perhaps, she would get implants, if she decided to go through with the operation.

Her legs, on the other hand, were perfect. Long and sleek, she played them up even more by wearing four-inch heels and a short matching red leather miniskirt and fishnet stockings. It would be cold, but she hoped she could do two quick blow jobs on passing motorists heading up Arlington Street to the Massachusetts Turnpike, then go home to a warm bed. She prepared a thermos of hot coffee, and walked the six blocks northeast to the corner of Columbus Avenue and Arlington Street. She set the thermos down, and leaned up against a telephone pole, one leg languidly extended outwards toward the street. Her stomach began to churn. It had been more than ten years since she had sold herself—it wasn't really like riding a bike.

And what about this whole AIDS thing? She had been on the sidelines during the entire epidemic because she had been faithful to Roberge. Would the men mind if she insisted on a condom? Would they expect it? Even for a blow job? She figured she would give a blow job without a condom; as for actual intercourse, well, the guy would be disappointed if he expected that anyway.

Maybe she should have gone to one of the gay clubs and looked for a trick there. It would have been safer because no one would be surprised to find she was actually a man, but she couldn't bear the thought of running into one of Roberge's friends and having him find out how she was supporting herself. So here she stood, shaking a leg at passing cars and offering blow jobs for $50.

And she had good luck early—a middle-aged Asian man driving a luxury sedan pulled over and quickly agreed to her price. They drove together to a schoolyard parking lot, where Charese skillfully performed with her tongue and lips. The man ejaculated quickly, the taste of semen filling Charese's mouth. She had never minded the taste, and tonight actually found herself aroused by it. The arousal at first amused, then saddened, her. *What has become of me*, she wondered, *when I get turned on by giving blow jobs to strangers?*

She took the money and walked back to her thermos of coffee. She poured herself a cup, both to warm herself and to take away the taste in her mouth. She refreshed her lipstick, and again dangled her leg toward the street.

But her heart wasn't into it anymore, and after a half-hour of unsuccessful efforts, she picked up her thermos and headed home. *What is happening with that damned lawsuit?*

14

[October 23, 1989]

Bruce and Marci had laughed their way through the Children's Museum. They blew bubbles with the children, crawled through mazes, and, Bruce's personal favorite, played Monopoly on a 1930s game board. When Bruce was a child, he and Grandpa often engaged in rainy-day Monopoly marathons. The loser had to do two things: pay the winner a dollar, and address the winner as 'Your Highness' for the rest of the day.

He and Marci had returned that night to Bruce's apartment, but he resisted the urge to make a pass at her (although he did chuckle at the thought of her addressing him as 'Your Highness' as he stood naked in front of her). Bruce knew that sleeping with a woman invariably led to expectations of a serious relationship, expectations that would have to be either fulfilled or dashed within a few weeks. Bruce wanted to take it slower, figuring that Marci's real estate knowledge might be useful for the next few months at least. Besides, he could always get casual sex from a bar pick-up or even by paying for it, so why deal with the emotional baggage if he didn't have to?

Over the next couple of weeks, he saw Marci three or four times for lunch and a Sunday afternoon sail on the Charles River. He was intrigued by Marci's insights into the real estate market. Prices had risen so far and so fast in Boston over the past few years that it seemed they would never come down. In fact, many so-called experts were citing demographic trends and historical models to argue that the real estate industry had become insulated from the cyclical nature of other economic sectors. Marci, however, offered a different perspective. A few of the more conservative property owners had begun selling their buildings, taking ninety or ninety-five cents on the dollar. And many others were no longer adding to their portfolios. Marci didn't agree with their positions, but then again it was her job to be optimistic about real estate values.

Meanwhile, Bruce continued to generate income for the firm, billing 50 to 60 hours of his time per week to firm clients. And nobody had reason to suspect that these bills had been inflated. Bruce made a point of being in the office every day between 7:30 and 10:00 in the morning, and 4:00 and 7:00 during the afternoon. This was prime "face time" and, along with at least one day of the weekend, was the time the partners tended to pop their heads into offices to see who was putting in the hours.

Bruce knew that he had put himself in an ideal position. As an associate at Stoak, Puck and Beal, he was cloaked in respectability. After only a couple of months on the job, he had won the confidence of the firm's partners—especially Bertram Puck—and would likely be called on to continue to work on matters involving the firm's institutional clients. He had a block of time during the middle of the day during which he could pretty much come and go as he pleased— he simply slung an extra suit jacket over his chair and left his light on, just as he would if he were in the library or conferring with another attorney. And, most importantly, the combination of the firm's arrogance and greed were the perfect shield for Bruce's activities. It would simply never occur to the partners that a lowly first year associate would be capable of pulling off a scam right under their noses.

15

[October 24, 1989]

Before she was even out of bed, Charese got a call from Shelby. "Listen, Charese, we need to meet." It was a Tuesday, Charese remembered.

"Is it about my case?" Charese cursed herself. *No, idiot, Shelby's calling for fashion tips.* "Actually, can you hold for a minute?" Charese ran to the bathroom and splashed water on her face, then to the kitchen to pour a cup of coffee from a pot that she had set to automatically brew the night before. The kitchen clock read 10:25. "Sorry, I'm back."

"Good. I only have a minute between classes. Are you free to meet for lunch?"

"Of course. At the office?"

"No, we can't meet there. Do you know 33 Dunster Street in Harvard Square? It's a restaurant. Say, 1:30?"

"Sure. I'll be there."

"Oh, and please don't tell Reese. I'll explain when I see you. Bye." The line went dead.

Charese put down the phone. It made no sense to her, but her intuition told her to trust Shelby. And Harvard Square was a great place to people watch.

*   *   *

Just after noon, Charese left her Clarendon Street apartment in the South End, walked north a few blocks and then east down Columbus Avenue toward the Boston Common. Her plan was to walk to Park Street station, then take the Red Line across the river into Cambridge. It was a brisk autumn day, but the walk would be good exercise, perhaps the last chance for a walk before the winter set in.

Charese arrived at the Park Street station a half-hour later, chilled but not really cold. She took the escalator down, and recalled her ride up the same escalator just two months earlier for her first meeting with Reese. Unlike her completely feminine persona that day, her appearance today was neither dominantly female nor male. She wore a purple sweatshirt and blue jeans over tennis shoes.

She had shaved and applied a little make-up to cover the razor stubble, but otherwise hadn't done anything to her face.

Not that it mattered. Nobody gave her a second look as she boarded the subway and spread out over a double seat for the fifteen-minute ride. At Harvard Square, a college-aged girl was playing a guitar and singing a folk song on the platform between the outgoing and incoming trains. Charese could hear her high-pitched, haunting voice, even over the sound of the train pulling away. The song was eerily hypnotic, a ballad about anger and love and passion. Charese walked over, saw a pretty porcelain-white face framed by dark brown hair. The singer was surrounded by a handful of other passengers, all equally enchanted by either the singer or her song.

Charese watched as a middle-aged man in a business suit dropped a twenty-dollar bill into her guitar case and walked slowly away, distant memories of a youthful love flashing in his eyes and flushing his cheeks. Charese moved into the spot he had vacated, listened to a few more songs, then handed the singer a five-dollar bill in exchange for a cassette tape. It was five dollars she couldn't afford to spend, yet the singer had soothed and comforted her. Adrienne was the singer's name, or so the cassette said, and she smiled a thank you at Charese as she sang. Charese smiled back, whispered a response. "No, thank you."

The incident reminded her of the time she and Roberge had watched Tracy Chapman, now at the top of the folk singer charts, sing in that very same subway station a few years earlier. The memory of Roberge angered her, but she was pleased that her anger was directed more at his intrusion into her happy moment than at his act of leaving her. Perhaps she was starting to get over him.

Buoyed by that thought, and humming an Adrienne ballad, Charese walked through the Square and over to Dunster Street. She was a few minutes early, which gave her the opportunity to see Shelby turn the corner from Mt. Auburn Street and make her way toward the restaurant. She counted three male heads swivel as Shelby walked the half block.

Shelby gave a friendly wave, then took Charese's arm as they walked down half a flight of stairs into the restaurant. Charese immediately noticed that Shelby seemed more at ease than she had in the LAP office with Reese around; she guessed that her theory about Reese coming on to Shelby was probably accurate.

They sat down, and Charese studied her further. At the LAP office, Charese had thought Shelby beautiful in a Parisian sort of way. But today, as they made small talk before ordering, Charese perceived Shelby differently. Smiling, animated, relaxed—Charese noticed that Shelby was not just beautiful, she was also cute and engaging. Shining eyes, dimpled cheeks, a playful toss of the head. Charese had known many woman in her life, and had envied a good number of them. Many were beautiful, and many more were cute, but few of them combined both qualities in quite the way Shelby did. Plus she was smart enough to get into Harvard Law School, and rich enough to pay for it. Simply not fair.

Charese would have been content to sit and study Shelby further, but she could tell that Shelby was eager to discuss the case. "So, what's up with my case?"

Shelby leaned forward. "Good question. There's some strange stuff going on." Shelby paused and played with her straw, then sipped at her Diet Coke. "I'm not sure about any of this, but I feel that I have to tell you what I know. But first, let me give you some background information.

"The way this whole LAP thing works is that there are a few full-time lawyers there. Reese is one of them. I think they're paid by the state and also supported by the big law firms. Anyway, they have a very liberal agenda—it's pretty funny, actually, because often they end up fighting big companies that are represented by the same law firms that support them. But that's not the point. The point is, most of the law students who work for them also are pretty liberal. Well, I'm not." Shelby stopped here, as if this were a confession of some sort, and started playing with her straw again.

Charese shrugged, unable to see the relevance of this revelation. And why should Shelby even care what Charese thought? "I don't get it. What does that have to do with me or my case?"

"I guess it really doesn't, I just want you to know where I'm coming from. I just don't believe that it's government's job to impose morals on its citizens. Government shouldn't be in the business of legislating morality—that's the job of parents and families and churches. People should be generous and care about the poor, but not just because Reese Jeffries and his liberal cronies force them to be by taxing them and redistributing the wealth to the needy. That only creates resentment and ill will, and charity is supposed to bring communities together, not divide them. Anyway, I thought you might not trust me if you knew I wasn't a bleeding-heart liberal."

"Not trust you? Honestly, Shelby, I trust you more than I do Reese. But I'm still lost here."

Shelby smiled gently, her turquoise eyes shining at Charese. "Of course you are; I'm not being clear. I guess I'm being a little defensive. People—or at least people in Cambridge—just assume that if you're not a liberal, you must be heartless and selfish and evil. Well, I'm not any of those things. I'm really not. And I need you to believe that. Because if you don't believe that, you're probably not going to believe the rest of what I have to tell you."

Charese stared at Shelby for a few seconds. Shelby's description of the liberal mentality in Cambridge reminded her of the sanctimonious bible-thumpers she had known in her Georgia childhood. You were either a churchgoer or a devil worshiper, no in-between. She spoke softy. "I'll believe whatever you have to say, Shelby."

Shelby put down her straw and grinned—a bright, dazzling smile that reached across the table and lifted the edges of Charese's lips as well. "Thanks, Charese. That's nice to hear. Now here's the story. After we filed your complaint, I got a call from Roberge. Actually, he called for Reese and I happened to pick up the phone. Reese wasn't there, but since I was familiar with the case I introduced myself and asked him what he wanted. Well, the upshot of the conversation was that he wanted to avoid any publicity because he didn't want to embarrass his father."

Charese cut in. "He means he doesn't want his little country club blue-blood bride to find out."

Shelby laughed. "Whatever his reasons, he made what I think is a very good settlement offer. He offered to give you the condo, which he owns free and clear, if you drop the case. The only thing is, he insisted on a confidentiality agreement so that there would be no publicity. He hadn't even hired a lawyer yet because he wanted to keep this as quiet as possible."

Charese was stunned. She knew the condo—a gift from his parents—was worth more than $200,000. She could sell it and start over again with a nice nest egg. Or just keep it and take in a roommate to help pay the bills. "So what's the problem?"

"Well, I wrote Reese a memo detailing the conversation before I left that day. When I came back to the office two days later, there was a message for me to see Reese ASAP. I thought he would be happy about the settlement offer, but instead he gave me a twenty minute lecture on how I hadn't passed the bar exam yet and how it was unethical for me to enter into settlement negotiations without his prior approval, blah, blah, blah. At first I thought he was just angry at me for something else, stuff not related to your case...."

Charese interrupted by nodding. "Yeah, I figured he came on to you."

Shelby gasped in amazement. "Charese, how did you know?"

Charese smiled back at her triumphantly. "Just woman's intuition. It comes with the hormone treatments!" Both women laughed, although Charese could tell that Shelby was a bit embarrassed at being so transparent. Not that Shelby seemed threatened by it in any way—in fact, she smiled at Charese with what Charese saw as a new-found respect.

"Anyway, I thought he was just using it as a way to re-inflate his male ego. But he went on for so long, I figured it had to be more than that. When he finally finished his little lecture, I think he expected me just to leave with my tail between my legs. Instead, I acted like nothing had happened and just asked him what he thought about the settlement offer. He turned real red and told me that Krygier had withdrawn the offer."

Charese slumped a bit in her chair. Shelby continued. "Well, that was a week ago. I hadn't heard anything about the case since then, and the whole thing just struck me as weird. I mean, the way it works is that I am supposed to negotiate settlements and make case decisions—that's the whole idea of the clinical program. So for Reese to be upset at me seemed totally, well, wrong. Then, yesterday, I got a call from a lawyer at one of the big firms downtown who said he was representing Roberge. He called to say he was preparing an Answer to our Complaint, and that we would have it by the end of the week. He asked me again if we would be willing to settle the case before it became public, because after it became public it would be too late. When I told him I thought Roberge had withdrawn the settlement offer, he totally denied it. He said Reese had called him last week and told him that you had refused to settle, for any amount of money."

"Me?! I haven't even spoken to Reese."

Shelby reached across and took Charese's hand. "Yeah. I figured."

16

[October 25, 1989]

Shelby slept late the next day, a rare luxury. She rolled out of bed at ten, threw on a robe and brushed her teeth, then opened the apartment door and grabbed the *Boston Herald* sitting on the stoop outside. Her friends teased her for reading the tabloid-style *Herald* instead of the *Globe*, but she found it a welcome counterbalance to the dry prose of her law studies. Besides, it did an equally good job on local news, and for national and international news, she read The *New York Times*. She folded the paper under her arm and carried it to the kitchen table.

The headline on page 3 almost knocked Shelby right off her chair:

Drag Queen Sues Real Estate Heir
Wants Krygier Son to Pay for Sex Change Operation

A picture of Charese standing next to Roberge's father, who had his arm around both Charese and Roberge, took up a quarter of the page. The caption identified the picture as having been taken at the senior Krygier's sixtieth birthday party the previous summer. The two Krygiers were dressed as upstanding citizens of Boston. Charese was dressed as a woman. Shelby recognized the picture as one of the group that Charese had given to Reese.

Shelby quickly read through the rest of the story. It quoted liberally from the Complaint Shelby had authored, recounting Charese's twelve-year relationship with Roberge, Roberge's request that she have a sex change operation and become his "wife", and Charese's subsequent pre-operation hormone treatments. It also recounted the recent announcement that Roberge would be marrying Megan French, even going so far as quoting from the engagement announcement that the *Globe* had published a few weeks earlier. It even contained a reaction from Reese, who questioned whether this was just another example of a wealthy property-owning family taking advantage of the less fortunate members of society. And in its most inflammatory paragraph, the article quoted unnamed sources who stated that Roberge had hidden the nature of the relationship from his father because he knew his father was "violently homophobic," so much so that the senior Krygier had once been heard to say that Hitler had been right to attempt to exterminate European homosexuals. The

71

Krygier family had no comment on the story, other than to deny that Wesley Krygier would ever condone the extermination of any group of people.

Shelby read the article a second time, then headed for the shower. She let the water run over her body for twenty minutes, trying to process the story and understand its ramifications for Charese. A few things were obvious. First, Reese had purposely leaked the story to embarrass the Krygier family—they were prominent in Boston social circles, and a picture of the senior Krygier with his arm around a drag queen would not play well with the afternoon tea crowd. Even worse, the Krygier family's position of prominence in the business community would surely suffer as questions were raised regarding Wesley Krygier's judgment and character—he had been duped by his son and, even worse, apparently was a closet homophobe and perhaps even a Hitler apologist. Second, Reese leaked the story now because he must have known that if he waited, Charese would insist on settling the case, a settlement that would also include an anti-publicity stipulation. Third, Reese had kept Shelby in the dark on purpose so that she wouldn't interfere with his plans. And fourth, now that the cat was out of the bag, there was less incentive for the Krygiers to settle Charese's lawsuit.

Shelby dried herself off, then poured a second cup of coffee. She still wondered whether she had made the right decision in coming back to law school after her family's death. The whole process of watching the drunk driver work the system for an acquittal had disgusted her. A team of high-priced lawyers simply paraded a chorus of high-priced experts in front a jury, while a pair of overworked and under-funded district attorneys valiantly fought, and lost, the good fight. It wasn't so much that a conviction would have brought back her family, but at least it would have ensured that Mr. Martini wouldn't climb back into a car and destroy someone else's life. In the end, she had returned to law school because she couldn't rebut the argument that the best way to change the system was to work from within it.

But was the system even worth saving? Not with lawyers like Reese Jeffries running around sacrificing clients at the alter of self-promotion. She shook her head—maybe Barry wasn't so bad after all. Sure, he was nothing more than a hired gun. But at least he didn't turn around and use that gun to shoot his own client in the back.

17

Hours before Shelby had even rolled out of bed, Reese Jeffries had purchased five copies of the *Herald* at the corner convenience store and had treated himself to a second chocolate croissant. He had single-handedly dealt a crippling blow to Wesley Krygier's reputation, and, by extension, to Krygier's personal crusade to repeal rent control in Boston. Krygier was currently the primary financial backer of, and the figurehead for, the repeal efforts, and he had been making headway recently in the political arena by contributing heavily in local political contests. Now he would become the subject of ridicule—from the conservative groups because of his son's lifestyle, from the liberals because of his apparent homophobia, and from both because he couldn't even tell that the "woman" he had welcomed so openly into his family circle had balls, not boobs.

Reese was sure that his own stature in the tenants' rights community would skyrocket. The group had been trying to damage Krygier for years, without success. Reese pictured himself arriving at Friday's tenant rally in Cambridge, people reaching to shake his hand, to pat his back, to whisper congratulations in his ear. He indulged in a third croissant.

18

[November 7, 1989]

Bruce, too, had seen the newspaper story. He had cut it out and kept it, and was in the middle of re-reading it when his office phone rang one evening almost two weeks later.

The digital display identified the caller: Bertram Puck. Bruce quickly picked up the handset. "Good afternoon, Mr. Puck." The rest of the world might view 6:30 as evening, but at the firm 6:30 was still afternoon.

"Come to my office." Click.

Bruce scooped up a clean legal pad and a pen and walked down the hall to the senior partner's corner office. Puck's door was open; Bruce knocked and waited until Puck motioned him in with an impatient wave.

Bruce surveyed the office as Puck, a file open on the desk in front of him, typed on a computer keyboard. He was surprised to see the computer in Puck's office—none of the other partners and only a few associates besides Bruce had requested their own terminals. Other than the computer, the office was decorated in a style that Bruce had labeled "Traditional Shipwreck"—prints of old naval battles and schooners being thrown against the rocks, pieces of driftwood mounted and displayed, a ship's clock on the wall, a navigational map of the coast of Boston circa 1800, an antique spyglass on the window sill. Bertram Puck, Sr. had practiced maritime law, Bruce knew, so the motif seemed appropriate enough; every time there was a shipwreck, old Bertram stood to profit from the ensuing legal work.

Bertram, Jr.—actually, there were few people left at the firm who even remembered there was a Bertram, Sr.—motioned for Bruce to sit, but did not raise his head from his work to look at the young attorney. Bruce had noticed that few of the partners actually looked at the younger associates. It was almost as if the partners reminded each other at their weekly meetings not to actually make eye contact with a young associate, lest the associate mistakenly take it as some sign of equality.

Sitting contentedly, Bruce studied the partner. He decided that Puck was misnamed—he looked more like a hockey stick than a disk of black rubber. He was tall and thin, and his head was perpetually angled forward as if from a lifelong effort to avoid making eye contact. His expression was rigid, his complexion rutted and knotty, his nose and mouth straight and hard. Even his closely cropped hair protruded splinter-like from the crown of his head. Only his eyes seemed animate, but even they were a shade of steel blue that Bruce had only seen once before, and then in a newborn wolf puppy.

Bruce studied Puck further as he continued to type—rather adeptly—on his computer keyboard. His clothes were timeless, as they had been every time Bruce saw him: heavy wool Brooks Brothers suit, speckled with flakes of dandruff; oxford shirt; blue and red tie; wing tips. Watching Puck hunched over his computer made Bruce think of some character from a Dickens novel who had discovered a futuristic device that made simple the act of stealing from widows and orphans.

And, from what Bruce had heard, many at the firm viewed Puck as some sort of modern-day Dickensian villain. Apparently an eighth-year associate, who had worked primarily on Puck's cases during his tenure at the firm, had recently come up for partnership vote. He had been rejected, despite stellar work habits and glowing yearly reviews. The scuttlebutt was that Puck had been concerned that some of his clients had been calling the associate directly, and that Puck had blocked the partnership election to prevent the possible loss of control of his client base. Even at a cutthroat firm like Stoak, Puck & Beal, it was considered extremely bad form to string an associate along for eight years with expectations of partnership and then to vote him down. And when the very partner who had profited from the associate's 80-hour work weeks and skillful legal representation had cast the deciding vote…; well, Bruce could understand why none of the other associates wanted to work for Puck.

Which is why Bruce was trying so hard to ingratiate himself with Puck. A vacuum existed, and Bruce figured the opportunity to work directly for a senior partner with a large institutional client base was an ideal set of circumstances for him. Usually at a large firm a first-year associate took assignments from a senior associate, who in turn worked directly with a partner. Bruce hoped that he could quickly win Puck's confidence, and that Puck—wary of again facing the loss of clients to a senior associate—would by-pass the traditional structure and work directly with Bruce.

As for winning Puck's confidence, Bruce had concluded it came down to one thing—ensure that nothing interrupted Puck's income stream from his client base. The unfortunate eighth-year associate had apparently threatened Puck's firm hold on the institutional clients he had inherited from his father. Such a threat was an inevitable result of the manner in which the firm serviced its clients—the associate or junior partner worked directly with the client on a daily basis, while the senior partner provided occasional oversight. This familiarity often resulted in the client contacting the junior partner directly when a new legal matter arose. Under the complicated formula used for calculating firm profit distributions, the senior partner would have to share profits from the new matter with the junior partner. Bruce, however, as a junior associate, was not entitled to any share of firm profits and therefore was not a financial threat to Puck.

Of course, Bruce realized that Puck would also be concerned that his clients be well-serviced. This could be a problem for Bruce. Usually, a young associate would get legal guidance from the senior associate assigned to the matter. Or, in some cases, the associate could go directly to the partner. But it didn't seem to Bruce that Puck would be receptive to frequent questions. And, because of the competitive atmosphere at the firm, Bruce doubted that any of the more experienced associates would be willing to waste valuable billing time to help a first-year associate. Bruce would have to be careful.

Puck interrupted Bruce's thoughts by finally speaking. Bruce looked at the clock—he had been waiting for six minutes. "I noticed that you have been working on the foreclosures for Yankee Bank. It seems that, since the real estate market has been so prosperous the last five years, none of the more senior associates have had any experience handling foreclosure cases." Bruce smiled to himself; when a senior associate had asked if any of the new associates wanted to work on the Yankee Bank foreclosure cases, Bruce had quickly volunteered. The other associates not only saw the work as boring and dry, they also dreaded the thought of actually having to stand out on a street corner in Lowell or Revere or Dorchester and auction off some piece of property like a pretzel vendor. But Bruce saw the cases as a perfect opportunity to obtain inside information on real estate opportunities.

Puck continued. "I have just received a request from Nickel Bank of New York that we handle their foreclosure work in Massachusetts. Apparently they made some rather, shall we say, ambitious mortgage loans over the past few years, and a number of the borrowers are delinquent. Nickel wants to move ahead quickly on the foreclosures, before it gets a reputation in the area for not being aggressive with its borrowers. That is why they have retained us rather than a smaller firm—they are looking for a show of strength." Puck paused at this point to display his long yellowed teeth, presumably as a show of that strength. "They have instructed me to take a hard line with all of the loans, and to move to foreclosure as quickly as possible. I have agreed to take the cases on a flat fee of $2,000 per foreclosure, plus costs."

Bruce took notes as Puck spoke, but his mind quickly found the meaning behind Puck's words. Puck wanted a young associate to whip through these cases as quickly as possible, the borrowers and their sad stories be damned.

Puck did not wait for Bruce to finish writing. "Nickel has given us 40 files to start with. Get a real estate paralegal to help you. Give me status reports twice a month. I expect that there will be more cases if these are handled appropriately."

Puck dismissed Bruce, who went back to his office. He reflected on the amount of time he had been spending on the Yankee Bank foreclosures. With a trained paralegal, he could complete a case in far less time than even Puck expected. Based on the $2,000 fee Puck was charging the client, Bruce calculated that Puck expected him to spend about 400 hours on the 40 foreclosure cases. Bruce was sure he could complete them in less than half that time. In other words, Bruce should have approximately 200 free hours to himself. Enough time to do all sorts of fun things.

19

[November 8, 1989]

Bruce spent the next morning at the law library reviewing every reference material he could find that related to foreclosure law and practice. Unlike the Yankee Bank cases, he would not have the benefit of a senior associate guiding him on the legal formalities in the Nickel Bank cases. Which was fine with Bruce—guidance also meant oversight.

As Puck had indicated, little had been written about foreclosure practice over the past decade because the booming real estate market made for little foreclosure activity. Bruce copied what he could find, and walked over to the Land Court to see if any of the older clerks of the court could give him any guidance. A desk clerk directed him to Eddie Sullivan, a red-nosed, white-haired caricature of the Irish civil servant that still existed in many parts of Massachusetts. But Eddie's eyes were clear, and he apparently knew all the ins and outs of foreclosure law. Bruce asked if he could buy him lunch. Eddie hesitated. Bruce suggested the Scotch and Sirloin restaurant. Eddie accepted.

The Scotch and Sirloin was located on the upper floor of an old warehouse building, midway between the Boston Garden and the edge of the financial district.

Customers—often businessmen on their way to or from the Garden to watch the Bruins or Celtics play—loaded onto an old freight elevator and were lifted upwards to enjoy thick cuts of steak and homemade bread. Not to mention one or two tumblers of Scotland's nectar. It was a favorite of the residents of many of Boston's neighborhoods, and Bruce had done well in Eddie's eyes by suggesting it.

Over lunch, Eddie laid out for Bruce—from beginning to end—the process of foreclosing on a piece of property in Massachusetts. The process was technical and cumbersome, and the slightest error could invalidate the entire process. But more amazing to Bruce was the absence of any court oversight. As long as the bank properly notified all the interested parties, no court permission was required before holding the foreclosure sale. And the sale was final. Bruce asked Eddie about it.

"Yeah, that's right." Eddie spoke in short sentences, sipping from his Dewar's between each one. "In most states, you have to get a court order before you can foreclose." Sip. "Or the court has to approve the sale afterwards." Sip. "But in Massachusetts, you just do it." Sip. "Don't need the court at all." Sip.

"So there's no oversight of the process at all? Nobody checks to make sure the bank did all it could to get the highest price?"

"That's right." Sip.

Bruce treated himself to a rare mid-day beer.

*   *   *

Two days later, Bruce took an early lunch in order to attend a foreclosure auction he had seen advertised in the *Boston Globe*. The ad had been stuck between one for a liquidation of Persian rugs and another publicizing the sale of restaurant equipment from an out-of-business oceanfront restaurant. The rug ad itself was reflective of nothing, but Bruce had noticed an increasing number of restaurant closings, and wondered if the economic boom was going to be followed by an equally severe bust. It wouldn't necessarily be a bad thing—chaos often created opportunity.

The foreclosure sale was held in the driveway of the mortgaged property, a single-family home on a cul-de-sac in Medford, a middle class suburb north of Boston. Bruce had driven by the house the day before and had seen a broker's "For Sale" sign in front. The sign was down now, but Bruce had called the broker, who told him the house was on the market for $289,000. When pressed, the broker had estimated that a more realistic value for the house was $235,000.

Bruce had researched the title on the property prior to the sale, and knew that the homeowners—Mario and Colleen Allante—had paid $260,000 in 1987 for a home that had sold in 1983 for barely half that amount. They had a mortgage of $247,000—Bruce calculated that the monthly payment, including taxes and insurance, must have approached $3,000. A commercial van with bright red "Mario's Carpet" lettering sat in the driveway. So, Bruce guessed, Mario made a ton of money installing carpet during the construction boom, then couldn't afford $36,000 per year just in housing costs once the boom ended. Bruce shook his head—who was more of an idiot, Mario for taking such a big mortgage or the bank for making such an aggressive loan?

From his title search, Bruce also knew that Mario owed another $15,000 to the IRS and $10,000 to a wholesale carpet supplier, each of whom had placed a lien on the property. No wonder Mario was asking $289,000—he needed that much just to pay the broker and clear the liens on the property.

Bruce approached the auctioneer, who was standing huddled under an umbrella with a man Bruce assumed to be the bank's attorney.

"Hello, sir. Are you here for the auction?"

No, Bruce thought, *I'm here to ask Mario for a loan.* "Yes, I am."

"Welcome, then. Do you have the ten thousand dollars?" A certified check—or cash—was a requirement for making a bid at the auction. Bruce wondered how many people actually showed up with an envelope full of cash.

"No, but I'd like to observe, if that's okay."

Bruce was not alone—there were seven or eight other people milling about in the driveway trying to stay warm in the November chill. Despite the crowd, Bruce could see that the auctioneer's sheet of paper entitled "Qualified Bidders" remained blank. Bruce guessed that many of the others in attendance were probably Mario's neighbors, drawn by a kind of morbid fascination. The scene clamored for Mario standing on the roof threatening to jump, a camera crew recording the drama for all of Boston to see on the evening news.

The auctioneer gave Bruce a copy of the Sale Agreement, which Bruce read through quickly. It seemed to Bruce that the bank's attorney had tried so hard to draft an agreement that was favorable to the bank that he had made it virtually impossible for a third party to be comfortable enough to make a bid. For example, prospective bidders were not allowed to view—much less inspect—the inside of the house. On top of that, it was the successful bidder's responsibility to evict the current owner and his family from the house. And the successful bidder had to close within 21 days, far too soon for anyone hoping to get a mortgage. Finally, the bidder was given no assurances that the bank even had clear title to the property. All in all, the terms of the agreement made it almost impossible for most people to make a serious bid.

Bruce shook his head. The draconian agreement drafted by the attorney was a classic example of the legal tail wagging the business dog. The attorney, in the name of zealous representation of his client (which zealousness, of course, merited a sizable fee), protected the bank from even the most obscure risk and transferred that risk to the bidders. No matter that the bank could easily have assumed many of these risks—for example, the bank had title insurance to protect against title defects, and therefore could easily have agreed that the bidders would not have to assume the risk of bad title. But avoiding risk was what lawyers did by nature. Usually there was an opposing attorney negotiating from the other side, and the tension of this negotiation resulted in a transaction where the parties shared the risks. In the foreclosure context, on the other hand, there was no opposing attorney. Just a zealous advocate with a wet dream-like opportunity to draft a completely one-sided agreement.

As a lawyer, it probably never occurred to him that the bidders would significantly discount their bids to cover these risks. The result was that the bank—which, of course, wanted to sell the property for the highest price possible—had the privilege of paying thousands of dollars in legal fees to an attorney who zealously ensured that the bank would suffer a sizable loss at the auction.

As ludicrous as the whole arrangement was in Bruce's eyes, he also realized that he could turn it to his advantage. If the banks expected to be "protected" by their lawyers to such an extent, well, then, he would just have to protect them.

The auctioneer, speaking into an electronic bullhorn, declared the auction open, interrupting Bruce's thoughts. Bruce had conducted a few auctions himself, and attended a few more, but he was again struck by the informality of the process. Just standing there in the rain on the side of the road selling somebody's home. Mario wasn't visible, but two small children were peering out from the living room window. One held a doll. Bruce looked away.

The auctioneer went through the formality of requesting for bids, even though there were no qualified bidders. Bruce understood the need to abide by these legal formalities, but when the auctioneer peered out expectantly over the sparse crowd, bullhorn in hand, waiting for one of the non-bidders to make a bid, Bruce almost burst out laughing. Like a stage actor in an empty theater expecting applause. Finally, the bank attorney spoke up—he seemed a bit less zealous now, standing in the rain next to an inane auctioneer while a little girl and her doll watched from the window. "The bank bids one hundred fifty-five thousand dollars."

"We have $155,000. Any further bids?" The auctioneer again surveyed the crowd, eyes magnified to twice their normal size by thick glasses, scanning for the slightest sign of movement from any of the non-bidders. "Is there anyone who wishes to display the required deposit money and increase the bid?" Everyone was now looking at their feet. Bruce wished he really did have the $10,000—it would have been fun to fumble in his pockets and then, with a look of profound shock, proudly display the wad of cash to the auctioneer. As if it had magically appeared through the sheer force of the auctioneer's will. "Going once, going twice, sold! To the bank."

As the auctioneer rolled up his auction flag, Bruce approached the bank attorney and offered his hand. "I'm Bruce Arrujo. I work for Stoak, Puck & Beal. We're looking for an attorney to help us with our foreclosure work. Are you interested? I was really impressed by the thoroughness of your Sales Agreement."

"Nice to meet you. Frank Macklin. Sure I'm interested."

"Great. Can I buy you lunch?"

Over lunch, Bruce listened as Frank described his foreclosure practice. "There's a bankruptcy case that governs this whole process. In that case, the court basically said that the bank has to bid at least 70 percent of the appraised value of the property." Frank was showing off his knowledge, and Bruce was happy to listen.

Bruce did the arithmetic in his head, working backward from the bank's final bid of $155,000. "So the appraisal today was $220,000?"

"Yup."

So, the value went from $260,000 two years ago to $220,000 today. "Would the bank have accepted a bid of $156,000?".

"Sure. They don't want to take this stuff back if they can help it."

Bruce did more arithmetic—over $50,000 in potential profit if he had bought the property and then re-sold it for the $220,000 figure, even after paying expenses. "How many auctions do you do per month?"

"Right now, only two or three, but I think it's gonna pick up. I got a lot more in the pipeline. Hey, how come you guys don't do the foreclosures yourselves? What do you need me for?"

Bruce sang him a song about the firm being concerned about protecting its image, which Macklin seemed to buy. Bruce grabbed the check, and got up to leave. "By the way, does anyone other than the bank ever buy at the auction?"

"Not yet. I mean, would you buy without an inspection and with no guarantee on the title? Plus closing in 21 days? And then evict the family? It's tough. You'd have to be a real shark to buy under those conditions."

20

After lunch, instead of driving south back to the office, Bruce headed north-east toward the North Shore. He took Route 128 all the way to Rockport, then headed back south along the shore roads. He had made this drive many times, yet was still awed by the size and majesty of many of the homes that rose up along the shores of the Atlantic. But this awe was mixed with resentment and bit of anger. As he approached Marblehead, specific homes became familiar to Bruce, and he allowed his childhood memories to wash ashore along with the waves of the Atlantic.

Bruce was twelve. Grandpa decided, over Bruce's father's objections, that it was time Bruce learned the truth: the woman Bruce called Mom wasn't really his mother. Bruce remembered feeling shock, then relief—the revelation answered a lot of questions that had kept a young Bruce awake deep into the night. It was tough to hear that your mother had abandoned you at birth, but it was a hell of a lot less traumatic than crying yourself to sleep because your mother kissed your brother goodnight every night and never did the same to you.

A few years later, Grandpa filled in the details. "Your dad was out at a convention in Las Vegas. I guess he had too much to drink or something, and the next thing he knows he's gone back to his room with one of the dancers. Your real mother. Now this kind of thing was way out of character for your father, but knowing your mother, I mean your stepmother, it's hard to blame him too much. Anyway, three months later, he gets a letter from Las Vegas. Of course, he does the 'right' thing—he flies your real mother into Boston, and he makes sure she gets proper medical care and all. The plan was for your real mother to live in Boston with you to be near your father, but after a few months it was clear that the arrangement just wasn't working out. Your stepmother was making life miserable for everyone. So your real mom agreed to fly back to Vegas and leave you here. They told everyone you were adopted—the truth would have been a bit tough to live with, your dad being a guidance counselor in town and all. But after that, we never heard from your real mother again. I tried to find her about five years ago, because I thought she should be part of your life. I tracked her as far as some modeling agency in Los Angeles, but then she seemed to have just disappeared. Somebody said they heard she went to Argentina."

Bruce remembered his response. "That doesn't sound like Dad."

His Grandpa had chuckled. "Well, your father wasn't always so…boring. And rigid. He used to have a fun streak. But he's not a happy person, I'm afraid. Your stepmother is not an easy person to live with, as you know. I think your father's way of dealing with his unhappiness is to simply refuse to have any emotional reaction to anything at all. It's like he's barricaded himself in a box—no emotions can come in, and none go out. He avoids the ocean, and the ocean avoids him."

Unfortunately, by the time Grandpa told Bruce the true roots of his family discord, a young Bruce had already reached some conclusions on his own. Things were different, he had noticed, at his friends' house. They ate dinner together at a table, instead of in front of the television. They sat cuddled together on the couch. They talked about their days. And they kissed each other good night.

And what made his friends' families different from his own? The answer was clear, arrived at with a degree of certainty that only a ten year-old, lying awake night after night listening to his parents fight about money, can attain: Bruce's family didn't have as much money as his friends' families. Other families went to Disney World. They belonged to the yacht club. They went on ski vacations. They had three bathrooms and a cleaning lady. All these things required money, and all these things were quite obviously necessary ingredients in the recipe for a happy family. The conclusion was unavoidable: Bruce's family simply couldn't afford happiness.

Looking back, Bruce was honest enough with himself to admit that his childhood could have been a lot worse. His father took a general interest in his life and well being. His mother provided three meals a day and dressed him warmly. And, on weekends, Grandpa picked him up and taught him how to sail and fish and laugh.

But, he also knew that at an early age his family's lack of money had become his obsession. He had vowed that someday he would return to Marblehead to raise a family in the style and fashion of the town's wealthiest residents. In retrospect, he knew that it was nothing more than an angry childhood promise, that the hardships he had suffered as a child were in reality unrelated to monetary issues. But a promise was a promise, and Bruce knew that his past was both who he was and who he had become.

21

[November 13, 1989]

It was just over two weeks since The Story had run, and Roberge had not spoken to his father since. Through his mother, Roberge knew that the *Herald* story—especially the Hitler comment—had seriously damaged his father, both professionally and personally. Megan, after her initial shock and a solid week of crying, finally agreed to go ahead with the wedding provided that Roberge immediately get tested for AIDS and that he promise never to speak to Charese again. Luckily for Roberge, Megan's family lived in California and hadn't seen the story, and most of her friends didn't read the *Herald*. For Roberge, The Story was starting to die.

But the repercussions were not. His attorney—actually, his father's attorney—had asked for a $25,000 retainer from Roberge to handle the case. And Roberge needed another $20,000 to pay for the wedding and honeymoon. He had planned to ask his father to pay for the wedding since his job as a museum curator only paid $30,000 a year and Megan's parents—well-off, but not wealthy—were currently paying close to $60,000 per year for her three younger siblings' private education. He had never doubted his father would pay for the wedding, and so hadn't bothered to ask yet. But now he knew that he would be lucky if his parents even attended—he and his mother were close, but his father had never taken much of an interest in his second son, especially as the young Roberge's interests had turned more and more toward the arts and away from sports and business. Finally, he and Megan planned to buy a house, for which they would need at least a $20,000 down payment, and he didn't relish the thought of telling Megan that because of Charese they couldn't afford it.

Roberge's first thought was to simply sell the South End condo. But to do so he would first have to evict Charese, and his attorney doubted a judge would order an eviction under the present circumstances. Still, Roberge had been around real estate all his life, and he knew that it would be a simple matter to get a mortgage of, say, $150,000 on the $200,000 condo. That would give him enough money to pay for the wedding and the legal bills, go on a honeymoon, and also to put a large down payment on a new house. They would put the house in Megan's name to protect it from Charese. Then, he and Megan would quickly produce grandchildren, hopefully before his father had time to re-write the will. By spring, everything would be on its way back to normalcy.

He picked up the Sunday newspaper and found an advertisement from an out-of-state bank. He called the 800 number and spoke to a loan officer. The bank would lend him an amount equal to 70% of the City of Boston property tax assessment. Or, if he chose, he could hire an independent appraiser to determine the value of the unit—the bank would then lend 80% of that apprais-al. Roberge tried to picture Charese greeting an appraiser at the front door of the condo with lemonade and cookies. No. The 70% figure would have to suf-fice.

The loan officer promised that a $147,000 mortgage loan would be ready to close in a couple of weeks.

22

[December 1, 1989]

It was the Friday after Thanksgiving. Charese had spent Thanksgiving alone, General Tsao's Chicken from the neighborhood Chinese restaurant the closest she could get to a turkey dinner. Now she was huddled on the bed in her apartment, wrapped in an electric blanket with the thermostat turned down to 50. Ever since the newspaper story had run her case seemed to have stalled, despite Shelby's efforts to speed it along. Only her hatred of Roberge—and now of Reese Jeffries—sparked her out of bed in the morning.

Shelby had phoned before the holiday to check on her and to update her on the lawsuit. As she was in the habit of doing, Charese had let the answering machine pick up the call. She had picked up the phone next to her bed only when she heard Shelby's voice on the machine in the living room; her laziness had the unintended effect of the machine recording their entire conversation.

Charese clicked off the soap opera she was watching and trudged into the living room. The play button on the answering machine felt cold as she pressed it.

Shelby's was the only message on the machine, so Charese was able to quickly fast-forward to the meat of their conversation. "The other reason I called was I've been trying to understand exactly why Reese sabotaged the settlement offer."

"You and me both, girl. You and me both." Charese cringed at the sound of her own slang.

"Well, I've asked around—professors who deal with LAP, a couple of friends of mine who were in the program last year, a classmate who used to date a lawyer on their staff."

"Not Reese, I hope for her sake."

Shelby laughed. "No, not Reese. Anyway, everyone's comments were strikingly similar. Basically, they all said that the LAP lawyers and staff have a liberal—one person called it socialist—agenda. As a matter of fact, other attorneys call LAP attorneys 'Lapdogs' because they're so devoted to their liberal agenda."

"Lapdogs. I like that."

"Well, the problem is that their agenda is more important to them than anything, even than their own clients. And the most important issue on their liberal agenda is the belief that housing should be publicly owned."

"All housing?"

"Pretty much. But definitely all rental housing. You saw the office—there was that 'Housing is for People, not for Profit' poster on practically every wall. It's like a moral issue for them. Anyone who owns property must be evil, or at least misguided. So they're big on tenant activism. They figure that, with enough political force, they can drive private individuals away from property ownership by removing any chance for profit. Heck, they've done it in Cambridge already. First they voted in rent control to keep rents down. Then the city hired these housing inspectors who harass property owners for things like drippy faucets and burned out light bulbs. Then, if the landlords try to go to court to collect the rent, they have to go in front of these hearing officers who are totally pro-tenant. It's amazing some of the stories I heard—judges and doctors and Harvard professors living practically rent-free in apartments owned by working class people. But that's the way it is in Cambridge—landlords are evil, and tenants are good, end of discussion." Shelby paused for a moment. "Is this stuff boring you?"

"No, not at all. I actually am sort of interested in it. I used to cut a woman's hair, and she lived in Cambridge and told me a story about buying a condo and the city telling her she couldn't live in it. Does that make any sense?"

"Believe it or not, it's true. In Cambridge, there are a bunch of condos that, if you own them, you can't live in them."

"What if you do?"

"The city actually hires people to go around and ring doorbells, check mailboxes, question neighbors, Big Brother kind of stuff. Trying to catch people living in their own property. If they catch you, they can fine you something like $100 a day for every day you lived there. Then they take you to court and evict you."

"From your own property?"

"Yup. The law is designed to force you to rent your property out. At a rent control rent, of course."

"Wow. But what does all this have to do with my case?"

"Well, I think what's happening is that LAP wants to get the same laws passed in Boston as they have in Cambridge. And to do that they need lots of tenants to vote for them. Like they have in Cambridge. But when those tenants turn around and buy a house or a condo, LAP loses their vote. That's why LAP never supports programs that help tenants buy their apartments when they get converted to condos. Bottom line: a LAP lawyer would never do anything to promote private ownership of housing."

"And that's what Roberge's settlement offer was. Give me the condo."

"Right. So any LAP lawyer would have trouble with it. But I think your case is about more than just the loss of a single vote on Election Day. I think Reese was looking at a much bigger picture. He had an opportunity to seriously injure Wesley Krygier. And Krygier is leading the fight to repeal rent control in Boston—both with his money and his clout with the local politicians. Reese knows that if he can knock Krygier out of the picture, that will tilt the balance in favor of the tenant activists."

"So what am I, some kind of foot soldier to be sacrificed for the greater good?"

"I'm afraid so."

"Well, I've got news for Mr. Reese Jeffries. I'm not his foot soldier, and I don't take kindly to being sacrificed."

Charese stopped the recording, rewound it quickly, hit the play button again. Her words echoed in the apartment a second time. Angry words. Defiant words. Inspirational words. "Well, I've got news for Mr. Reese Jeffries. I'm not his foot soldier, and I don't take kindly to being sacrificed."

But as she plodded into the kitchen to warm herself by the open oven, she prayed that Shelby would be able to come up with some kind of strategy to save her.

*　　　　　*　　　　　*

Pierre stood blowing on his hands under a dim autumn sun. The play was designed for the quarterback to throw the ball to him, and he wanted to make sure he had feelings in his fingers. He glanced over at the bleachers—Carla and Valerie, almost a year old now and already beginning to walk, were bundled under a blanket with the other wives and girlfriends. The spectators were getting bored and cold, and Pierre and his old high school friends had agreed that this would be the last play in this year's annual Turkey Bowl game. After the game they would all go home and shower, and then meet in the North End for dinner. It was a Thanksgiving Friday tradition, and Pierre wondered how many more years he could pressure the group—already complaining about sore backs and pulled muscles—into playing.

And it wasn't as if he was dealing from a position of strength. He had been the one to break ranks on the first part of the Thanksgiving Day tradition—the group serving meals to the homeless at a homeless shelter. Not that he really had a choice; Carla's mother had insisted they come to Connecticut. *We think it's wonderful that you kids want to help the unfortunates. But this family has been celebrating Thanksgiving together since, well, since there was a Thanksgiving. You know that there were Spurrs on the Mayflower, don't you Pierre? Now we'll expect you here by noon, that's when the Bordens will be here. And we'll send you a nice check that you can forward to the homeless center.* Pierre had to tip his hat to Carla's mother—she never missed an opportunity to zing him, and to do so expertly. Pierre was zero for three on the Spurr family checklist: his blood wasn't blue, he wasn't rich, and he wasn't Chip Borden. There was nothing he could do about his lineage, but maybe he could someday out-earn the chinless Chip and gain some measure of acceptance from Carla's parents.

At least they had returned from Connecticut in time for the Turkey Bowl. The quarterback stood behind the center and coughed out the signals. "Hut, hut, hut." Pierre ran diagonally down the field, on an intersection course with one of his teammates running diagonally from the other side. The plan was for Pierre and his teammate to lock arms as their paths crossed, spin each other around, and slingshot past the bewildered defenders to catch a pass for a sure touchdown. This was the famous "do-si-do" pattern that Pierre had invented when they were kids after seeing a square dance on TV. And it still worked years later—not so much because the play deceived the defenders, but because the defenders were so busy laughing that one of the receivers was usually able to break open.

Pierre and his teammate ran toward each other, locked arms, spun around, and broke apart. The quarterback arched a wobbly, high pass in Pierre's direction, and he sprinted toward it. As he made his cut, he felt his sneaker land in something mushy, and his leg slipped out from under him. He tumbled to the ground and skidded a few feet, knowing without looking at his foot that some jerk hadn't cleaned up after his dog. The defender continued running another few yards, then turned just in time to see the football falling from the sky. The defender reached up to grab the ball, but his reaction wasn't quick enough, and the ball bounced off his shoulder. Pierre, still lying on the ground, raised himself to one knee and lunged toward the ball, catching it just inches from the ground. He rolled to his feet, whooped in delight, and scurried into the end zone for a touchdown.

Carla was waiting for him on the sideline. "Take off that shoe and Valerie and I might give you a kiss."

Pierre removed the shoe and tossed it into a garbage can. "Now, where are my hugs and kisses?"

Valerie wobbled over to him, and he scooped her up. She wrapped her little arms around his neck and buried her head on his shoulder. "Da, da," she cooed.

Carla was right behind her and kissed Pierre tentatively on his dirty face. "You'll get a real kiss after your shower."

"Just a kiss?" They exchanged a naughty smile. "What'd you think of that last play?"

"Want the truth?" Carla didn't wait for a reply. "Stuff like that scares me. Ever since I've known you, I've seen you step in shit and come out smelling like a rose. But those things tend to even out in the long run."

Carla had said it in a light tone, but Pierre could see that she was semi-serious. He thought about how his business had slowed over the past few months. Was his luck turning bad?

*   *   *

At dinner that night, Pierre made a point of sitting next to Patti, the new girlfriend of one of his old friends. Patti was a legal secretary at a medium-sized downtown firm, and Pierre knew that she worked for a partner who represented a number of local mortgage lenders. Pierre was curious to hear how the mortgage lending business was doing.

"Hey Patti, mind talking shop for a minute?"

Patti smiled at Pierre. Pierre had been one the first of the group to make her feel welcome. And it flattered her that Pierre seemed to value her insights into the mortgage lending business. The only time any of the lawyers asked for her opinion at work was when they needed to buy a gift for their wives. "Talk away."

"I was just wondering how busy you guys are. Real estate has been dead the last few months."

"Yeah, us too. We used to do seven or eight closings a day. Now maybe it's two or three. This one New York lender we represent, they just called to say they weren't doing any more loans."

"Really? None at all?"

"Well, they were doing second mortgage loans. You know, poor people in Roxbury who need money right away. This lender would close the loan quickly, and charge like twenty points."

"Did you say 'twenty'?"

"Yeah. Unbelievable, huh? But that's not the half of it. Check this out." Patti pushed her plate away and picked up her glass of wine. "I can't use any names, but here's the story. The partner I work for gets a list every week of the people who are in trouble—you know, being foreclosed on or filing for bankruptcy. You know there's a newspaper that lists this stuff every week?"

Pierre nodded.

"Anyway, we send a letter to them offering them a loan. Like I said, they pay like twenty points, and the interest rate is 18 percent, and my boss charges them $3,000 for the legal work." Pierre knew that a 'point' on a mortgage loan was an up-front fee paid by the borrower. Each point equaled one percent of the loan, and a normal mortgage lender usually charged two or three points, not twenty. So, for example, for a $50,000 loan, twenty points would equal $10,000. Pierre also knew that the normal fee for legal services for a loan was around $800, not $3,000.

Patti continued. "But what are they going to do? Say 'no' to the loan and lose their house? So they pay the fees. But here's the other thing. The lender—it's some group of investors in Miami—requires that we get an appraisal before making the loan. The appraisal has to show that the property is worth at least twice the amount of all the mortgages on the property. That way, the lender knows it has security for the loan. So my boss hires his wife to do the appraisals! She gets paid another $500 for each appraisal. So how many times do you think the appraisal comes in too low?" Patti looks at Pierre to make sure he sees the point.

"Let me guess. Your boss' wife loves to shop, and the $3,500 per loan comes in handy. I would guess that most appraisals come in okay."

"Boy, does she like to shop. And instead of 'most', try 'all'. Not a single property hasn't appraised out. And it gets even better. Guess who keeps half of the twenty points?"

Pierre shrugged his shoulders.

"My boss' ex-wife, because she's friendly with the people in Miami and she set the whole deal up. They call it a 'finder's fee' and she puts it into a college fund for their kids—you know, my boss' and his ex-wife's."

"That's unbelievable. He gets the attorney's fee and his wife gets the apprais-al fee and his ex-wife gets the finder's fee. Good thing this guy was only married twice. So what made the lender stop making the loans?"

"All the borrowers stopped paying. It used to be that maybe ten or fifteen per-cent of the borrowers wouldn't pay. Now it's like sixty or seventy percent. And now when the lender tries to foreclose, it turns out that the property isn't even worth the amount of the first mortgage, never mind the second. Guess those appraisals weren't so accurate, huh? So the lender's losing tons of money."

Pierre shook his head. Patti took a sip of wine and continued. "But it gets even better. So now, the lender has no choice but to foreclose. And guess who gets paid for doing the foreclosure work?"

"Did the lender know your boss' wife was doing the appraisals?"

"I don't know for sure, but I don't think so. She used her maiden name on them, even though she usually uses her married name."

Patti's boyfriend interrupted them, and Pierre leaned back in his seat and did some arithmetic in his head. If Patti's boss had been doing just one closing a day for this lender, he would have earned over a million dollars a year just from that one client. Pierre himself had made decent money during the real estate boom, but he was beginning to see that his $100,000 per year was chump change com-pared to the small fortunes made by players like Patti's boss and the Baron of the Brownstones. They may have been operating in that gray area between sim-ple immorality and outright illegality, but they sure got paid well for it.

23

[December 14, 1989]

Puck's secretary wheeled a shopping cart full of files into Bruce's office. "We're having a special this week on canned corn and paper towels," she said with a wry smile.

She was a mature woman, but still attractive in a leggy, big hair kind of way. Like Bruce, she was dark-eyed and dark-complexioned, though Bruce could tell her hair had been chemically lightened. When Bruce was younger, he used to fantasize about his birth mother appearing at his doorstep one day to re-claim him. In his fantasy, she looked a lot like the woman standing framed in his office doorway.

Bruce chuckled good-naturedly, resisted the urge to be flirtatious. "Thanks, Jan. Just leave them there in the check-out aisle."

She wheeled the cart alongside Bruce's desk, smiled, and spun on one heel to leave. She was carrying Mr. Puck's mail, and as she turned Bruce could see that the top letter bore the return address "Lloyd's of London". Was Lloyd's a client of the firm? Bruce was sure he had not seen it on the list of firm clients. Was it possible that Puck was one of the shareholders, known as "names", of the company that was willing to insure almost anything? Rich old bastard.

Bruce turned in his chair and eyed the Nickel Bank foreclosure files. He knew that each of them told a story—of greed, of shattered dreams, of stupidity, of desperation. Collectively they told of fortunes lost and, Bruce hoped, of fortunes to be gained.

There were 40 of them, as Puck had said there would be, and Bruce guessed that at least a couple would offer an opportunity for profit. Bruce grabbed a handful of files and began skimming through them. Nickel's previous attorney had done some preliminary legal work, but the cases were still two or three months away from the actual foreclosure sales.

All of the borrowers had been in default for at least six months, some because of job loss and some because they simply had too much debt to cover. Still others, usually the owners of investment properties, seemed to have thrown up their hands and simply walked away from their properties. Whatever the case, the slumping economy and real estate market had shattered these American Dreams.

Bruce was also interested in what the files did not contain. None of them contained a current appraisal, so the bank really had no idea what the properties were worth. Bruce would have to order appraisals for each property before conducting the foreclosure sales. Was there an angle to play here?

He took the files and divided them on a geographical basis. Six of the properties were single family homes in upscale suburbs. Eight were condominiums in affluent neighborhoods of Boston—the Back Bay, Beacon Hill, parts of the South End, the Waterfront. The remaining twenty-six were houses and condominiums in neighborhoods or suburbs Bruce characterized as undesirable. He tossed them back into the shopping cart—he would let the paralegal handle these.

He looked at the remaining files. Fourteen pieces of property, each worth at least $100,000, and each under his control. Here was the opportunity, but where was the profit? What was the play?

*   *   *

Over the weekend, Bruce visited all fourteen properties. Some of the suburban homes were choice pieces of property, but, to Bruce's disappointment, none of them had "For Sale" signs in front. Apparently the owners realized that they were so far under water with their mortgages that it would be futile to attempt to sell the property. Or they were simply in a state of denial. Either way, Bruce realized that he was not qualified to form an opinion about a property's physical condition and structural soundness simply by viewing it from the outside. And there was no opportunity to pose as a buyer and get a tour of the homes since they weren't for sale. Bruce reluctantly concluded that the purchase of any of the suburban homes at a foreclosure auction would be too risky.

The condominiums units, on the other hand, were easier to access. Bruce, dressed in wool slacks and an argyle sweater and struggling under three bags of groceries, went unchallenged as he slipped into the condominium buildings as residents entered and left on their weekend errands. Once inside, Bruce stashed the grocery bags and inspected the heating and electrical systems in the basement. Posing as a potential buyer of a unit in the building, Bruce spoke with other building residents and obtained information regarding the condition of the units and the financial strength of the condominium association. From the mailboxes, he determined whether the unit he was foreclosing on was occupied by the owner or by a tenant. By the end of the weekend, Bruce had a fairly complete profile of each of the condominium units.

On Sunday night, he called Marci and invited her out for a drink. They had settled into a comfortable routine of dating once or twice a week, but Bruce could tell she was growing impatient at the lack of progress in their relationship. They had been seeing each other for over two months, and Bruce had done nothing more than kiss her goodnight. He had responded to her probing tongue one night by making the false revelation that he had recently discovered that an ex-girlfriend had AIDS. He had scheduled an AIDS test, he explained, and did not want to initiate any intimacy until after the results were back. It was an ideal, though temporary, excuse.

"Hi, Mars, how was your weekend?"

"Probably just like yours. I worked both days. The end of December is dead because of the holidays, so this is probably the last chance to make a sale this year. And don't call me Mars—I prefer Venus, if anything." Bruce could see she was tired and a bit depressed, and appreciated her effort at spunkiness. He looked at her closely, surprised that she stirred him sexually. He sighed softly. Another time, another place, maybe they could have worked. But he had lied to her and misled her and manipulated her. It was too late for love.

"Venus it is, then," he said, knowing that it wasn't. "Any luck making a sale?"

"No. The only things that are selling now are the really nice properties in good locations—and only if they're priced right. There are still a few buyers out there, but they're being really careful. What about you?"

"I worked. I've actually got some new foreclosure cases. Some condos in Boston."

"Oh yeah, where?"

Bruce gave her the addresses. She knew most of the buildings. Bruce teased her. "Tell me what you know, and I might be able to get you the listings to sell the properties after the foreclosure sales."

By the time they had finished their second drink, Bruce knew that of the eight condo units, six were desirable units in solid buildings. Even in a down market, they could be quickly re-sold if priced correctly.

*   *   *

First thing Monday morning, Bruce telephoned five different appraisers to discuss the Nickel Bank work. Two he dismissed immediately because they had been in business less than five years—Bruce wanted someone who had seen busts as well as booms, someone who remembered when condos sold for $25,000.

He set up three appointments for the next day, all in the Stoak, Puck & Beal offices. He reserved the most impressive conference room and sheepishly requested that his secretary refer to him as 'Mr. Arrujo' rather than 'Bruce' in the presence of the appraisers. These appraisers were attempting to do business with Boston's oldest and largest law firm, and Bruce wanted them to be appropriately humbled.

His first meeting was with a large, established real estate management company that had been doing business in Boston for decades. The company managed many commercial and residential buildings in the city, and had begun doing appraisals and brokerage for their clients in an effort to offer "one-stop" real estate shopping. They sent the son of the company's owner, who was respectful of, but by no means cowed by, his potential client. Bruce knew immediately they were the wrong choice. They were simply too intertwined with the health of the Boston real estate market to admit that the market was experiencing anything more than a "minor correction". They spent most of their time assuring their clients that the market would stabilize and rebound. Their appraisal valuations would inevitably reflect the most optimistic of assumptions.

His second meeting was with Samuel Leumas, principal of Leumas Auctioneers and Appraisals. Samuel was in his late-sixties, and was not the least bit intimidated by the firm or anyone in it. He sat down without invitation, threw his card on the table, and simply began talking. He was a slight man with thick, dirty glasses. He wore a checkered blazer and a blue tie with a thick, uneven knot.

"Name's Samuel Leumas. Actually, Leumas is the name they gave me at Ellis Island in 1936. It's Samuel spelled backwards. They asked me my name, I tell them 'Samuel'. They ask my surname, I shrug. Who asks a fifteen-year-old kid who doesn't speak any English what's his surname? I mean, what the fuck is a surname? Anyway, here I am, kid. Came all the way up to your fancy office. Whad'ya got?"

Bruce laughed to himself. "Before I get into that, Mr. Leumas, please tell me about your business."

"What's to tell? When the market is good, I do appraisals for the banks. When the market is bad, I do auctions for the banks. In between, I do both. Thank God for the banks. Just don't put your money in them."

Bruce couldn't resist. "Why not?"

"Have you seen some of the loans these idiots are making? They got their 'No money down' loan. They got their 'No income verification' loan. They got their 'No personal recourse' loan. They got no brains, is what they got. Hey, that's your money they're making those loans with."

Bruce looked down at his notes. He had certain questions he wanted to ask, but Leumas had thrown him totally off balance. He went back to his script. "I see your point, Mr. Leumas. So what do you think is the future for the real estate market?"

"Listen, sonny, here's the thing. What goes up must come down. It's the law of nature. These prices are crazy. So if you're looking for me to give you some happy, cookies and ice cream appraisal so your bank client can fool itself into thinking it's loans are still good, you got the wrong guy. But if you want my opinion on what your bank can expect to sell these properties for at a foreclosure sale, I'll give it to you. But your bank isn't gonna like my numbers."

Bruce canceled his appointment with the third appraiser.

*   *   *

Puck had asked for regular updates, and Bruce was diligent about providing them. He summarized his recent work on the cases (leaving out his weekend visit to the properties), informed Puck of the need to get current appraisals, and concluded the memorandum with the following:

"I have attached a memo I have drafted which I feel should be forwarded to the client. The memo summarizes the various risks associated with the client taking the properties back at the foreclosure sale, and advises the client to adopt a bidding strategy in which the client bids 70% of the appraised value of the property. The highest bid by a third party above the 70% amount would be the successful bid. As detailed in the memo, the risks associated with the client taking the properties back at foreclosure sale include: 1) environmental contamination of the properties, including lead paint, asbestos and underground fuel oil storage tanks; 2) tenant protection laws which give protections to tenants (including owners who have been foreclosed on), including rent control and eviction bans; 3) market risks if the market continues to slump; and 4) costs of ownership and eventual disposal of the properties, which include property taxes, condominium fees, utility costs and broker's fees. These risks can all be transferred to a successful foreclosure sale bidder."

The next day, Puck's secretary delivered a copy to Bruce of a letter Puck had sent to Nickel Bank. The letter included Bruce's memo, unedited.

24

[December 21, 1989]

Shelby tried not to gasp when Charese sat down opposite her. She had just finished finals and was herself looking a bit haggard, but Charese's whole being oozed despair and neglect. Her skin was blotchy, her features drawn, her shoulders slumped. Shelby decided to confront her.

"You look terrible. What's going on?" They hadn't spoken in a few weeks, and Shelby was glad she had suggested this lunch before leaving town on Christmas break.

"That bad, huh? I just don't seem to have any energy. It's like the thought of getting my revenge on Roberge had pumped me up, and now I can't even get out of bed in the morning. So some days I don't."

"Are you doing drugs?"

"Yeah, I've been shooting a little. Heroin. But please, no lectures. When we win this case, you can stick me in some rehab center. Until then, I'm just trying to get by."

Shelby and Charese held each other's eyes for a few long seconds. "All right, no lectures. But please be careful. Are you working?"

"Just the streets. It's my best talent."

Shelby took another long, hard look at her. What was her role here? Lawyer? Guardian? Social worker? Friend? They didn't teach this stuff in law school. "All right, look. You've got to hang in there. Just because Reese fucked up the settlement, you've still got a good chance in this lawsuit. But it's going to take some time, and all the money in the world won't do you a damn bit of good if you get AIDS in the meantime or die of an overdose. Can't you get a job cutting hair or something?"

"I've looked, but it's not like the economy's so great right now, you know?"

Charese was getting defensive, so Shelby backed-off a bit. "How are you set on cash?"

Charese seemed to relax a bit. "Not great, but if I need some, I just go down to the ATM on the corner at around eleven at night. I don't even need a bank card, just my tongue. Works every time. You've heard of living 'hand to mouth'? Well, I'm living 'mouth to mouth'."

Shelby smiled and rolled her eyes. "You have a sick sense of humor. What about protection?"

"Nah, the guys won't wear anything for blow jobs, you know?" Actually, Shelby had no idea whether johns wore condoms or not. "I mean, they figure they can't catch it from my mouth, right? Anyway, enough girl talk. Any news on the case, counselor?"

"Roberge took a mortgage out on the condo. Our injunction prevents him from selling it out from underneath you, but he can still mortgage it."

Charese nodded her understanding. "His daddy probably cut him off, so he needed cash. Anything else?"

"Not really. This is the stage of the lawsuit called 'discovery' where both sides try to gather information from the other side. What it really is, is a good way for the lawyers to run up their fees by fighting over trivial little issues. And it also causes lots of delays. Right now I'm fighting over whether we have a right to question Roberge's new wife about what she knows about his relationship with you. Not that I think she knows anything, but it will make life miserable for Roberge and he might be more willing to settle this thing."

"Do you think he might still settle?"

"It's possible, but my sense is that his father is so pissed that he wants to keep fighting it in hopes of clearing his name. I mean, from the father's point of view, the damage is already done, so why not keep fighting?"

Charese was silent for a moment. "There are some other pictures which I didn't show to Reese. It's a video of Roberge with some boys on a vacation we took in Mexico five years ago. The boys were maybe thirteen, fourteen years old. He thought I threw it away, and I was going to, but I never got around to it. Actually, I taped over some of it, but the end of the tape is still Roberge and the boys."

"Is it graphic stuff?"

"Yeah, it is. It's pretty rough. At one point, one of the boys starts crying and Roberge just slaps him and tells him to shut up and bend over. It was a side of Roberge I never saw before, but he just blamed it on too much tequila."

"Are you in the tapes also?"

"No, young boys aren't my style. You know, Roberge was the dominant partner, always wanting to be George. I was happy being Martha."

Shelby pondered this new piece of information. It was an effective leverage point in the litigation posturing, which was a nice way of saying it was good blackmail material. Did she want to be that kind of lawyer? Of course not. But could she make an exception in this case? Did the ends—saving Charese from AIDS or overdose—justify the means?

"Well, put it in a safe place. But don't show it to Reese, whatever you do."

"Come on Shelby, I'm not that stupid. Although it might be a way to get rid of him for a while."

"What do you mean?"

"Well, he might watch it and then catch the next plane to Mexico. Maybe the boys have little sisters."

Shelby laughed, pleased to see the improvement in Charese's spirits just in the few minutes they had been together. She motioned for the waitress and smiled coyly at Charese. "I've changed my mind. Could I change my order to a burrito? I'm suddenly in the mood for Mexican."

*   *   *

Shelby dawdled after lunch, popping into shops around Harvard Square and doing errands she had put off during finals. She knew she was just killing time because she didn't want to go back to her apartment to pack. She had agreed to go visit a college friend for the Christmas break, but a week in the malls of New Jersey appealed to her about as much as re-taking her finals. The whole thing was silly—she had agreed to go because she couldn't really think of an excuse not to, and she was pretty sure that her friend had invited her mostly out of a sense of pity.

But she was tired of pity, tired of being passed from cousin to friend to cousin during the holidays. What she really wanted was to turn back the calendar and just tweak the past ever so slightly. Maybe the waiter could stop at another table before bringing her father the check, or her mother could go freshen up in the bathroom before leaving the restaurant, or her brother could order desert, or the hotel valet could take an extra drag on his cigarette before retrieving Mr. Martini's BMW. The randomness of the events leading to her family's death overwhelmed her. How could the decision not to have another cup of coffee be the difference between life and death? Does every choice we make in life—what time to eat or when to cross the street or where to study—have such drastic consequences? She pushed the palms of her hands into her eye sockets, trying to force the inquiry back into the recesses of her consciousness. She knew it was the type of thing that, if analyzed too much, would paralyze her.

She sighed. The calendar would not turn back, just as it would not skip the last week of December, would not skip Ski Week.

Since she was four years old, her parents had bundled up her younger brother and her and headed for the Vermont mountains for a week of skiing during the Christmas break. The four of them would stand together arm-in-arm at the bottom of the trail after the first run on the first day and ask a stranger to take their picture, and 51 weeks of job pressures and adolescent hormones and mid-life crises were miraculously buried and forgotten under a two-foot shroud of packed powder.

For parts of the week uncles and aunts and cousins would join them, and the family would commandeer a large table near a roaring fireplace in the ski lodge and feast on hot chili and cold beer and baskets of French fries. One year, Shelby's father had convinced a vacationing policeman to arrest and handcuff her uncle on bogus charges of not paying for a tray of food. Her uncle responded by paying a snow-plow operator to bury Shelby's family's car, which was countered the following year by Shelby and her brother—at their parents' prompting—stealing their uncle's and aunt's towels as they sat naked in an outdoor hot tub. The practical jokes became a yearly tradition, and every year at least one member of the family good-naturedly bore the brunt of their loved ones' pranks. Shelby's cousins still teased her about the time when, as a fourteen-year old, she breathlessly recounted her story of being approached on the slopes by an Olympic ski team coach who invited her to try out for the 1980 team, oblivious to her audience's smirks and giggles.

She had hoped that her extended family would continue the skiing tradition even after her parents' and brother's death. But her parents had always been the impetus behind the event, and it was becoming more and more difficult to accommodate the group now that some of her cousins had young children of their own and the aunts and uncles were getting older and preferred warm weather vacations. In the end, it just simply didn't get done. And Shelby was stuck going to New Jersey.

25

[January 2, 1990]

Pierre turned over onto his left side, careful not to disturb Valerie sleeping peacefully next to him. The good news about the slowdown in Pierre's business was that he had been able to spend more time with Carla and Valerie in the last four months than most husbands/fathers did in a year. The bad news was that they were unable to fill this time with any activities that cost any money. For now, cuddled up with his little girl asleep against his shoulder on a lazy Friday morning, Pierre considered it a wonderful trade-off. He drifted back to sleep.

Later that day, however, Pierre went into the office, hung up his new 1990 calendar, and forced himself to focus on the realities of their financial situation. Over the past four months, he had earned a grand total of $7,000, and the market was so slow that Pierre doubted he could even keep up that pace. The market had simply gridlocked—sellers wanted to sell, but most of them couldn't afford to accept an offer that was less than their mortgage balance. And those that could afford it were unwilling to do so. Why bother selling your house if you have to go to the closing and pay ten or twenty thousand dollars? Hardly the American Dream.

In fact, Pierre was trying to broker one of these gridlocked deals right now. A young couple was trying to sell a one-bedroom condo they had purchase two years ago. They had paid $130,000, and had taken a mortgage of $117,000. They now had a child and wanted to move to the suburbs, but the best offer Pierre could get them was $107,000. After paying Pierre's commission and their other closing costs, they would be taking a $30,000 loss. As much as it killed them, they were willing to walk away from their $13,000 down payment, even though it was almost their entire savings. But they simply didn't have another $17,000 to bring to the closing. They had asked the bank to take less than it was owed, but the bank refused. So the deal had died, even though the seller wanted to sell and the buyer wanted to buy at the $107,000 price. Even worse, Pierre understood, was that this type of grid-lock had a domino effect throughout the market—since this young couple couldn't sell their condo, they couldn't in turn buy a small house in the suburbs that would in turn allow another growing family to trade-up to a larger house. The result was that there were tons of sellers, and even a decent number of buyers, but very few transactions.

Anyway, on a personal level, with Carla not working and a mortgage payment of over $2,000 per month, they were spending more than they earned. Worse, they had little savings on which to draw. They had put most of their savings—$30,000—into buying the condo, and it was stuck there unless they could find a buyer, which Pierre was having trouble doing. Even then, the $30,000 had probably shrunk to $15,000. The remainder of their free cash had gone toward tastefully furnishing the condo. The decision hadn't seemed overly irresponsible at the time, but it wasn't as if they could have a garage sale and expect to get much back for it now. In short, they had spent freely through the boom years, and now were suffering for it.

And Pierre preferred that Carla not go back to work. Valerie was thriving under her mother's care, and both Pierre and Carla agreed that her welfare was paramount. Even so, Carla had been scanning the help wanted ads for the past few weeks. Unfortunately, after paying for daycare and transportation, Carla's salary—even if she could get a job in this slumping economy—was not likely to make much of a dent in their financial problems.

Carla had considered just asking her parents for an advance on her inheritance, but she knew that Pierre would feel that such a request would cost him any chance he had at ever winning them over. Even then, she wasn't sure if her parents had anything to spare. They had invested heavily in some bank stocks that had recently tumbled, and for the first time since Carla could remember they had decided not to winter in West Palm Beach with the Bordens.

But things were actually starting to look up. Bruce's letter had successfully extricated Howie from his apartment building deal, so, with the promise of Howie's money behind him, Pierre had attended a number of foreclosure sales over the past couple of months. He had not purchased anything yet, mostly because the banks seemed oblivious to the fact that the real estate market was slumping and still had 1988 expectations. It was as if the bankers, insulated downtown in their air-conditioned towers and underground parking garages, were the last to know what was going on in the neighborhoods around them. Pierre imagined a chinless Chip Borden in a Brooks Brothers suit, sitting at his antique desk in front of his prep school and Ivy League diplomas, pulling out an appraisal from 1987 and stating: "But it says right here the property is worth $250,000. I'm sorry, but I can't take less than that." Recently, however, Pierre had noticed that a few banks, mostly the smaller ones, had finally adopted a more realistic bidding strategy at their auctions.

Pierre pulled out the auction sections he had been saving from the previous week's Sunday newspapers. He had already circled the auctions that interested him; now, using an exacto knife he meticulously cut out a couple of dozen foreclosure sale advertisements and taped them into his daily calendar. It was time to buy.

He rang Howie. "Howie, it's Pierre. How you doing?"

"Pierre! Great. Hey, I got a joke to tell you. I read they just discovered fossils of a new kind of dinosaur. Funny thing is, they were all gay males. The scientists named them 'Tyronta-sore-ass'."

"Let me guess," Pierre responded. "They found the fossils out in San Francisco?" Howie laughed. Pierre knew Howie would incorporate this geographical twist into the joke when he told it again—probably within the half-hour. "Anyway, Howie, I wanted to talk to you about these foreclosure sales I've been going to."

"Yeah. You bought anything yet?"

"No. But I think some of the banks are realizing that they're going to have to take a haircut or they're going to get stuck with these properties. I just want to make sure you're still on board for this."

"Definitely. I'll put up the cash and you do the work. We split it fifty-fifty, right?"

"That's the deal. When I find something, we'll probably have only a few weeks to close."

"That's fine. I'm pretty liquid. Just let me know. And good luck."

"Thanks. I'll keep you posted."

26

[January 11, 1990]

Bruce looked at his time sheets for the first 11 days of the new year. He had billed almost one hundred hours already, most of it on research items for a few big closings he was working on and the remainder on general background work for the foreclosure cases. And it was mostly legitimate time—he had decided to cut back on his creative billing practices, seeing them as an unnecessary risk. Even without excessively padding his time, he was one of the top associates in terms of monthly billable hours. Not he that cared about this statistic in the same way the other associates did—that is, as a way to gauge themselves against each other in the race for partnership. But keeping his hours high was important to Bruce for other reasons. First, it made him a profit center for the firm's partners, which, he hoped, would give them less incentive to keep a watchful eye on him. Second, it indicated to the partners that pending matters were fully occupying his time and they should not expect him to take on any more major projects. The last thing he needed right now was to be sent out of town on some major closing.

Bruce pulled out his December billing sheets. They were a little bit lower than he would have liked, especially because they were the last month of the billing year. He had an idea: why not put some of the January time onto the December sheet? Nobody would have any way of knowing whether he had done the research on December 30 or on January 2 and, more importantly, nobody would care. As long as the work had been done, the distinction was only administrative. It would put him behind in his 1990 billing, but, if necessary, he could just borrow from 1991. More likely, it wouldn't matter by then.

Bruce smiled as he worked, transferring about fifty hours from calendar year 1990 to calendar year 1989. It was like the federal government, except this was deficit billing instead of deficit spending. And it sure made his billing numbers look great for 1989.

27

[January 19, 1990]

The red auctioneer's banner, attached to a tree in front of the Victorian-era brownstone by two bungee cords, was barely visible under a coat of dust-like snow. The snow was more like sand on this windy winter day—small and dry, pellet-like as it whipped against exposed skin. It made Bruce smile. He loved the extremes of nature—he saw them as mythical battles between order and chaos. These battles were like prisms for Bruce, bringing back into focus the earth's continuing conflict between the order of the landmass and the chaos of the sea. History had made it clear that there would be no winner in this battle, that the fight would continue endlessly.

But Bruce could win. He could win by harnessing the power of each, by bringing chaos to the orderly world and order to the chaotic one.

So he had hoped for a stormy day when he had scheduled the foreclosure sale, an auction process that was technical and rigid and regulated and orderly. It was a process that wanted a little chaos.

The Marlborough Street condominium unit was an 'A' property—prime location, in the heart of the Back Bay. Of course, Samuel Leumas remembered when hookers and other vagabonds frequented the first block of Marlborough Street, now considered Boston's best address. "It may be popular now, Mr. Lawyer, but I remember when you avoided this part of town after dark. The city finally had to make the first block one way in the opposite direction from the rest of the street just to keep the johns from cruising up and down it all night long. Bet you didn't know that's why the traffic pattern is so ridiculous, did you?"

Bruce didn't, nor did he really care. What he did care about was that Leumas had appraised the condo—a one-bedroom unit in the front part of the second floor of the building—at only $120,000. His comment to Bruce: "For Christ's sake, it only has 550 square feet, even if it is done up all nice and fancy. How can it be worth more than that? It's no bigger than a walk-in closet."

Closet or not, the unit had sold for $187,000 only three years earlier. Marci was convinced she could sell it today for at least $145,000. And Nickel Bank had apparently heeded Bruce's warnings about the dangers of property ownership: they had instructed Bruce to bid $84,000 on their behalf, equal to 70 percent of the $120,000 appraised value. Any higher bid would take the property.

Bruce was hoping that the weather would keep people away. His plan was simple—do everything he could to discourage bidding at the auction.

He reviewed in his mind the steps he had taken so far. First, he had scheduled the auction for 4:00 in the afternoon on a Friday in January—potential bidders would have to fight rush-hour traffic, and hopefully a little snow, to get to the auction. Second, in a purported effort to keep costs down, he had advertised the auction only in the *Boston Herald*, not the more widely read *Boston Globe*. Third, he had required a $20,000 deposit in order to bid at the auction, twice the usual amount. ("That way," he had explained to the bank officer, "we'll be sure to weed out bidders who don't really have the financial ability to close.") And fourth, he would make it clear that the bank would not agree to any extensions— close in twenty-one days or forfeit the $20,000 deposit.

But Bruce knew that the prime location of the property would counterbalance his efforts—some people were still likely to attend and plan to bid. Bruce had a few tricks in store for them.

By four o'clock, a total of four people had registered to bid at the auction. One was Pierre, and he went right over to Bruce to re-introduce himself.

"Of course I remember you, Pierre. How have you been?"

"Great, thanks. And thanks again for helping out Howie. That was a beautiful move, the letter to the bank."

"Don't thank me, I appreciate the referral. Are you guys still looking to buy? Actually, that's a stupid question—I doubt you came out here in this storm just to watch my nose run."

Pierre laughed. "Yeah, we're actually using the money Howie didn't spend on that last deal to try to buy some foreclosure stuff. That's why I'm here, obviously. I was hoping the weather would keep other bidders away."

So, Bruce thought, *Pierre had the same thought. Good for him.* Bruce laughed and nodded at him. "Yeah, I bet you were hoping for that." He paused for a moment, as if weighing something in his mind. "Listen, Pierre, you seem like a good guy. I don't want you to get burned on this one. Take a look at this." He pulled a manila folder from his briefcase and handed it to Pierre. There was a single sheet of paper inside. It read:

Dear Potential Bidders:

I am the tenant in the condominium unit being foreclosed on today. I live here with my four-year old son. He has been diagnosed as having lead poisoning. This

lead comes from lead paint in the apartment. My lawyer has advised me to notify you that we will expect the new owner to de-lead the apartment immediately.
Sincerely,
R Kessler

Bruce let Pierre read it, and was pleased to see that other bidders had begun to gather around them. Bruce made a half-hearted attempt to shield the letter from the other bidders, then, moving away from the group, addressed Pierre in a whisper he knew would carry in the wind. "This was taped to the front door when I got here. I wish I had known about it before the auction; it might have affected the bank's bidding strategy. The worst part is that the new owner could be liable to the tenant if the kid really is poisoned. And you're talking some pretty big damage awards in these lead paint cases. By the way, peak through the front door and check out the pictures taped to the walls in the foyer."

Bruce watched Pierre and the other bidders walk up the stairs and peer into the foyer. He knew what they would find—three crayon pictures hung on the walls, all with the name "Brad Kessler" written across the bottom. They were Bruce's first crayon drawings in almost twenty years, and he was pleased with them. Maybe he would be able to slip back into the building later on and retrieve them—his refrigerator could use some decoration.

Meanwhile, he took the letter back and filed it in his briefcase. 'Kessler' was indeed the name on the mailbox, but last week Bruce had learned that Ms. Kessler was actually a college student with no children who had vacated the apartment in December, at the end of the fall semester. He would throw away the only copy of the letter before he returned to the office.

One more trick. Fumbling with his bulky gloves, he rested his briefcase on one knee and re-filed the lead paint letter. He waited a moment for the wind to let up, then grabbed in vain for a sheet of paper as it slipped out the side of the briefcase. The paper floated to the ground with the other snowflakes, landing face up in a snowy footprint. *Heads, I win*, Bruce said to himself. In big, block letters, the paper read:

BID INSTRUCTIONS: BID UP TO $165,000

Bruce knew everyone would see it immediately; foreclosure bidders were like sharks, circling the attorney and auctioneer, hoping to feast on stray pieces of information. The paper had as little chance of going unnoticed as bloody chum in a shark cage. Awkwardly, Bruce bent over and picked up the paper, trying to shield its contents with his body. He stuck it back in his briefcase—it, too, would be destroyed.

It was now 4:15, and the auctioneer was eager to begin reading the required legal notices and terms of the sale. Normally he would have begun doing so right at 4:00, but Bruce had asked him to wait until 4:15, "just in case anyone is stuck in traffic."

Finally, Bruce authorized the auctioneer to begin his readings. Bruce had drafted an especially lengthy set of documents, and it took the auctioneer a full twenty minutes to complete the readings. Many of the bidders were now stomping their feet and covering their ears with gloved hands. One man's mustache had turned white from a frozen coat of snow, and another had removed his snow-caked glasses. Only Bruce seemed unaffected by the weather—electric socks, thermal underwear, and thoughts of profit were keeping him warm.

Bruce addressed the group. He folded his hands behind his back, striving to strike a pose of candor and openness. "Some of you may have seen a letter from the tenant regarding lead paint poisoning. Just so there is no confusion here, the bank makes no representations regarding this letter. But to be fair, I have to tell you that if you buy the property, you are responsible for any claims the tenant may have against the property. Also, as the auctioneer announced, you are buying this property in 'as is' condition. You are also buying this property subject to any title defects. Finally, your inability to obtain a mortgage or otherwise close in twenty-one days will not excuse you from performing under the terms of this sale. In other words, if you don't close in twenty-one days for any reason, you lose your $20,000." Bruce paused here, lightened his tone. "Look, I just don't want anyone to get hurt here. Twenty grand is a lot of money, and I would hate to see you lose it. Just make sure you know what you're getting yourself into." Bruce almost laughed out loud—who would bid when the big firm attorney for the bank had done them the favor of hinting that it would be imprudent to do so? Free legal advice was hard to ignore.

Bruce then leaned over and pulled a cellular phone out of his briefcase—the firm had recently purchased a few cell phones for the lawyers to travel with. He removed a glove, feigned dialing a number, then spoke loudly into the phone. "Hi, this is Bruce Arrujo, from Boston. We're ready to begin the bidding." Bruce hoped the others would assume he was on the line with a representative of the bank.

He spoke to the auctioneer. "You may begin the bidding."

The auctioneer stepped onto the front stoop and called out, "What am I bid for this property. Do I have an opening bid?"

Bruce immediately spoke. "I have a bid here for $88,756.17. Also, Nickel Bank reserves its right to increase this bid." These two sentences were crucial for Bruce, and he had struggled with their wording for days.

He had informed the auctioneer that a wealthy Arab investor from New York had qualified by mail and would be bidding by telephone; since the auctioneer was technically officiating at the auction, Bruce needed the auctioneer to understand that the $88,756.17 bid had come from this Arab bidder. To the auctioneer's ear, he hoped the second sentence would sound unrelated. That is, the Arab bidder made an opening bid, and, by the way, Attorney Arrujo, young and a bit nervous, was making it perfectly clear to the bidders that the bank reserved the right to enter into the bidding at any time.

On the other hand, he wanted the other bidders to believe he was talking on the cell phone to the bank, against whom they were less likely to bid in light of their knowledge of the bank's ultimate bidding strategy. Which is why he chose the $88,756.17 figure—he hoped the other bidders would conclude it was just some random opening bid the bank's accountants had come up with, followed by a second statement from the bank that it reserved the right to increase its bid.

The auctioneer looked at Bruce quizzically—where had the Arab bidder gotten that number? Bruce just shrugged and smiled, as if to say: "Who knows where those crazy Arabs get their numbers?" To the bidders, he hoped it said: "Who knows where those crazy bankers get their numbers?"

The auctioneer asked for further bids, and Bruce froze for a second as the man with the mustache lifted his hand. But he was just brushing snow off his shoulder, and as the group stood impassively, Bruce knew he had won. The temperature had dropped even further as the sun had begun to set, and the bidders had been standing outside in the cold for over forty minutes now. Their body language told Bruce they were far more interested in getting into a warm car and beginning their weekends than they were in prolonging the auction. The sale had been chilled, both literally and figuratively. Bruce knew that nobody would take the extra time now to engage in a bidding war when they all knew the bank would bid up to $165,000. Especially with the lead paint issue. "Going once, going twice, sold for $88,756.17."

Bruce said good-bye to Pierre and climbed into the auctioneer's car. He pulled out a document entitled "Sales Agreement", and began filling it out. In the blank next to the word "Buyer", he wrote "Arabian Acquisitions, as per tele-

phonic bid authorized by attached letter". He filled in the purchase price, and
handed it to the auctioneer to sign as agent for the seller. From his briefcase, he
pulled out a letter on Arabian Acquisitions letterhead and stapled it to the Sales
Agreement. The letter requested that Bruce contact them by cellular phone from
the auction and allow them to bid by phone. Attached to the letter was a
Citibank cashier's check made out to Nickel Bank in the amount of $20,000, to
be used as a deposit in the event they were the high bidder.

He turned to the auctioneer. "Well, that should do it. Some rich Arab just
bought himself a piece of Boston. Thanks for your help."

"My pleasure, Mr. Arrujo. Say, do you mind if I offer a piece of advice?"

"Please, I'd appreciate it."

"It seems to me that you were too nice to those bidders. Maybe one of them
would have bid higher if you hadn't shown them that lead paint letter. Not that
I care, I'm not working on commission anyway, so I don't care how much you
sell the property for."

*Of course you're not on commission, you idiot, for that very reason. You're simple-minded
and content—fat, dumb and happy. That's why I hired you and not Samuel Leumas.* "Yeah,
I guess you're right. It just seems unfair to not tell them. Besides, I don't want
my client to be sued by one of them later on because I didn't disclose something
I knew."

"I see your point. You're the attorney, you know best. Sit tight, I'll give you a
ride back to your office." Bruce sat back, closed his eyes, and enjoyed the slow,
slippery ride through Boston's snowy streets.

*   *   *

Pierre, meanwhile, was feeling pretty good about things. He had struggled
with the problem of trying to minimize the risks of buying at foreclosure, but
had been unable to find a solution. It simply wasn't economically feasible to hire
an attorney to review the title to every property before every auction, and Pierre
wasn't yet fully confident in his own title searching skills. Maybe Bruce was the
solution.

There was no reason for Bruce to have told Pierre about the lead paint problem—it was exactly the kind of risk that a foreclosure bidder was required to
assume at an auction. But Bruce seemed to have a sense of loyalty to Pierre. Was
it just because of a single client referral? Could be. Clients in a shrinking economy were a rare find for a young attorney.

Whatever the reason for Bruce's loyalty, Pierre was thankful for it. He knew Bruce had scheduled a number of foreclosure sales over the next few months. If he could count on Bruce to warn him away from the risky properties, he could bid aggressively on others. He would make it a point to attend all of Bruce's auctions.

*   *   *

Bruce went home that night, ordered a pizza for delivery, and sat in front of the television set with the channel clicker. He was interested in the late-night sitcoms and old movies. Or more accurately, in their commercials. He needed an attorney to front for an Arab company, one who wouldn't ask too many questions. It seemed to Bruce that the attorney he was looking for would be the type to advertise on The Three Stooges or an old Jerry Lewis movie. Too bad Roller Derby wasn't on anymore.

By the end of the night, in addition to a headache, he had a list of seven law firms, three of which specifically advertised that they did real estate work. One in Springfield, on the other side of the state from Boston, particularly interested him—it actually seemed like a real firm, anxious for clients but still trustworthy. And far enough away to stay out of the way.

He woke up the next morning and pulled out a stack of checkbooks issued by different credit card companies. Since he had officially been admitted to the bar back in November, banks and financing companies had inundated him with offers of pre-approved credit cards and lines of credit. He had signed up for every one of them. Together, they offered him a total of $55,000 of unsecured credit. He had $34,000 left from the sale of the Manet, $20,000 of which he had used to buy the Citibank cashier's check. He needed almost $90,000 to close, so by using his next couple of paychecks, he should make it. Barely.

*   *   *

[January 22, 1990]

First thing Monday morning, Bruce called the Nickel Bank employee in charge of Massachusetts foreclosures. His name was Chris Jones, and Bruce had immediately concluded that he had a personality to match his name. He was the quintessential "empty suit"—recent business school graduate, at work by 7:30, intent upon climbing the corporate ladder through sheer tenacity. Chris Jones understood his assignment perfectly: work through the bank's list of Massachusetts foreclosure cases as quickly as possible, and then to come back for another assignment.

Bruce felt comfortable dealing with Chris Jones, as well as with the bank as a whole. It was all a matter of knowing which buttons to push. Bruce had learned long ago that it was a mistake to assume that large institutions such as banks would act in a purely rational manner. In a political science course in college, Bruce had read *Essence of Decision,* an analysis by Graham Allison of how governments made decisions. Allison theorized that governments often did not act "rationally"—that is, they did not base every significant decision on an objective cost-benefit analysis. Instead, sometimes they simply acted under pre-established standard operating procedures, rational or not. On other occasions, the actual individual making the decision for the government would act in a way that would benefit him or her personally, but might not be in the best interests of the state as a whole. Bruce had found the book to be a brilliant insight into governmental behavior. More importantly, Bruce believed that Allison's decision-making models worked equally well in analyzing—and predicting—decisions of large institutions like corporations and banks.

In the case of Nickel Bank, Bruce knew that the bank was not making decisions relating to the Massachusetts foreclosure files in a strictly rational manner. For example, a smaller local bank with the same bad loans as Nickel would assign a senior bank officer to each loan. That officer would study each property carefully before making a decision on bidding strategy. That is, the bank officer would do many of the things Bruce had done when Puck had given him the foreclosure files—visit the properties, speak to the local brokers, investigate the tenant situation. Then the officer would determine a rational bidding strategy based on his experience and on the information he had obtained. The small bank's bid would have probably been in the neighborhood of $125,000 for the $145,000 Marlborough Street condo, a 15 percent discount reflecting the risks, costs and loss of liquidity associated with re-marketing the property.

Nickel, of course, did not behave this way. They were simply too big, and had too many bad loans spread out over too wide a geographical area. Instead, Nickel established a set of operating procedures which governed how to handle its foreclosures: hire a local attorney, rely on him to hire a local appraiser, foreclose as quickly as possible, and then, as Bruce himself had suggested in his memo, bid 70 percent of the appraised value at the auction. Put the whole process under the oversight of a junior employee, and reward the employee for disposing of the properties as quickly as possible. It was how large companies often behaved, and nobody ever even gave it a second thought.

Except, of course, Bruce. He understood the bank's operating procedures, and was careful to operate within them. But it was their choice to rely on these procedures instead of expending the time and effort to perform a more thorough cost-benefit analysis. And if their choice to operate in a less than rational manner resulted in a less than optimal recovery, well, that was their fault, not his.

As for Chris Jones, he was thrilled that Bruce had sold the property for more than the $84,000 minimum bid. It was one less file on his desk, and the extra four thousand dollars was an added bonus. It never occurred to him to ask Bruce why nobody bid more, or even how many people attended the auction. His task was to dispose of the property as quickly as possible for at least $84,000, and he had succeeded. The fact that the bank had lost $70,000 on the loan was somebody else's problem, not his—he had been at Princeton when some loan officer had approved the original loan. If Bruce could keep it up, or, more accurately, if Chris Jones could continue to manage both the assets and Bruce in an efficient manner, he knew a bonus—and maybe even a promotion—would be in his future.

*   *   *

Later that day, Bruce's phone rang. The display identified the caller as Bertram Puck, Jr.

"Yes, Mr. Puck."

"You wished to see me?"

"Yes, sir. I wanted to update you on Friday's foreclosure for Nickel Bank."

"Young man, I do not need to have a conversation with you after every auction. This is a law firm, not a support group."

"Of course, sir." Or should he have said, "Of course not, sir."? It was all in the delivery anyway.

"I do, however, expect a written summary after every auction. By the following day. If it's not too much trouble, Mr. Arrujo."

Bruce saw Puck's extension disappear from the display, indicating that Puck had hung up. Puck seemed like he was in a worse mood than usual, and Bruce couldn't help being bothered by the fact that he really didn't understand the old man at all.

28

Pierre's conversation with Howie wasn't going exactly as Pierre had planned.

"Pierre, I don't know why you're upset. It seems to me that Bruce is really going to help us."

Pierre took a deep breath, counted to three. "I totally agree, Howie. It's just that I thought we were going to buy stuff at auction, and then flip it. I really think we can make some good money doing this."

"Maybe so, Pierre, but why do it that way? Why not buy and hold? If you're right, and the market eventually will come back, why not put together a portfolio of properties and hold onto them for a few years? Then we can sell after prices have really risen." Pierre knew that Howie had read a lot of books on investing, and they all said to buy low and hold, not buy and sell. "If we sell, then we just have to pay the taxes on the gain and then go buy something else to sell and pay the taxes again. And I'm in the top bracket, so that's almost 50 percent for me. Why not just keep the first thing and pay the taxes only once?"

Howie's strategy made sense for Howie—he was single and earning six figures. And Howie's strategy would allow Pierre to pay for Valerie's college someday. But Pierre was more concerned right now about next week's groceries. He took a deep breath. He knew how stubborn Howie could be about certain things, especially things he had read in investment strategy books. They were like the bible to Howie. "Look, I've got to generate some income. I can't wait a few years for our profit."

"Sorry, Pierre." Howie was pretty sure Pierre didn't have another money source. "I'm not going to take all this risk and then give Uncle Sam half my profit."

Pierre decided to try a different tack. "What you say makes sense, Howie, but I'll be honest, my brokerage business is dead. I've got to put food on the table. Would you be willing to lend me, say, $20,000, short term so I can do a quick flip? I can give you a second mortgage on my Brookline condo, and I'll pay 14 percent interest."

Howie was silent for a moment. Pierre knew he was excited about buying foreclosure property with Pierre—Pierre had proven his trustworthiness, and Bruce the lawyer was a valuable connection. And he must have understood that

Pierre needed to eat. "Okay, Pierre. My money's just sitting in a money market anyway. But I want twenty-two percent, and only for six months."

"Twenty-two's a bit steep, Howie."

"Not really. It's the same as some credit cards. Look, Pierre, I want to help you out, but business is business."

Business is business? Anybody remember a certain $45,000 commission I sacrificed? "All right. I have no choice."

"I'll call Bruce and ask him to draft the paperwork. Then I'll just send you a check."

Pierre hung up the phone. He had just added $400 to his monthly debt.

29

Over the next few weeks, Bruce scrambled to consummate the purchase of the Marlborough Street condo. He drove to New York late one Friday night and opened a bank account the next morning. He deposited a total of $73,000, the sum of his credit lines and savings. The name on the account was Arab Acquisitions, with himself as the sole signatory. He knew the account could be traced to him if somebody looked hard enough, but by putting the money in an out of state bank under the Arab Acquisition name, and by using only bank cashier checks, he hoped to gain a measure of anonymity.

While in New York, he also rented a post office box and made arrangements with a telephone answering service to provide Arab Acquisitions with a private line that an operator would answer during business hours.

He also called the law office in Springfield. He adopted a Middle-Eastern accent, hoping that not too many Egyptians or Syrians passed through Springfield. The receptionist put him through to a lawyer.

"Hello, yes, excuse me, I am looking for a lawyer who can assist me in a real estate purchase in Massachusetts. In the city of Boston."

"Well, you know we're located in Springfield, right?"

"Oh, my mistake. I am terribly sorry. An associate of mine referred you to me—I am new in this country. This Springfield is far from Boston?"

The attorney backtracked. Business was slow right now, especially for a real estate lawyer. "Well, not too far. Maybe we can help you. What do you need?"

"Thank you. My name is Ahmed Bahery. My company is Arab Acquisitions. I am buying properties for my family in Saudi Arabia. I am successful bidder at auction for foreclosure. The property is condominium on Marlborough Street in Boston. You can help me with the closing?"

"Yes, I'm sure we can. When are you available to come to Springfield to meet with me?"

"Oh, yes, that is the problem. I am traveling very much—to California and also to the Middle East. I am leaving tomorrow for one or two months."

"Well, when is the closing?"

"I believe in two weeks—yes, in sixteen days."

"So you would need me to attend the closing in your absence?"

"Yes. I suppose I need many services from you. In California, my attorney has formed a trust for me and he is the trustee. That way he can control the property while I am away. Is this possible?"

"I suppose so, although most attorneys don't like to act as trustees in real estate deals. Too much liability."

Bruce could tell the lawyer was torn between servicing his new client and a hesitancy to assume the risk of having his name on the deed. "I have bought insurance for my California attorney to deal with any liabilities. Also, I pay him a monthly fee for being trustee." That should tip the balance—remove risk from one side and add money to the other. "But if you are not comfortable, you can perhaps recommend another attorney for me?"

"No, what you've proposed sounds like an acceptable arrangement. Why don't you send me the documents, and I'll get started. I'll need a retainer—say, $5,000?"

Why not stick it to the rich Arab? Maybe I should have been German instead. "Of course, that is more than fair. I will send it to you by Federal Express."

They exchanged additional information, and Bruce hung up. Done. As far as the world would know, the property would be owned by a trust, the trustee of which was some attorney in Springfield. And the attorney believed his client was some rich Arab in New York who paid all his bills with bank cashier checks. Bruce's involvement was completely hidden. After the closing, he would instruct the Springfield attorney to hire a real estate broker to sell the property. Even after paying the broker's commission, the attorney's fees and the 16 percent interest on the lines of credit, Bruce was confident that his profit on the deal would approach $40,000.

Not bad for a start, but Bruce hadn't sacrificed the last four years of his life for a five-figure, or even a six-figure, payoff. Bruce needed at least a million. Invested conservatively at ten percent, he could live off of the $100,000 yearly income and never have to work again. He would buy a large sailboat, moor it on the Boston waterfront, and live on it year-round. In the winter, he could rent a furnished apartment for a few months to escape the cold, maybe do some volunteer work at a museum. And when he found the right woman, he'd settle down, have 2.2 children and live the yacht club life in Marblehead. But whatever he did, he would have money in his pocket, and money in the bank. And he would answer to nobody.

But first, he needed to find his million.

Pigeon on the Bow

30

[February 8, 1990]

Bruce knew he was tapped-out for a while, and regretted having rushed to hold the foreclosure sales on the other Nickel Bank properties so quickly. If he had held one or two properties back for a few months, he could have rolled the profits from the first deal into a second one.

As it stood now, he had scheduled two auctions in early February and one in early March. All of the properties were solid properties in good locations, and all of them had been under-valued by Leumas and thus would be under-bid by the bank. What had originally seemed like a sound strategy was becoming a problem for Bruce—he did not want these properties to sell at a substantial discount. If word got out that investors were scoring big profits at Nickel's auctions, Bruce would never be able to duplicate his Marlborough Street coup. Yet to keep Chris Jones satisfied, he needed to sell the properties.

The first of the auctions was scheduled for later that day. The property was a three-family brownstone in the Back Bay section of Boston, which had been converted to three condominium units by a small developer, though the units were still owned by the developer. But because the developer had not obtained the bank's permission to convert the building to condominiums, Nickel's foreclosure would "wipe out" the condominium conversion. Therefore, after the auction the building would legally revert back to apartment status.

Bruce understood the ramifications of this. In an effort to protect tenants, Boston had made it extremely difficult to convert apartment buildings to condominiums. As a result, a three-unit condominium building was far more valuable that an identical three-unit apartment building. The Leumas appraisal (valued the property as an apartment building, at Bruce's instruction) placed the market value at $270,000, which meant the bank's bid would be $190,000. Bruce wished he could have kept this one for himself, but he simply did not have that kind of money and did not dare take the risk of bringing in a partner who might later turn on him. But it was tempting—Bruce estimated that building was worth $300,000 as an apartment building and about $400,000 as three condominiums. It killed him to think that so much money was just sitting there, and he couldn't grab it.

Unlike the last auction, the weather was clear and comfortable. Seven people registered to bid. Bruce recognized Pierre among them and nodded a return to Pierre's wave. Bruce didn't want to speak to Pierre just yet, so he grabbed the auctioneer and huddled in a conference.

Bruce stayed huddled with the auctioneer until it was time for the auctioneer to read the legal announcements. Even then, Bruce's body language made it clear to Pierre and the other bidders that he did not want to be approached. When the auctioneer finished his readings, Bruce stepped forward.

"I have an announcement to make. Just so there is no confusion here today, the mortgage being foreclosed on is senior to the condominium conversion documents filed for this property. What that means is that this foreclosure will legally wipe out the condominium status of this building and what you'll be left with is an apartment building. Is that clear to everyone?"

The bidders and hangers-on seemed satisfied with this statement, so Bruce stepped aside to let the auctioneer continue with a few more announcements. Bruce caught Pierre's eye and moved away from the group. Pierre understood and followed.

Bruce wanted to help Pierre without being too obvious about it. "Hi, Pierre, how are you?"

"Great, thanks. And thanks for doing those loan documents for Howie so quickly. I appreciate it."

"No problem. Hey, I'm curious—what do you think this property's worth?"

"Well, I was in the building last year. The units are in good shape, they did a nice job on the renovation. It all depends on whether you own the building as three condos or as just an apartment building with three units. If it's three condos, you can sell the units off to individual buyers, so it's probably worth close to $400,000, maybe a little more if the spring market's any good. But if it's just an apartment building, it's worth high 200s maybe."

"Wow, $100,000 difference just because you call them condos instead of apartments?"

"Yeah, it seems strange, I know. But there are a lot more people looking to buy condos than apartment buildings. I mean, every Yuppie in town wants a two-bedroom condo with a Jacuzzi and a deck. But there aren't many people interested in being a landlord—it takes too much time, plus the city's always busting your balls about something."

"All right, so I understand why the building is worth more as condos. It makes sense—you can just go out and sell the units. So why can't somebody just buy it as an apartment building and convert it to condos?" Bruce didn't completely understand the interplay between the legalities and the economics, and wasn't ashamed to ask for an explanation. And he sensed that Pierre would be a bit flattered to be relied on for the answers.

"Good question. The answer is that the conversion process is a nightmare. I mean, you have to buy out the tenants first, and that alone can cost twenty grand per tenant. Then you have to get the conversion approved by the city's rent board, and that can be a major hassle. When you figure in the lawyers and the architects and the delays, it adds up quickly. Maybe $100,000 is a bit overstated, but not too much." Pierre looked past Bruce and studied the building. "It really is too bad that the conversion gets wiped out. It's a great building for condos."

"Well, thanks for the info. If the bank is the high bidder today, I'll make sure to file a document consenting to the conversion. It's any easy document to draft." *Slow, fat pitch. Now hit it, Pierre.*

"You mean the bank could just file a document and the building would stay a condo?" Pierre spoke in an excited whisper.

"Yeah." Bruce paused for a moment, then laughed. "Oh, I see what you're thinking. I hear you, Pierre, I hear you. If you're the high bidder.... I can't make any promises, but I don't see why not. Okay?"

Pierre nodded, an appreciated grin on his face. Bruce smiled to himself—make a man rich, and he'll be your friend for life.

*   *   *

The auctioneer announced the opening of the auction, and Bruce immediately opened the bidding at $190,000. Pierre expected the bidding to move up quickly into the $250,000 range. That would give a buyer a ten or twenty percent discount off the value of the apartment building. Pierre, on the other hand, was bidding for a three-unit condominium building, and was therefore prepared to bid higher.

Pierre decided to be aggressive in his bidding in hopes of intimidating the other bidders. Ideally, he and Howie would pay less than $300,000 and then flip the individual units for a total of $400,000. After costs, they would split $70,000 to $80,000. Unfortunately, Howie had made it clear: he wanted to hold the properties until the market rebounded. Pierre did some quick arithmetic in his head—if they paid $280,000 and then got a mortgage for $190,000, the rents should be more than adequate to cover the expenses. Pay more than that, with interest rates as high as they were for investment properties, and it might get tight.

In a loud, clear voice, Pierre called out his bid: "$200,000."

After a few seconds, another bidder increased the bid to $205,000.

Before the bid was even out of the other bidder's mouth, Pierre yelled out again: "$210,000."

The ping pong match continued, each increasing the other's bid by $5,000, until Pierre reached $240,000. The other bidders were now watching, hands in their pockets. Pierre's opponent hesitated for ten or fifteen seconds, spoke to his companion, and then raised the bid by only $1,000, to $241,000.

Pierre sensed his opponent's weakness, decided to go for broke. "Two hundred fifty-one thousand dollars." He had raised the bid by a full $10,000. It was a bold move, since his opponent had just decreased the bidding increments to $1,000. Most bidders would have just raised by another $1,000, but Pierre had sensed his opponent's hesitation and had decided to deliver a knockout punch. Maybe Pierre would have won the bid at $242,000 or $244,000, but it was also possible that his opponent would have continued making $1,000 increases for another twenty or thirty thousand dollars.

The other bidder turned to Pierre. "All right, buddy, obviously you want it more than me. I'm not gonna keep bidding you up. Good luck."

Pierre had a momentary feeling of panic—why had nobody else been bidding!? But it quickly passed. He was a real estate professional, and he knew this was a good—no, great—deal. A $400,000 property for $251,000. Bruce came over, smiled reassuringly, and shook Pierre's hand. "Congratulations, Pierre."

"Thanks, Bruce. Thanks a lot."

31

[February 9, 1990]

Bruce held the deed to the Marlborough Street condominium in his hand. Later that day—exactly 21 days after the foreclosure sale—he would slide the deed across a mahogany table to the Springfield attorney, and the Arrujo family would once again enter the world of real estate ownership. It would be a symbolic step, like the son of a downed fighter pilot enlisting in the Air Force.

But Bruce was feeling a bit melancholy. His grandfather had been dead almost seven years, and Bruce still felt cheated by it.

Cheated by the loss of Grandpa. But also cheated by the fact that he had no memory of the brawl after Grandpa's heart attack. No memory of his fist smashing into the cartilage of one of the activists' nose, breaking not only the nose but part of the cheekbone. No memory of his work boot burying itself into the mid-section of another activist, fracturing three of her ribs and rupturing her spleen. No memory of grabbing the pony-tailed hair of another and smashing his head down onto the back of a metal chair, opening a gash on his forehead that squirted blood into the air like a garden hose. And no memory of being wrestled to the ground by a group of Cambridge police officers. He had memorized the police reports, and one of the cops even had been willing to give him a blow-by-blow description. But it simply wasn't the same as being able to re-live his vengeful fury over and over again in his mind.

Grandpa's dispute with the city actually had begun nine years before the fateful hearing, although no one knew it at the time. Grandpa lived in a triple-decker in a working class neighborhood of Cambridge, and also owned a few other investment properties in neighboring Somerville. He had owned them since before Bruce was born, and prided himself on being a caring and compassionate landlord. In the late 1960s, when Cambridge first enacted a rent control law, Grandpa had been unconcerned since the law specifically exempted three-family homes that were occupied by the owner.

And so it went for years, Grandpa continually upgrading and improving the properties. On Christmas he brought the tenants turkeys and hams, and in turn the tenants maintained their apartments and policed themselves. The properties provided him with a comfortable income, and he planned to pass them on to Bruce when he died.

But the tenant activists in Cambridge were fanatical. And savvy. And greedy. They wanted rent control to extend to all properties, even the small ones. At a certain point, it became almost a competition between the activists—every landlord a potential notch in their belt, every tenant paying market rent a soul to be saved, every clause in the rent control law a candidate for an Alice in Wonderland type of re-interpretation.

Then Grandpa made what turned out to be his fatal mistake: a widow who owned the triple-decker adjacent to his approached him one day. Her husband had recently died, and she could no longer take care of the property. But she didn't want to move out, either. Would he be willing to buy it from her and let her rent her apartment back from him? They agreed on a fair price, and Grandpa purchased the building.

The rent control law stated that any building with three or fewer apartments that was occupied by its owner was exempt from rent control. But the drafters of the law were concerned about a situation in which a triple-decker might have a separate, detached garage that had been converted into a fourth apartment—they wanted to make sure that this type of property would be considered a four-apartment building and be subject to rent control. And so the definition of a "single building" was redefined in the statute so that it also included any adjacent building owned by the same owner. Late one night, poring over the property tax rolls while picking at cold Chinese food, one of the tenant activists noticed that the same person owned a pair of adjoining triple-deckers. A light bulb went on, and from that moment on Grandpa found himself trying to fight the tide with a shovel.

Grandpa was just never willing to deal rationally with the activists' attempts to have both buildings subjected to rent control. Instead of hiring a lawyer to argue the technical interpretation of the law, Grandpa personalized the attack and reacted like an innocent man accused of child molestation. And instead of simply paying a fine and agreeing not to raise the rents above current levels, as the city proposed, Grandpa dug in his heels. Bruce could still remember his words. *This is a matter of principle, Brucie. A man has to stand up for what is right. These people are lunatics—how can two separate buildings be a 'single building' for Christ's sake? The way to treat these people is to not even dignify their arguments with a response. Like the Israelis say, you don't negotiate with terrorists.*

But negotiation was the last thing the activists wanted. They wanted—and Grandpa was right here—terror. They wanted every landlord in Cambridge to fear them, every real estate investor to redline Cambridge, every tenant to see them as Robin Hood and to vote for their candidates at the next election.

Grandpa had been collecting market rent on the two three-family buildings for the nine years since buying the property from the widow. The activists argued that this entire nine years of rent must be returned to the tenants since it had been illegally collected. Never mind that none of the tenants had requested the rebates. "As a matter of public policy," the activists argued, "the rent must be rebated as a message to other unscrupulous landlords."

The hearing officer delayed his decision for a few months after Grandpa's death, but in the end he sided with the activists' arguments and ordered that the rents be rebated to the tenants—in an amount totaling close to $400,000.

Meanwhile, the injured activists had sued Bruce for damages from their injuries, some of which were permanent and substantial. Grandpa's buildings, which he had left to Bruce in his will, had become Bruce's property, and the court ordered them conveyed to the activists as compensation for their damages. However, the tenants had first claim on the $400,000. The activists immediately sold the four buildings (two of which were now subject to rent control), but after deducting the $400,000 that was owed to the tenants and paying their lawyers and their medical bills, the activists walked away with next to nothing. It was little solace for Bruce for the loss of his inheritance, but it was something at least.

32

[February 13, 1990]

Charese was in the habit of staying in bed until the mailman arrived. The doorman would ring her, and she would rush downstairs in her bathrobe and a baseball cap. A year ago she wouldn't have dreamed of leaving the apartment before she had showered and applied make-up. She just didn't care that much anymore.

She was hoping for a letter from her sister. It was the only contact she had with her family, and it was irregular, but Charese longed to feel that she belonged to something, even a family as self-righteous and hypocritical as her own. Her father was a minister in a small Georgia town, and her mother a teacher at the local elementary school. On Sundays Reverend Galloway preached the words of God—messages of compassion and kindness and understanding. During the week Mrs. Galloway taught the lessons of American history—mandates of tolerance and open-mindedness and the individual spirit. At home, however, the parents Galloway forgot these messages and these lessons; after spending the entire day nurturing and caring for the congregation and community, it was as if they simply had nothing left to expend on Charese—actually, Charles at the time—and his sister. Theirs was a strict and joyless household, one that stressed discipline and order and obedience.

Looking back, Charese realized that she had been stupid to embarrass her father by publicly announcing her homosexuality the day before Easter. Especially with the bishop in town for Easter services, and her father hoping to increase his influence in statewide religious affairs. But adolescent emotions run strong, and the seventeen-year-old Charles had been waiting for years to avenge the humiliation caused by his father sermonizing about "the evils of teenage masturbation in the very household of the messenger of the Lord". So when 'Master Charles', as he was referred to at school after the sermon, saw the opportunity for a little Easter Massacre of his own, he didn't exactly contemplate what the repercussions of his actions would be twenty years down the road.

The repercussions, not surprisingly, had been that his parents kicked him out of the house and never spoke to him again. His sister, against the mandate of their parents, corresponded occasionally, but only to convey news of the family and never to hint that there was even the slightest chance of a reconciliation.

Charese knew that perhaps the clearest evidence of the desperate state of her own life was that she had written to her sister about possibly moving home to Georgia, and that she now fervently prayed for word that her parents would welcome her. She understood that her desire to go home was similar to the desire of a starving man to catch a rat for dinner. Neither choice is in the least bit appetizing, but both are proof that the survival instinct runs strong.

It had been six weeks now, and she still had not heard back from her sister. Easter was in three weeks, so maybe this wasn't the best time to go home anyway.

33

[February 16, 1990]

Pierre had just put Valerie down for the night, then sat for ten minutes and watched her sleep. It continually amazed him how strong—almost violent—his love was for her. He had no doubt he could kill on her behalf if necessary. He came downstairs. "Carla, Sweetie, we have to talk," he said as he poured them each a glass of wine.

"Uh oh. Last time a guy said that to me, I ended up throwing my engagement ring at him. Of course, I'm safe this time—you know if you try to divorce me, I'll murder you."

Pierre laughed. "No, that whole New Hampshire thing doesn't appeal to me." Carla looked at him quizzically. "You know, 'Live free or die'. I'll stay right here as your slave, thank you very much." Of course he would stay—how many women would be able to joke about their fiancee breaking things off just two months before the wedding?

"Okay, slave, what's up?"

"We need to have another of those money talks. First of all—the good news. We bought another property today. It's just a condo, but I think we got it at a good price."

"Great. Was this one of Bruce Arrujo's auctions?"

"Yeah. The guy's been incredibly helpful. This condo is on the first floor and has nine hundred square feet according to all the legal documents, so it's worth today maybe $140,000. Good location by the Bunker Hill Monument in Charlestown. But Bruce pointed out to me some obscure provision in the con-dominium documents—the owner of the unit has the legal right to annex part of the basement and expand his unit to make the unit fifteen hundred square feet. I went down into the basement—it's already semi-finished space. So you spend maybe another twenty grand to finish it and, presto, the unit's worth $210,000."

"So what did you get it for?"

"Hundred ten. There was one other guy bidding me up, but I would have gone up another ten or fifteen. It was a clean deal—no owner to evict and Bruce said the title was clear."

"This is a deal with Howie, I assume?"

"Yeah. That's what I wanted to talk to you about. You know we've bought two properties so far, this one and the three-family. Which, by the way, Bruce did get the bank to sign the document we needed to legally keep it as three condos. So I figure for both properties we've made about $150,000 in profit already, which we split with Howie fifty-fifty."

"Really? Our share is $75,000? That's great."

"Yeah, and those are pretty conservative numbers. But the problem is that Howie doesn't want to sell for a couple of years. So our profit is tied up, and in the meantime we have no income."

"What about the rents?"

"Unfortunately, we need the rents to pay the mortgages. Howie's got a chunk of money, but it's not unlimited. Plus, he's really into the concept of leverage. So what we're doing is paying cash for the properties and then taking a mortgage so that we can free up Howie's cash to do more deals. And it's tight—there aren't many banks looking to make real estate loans right now, especially to investors. And the ones that do are charging pretty high interest rates. So, like I said, we need the rents to pay the mortgages. And what's left we're putting back into the properties. I think you agree with me on this—I don't want to be in this business if we're just going to be slumlords, so I told Howie we need to fix them up a bit."

"Of course I agree." It was a subject they discussed often. Many people in society simply fought for a piece of the pie; Pierre and Carla agreed that they should try to increase the size of the pie, not just eat from it. And, in real estate, growing the pie translated into putting money back into the properties for renovations and improvements.

Carla continued. "And, Pierre, I don't mind cutting back for a few years. But we need some income. I mean, come on. We've got nothing coming in except a few hundred bucks from the brokerage business."

"I know, Sweetie, and I have an idea. But I wanted to talk to you about it first. Howie has no problem if I go out myself and buy a property and flip it. The problem is that I've talked to a few banks, and none of them will do the loan. We have too much debt and too little income."

"Really? I hadn't noticed."

"Well, the bankers did. Anyway, I found a guy who will lend me the money, but he wants twenty-one percent interest. I thought I should talk to you first."

"What, and if you don't pay, he breaks your legs?"

"Something like that."

"Pierre, are you crazy?"

"Seriously, Carla, he's not the leg-breaking type. He's more the foreclose and then sue us for everything we have type. But I still thing it's worth it. If I buy a property and then flip it in two or three months, who cares about 21 percent interest? I mean, it's actually a better deal for us than splitting it 50-50 with Howie."

"And what if you can't sell it in a few months? Isn't the market still terrible?"

"It's still bad, but the better properties are selling. Values dropped like twenty-five percent over the winter, but now they're holding pretty firm. At least some people have realized that Boston's not going to turn into Newark, that it's still a world-class city. And they're starting to buy in the good neighborhoods and the better suburbs. It's the properties in the bad neighborhoods that are still in a free-fall. So if I have trouble selling, I'll just cut the price."

"Famous last words. I'm not kidding, Pierre. We can't afford any more debt—hell, we can't even afford our current debt."

"I know, honey. But listen to me. We're pretty much insolvent anyway right now. If this doesn't work, we'll really be no worse off then we are now. But if it does work and I can make thirty or forty thousand in a flip, that will give us the breathing room we need so that I can keep doing these deals with Howie. I've been thinking about this a lot, and it really is the only way."

Carla studied Pierre intently. He knew she believed that his business sense was generally good—he tended not to be ego-driven like so many other real estate investors. She sighed. "Okay, honey. But please be careful. And the same rules, right? I don't want to get involved with putting a family out onto the street. I mean, that might be us someday."

Pierre reached over and took her hand. They had gone through a number of bottles of wine over the past few months discussing the morality of profiting over someone else's misfortune. "I agree, same rules. As a matter of fact, most of the things I've been looking at are investment condos. The owners don't even live in the units—they're either empty or there are tenants that can just stay until the end of their lease."

"All right. I can live with that."

"You know, Carla, I hope I'm not just rationalizing, but I'm starting to believe that 'bottom feeders' like me and Howie actually serve a useful purpose."

"Yeah, so do hyenas and vultures, but that doesn't mean I want to sleep with them."

Pierre leaned over and nibbled on her shoulder. "Mmmm, fresh meat. But seriously, prices were in a free-fall for a few months, then all of a sudden a few people like me have started bidding at the auctions and buying from the banks and now things seem to be leveling out a bit. Somebody's got to buy at the bottom; otherwise the market just keeps falling, and there is no bottom."

Pierre watched as Carla mulled this over. He knew his analysis made sense, but he doubted that Carla's college economics textbooks ever made a point of lauding the economic benefits of bottom feeding. "You know what, I'll buy it. I'm not going to go around bragging that my husband is a real estate vulture, but as long as we're not putting families out on the street, I think you're right—it's no different than people who buy stocks when they're cheap. And it's better than the people who choose to save a buck or two on a shirt even though they know it was made by ten-year-old slave laborers in Asia somewhere. So come on, Mr. Hyena, let's go to bed."

34

[February 22, 1990]

"Please, Shelby, I promise not to make a scene."

"Hey, Charese, this is your case, so you don't have to ask my permission for anything. I just thought you might be more comfortable waiting in another room. But if you don't mind seeing Roberge and Megan together, I'd love to have you in there with me. It'll help keep them honest when I ask some tough questions.

"Great. I want to watch the son-of-a-bitch squirm. And I can't wait to see his little trophy wife."

Shelby laughed. She hadn't seen Charese so energized since before Thanksgiving. She hoped it wasn't because she was high. "Okay then. But remember, you have to behave."

"You mean I can't stick a pen in his eye?"

"Actually, feel free to get under their skin a little, especially Roberge. You know, glare at him, roll your eyes, that kind of stuff. I'm sure his lawyer has rehearsed his answers with him—maybe you'll be able to throw him off script."

"You got it."

Shelby squeezed Charese's arm, and they entered the conference room. Roberge, Megan and Roberge's attorney were seated in a row on the opposite side of a long mahogany conference table. Shelby walked around the table, shook hands with Roberge's lawyer.

"Shelby, this is my client, Roberge Krygier. And his wife, Mrs. Krygier." They looked like they had come straight from the country club—he in a blue blazer over a white turtleneck, she in a cardigan sweater over a button-down shirt.

Shelby shook their hands, noticed their manicured nails, wondered what kind of woman would allow herself to be introduced as "Mrs. Krygier". She introduced Charese, greeted the stenographer and walked back around the table to sit down. She addressed Roberge's attorney. "I'll start by taking the deposition of Mr. Krygier. If we finish in time, I'll begin with…." She turned and looked at Roberge's wife. "I'm sorry, I didn't catch your first name." Shelby knew it was Megan, but wanted to gauge her a bit.

Megan glared at Shelby, deep-set eyes firing at her over round, protruding cheeks and a pink button nose. Shelby thought she looked like an angry rabbit.

Actually, Shelby felt some sympathy for her. She had gone from giddy fiancée to the object of widespread ridicule, and had every right to feel cheated by it. After a few seconds, when it became apparent that Megan had no intention of answering, Roberge answered for her. "My wife's first name is Megan."

Shelby continued. "Thank you. As I was saying, if we have time today, I'll move on to Mrs. Krygier's deposition. Otherwise, we'll do hers tomorrow."

Krygier's attorney interrupted. "I can't see why we can't finish both of these today."

Shelby knew he was testing her. "I hope you're right. And if you're clients are cooperative in answering my questions, we might be able to finish today. If not, it might take longer. Or we might have to go see the judge."

Roberge's attorney leaped to his feet, bellowed in his best courtroom voice. "Are you threatening us? Because we're not going to stand for it." Shelby tried not to laugh—she knew this was just a show for his clients, an attempt to intimidate the young female lawyer. What would he do next, go urinate in the corners of the room?

Shelby simply ignored him, turned to the stenographer. "I believe it's time to begin the deposition of Roberge Krygier. Please put us on the record." Shelby guessed that Roberge's attorney wouldn't be so bellicose now that his words were being transcribed.

Shelby ran through some background questions for Roberge, gauging him as she slowly worked her way to the issue of his relationship with Charese. As she questioned him, she watched him carefully. He answered her questions quickly, as if trying to portray an attitude of impatience, or even indifference, to the proceedings. But she peaked under the table once, under the pretense of picking up a file, and saw his leg bouncing up and down nervously.

After about fifteen minutes, Charese slipped her a note. *When he puts his hand on his chin, it means he's lying.*

Shelby decided to move to the good stuff. "Mr. Krygier, did you have a sexual relationship with Charese Galloway?"

"If you're referring to Charles Galloway, the answer is yes." Shelby noticed that Roberge had not once looked at Charese. She also noticed that Megan refused to look at anyone; she just stared at a painting on the wall and played with her wedding ring, sliding it up and down her finger.

"You're not familiar with the name 'Charese Galloway'?"

"I am. It's the name Charles started calling himself when he decided he wanted to be a woman."

"And did you support Charese in that decision?"

Roberge put his hand to his chin. Shelby noticed he had small, flabby fingers, which surprised her because he was otherwise thin and a little taller than average. "Not really. But hey, whatever turns him on."

"You say 'not really', but isn't it true that you asked Charese to wear women's clothing when the two of you attended events with your family?"

"Yeah. It was easier than telling them I was gay."

"So you just introduced Charese as your girlfriend?"

"Yes."

"You never referred to her as your fiancee?"

"No."

"Never told her you would marry her if she had a sex-change operation?"

"No." Hand back on chin.

"I see." Charese passed Shelby another note. *Buffy is wearing the engagement ring Roberge gave me. It's his grandmother's. It's the same one I'm wearing in the picture that was in the newspaper.* "So you never did anything to make Charese think that the two of you were to be married?"

"Nothing I'm aware of."

"You know that you're under oath, don't you Mr. Krygier?"

"I do."

Shelby reached into her briefcase, pulled out a stack of photographs. As she did so, she looked under the table again; Roberge's leg was bouncing like a jackhammer. "Mr. Krygier, I want to show you a photograph—it's the original of a picture that appeared in the local newspaper recently." Shelby handed the photo to Roberge. "Do you recognize it?"

"Yes."

"Who's in the picture?"

"My father, myself and Charles."

"Could you look carefully at Charese's left hand, specifically her ring finger."

Shelby waited a few seconds, but Roberge did not respond. "Mr. Krygier? Do you recognize the ring on Charese's finger in that picture?"

Roberge again remained silent, his head down. Suddenly Megan jumped from her seat and grabbed the picture, stared at it, then threw it on the floor. She glared down at Roberge. "You bastard! That's my ring! You gave me a fucking hand-me-down ring?!" Megan ripped the ring off her finger and hurled it at Roberge; it struck him on the cheek, then bounced to the floor. "You're a lying piece of shit, Roberge Krygier!" Roberge remained in his chair, motionless, his head bowed.

Megan ran from the room, slammed the door.

The slam of the door jolted Roberge from his cower. He exploded out of his seat like a greyhound out of the starting gate and raced around the conference table in pursuit of his wife.

As he reached the door, Charese called to him. "Hey Roberge. If you catch her, tell her that I'm sorry I didn't have a chance to wish her luck in her new marriage. She's gonna need it."

Roberge stopped at the door, spun around and pointed a fat finger at Charese. The finger shook, and Shelby could see a vein bulging in his forehead. The words came out from behind clenched teeth. "Fuck you, Charles. You're nothing. You're nothing but a little piece of shit."

35

[March 1, 1990]

Bruce heard a soft knock on his door. "Come in."

Puck's secretary, Jan, opened the door and smiled. Lately, Bruce had noticed that she seemed to look for opportunities to visit his office. Today was the first spring-like day of the year, and, warm as it was in the office, it seemed to Bruce that her blouse needed one or two more buttons at the top and her skirt one or two more inches at the bottom. Had her strategy shifted from looking for opportunities to see Bruce to giving Bruce opportunities to see?

Whatever the case, he smiled appreciatively back at her. *Not bad for north of forty.* "Hi, Jan. Have a seat for a minute—I was just about to take a break."

She glided over to a side chair and gracefully sat down, her skirt riding even higher up her legs. Bruce saw upper thigh, then a flash of red panties. They matched—exactly—her lipstick and fingernail polish. Jan watched his eyes and re-crossed her legs, and again a red target flashed in front of Bruce's eyes. He sighed quietly and forced himself to resist the urge to charge. *In the battle between skilled matador and raging bull, the odds were long on the bull.* Besides, what he wanted from her was between her ears, not between her legs.

Still, he eyed her appreciatively. He wanted her to think that he was making small talk just as an excuse to look up her skirt and down her blouse.

"So, how did a nice girl like you end up in a place like this?" It was a terrible line, but Bruce wanted to play the role of the clumsy, inexperienced stallion.

"Well, first of all, I'm not so nice." She smiled knowingly at Bruce, who bit his lip and smiled shyly in return. "But if you must know, I've been here since I graduated secretarial school…, well, many years ago."

"Have you always worked for Mr. Puck?"

She turned away and her face darkened slightly. Bruce guessed she would have preferred to continue the flirtation rather than discuss her boss. "No, only the last seven or eight years."

"What's he really like? I mean, what does he do for fun, other than try to act British?"

Jan let out a single, sharp laugh. "Fun? Mr. Puck? For fun he comes into the office on the weekends and plays with the computer. That's really his whole life—his law practice and computers. He's got this firm as high-tech as any firm in the city. Oh, and he also reads crime novels—he's really into forensics, you know, fingerprints and that kind of stuff. He's actually considered a bit of an expert."

His interest in forensics made sense to Bruce—Scotland Yard and Sherlock Holmes and all that. But the computers surprised him. "Puck knows computers?"

"Better than anyone else here, even the technical people. One of the older secretaries said that he originally had wanted to be a scientist, but his old man—the original Puck—forced him into the law practice."

"He doesn't seem very happy."

"You're telling me. And it's been worse the last few months. He's lost a few big clients because of the economy, and he's not exactly taking it well."

"Does he have a family?"

"None that I know of. He lives in an apartment building on the waterfront and drives his Mercedes to work every day. And I mean every day, including weekends. Once a year he takes a vacation to London, but that's it." She shifted gears, angled her head teasingly. "And what do you do for fun?"

Bruce almost didn't answer; he had been thinking about the London comment. He knew Puck was an Anglophile, but could the London vacation be related to the Lloyd's of London correspondence? And didn't he read recently that Lloyd's was having financial problems due to pollution claims, problems so bad that its shareholders—the famous "names" of Lloyd's—might have to write hefty checks to cover the losses? If Puck was a "name", it wasn't a great time to be losing clients.

He refocused on Jan. "What do I do for fun? I pry into my boss' personal life. When I'm really in a crazy mood, I steal pens from his office."

Jan smiled politely, but Bruce could tell she had hoped for a response with a little more innuendo. She got up to leave. "Be careful, then. I'm in charge of the pens. And you should see what we do to pen thieves."

Bruce knew he would surprise her with his answer. "Let me guess—you write all over us?"

Jan stopped in mid-stride and turned slowly around. "Yup. Then we stick you in a bubble bath to clean you up." She winked and left the room.

CHAPTER

36

Bruce had noticed a rotund, loud-voiced woman talking to bidders and taking notes during the auction. She had even interrupted one bidder as he was about to make a bid. So Bruce was not surprised when, after the auction, she wedged herself between Bruce and the auctioneer.

"Name's Bailey Gray. Write for the *Herald*. Doing a story on foreclosure auctions. Ask a few questions?" Her hair was pulled back from her round face, and she was carrying a large plastic cup of coffee, which he had noticed she sipped through a straw on those rare occasions when she wasn't either talking or scribbling on her notepad.

Bruce instinctively adopted her clipped manner of speech. It was an interpersonal skill he had learned while working as a telemarketer his senior year of high school. "Not at all. Bruce Arrujo. Nice to meet you." Bruce offered Bailey an easy smile and an outstretched hand, both of which Bailey accepted quickly and then returned.

"Been to four of these auctions now. No action. Bank took back each one. Anyone ever buy anything? Not much of a story so far."

"See your point. Doing some kind of 'how-to' story on buying foreclosures?"

"Trying. Editor is tired of doom and gloom real estate stories. People don't want to keep reading that they lost fifty grand on their house. But so far, nothing to write about."

"Properties in places like this aren't going to sell at foreclosure." They were in Malden, a working-class suburb of Boston that had seen better days. The paralegal, whom Bruce had trained personally, had done all the work on the file—Bruce had merely shown up to supervise the auction itself. "A few properties sell downtown, or in the western suburbs."

"Yeah? Who buys 'em?"

"Put it this way. Not Mr. and Mrs. Smith buying their dream home for half-price. Doesn't happen. Too risky."

"Could you explain what you mean?"

"Sure." Bruce took a few seconds to word his answer correctly—he wanted to be clear and quotable, yet he wanted his answer to be intimidating. "The only people who should be trying to buy property at foreclosure sales are professional real estate investors. By professional I mean people who devote themselves full-time to researching the properties and who can afford to walk away from ten or twenty thousand dollars if the property ends up having problems. Remember, people bidding at foreclosure sales don't get to inspect the inside of the properties, don't know if the title is clear, and don't have time to get a mortgage. Then, if they do close, they have to evict the previous owner and his family. It's very risky."

Bruce waited as Bailey scribbled for a few seconds, stubby finger tight on the tip of her pencil, lower lip tucked under her coffee-stained upper teeth. "Thanks. Well said. So you think people should just forget about auctions?"

"Actually, no. I would recommend that people call the banks after the auctions and try to buy the properties then. The banks don't want to keep the properties, and after the auction a buyer can structure a normal transaction that minimizes the risks."

Bailey looked disappointed. "Maybe good advice. Not a very juicy story."

"Well, I know a guy who buys a lot of property. Could introduce you. Pretty interesting."

"How so?"

"Goes to the auctions on roller blades. Stands right there on the sidewalk in them and bids. Expert on buying foreclosures. Taught himself how to do title searches. Knows all the brokers in town, gets the scoop on all the properties. Got good money behind him, too. Entrepreneur type. An American Original."

"Name? Might be the angle I'm looking for."

               *   *   *

Bruce returned to the office and phoned Pierre.

"Hi, Bruce, nice to hear from you. What's up?"

"There's a reporter from the *Herald* who's doing a story on buying at foreclosures. I hope you don't mind, but I gave her your name, told her you were the expert in town. I also told her about the roller blades. I think she wants to profile you."

"Of course I don't mind. But you told her I was the expert?"

"Yeah. I mean, you are. You're the best prepared and, as far as I know, you've bought twice as many properties at foreclosure as anybody else."

"You mean 'twice as many', as in two?"

Bruce laughed. "I don't mean to be technical, but do you know anybody else who's bought more than one?"

Pierre paused for a second. "No, I guess I don't. All right, so I'm the expert. What does she want to talk to me about?"

"Well, she wanted to do a story telling readers how to buy at auction, but I discouraged her because I think it's too risky for most people. My advice was that they wait until after the auction and try to make a deal with the bank then."

"That's probably good advice. Anyway, of course I'll talk to her."

"Good. I figured the publicity wouldn't hurt."

"Course not. Hey Bruce, mind if I ask you a question?"

"Shoot."

"You've been incredibly helpful to me. Mind if I ask why?"

"Well, first of all, I think you're a decent, honorable guy. Not many people would have sacrificed their commission like you did when you thought Howie was overpaying for that building. But it's not like I don't have selfish motives. The way I see it, you're going to be a big player in Boston real estate for a long time, and you're going to need a lawyer. Hopefully, you'll think of me, which might help my career, too."

37

[March 14, 1990]

Pierre had mixed feelings about waking to the sound of the birds singing in the tree by his window. On the one hand, spring was historically the best time of the year to sell real estate. His brokerage business was virtually non-existent, and he could sure use a little mid-March flurry. On the other hand, those same spring buyers might become competitors of his at foreclosure sales. In the past few months, Pierre had witnessed more and more activity at the auctions. People were simply getting more comfortable with the process and were finding ways to minimize the risks.

And Pierre was getting more comfortable as well. He no longer limited himself to Bruce's auctions. He was still cautious, but a few of the larger auctioneers had been able to persuade some of the banks to give bidders assurances on title matters. And Pierre had been able to further cultivate his network of rental brokers who, unbeknownst to the landlords in town, seemed to have a key to every building in Boston. Pierre still had to assume some risks, but at least he could bid feeling comfortable about title and property condition.

But even Pierre's increased comfort level was a two-edged sword. A small group of individuals had begun traveling the auction circuit on a regular basis, attending ten to fifteen auctions per week. Pierre was part of this group, and he had already gained a reputation as a well-connected and savvy bidder. In fact, some bidders had begun to ride his coattails—if Pierre bid, they figured it was probably safe for them to bid as well. They simply raised Pierre's bid by a hundred dollars—if it was worth $123,000 to Pierre, it stood to reason that it would be worth $123,100 to them.

And then the *Herald* story hit. The story featured a large picture of Pierre in his roller blades, standing outside a Back Bay brownstone, and referred to Pierre as "the most experienced and successful foreclosure bidder in the city". Pierre had officially become the largest fish in a small pond.

Pierre took a shower, then sat down at the kitchen table and shared a banana with Valerie. Carla teased him. "So, how is my King of the Vultures doing this morning?"

"Don't laugh. This celebrity status is killing me at the auctions."

"What do you mean?"

"Three times in the past couple of weeks I outbid the bank, only to have some 'coattailer' jump in at the last minute and raise the bid. It happened at that Charlestown condo that I bought with Howie—it cost us an extra $12,000. And the last two times I lost the property entirely. And I know the guys who outbid me—they never would have bid if I hadn't bid. But when I did, they figured it must be a good deal. One guy even came up to me after the auction. Told me he knew it must be a solid property or else I wouldn't have been bidding."

Carla was silent for a moment. "Remember how you explained to me once the whole idea of wrestling? You know, using the other guy's leverage and momentum against him?"

"Yeah. If you've got a guy who's pushing toward you, it's easier to just pull him along and get him off-balance than it is to push him back."

"Well, I have an idea. But you have to be willing to do a little acting."

"Fine. I've been playing it straight so far, unlike most of the guys. You should hear some of the stories they make up to try to scare the other bidders away. One guy last week was telling a couple of women that a convicted rapist was living in the building. Anyway, I'll give it a shot. What's your idea?"

Carla relayed her idea to Pierre.

He nodded. "It's a good plan. It really could work. But it seems a little dishonest. I'm not sure I'm totally comfortable with it."

"Honey, listen. I know you set high moral standards for yourself, but this is the real world out there, and times are getting a little desperate. You did right by Howie, walked away from a $45,000 commission, saved him hundreds of thousands of dollars, and what did it get you? A twenty-two percent interest rate. You work hard and carve a nice niche for yourself at these auctions, and what happens? The other bidders attach themselves to you like a leech. It's nice to be a good guy, but people are taking advantage of you. I'm not saying you need to turn into a criminal, but you have to be willing to take at least one step into the gray area or we're going to have to move in with your parents."

Pierre knew that Carla was right. His first responsibility was to his family. Even if it meant the loss of a little self-respect. "All right. There's an auction scheduled later that week, and I know it'll be well attended. It's a condo in the South End. I haven't been in the unit, but I've been inside other units in the building. The building's an old brick church—it was renovated by a pretty well-respected developer. Even won a few architectural awards. There'll be a decent crowd."

The next morning, Pierre slipped into his roller blades, threw on a windbreaker and, darting around pedestrians and between cars, skated downtown to the Registry of Deeds building. Bruce was not the attorney for this auction, and the first thing Pierre wanted to do was make sure the title was clear. He quickly found what he was looking for—the property had been purchased four years earlier in an all-cash transaction. Then, last December, the owner took out a mortgage for $147,000. There were no other mortgages or liens on the property.

This seemed odd to Pierre. He was used to seeing foreclosures where the property was "under water"—that is, where the property was worth less than the mortgages. Here, Pierre guessed that the property was worth about $210,000, or $60,000 more than the only mortgage. Why didn't the owner just sell the property and pay off the mortgage? And why was the foreclosure occurring so soon after the mortgage was given?

Pierre looked again at the documents—the owner's name was Roberge Krygier. Wasn't there a newspaper story last fall about one of the Krygiers being sued by his transvestite lover? Could this be the same Krygier? It might explain the foreclosure—if his ex-lover still lived in the condo, Krygier might have stopped paying the mortgage.

Pierre wanted the rest of the story. He took the elevator down to the street level and slipped into his roller blades again. He navigated his way between the moving cars and roadside slush of Beacon Hill, careful to avoid puddles that would cause his wheels to lose traction. The pathways in the Common had been cleared of snow, and he cut across Beacon Street into the park. He glided downhill, away from the State House and diagonally across the park, dragging his right heel to keep from gaining too much speed. On the opposite corner of the Common, he passed through a wrought-iron gate and onto Boylston Street. He turned right and skated toward the Public Library, barely visible five blocks away in Copley Square.

He reached the Library, then sat on the front steps to remove his skates and put on his shoes. While he did so, three homeless men approached him separately for money—more evidence of the slumping economy. Years ago, Pierre and Carla had stayed up late one night with some friends and argued over what to do when asked for money by a homeless person. To do nothing, they agreed, was simply immoral. But to give them money, which many would simply use to buy alcohol, was often counter-productive. Their solution had been to purchase McDonald's gift certificates. So today, as always, Pierre handed out a couple of one-dollar gift certificates to each of the homeless men—enough for a sandwich and a cup of coffee. As bad as things were financially for him and Carla, at least they weren't living on the street.

Once inside the library, he quickly found the newspaper article about Roberge Krygier and his transvestite lover. The story was accompanied by a picture of Krygier, his father and his lover, Charese. Pierre scanned the article quickly— sure enough, Krygier and Charese shared a condo together in the South End. Then came the breakup, followed by the filing of a lawsuit in the Suffolk County court. Pierre made a copy of the article and stuck it in his backpack.

The Suffolk County courthouse was located in the same building as the Registry of Deeds, so Bruce simply reversed his course and headed back up Beacon Hill. It was a tougher skate, uphill, but Pierre didn't mind. It was a great day to be outside, and a little exercise was always welcome.

Pierre waited ten minutes before a clerk of the court shuffled into the file room to retrieve the litigation file for him. He read the Complaint. It made for fascinating reading—blue blood real estate heir leaves transvestite lover to marry country club preppie. As far as Pierre could see, nothing much had happened in the case since it was filed last September, other than an injunction issued by the court preventing Krygier from selling the condo until the suit was resolved. Just a lot of arguing between the lawyers about whose deposition could be taken and what questions could be asked. But one thing was clear—Charese's address listed in the Complaint was the address of the condo being foreclosed on.

Pierre returned the file to the clerk, then walked over to a pay phone and called information—they had a listing under Krygier's name. Pierre dialed the number. On the fourth ring, a tired-sounding voice answered. Pierre couldn't decide if the voice sounded male or female.

"Could I speak to Charese please."

"This is Charese. Who is this?"

Pierre hung up the phone. So she was still there.

*   *   *

The next morning, Pierre and Carla dropped Valerie off at his parents' house, then swung by the bank. They withdrew the $20,000 they had borrowed from Howie and purchased two separate bank cashier's checks, each in the amount of $10,000. One check was made out to Carla, the other to Pierre.

From the bank, they drove to the local BMW dealer. Pierre was friendly with the owner, and he had arranged to rent a top of the line model for the day. Bright red.

Carla drove, inbound on Route 9, careful not to ding the BMW. When they reached Copley Square, Pierre jumped out. He put on his roller blades and began skating toward the South End. It was 10:50—the auction was scheduled for 11:00. At 10:55, Pierre glided to a stop in front of the building.

Pierre saw three other auction regulars who, like himself, had made attending foreclosure auctions a full-time job. The three other regulars and Pierre exchanged greetings—they were competitors, but also potential allies. One of them had already suggested that the four of them—along with a fifth regular who was absent from today's auction—agree to work together in some kind of syndication. "Why bid each other up?" he had asked. "If we work together, we can all benefit by keeping the bidding down. I mean, most of the time, one of us buys the property if the bank doesn't. If we don't bid against each other, the only one who loses is the bank." The idea was strategically sound, but Pierre was a little uncomfortable with it, and he had been non-committal.

Pierre leaned against a railing and removed his skates. He kept an eye out for Carla, and she appeared a few minutes later. She played it perfectly. She stopped the red BMW in front of the building, double parked, put on her flashers, and stepped out of the car. With an attitude. Fur coat, leather pants, heels, sunglasses. Big hair and even bigger jewels.

Pierre looked over. "Hey, look. A rich bitch has come to buy a condo. I wonder if Daddy gave her the money?" He didn't usually use such crude language, but he figured, well, he was referring to his wife, and the whole thing was her idea, so it was okay. The other auction regulars laughed. Pierre continued. "Well, I bet she doesn't know what she's getting herself into. Check this out."

He handed a copy of the newspaper article around. The other regulars eyed it warily—they had never know Pierre not to play it straight, but you never knew. As they scanned the article, Pierre watched Carla register to bid. She was now holding a cigarette with an ebony cigarette holder. He laughed to himself. Had she found that in his mother's closet along with the fake fur and the costume jewels?

One of the regulars turned to Pierre. "So this is Krygier's condo?"

"Yeah. I actually went to the courthouse to check out the lawsuit. I mean, the Krygiers have more money than God. So why would Krygier be getting foreclosed on? Well, it turns out that his transvestite lover is claiming that she should get to keep the condo. You know, like if you divorce your wife she tries to keep the house. The court put an injunction on Krygier so that he couldn't sell it, so she must have a pretty good case. Plus, what are the chances a transvestite in the South End doesn't have AIDS? Try to evict her, and watch the gay groups rush to her defense. I'm staying real low on this one; you guys can buy it if you want."

The others eyed Pierre. One of them challenged him. "Well then why did you register?"

Pierre turned to him. "You're right. If it goes for fifty grand or something stupid like that, I probably would buy it. Otherwise it's yours."

The group continued to study him. Was he bluffing? If so, it wasn't a very smart bluff. They could call him on it by simply waiting five minutes until the auction began to see how he was bidding.

Pierre had guessed that the bank would bid close to the $150,000 they were owed. He had instructed Carla to bid up to $155,000, but no higher. Based on a property value of $210,000, that would give them a profit margin of $55,000, although they would still have to deal with Charese. But Pierre figured they could buy Charese off for five or ten thousand, or else just evict her if they had to. He had embellished the story a little bit for the other regulars—as far as he knew, Charese didn't have AIDS. Then again, he hadn't actually come right out and said she did.

Other than Carla, Pierre and the other regulars, there was only one other registered bidder, a young couple with a baby. They were asking a lot of questions, and couldn't understand why they weren't being allowed to go inside to view the unit. The auctioneer was trying to be patient with them.

"We can't let you in because we don't have a key. Remember, the bank doesn't own the property yet—it's just foreclosing on the mortgage. After the auction it will own it, unless one of you buys it today. All I can do is show you a copy of the floor plan—it shows that there are two bedrooms and two bathrooms and that the unit is 1150 square feet. And it comes with an underground parking space."

The couple seemed frustrated by the process—they were used to being coddled by a broker. Pierre guessed it was their first auction. Still, he was worried. He had overhead them talking—apparently they had almost purchased another unit in the building. So they knew the building, and they knew what units were worth. He hoped they would be too nervous to pull the trigger. He walked over and handed the wife a copy of the newspaper article, smiled kindly, and walked away.

The auctioneer declared the auction open and asked for an opening bid. Nobody moved—it was a common scenario, bidders hoping to gain some kind of advantage by waiting until the last possible moment to make their bid. The auctioneer knew Pierre from previous auctions, and looked to him for an opening. Pierre usually complied; it was a good way to curry favor with the auctioneers. "Mr. Prefontaine, do you have an opening bid?" The other auction regulars also eyed Pierre, waiting for his move.

Pierre responded. "First, I have a question. My understanding is that the property is the subject of litigation between the owner and the current occupant. Is the bank willing to guarantee that the property will be vacant at the time of the closing?" Pierre knew the answer, but he wanted the young couple with the baby to hear it.

The bank attorney stepped forward, right on cue. "The bank makes no representation regarding the occupancy of the property. It will be the successful bidder's responsibility to evict any occupants of the property."

Pierre sighed disappointedly. "All right, I'll start then. But you're not going to like it. I bid $50,000."

The auctioneer didn't like it at all—he was working today on a commission basis. "Fifty thousand? Please, sir, we are here today to sell the property, not to rent it."

Pierre quickly responded, good-naturedly but with an edge to his voice. "That's fine, but you'll have sell it to someone else then. I'm not getting into the middle of this mess. That's my final bid." He knew he was jeopardizing his relationship with the auctioneer, but so be it.

Carla glanced disdainfully over at Pierre and the other regulars. Haughtily, she spoke. "I'll make a bid." She raised her chin slightly. "One hundred twenty thousand dollars."

Pierre snorted derisively. He whispered to the other regulars in a squeaky voice. "And Daddy will make sure that naughty tenant leaves." They all laughed. They were with Pierre so far.

The bank attorney stepped forward again. "The bank bids one hundred forty-one thousand, three hundred twenty-two dollars."

Pierre laughed out loud. In fact, he hoped he did so rather rudely. In a voice loud enough for Carla to hear, he spoke. "Well, that's it boys, the bank wins again. Even the princess over there can't be that stupid." He sat on the ground, took off his shoes and began putting on his roller blades.

But the princess was exactly that stupid, and she raised her bid to $142,000. As she made her bid, she folded her arms across her chest and glared at Pierre. The perfect petulant spoiled brat. The other regulars laughed—they were enjoying watching Pierre bait her. So far, they were ignoring the auctioneer, who was asking for further bids. Even so, Pierre was concerned. They all knew the property was worth over $200,000, and they all knew that the bank's odd-numbered bid usually was a sign that the bank would bid no higher. So somebody still might jump in.

Pierre played the last card in his hand. He stood up, rolled forward a few inches, and spoke to Carla. "Listen. You have no idea what you're getting yourself into. You should withdraw your bid. It's not too late. Just say 'I withdraw my bid.' Trust me on this."

Carla began to respond, but before she could, the auctioneer raised his voice. He saw his fee disappearing—he earned no commission if the bank was the high bidder, and three percent if the property sold to a third party. "Going-once-twice-sold." He spit out the four words as if they were one.

Pierre looked at Carla and laughed. "Sorry, too late. Looks like you just bought the farm. Good luck." And he skated away.

                    *   *   *

An hour later, Carla arrived at their Brookline apartment. She immediately called Pierre's mother and asked her to keep Valerie for a few more hours.

Twenty minutes later, she heard Pierre's key in the door. She opened the door for him, saw the sadness in his soft brown eyes. She greeted him with a long, deep kiss, then wiped the sweat off his face.

She took his hand and led him up to the roof deck, motioning to him to remain silent. When they had first bought the condo, they had agreed to splurge on a hot tub for the deck. They hadn't used it much since Valerie was born, but they kept it clean and full of water. Carla had started it immediately upon getting home; it was now hot and bubbling.

Silently they undressed and hopped into the tub. Carla reached up and grabbed a container of strawberries from a ledge. She put one in Pierre's mouth and, before he could finish chewing, pulled him to her in a sweet, juicy kiss. They finished off another dozen strawberries in the same fashion, then a cool wind blew over them and they sank deeper into the hot bubbles.

Twenty minutes later they cried out in relief, as hot bubbling water splashed over the sides of the frothing tub.

38

[March 19, 1990]

Bruce had been half-expecting it for months, but the headline still screamed at him when he picked up the *Boston Globe* early Monday morning:

$200m Gardner Museum art theft
2 men posing as police tie up night guards

So Gus had pulled it off, just as he said he would. The biggest art theft ever in the United States. Even if he had to dump the pieces at only a penny on the dollar, it was still two million bucks for Gus and his partner to share. More likely, the son-of-a-bitch had lined-up a buyer and would receive many times that amount. If he didn't get caught.

But for Bruce, the theft was sure to be a major pain in the ass. His name would be near the top of any list of local suspects, and it would likely mean that he would be the subject of constant attention and surveillance. Luckily, he had a solid alibi for the previous night—he had let Marci strong-arm him into escorting her to a St. Patrick's Day party. They still dated sporadically, but Marci had sensed that the wall around Bruce was both steep and solid, and she had come to accept that Bruce would be nothing more to her than an occasional handsome and charming escort to some function or another. Still, the evening spent with Marci didn't mean that Bruce wouldn't be considered a suspect—he could have masterminded the theft and simply used Marci as an unwitting alibi.

39

[April 2, 1990]

Bruce wished he had somebody to share his little April Fool's prank with. He would get a laugh over it, and also probably make a nice profit, but it would be even more fun if he had somebody waiting at home to share it with. Maybe Grandpa, wherever he was, would be watching and get a chuckle out of it. The only problem was that Bruce had to wait until April 2, a Monday, to spring it.

Bruce walked the short distance from his office to Beacon Hill, cut up a narrow brick alley, and emerged into a small, square courtyard framed by wrought iron fencing. A brick pathway cut through the courtyard, illuminated by a row of gas lights and bordered by a series of wooden benches. The trees were taller, as were the buildings in the background, but otherwise the scene had probably changed little over the past 150 years.

Bruce was foreclosing today on one of the condos in a brick, federal-style building in one corner of the courtyard. It was a typical Beacon Hill condo—two bedrooms, living area, kitchen and bathroom squeezed into an area the size of a typical suburban living room. It had sold for $170,000 two years earlier, and Marci had told Bruce she thought it was worth about $130,000 today. Leumas, reliably crotchety, had appraised the unit for $112,000, and Nickel had instructed Bruce to bid 70 percent, or $78,000.

Bruce figured he could pay up to $90,000 and still make a comfortable profit, and was planning on doing so through his Arab Acquisitions front. He simply couldn't let another property slip away—there weren't that many good ones left. If he had to, he knew he could delay the closing until the sale of his Marlborough Street condominium, scheduled for later in the month, had been consummated.

By ten o'clock, seven bidders had qualified to bid by showing the required $20,000 deposit, and Bruce instructed the auctioneer to begin reading through the necessary legal notices and announcements. At 10:20, the auctioneer finished the readings. Bruce took the cell phone from his briefcase, feigned dialing a number, put the phone to his ear, and walked away from the crowd. After five minutes, he returned.

"Ladies and Gentlemen, I'm sorry for the delay. I have just spoken to counsel for the borrower, and he assures me that the borrower is on his way into town

154

with funds necessary to cure the mortgage default. I have agreed to postpone the auction until 11:30 this morning, approximately one hour from now."

Bruce ignored the grumblings from the bidders, slung his jacket over his shoulder and began walking back to his office. He could have stuck around at the auction site, but he decided that he should make a show of returning to his office to meet the borrower "on his way into town" with the funds. He exited the brick alley, worked his way over to Myrtle Street, then passed under the State House driveway arch. It was a familiar walk—he had passed under the arch less than an hour ago on his way to the auction.

Bruce looked up—a few yards ahead, leaning casually against a pillar, stood Gus. Gus caught Bruce's eye, dropped a gum wrapper on the ground, and walked away. Bruce maintained his pace, cursed to himself, then stopped near the gum wrapper. He bent over to tie his shoe, casually looked around, and pocketed the gum wrapper. He walked another fifty yards before pulling it out of his pocket. He recognized Gus' left-handed handwriting: "5:00—One Beacon Street pay phones." He gave Gus credit—unlike the bathroom meeting, this was a safe way to talk, assuming Gus was smart enough to call from his own pay phone.

Forty-five minutes later, the group re-congregated on Beacon Hill at the auction site. Only five of the bidders were now present. Bruce instructed the auctioneer to re-read the legal notices.

A couple of the bidders grumbled. The auctioneer addressed Bruce. "But Mr. Arrujo, I just read the notices. Are you sure I need to read them again?"

"I'm sorry, but just to be safe, please re-read them. You know how the courts can be."

At 11:50, the auctioneer completed his reading, and Bruce again retreated with his cell phone. Five minutes later, he made another announcement. "Ladies and Gentlemen, I again must apologize. I have just spoken to counsel for the borrower, and he assures me that the borrower, although not here just yet, is indeed in his car and on his way into town with funds necessary to cure the default. I have dealt with this attorney before, and I believe him to be trustworthy. Therefore, I have agreed to postpone the auction again until 1:30 this afternoon, approximately one and one-half hours from now." Bruce knew the bidders would be getting impatient and frustrated—in fact, he was counting on it. But he also knew there was nothing they could do about it.

At 1:30, the group had dwindle to only two qualified bidders. Bruce went through the charade again, once more postponing the auction, this time until

3:00. He hoped the remaining two bidders would finally drop out; he wasn't sure
if he could justify yet another postponement.

He didn't have to. At 3:00, only he and the auctioneer appeared at the auction
site. Bruce made his phone call to the Arab investor, entered a bid of $82,000
on his behalf, and signed the necessary documents. Bruce looked closely at the
auctioneer—Bruce was the auctioneer's meal ticket, but some damage control
might be a good idea anyway.

"You know, banks are funny sometimes. If it were up to me, come the day of
the auction I would just go foreclose—no last minute negotiations. But they're
really sensitive to public relations issues; remember, they're regulated by the government. So Nickel has a policy that we should postpone the sale if we feel there's
a legitimate chance the borrower is on his way with the money. It seems silly to
me—I mean, unless the guy hit the lottery last night, what could have changed
since the day before? But the bank is the boss, and I do what they tell me, you
know?" The auctioneer nodded, apparently satisfied with the explanation.

Bruce killed an hour at his office, then walked to a neighboring office tower.
He was pretty sure nobody had followed him, but to make it look good he
stopped at the bank machine on the ground floor and withdrew fifty bucks. It
felt good to have money in the bank. After today's auction, he would soon have
forty grand more.

At a few minutes past five, one of the three pay phones in the ground floor
lobby rang. Bruce casually walked over and picked it up.

Gus spoke first. "Howdy, counselor. Those foreclosure auction ads you put
in the Sunday newspaper sure make it easy to find you on Monday morning."

"Can't say I'm glad to hear from you. I thought you'd be long gone by now.
Bought your own island or something."

"Funny thing about that. I always planned on just ransoming everything back
to the insurance company—that's why I took the Vermeer. I mean, there's no
way to sell something that rare. But you know what? There's no fucking insurance. Ain't that a pisser? Some of the best art in the world, and no insurance.
Newspapers say the museum couldn't afford the premiums. And I got no buyer,
so I'm stuck with the stuff."

"Sounds like you fucked-up, Gus. You took too much, and you took the good
stuff. The whole world knows those paintings are hot. There you were, like a kid
in the candy store. But you didn't know when to stop. And now you've got
chocolate all over your face and a big tummy ache. Let me guess—now you want
me to try to sell the stuff for you."

"No, I know better than to expect Mr. Lawyer to do something illegal." Bruce heard a tone of resignation he'd never before heard in Gus' voice. "But Bruce, I need you to set up a meeting for me with your buyer from Columbia."

"The cocaine guy?"

"Yeah."

"No fucking way. That guy is crazy. I dealt with him once, and I swore I'd never do it again. I mean, he showed up at our meeting in Philadelphia with six guys carrying Uzis. Like it was a fucking drug deal or something. It's one thing to steal paintings, but I don't like getting shot at."

"Look, I'm desperate. My partner's ready to kill me for not knowing about the insurance—he wants to cash-out already. So I've got to move these paintings, and your cocaine friend's the only one I can think of who's ballsy enough to come to this country to do the deal. I'll drive to wherever he wants, but I just can't risk flying anywhere with all this stuff."

"That's a hard meeting to set up, Gus. It took months last time—those guys are pretty paranoid. Sorry, can't help you."

"Wait, Bruce, please don't hang up." Bruce wasn't planning to, but Gus didn't know that. "I understand it's risky. But I've got to try something. And I know this isn't a freebie, Bruce. I'll do whatever you want."

"What do you mean, 'whatever I want'?"

"Just what I said. Whatever you want. What I can't handle, my partner can. He can fix things, fix problems, you know?"

"You mean, broken legs and that kind of stuff?"

"That, or worse. Whatever you need."

"Sounds like quite a partner."

"Well, my last partner dumped me and went off to law school."

"A lot of good it did me. You still need me to clean up your mess." Bruce contemplated Gus' request. He didn't give a shit about Gus' problems, but he realized he was stuck with the fact that his past with Gus was a threat to his future without him. Gus sounded desperate, and the last thing Bruce needed was for Gus to go off and do something stupid and get caught. Who knew what he might say to the cops to get a lighter sentence? Plus, maybe Gus' offer would be worth something someday—Bruce didn't need anybody roughed up or killed at the moment, but who knew what the future might bring? "All right, I'll find out how to contact him. Call me here in one week. Same time. But you owe me, Gus."

"Thanks, Bruce. And you know I always pay up. You gotta admit that about me, Bruce. I always pay up."

CHAPTER

40

[April 16, 1990]

Pierre was beginning to wonder if he had the stomach for this foreclosure stuff. He had barely been able to close on the Clarendon Street condo the previous Friday—the thirteenth, no less. The sales agreement required him to come up with the money and close within thirty days, and the private lender he was dealing with had been more than willing to leverage this deadline to his own advantage. He knew Pierre either had to accept his terms or forfeit his $10,000 deposit—he had Pierre by the balls and was not at all shy about squeezing. So he charged Pierre for "inspection fees" and "underwriting fees" and "condominium document review fees", adding thousands of dollars to Pierre's closing costs. In the end, Pierre paid the fees and was able to close (putting title to the property in the name of a trust, lest his auction cohorts discover his ruse), but he had had to borrow money from his parents to do so.

They couldn't really afford to lend it and, Pierre could tell, they were more than a bit surprised to be asked. They had always thought of their son as a successful businessman, and it killed him to see the concern in their eyes as they handed over the check. He promised himself he would pay it back quickly, with interest.

But what was quickly? It seemed as if he owed everyone in the world money, and there was very little income coming from the brokerage business. And taxes were due today—they didn't owe much, but it was still a couple thousand bucks. It was a strange feeling—his net worth had grown by six figures over the last few months, but he had never felt poorer.

To make matters worse, he had just gotten off the phone with the tenant, Charese Galloway, and she was being totally uncooperative. She had agreed to let him come up to see the condo in two hours, but only for five minutes and only this one time. He didn't even have a chance to bring up the subject of her leaving before she hung up the phone. And he had to get her out so that he could begin to try to sell the condo.

He hopped into the car and drove toward the South End. No roller blades today—he wanted to appear professional and serious. He had even put on a tie.

He parked at a meter and entered the building. Pierre had been in the building many times, but still appreciated the effort that had gone into preserving the architectural details of the original church. Most of the front face of the church had consisted of a large stained glass window, and the architects had preserved this feature and made it the focus point of the building. Standing in the entry foyer, a visitor could turn back toward the street, look up and see the entire window stretching heavenward. The use of the atrium ceiling to allow for this vista had cost the architects thousands of square feet of potential living space, but the result was one of the most dramatic residential buildings in the city. Pierre actually felt pride at owning a part of it.

The doorman called up to Charese, and after a fairly lengthy conversation, hung up and turned to Pierre. "She says you can go up, but that I should call the police if I haven't heard back from her in fifteen minutes." His tone was nonthreatening, but Pierre did not doubt he would do as he was told.

Pierre simply nodded and walked toward the elevator. He pushed the "3" and was quickly whisked upwards—he would take the stairs back down and continue to the basement to inspect the systems. He stepped out and knocked on the door marked "303".

*   *   *

Charese answered the door. She had spent the past hour and a half dressing and making herself up, spending extra time trying to cover a bruise she had received from an ornery customer a few nights earlier. And she had kept her promise to Shelby and was straight for the meeting. The look of surprise in Pierre's eyes as he searched her face for signs of masculine qualities pleased her. She knew he would find none. What she hoped he would find would be strength and resolve—a formidable, conservatively dressed woman. She had thought about playing the sympathy card, but, in discussing it with Shelby, had decided that she'd likely have better results with a more confrontational approach. That approach was fine with her—she was tired of getting pushed around by the men in her life.

"Please come in, Mr. Prefontaine." Charese conjured up memories of how her mother used to sound when local parishioners would come to seek her father's counsel or forgiveness.

"Thank you. I'd like to look around the apartment if you don't mind."

"As a matter of fact, I do mind. You are here as my guest, and you may sit on the sofa here in the living room. If you want to inspect the property, you may get a court order. Now, what is it that you wanted to discuss?" Charese sat in an armchair across from the sofa, legs crossed, hands folded in her lap. A cultured lady.

She could tell that Pierre was a little flustered—he was probably not used to tenants telling the owner what to do. He sat down as instructed and took a moment to gather his thoughts. "Well, to get right to the point, I am the new owner of this condominium. Here's a copy of the deed." He put it on the coffee table in front of Charese. Her eyes remained level with his. "So, basically, I'd like to talk about a time frame for you leaving. And about rent payments in the meantime."

"First of all, Mr. Prefontaine, I am not leaving. I have lived here for a number of years, and this is my home. As for rent, I am not in a financial position to pay you much of anything." She pulled her checkbook out of her purse and wrote out a check for $200 and handed it to Pierre. On the bottom left, she wrote "April rent". "But, I am not in the habit of accepting a stranger's charity. Here is $200 for April. It is all I can afford." Actually, it was more than she could afford. But Shelby had been adamant that she should try to get Pierre to accept something that said "rent" on it. Then they could argue later in court that the $200 was the agreed-upon rent and that Pierre had no right to raise it under Boston's rent control laws because Charese was a low-income tenant. It was a sneaky tactic, but Shelby was willing play a little hardball to help Charese.

"The rent for this place is much more than $200. You know that. This place rents for over a thousand."

Charese began to put the check back in her purse. "You can quote any number you like, Mr. Prefontaine, but the fact remains that this is all I have to give you right now." She saw his eyes following the check on its journey away from his pocket. "If you don't want it, I'm happy to keep it."

*   *   *

Pierre closed his eyes. This meeting was not going at all as planned. He opened his eyes and focused on the check.

"No, wait. I'll take it." He reached out and Charese handed him the check. It was better—barely—then nothing, and he needed the money. He struggled to control the anger in his voice; he was willing to be reasonable with her, but she was acting like she owned the place and he was the tenant. "Look, I'd rather not evict you. But you know, one way or another, you're going to have to leave. And in the meantime, the rent for this place is a lot more than $200."

"Mr. Prefontaine, I am not at all convinced that I have to leave. This apartment is the subject of a lawsuit between myself and the prior owner—you may discuss the legalities of the matter with my attorney. In the meantime, the $200 is what I can afford. You may contact my attorney if you would like to discuss this further." Charese gave Pierre Shelby's name and phone number, and stood up. "Now, if you don't mind, I have another appointment."

Pierre stood up with her, and walked toward the door. He really didn't know what to say; nothing had been resolved at all. He hadn't even had a chance to make her a cash offer to leave—not that he had cash to give her. But it didn't feel right to make the offer now. It was time to leave and regroup. He needed to figure out a strategy to get her out, and soon. It was costing him over $3,000 a month in interest to carry the condo, and he simply didn't have the money. And $200 in rent barely made a dent.

Pierre left the building and walked across the street to a BayBank branch. He deposited the check into his checking account. At least he and Carla could buy groceries this week.

*   *   *

Pierre returned to his office and checked his answering machine. His mind was still on his meeting with Charese, so he only half heard the lone, short message.

"Sebastian Felloff calling for Pierre Prefontaine." He left his number and hung up.

The message intrigued Pierre, momentarily took his mind off Charese and his money problems. Sebastian Felloff was a big Boston developer who concentrated mostly on renovating older apartment buildings and turning them into condos. Unlike the Baron, he actually put some money into his renovations. Pierre had met him a few times—he was a round, jowly man who spoke in a squeaky voice and was constantly filing his already-manicured nails. He was known to be a collector of old furniture, and was rumored to be a collector of young Philippine brides.

Pierre immediately returned the call. A secretary put him through. "Felloff here."

"Yes, Mr. Felloff. Pierre Prefontaine returning your call."

"Yes, Pierre. I'll get right to it. This is a delicate matter, so I would appreciate your discreetity."

Pierre wasn't sure 'discreetity' was a word, and wasn't sure the sentence was a question, but there was a pause in the conversation. So Pierre filled it: "Of course."

"I am involved in a condominium project in the Fenway area. Fenway Place. Are you familiar with it?"

"Yes, I am." Pierre had toured the project during the early stages of renovation. The project consisted of an entire city block of four-story brownstone apartment buildings, each of which contained fifteen to twenty apartments. There were probably 250 apartments in total. It was a well-conceived project in a solid area of town. But its timing had been terrible.

"The lender failed. Taken over by the government. You know, the RTC. That's the agency that takes over insolvent banks. Just took over a couple of months ago."

Pierre remembered the incident. The bank failure had been big news—the first of maybe half a dozen that had failed already this year. Only last year the stock prices of the banks had been soaring. Now, bank employees had begun taking their personal items home on the weekends—it seemed like almost every week there was news of SWAT-like teams of men in dark suits, cowboy boots and federal identification badges ushering bank employees out the door and permanently closing a bank's doors at four o'clock on a Friday afternoon. The teams had finished closing most of the banks in Texas; now they had been transferred up to New England. "Howdy, we're here to close this here bank," had become the punch line on a score of bank jokes making the rounds in the nervous office towers of the city.

Felloff continued. "So now the RTC wants to liquidate the project. Bulk sale. All two hundred forty-five condos in a sealed bid auction. These bureaucratic cowboys want to prove to Congress they can turn these bank assets into cash, sort of like justifying their existence. Anyway, I know you've been an active buyer lately—I saw the article in the *Herald*—and I hear you have some money behind you. Are you interested?"

"Of course I am." Pierre wasn't sure what he was supposed to be interested in, but he was curious to here where Felloff was going with this. And it flattered him that Felloff had heard of him. He knew he had become a big fish, and maybe the pond wasn't as small as he originally had thought.

"Can you come over tomorrow, say ten o'clock?"

"See you then."

*   *   *

Pierre hardly slept that night. Valerie had a cold and was up all night coughing; Pierre tried elevating her head on a pillow, but she kept rolling off. In the end, the only way she could sleep was if Pierre held her vertical while he rocked in a rocking chair. Every time he tried to lay her down, the coughing began again and she woke up. Still, there were worse ways to spend the night than with a little angel's head perched on your shoulder.

Pierre doubted he could have slept anyway. The irony of his current situation amazed him. On the one hand, he faced financial ruin because a transvestite tenant refused to move out of the condo he just bought. On the other hand, he had a meeting tomorrow morning with a prominent developer who had contacted him to discuss purchasing a multi-million-dollar condo complex. It was hard to reconcile the two, but one thing was becoming clear to Pierre: He had timed the market perfectly—if he could just survive the next few months without declaring bankruptcy....

*   *   *

[April 17, 1990]

He arrived at Felloff's office right at ten. The corner office was on the top floor of the four-story Fenway Place condo complex; it offered views of both historic Fenway Park to the north and the Back Bay fens and Boston skyline to the east. It was a unique view in Boston, and Pierre was impressed.

He was also impressed with the opulence of Felloff's office, although the antique furnishings and finely woven Persian rugs seemed a bit out of place in a neighborhood comprised predominantly of students and young working people. Felloff was known to skim a bit off the top to support his lifestyle, and Pierre was not surprised that the RTC had taken over the project.

To Pierre's surprise, Felloff saw him immediately. As a broker, he was used to being treated in an inconsiderate, if not rude, manner by most developers. He doubted he even could have gotten a meeting with Felloff a year ago.

Felloff was as obese and well groomed as Pierre had remembered. It seemed incongruous to Pierre that a man who took such pride in his dress and grooming would allow himself to become so obese. Didn't he understand that when people looked at his hands, they didn't noticed the finely manicured nails but the rolls of fat covering his knuckles instead? Pierre was surprised he was able to climb the three flights of stairs to his office every morning.

Felloff offered Pierre a croissant, which Pierre refused. Felloff ate gingerly, using a silver fork and knife; between bites, he wiped his mouth with a linen napkin. He did not speak, but as he chewed he eyed Pierre. Pierre was glad he had shaved and put on a shirt and tie—Felloff seemed to be the type that might judge a book by its cover.

Finally, Felloff spoke. "You must be wondering why I contacted you, out of the blue." Pierre nodded—he had been wondering. "Well, I have a long memory. Six or seven years ago, you rented an apartment for me. I had forgotten about it until I began making inquiries as to who was buying real estate right now. You know, by the way, they're aren't many buyers out there—most of us are just trying to keep our heads above water. Anyway, two different people mentioned your name, and it sounded familiar to me. Because you had rented that apartment. I was a small landlord at the time, just starting out, and you probably don't even remember the incident. But the old tenant was supposed to leave on the 31st, and the new tenant was supposed to move in on the first. Well, the old tenant didn't leave on time, and the new tenant showed up with a U-Haul ready to move in. Well, she was extremely agitated that she couldn't move in, and I had no other apartments available for her. I was ready to put her up at the Howard Johnson's at eighty dollars a night, which I really couldn't afford at the time. But than you spoke up and offered to let her stay at your place until the old tenant moved out because your roommate was away or some such thing. And the thing I remember is this—you never squeezed me for anything. You could have convinced me to give you half the eighty dollars for every day she stayed with you— I would have paid it and still come out ahead. But you didn't. And I said to myself: 'That man is a mensch. That man understands that what goes around comes around.' Well, Mr. Prefontaine, it has just come around."

Pierre tried not to laugh out loud. Of course he remembered the incident— he had been more than willing to let the young woman move in with him for a couple of weeks. But his motives had been purely selfish—she was attractive and fun loving and new to the city, and there had been an instant chemistry between them. "Actually, I do remember the incident. And I'm glad to hear my efforts were appreciated." Pierre thought it best not to mention that the angry tenant had become his wife.

"Okay then. Here's the deal. The RTC is taking over Fenway Place in a few weeks—I've agreed to let them, and the lawyers are just finishing up the details. Their plan is to immediately have an auction to sell the entire 245 units. It'll be one of those sealed bid sales—you know, everyone submits a bid in writing, and the high bid takes it. But here's the catch—they're willing to give 90 percent financing to the high bidder. So, really, anyone who's got five or six hundred thousand sitting around could probably do this deal, assuming the high bid will be around five or six million."

Pierre shifted forward in his seat. Howie could come up with five hundred thousand for the right deal, and to be able to buy this project at twenty thousand per unit would be a steal. If Felloff was right, and it really would sell at that number, it could be a home run deal. "What makes you think it will sell so low?"

"Please allow me to answer that later. First, let me tell you what I'm proposing. I'm proposing that I help you do this deal, and in exchange you hire me as a consultant."

"What do you mean by 'help me'? Can't I just bid without you? And what salary would I be paying you?"

"Those are all legitimate questions, and they tell me that you might be interested, right?"

"That's a fair statement."

"Then I'd like to bring my attorney in to explain some things to you about this deal. He's waiting in the hallway right now. Is that okay?"

Pierre nodded. He was a little apprehensive about meeting with Felloff's attorney, and it was strange that he was waiting in the hallway. But what the heck, it wouldn't hurt to listen.

Felloff buzzed his secretary and told her to send the attorney in. He was a large, tanned, handsome man wearing a tailored double-breasted suit. The aroma of expensive cologne accompanied him into the room. "Mr. Prefontaine, my name is Mitchell Siegelman. I'll be straight with you right away. I know very little about real estate, and even less about Boston real estate, since I live and work in New York. What I do know a lot about is litigation. I am a litigator; that is, I spend most of my time in the courtroom. Or, more accurately, trying to keep my clients out of the courtroom. It probably seems strange to you that a New York litigator would be meeting with you to discuss a Boston real estate deal, but it will make more sense as we go along."

Pierre was impressed by the lawyer, as he knew he was supposed to be. The attorney was smooth and charismatic, although a little too slick and a little too theatrical for Boston's Puritan-rooted sense of propriety. He was full of himself, but apparently with good reason. Pierre could see where a jury would be swayed. "I'm here to listen. Do you mind if I take notes?"

The lawyer smiled at Pierre—the proud father beaming at his brilliant boy. "Normally, I would think that's a great idea, Pierre. Oh, do you mind if I call you Pierre?"

"That's fine."

"Thank you." The attorney bowed slightly to Pierre. "But I'm afraid on this one occasion I will have to ask you not to take any notes. Again, it'll make more sense later."

Pierre put down his pen and sat back in his chair. "All right, I'll just listen then."

"And one more request. I need you to sign this confidentiality agreement. It's very simple, but it does state that you won't repeat any of this conversation to anybody." Pierre read it—it was as simple as the lawyer said it would be. He shrugged and signed it, his curiosity now peaked.

"Thank you very much. I'm going to tell you this story from the beginning, but first of all, I'm going to tell you why I'm telling the story instead of Sebastian, who clearly knows it better. If Sebastian were to tell you things that would be incriminating to him, you could be called as witness at a later date and, in all likelihood, be allowed to recount your conversation with Sebastian on the witness stand. However, if I tell you a story about Sebastian, and you were later asked to testify as to what I have told you, your testimony would be inadmissible as hearsay. This is a very basic summary of the law, but I gather you generally understand the distinction between me telling the story and Sebastian telling it."

Pierre guessed it was a little more complicated than that, but he understood the basic distinction.

"Because of that, I would like Sebastian to leave to room." Felloff hoisted himself out of his chair and ambled out of the room. "And, of course, being a lawyer I have yet one more caveat before diving in. And that is this: what I am about to tell you is purely hypothetical. None of it is true. It is all merely a figment of my fertile imagination. In other words, if somehow the government is able to get around the hearsay problems and compels you to testify against Mr. Felloff, I will in clear conscious stand on the witness stand and swear that you and I both knew that this conversation was a purely hypothetical one."

The attorney paused, then smiled at Pierre. "Do you have children?"

Pierre nodded. "A little girl."

"Ah, then you must read her bedtime stories."

"Every night."

"Good. Then think of what I am about to tell you as nothing more than a fairy tale. Do I make myself clear?"

Pierre nodded again. Last night he had read Valerie the story of the wolf dressed in sheep's clothing.

"Now, here, finally, is the story:

"We know to be true that Sebastian borrowed approximately seventeen million dollars on the Fenway Place project. And we also know that it is now worth far less than that amount—say eight million for argument's sake. Along the way, Sebastian paid himself fees that reflected his unique expertise in residential development—fees that totaled in the neighborhood of three million dollars. Now, the bank had approved all these fees, but in hindsight, it seems rather, shall we say, awkward for Sebastian to have pocketed this amount of money when the bank ended up underwater by about nine million dollars. At least, the federal government, which insured the deposits and therefore knew it would have to pay the nine million if the bank failed, at one point began to think so.

"Well, about six months ago, Sebastian saw the writing on the wall and realized that the project would not be profitable and that the bank might try to recover the three million, and more. After all, Sebastian had personally guaranteed the seventeen million-dollar loan, and so was technically on the hook for the nine million shortfall. So he did something smart. He called me. And my job is to make sure the government gets as little money from Sebastian as possible.

"So, what if, to make our story more interesting, six months ago, Sebastian started hiding his money. It doesn't matter how much money he started with, but let's just say it was in excess of the three million he took from Fenway Place. And when I say hiding, I don't just mean putting it under the mattress. I mean putting it into Swiss bank accounts or gold coins or other untraceable assets. But even that wouldn't be enough, because there's plenty of evidence from a year ago that these millions existed—brokerage accounts, that sort of thing. So, in our little fairy tale, Sebastian not only had to hide the money, he had to make the government think it had been spent and was now gone. Otherwise the government would just keep looking for it. The government, by the way, I have found to be not very efficient in these matters, but extremely persistent. So Sebastian, at that time, would have been wise to take weekly trips to Atlantic City—not to gamble and lose, but to support his story that he had gambled and lost. Huge amounts of money, of course, with hotel and flight records to document the trips. Once a trip, under this scenario, he would have made a $20,000 bet on some athletic event or another, something big enough so that there would be a permanent record of it. And every trip, he would have bought fifty grand worth of chips on his credit card, spent on hour or so at the blackjack table to make it look good, then just put the chips in some safe deposit box for safe-keeping. (God help him in this hypothetical scenario, by the way, if the casinos were to fail.) Perhaps he would have even checked himself into a drug rehab center— not because he had a problem, but because he would have wanted the government to believe his story that wads of money had gone up his nose.

"And, of course, we know the government does nothing quickly. So when it finally would have come time for Sebastian to sit down with them a couple of months ago, after they had taken over the bank, most of Sebastian's money under this fictional account of ours would have been gone. Poof. Disappeared. The government would have screamed and hollered, and I'm sure spent tons of money on a private detective, but Sebastian would have been careful and in the end they would have had to admit that all they could find was the half million Sebastian had left for them to grab. And, of course, the Fenway Place property would have still been here for them to grab.

"But before sitting down with the government, let's for a minute imagine that Sebastian had done one other thing. I mean, he wouldn't have known if he would be successful in hiding the money from them. And if not, he would have wanted to at least put himself in a position where he could start over again by keeping Fenway Place. So maybe Sebastian would have come up with a back-up plan to give the government all the money he owed, but in exchange make them agree to let him keep Fenway Place. That would explain why he never would have sold any of the units—if he bought the project back, it would be easier to get financing if he had the whole thing. And of course, if Sebastian were to buy it back under this hypothetical, he would want to keep the price down as low as possible. That's obvious—if Sebastian could convince them that Fenway Place was worth five million rather than eight, and could buy it back at that price, that would be so much the better. Are you with me so far?"

Pierre nodded. He was impressed that anyone had the foresight to plan six months ahead for a potential financial calamity. He knew he didn't. He knew he hadn't. Hypothetically, of course.

"So, Sebastian would have wanted to plant some warts on the project—you know, things that would lower the value of the project in the government's eyes but that could be removed by Sebastian later if he ended up owning it. 'Removable warts', if you will. Actually, Sebastian might call them warts, but I might call them poison pills, like the things that companies do to themselves that poison the company if an outsider tries to take over. Later, Sebastian could get into the specifics on what kinds of warts a developer in this hypothetical situation might put on a property, if you're interested. Suffice it to say that, in this case, the RTC is aware of a seven-figure lawsuit brought by an abutting property owner because of contamination from leaking underground fuel oil tanks. But what if, hypothetically, the abutting property owner happened to be a corporation controlled by Sebastian? And the government is aware in this case that the thousands of pages of documentation required to establish that each and every unit in the project is exempt from the Boston rent control laws have mysteriously disappeared from the city hall offices—the nefarious work of tenant activists, no doubt. But what if, hypothetically, Sebastian had the original certificates issued by the Rent Control Board hidden securely in his safe? You understand my point."

Pierre nodded.

"So, anyway, that could have been a back-up plan in this hypothetical, in case Sebastian needed it. But what if it turns out he didn't need a back-up plan, because the RTC bought the whole story that Sebastian lost all his money gambling and snorting? And what if the RTC is willing to take the half million and let Sebastian walk, but only if he pays them another three hundred grand in two years? Now, as an aside, what they'd be doing with the three hundred is trying to get cute. It's not so much that they would want the money, it's that they would want to see where Sebastian gets it. And when I say 'they', I mean the FBI now. See, the way it works in these cases is that the FBI would tell the RTC to make Sebastian pay a chunk of money in two years, and in the meantime they'd follow him around and see where he gets the cash. If he were to get the three hundred from some Swiss bank or something, they'd nail Sebastian for fraud and throw him in jail. Pretty cute idea, I must admit, but what if the idiot negotiating for the RTC was so insistent on the three hundred that an experienced negotiator like myself began to smell a rat. So then I might offer to pay two fifty up front instead of three hundred in two years, just to see what the RTC would say. I mean, anyone would take the two fifty today—it's a sure thing. But what if the RTC negotiator didn't even ask where the two fifty would come from? Then I would know something was up.

"And that's where somebody like you would come in. Under this hypothetical, Sebastian could go out onto Wall Street or something and try to clear three hundred grand over the next two years so he could pay the RTC. But why should he do that? The guy's got millions; he wouldn't need that bullshit lifestyle. Plus, there'd be no guarantee he could even pull it off. And his credit would be ruined, so he couldn't even get back into real estate for a while. So he would need to find some way to earn a legitimate three hundred grand over the next two years. And in exchange for that, he could help somebody buy an eight million-dollar property for five million because he would know where the warts are. And how to get rid of them. But that somebody would have to have no prior connection to Sebastian, or else the FBI would think he's just playing games, trying to keep the property by using a straw."

Pierre tried to wrap his mind around this bombardment of information. It was clear to him that he was dealing with some brilliant minds and that he better be careful. "Let's assume that somebody like me would be interested in this kind of theoretical situation. The FBI involvement would obviously scare me."

"Fair enough. But remember, as sordid a tale as this is, you would not be involved in any of it. I made up this hypothetical story so that you'd understand what might be motivating someone like Sebastian to call you and propose an...arrangement.

"But whatever the realities of Sebastian's current situation, it's important you understand that we wouldn't be asking you to do anything illegal here. All you'd be doing is hiring Sebastian as a consultant for two years at two hundred per year—that would net him one fifty after paying taxes. You'd get together once every week or two to make it look good. Hey, he might even be able to help your real estate business. Whatever. It'd your decision how high to bid at the auction, and if you're not the high bidder you wouldn't have to pay him a penny. And don't forget—you'd really have him by the balls. He'd deny everything, of course, but there's no doubt you could make his life miserable if you wanted. But that's why he chose you to hear this little tale; he really checked you out thoroughly. He believes you're an honest and decent man that will do what he says. And, apparently, there aren't many people like that in real estate right now. Everyone's too busy trying to save their skin."

"Including your client?" Pierre couldn't resist.

The lawyer nodded and spoke softly. "Oh, yes. Including my client."

41

[May 3, 1990]

Bruce was starting to get impatient. He had been at the firm almost eight months now, and all he had to show for it was $42,000 in profit from the sale of the Marlborough Street condo, which he would soon pour back into the Beacon Hill condo. Even if he made another $40,000 from that deal, he was still only up about fifty grand after paying taxes. It was nice money—his landlocked father would have thought it a fortune. But it was hardly the million-plus he was looking for.

And it was getting tougher to control the foreclosure auctions. The market was still flat, but there were a growing number of investors looking to grab property now and wait for a market recovery. Vultures, sharks, hyenas, bottom-feeders—whatever you wanted to call them, they were growing in number and becoming more aggressive in their search for food. And he was running out of tricks.

His best hope now was that one of his pigeons would come home to roost. Pierre Prefontaine was his best bet—he was actively buying and had good money behind him. More importantly, he seemed to trust Bruce. But so far Pierre hadn't done anything big enough to warrant a play by Bruce.

He looked at his calendar—May 3. He would give Pierre and the other pigeons three more months. If none of them had locked onto something big by then, Bruce would have to consider another strategy. Perhaps finding a money partner. Bruce was sure Nickel would be willing to sell the entire loan portfolio at a significant discount. He could then foreclose and liquidate the properties; it would be easy money. But bringing in a partner would be difficult and expensive—it wasn't as if there was a lot of free cash out there. Most investors with an interest in real estate were probably still reeling from the last twelve months of turmoil. And those that were stable were probably happy to remain on the sidelines until the dust settled, or could only be lured into the game with the promise of a huge cut of the profits.

Even worse, partners were dangerous. Gus, for example. He could still screw things up for Bruce. If Gus got caught, Bruce had no doubt he would sing in exchange for a reduced sentence.

No, no more partners. It was safer to operate alone. Wait in the shadows, then move in with a surgical precision so seamless that even the victim himself would be unaware that he had been violated. A painless incision, an extraction of money, no scar or other trace of the wound.

42

[May 10, 1990]

Shelby already had taken a job at the District Attorney's office after graduation, so she figured she could just tell Reese to go fuck himself if she had to. She hoped it wouldn't come to that, but she just couldn't sit around any longer while Reese ignored Charese's case. Charese looked barely human the last time Shelby had seen her, and Shelby was sure she had seen more than the usual number of needle tracks on Charese's arm.

And it had been Roberge's choice to play hardball. If he didn't want to pay the mortgage on the condo, that was his business. Shelby couldn't really blame him for that. But when he went out of his way to let the bank foreclose right away, instead of taking the usual four or five months, she knew he had done so just to punish Charese. Roberge knew he couldn't evict her while the lawsuit was pending, but he figured—correctly—that the new owner would try to kick her out right after the foreclosure. He probably thought that if she were homeless and destitute, the lawsuit might just go away. And if she died on the street, better yet. It was just a sleazy move all around, and in Shelby's mind it justified anything she might do in return.

She phoned Roberge's attorney. She skipped the pleasantries. "Tell your client that he's a sleazeball. That little stunt with the bank is going to cost him."

"Hey, Shelby, slow down. I don't even know what you're talking about." Roberge's lawyer wasn't a bad guy—a typical suit in a downtown firm. Every city had thousands just like him. Shelby decided to give him the benefit of the doubt.

"The condo that your client owns, the one Charese lives in."

"What about it?"

"It got foreclosed on. He stopped paying the mortgage."

"I didn't know, but so what? I mean, it's not like that's a crime or anything."

"Well, do you know how long a foreclosure usually takes?"

"Yeah, it's a pain in the ass. Six months maybe, start to finish."

"Except if the borrower signs a waiver allowing the bank to foreclose right away."

Roberge's attorney was silent. When he spoke, he did so in a tone of incomprehension. She guessed that he had made a career out of advising his clients never to concede or waive anything. "Did Roberge do that? Are you sure? That can't be right."

"He did. I'm sure. That's right." Through her anger, Shelby was actually enjoying this. "When the new owner showed up at my client's door last month, she called me. I called the bank. They just sent me the papers—your client signed the waiver."

"I really know nothing about this."

Shelby believed him—she could tell he still hadn't figured out why Roberge had done it. "Well, be that as it may, please convey a message from my client to yours. Ask him if he wants a copy of the video they took when they were on vacation in Mexico. She has a couple of extra copies."

"What's that supposed to mean?"

"I have no idea. My client just asked me to convey the message. Maybe now that the condo's been foreclosed on, she's started packing up her things and found some old momentos. But I'm just guessing."

Shelby was on a roll now. She pulled out a nine- by twelve-inch envelope she had been carrying around for a couple of weeks. It was a Board of Bar Overseers complaint form. The BBO was the organization that regulated the conduct of Massachusetts lawyers. Non-lawyers tended to laugh at the idea of a code of conduct for attorneys, but it was actually rather strict and the penalties for misconduct severe.

Shelby had been undecided whether to suggest that Charese file the complaint against Reese. She clearly had grounds to do so, but it would be a difficult case to prove. After all, the offer of settlement from Roberge's attorney had not been in writing, so it would be difficult to prove it had ever been made. Even then, Reese would surely claim that he had communicated the offer to Charese and that she had rejected it. Shelby would testify on Charese's behalf, but she had no doubt that the other Lapdogs would circle the wagons and hire the best lawyers to defend Reese. It would be a tough case to win, and even if they won, Reese would be punished but it wouldn't necessarily help Charese.

But that was not why Shelby had hesitated to file the complaint. She had hesitated because she knew that, once she did so, Reese would withdraw from Charese's case. And Charese could not afford to pay another lawyer; even if she could, the case would be further delayed while the new attorney got up to speed.

Shelby's last meeting with Charese had removed this hesitation. Charese would simply not survive much longer. Drugs and hooking—and, if she got evicted, homelessness—would likely kill her. Her only hope was for Shelby to force Roberge and Reese into an immediate settlement. With a chunk of money, Charese could hopefully pull herself together and start a new life somewhere.

Shelby guessed that the threat of revealing the Mexico video would bring Roberge back to the settlement table, but she feared that when Reese heard about the video, he would resist settlement until after he had used the video to further damage the Krygier family. Shelby would try to change Reese's mind by agreeing not to file the complaint with the Board of Bar Overseers if he produced an acceptable settlement.

She knew she was burning the candle at both ends; she would have to take care not to get singed.

She picked up the phone for her last piece of Charese business. She had received a message from Pierre Prefontaine and needed to return his call. She had yet to build up a dislike for Pierre; he actually seemed like a decent guy.

"Premier Properties. Pierre Prefontaine speaking."

"Mr. Prefontaine, this is Shelby Baskin returning your call."

"Yes. I was calling to talk about Charese Galloway."

"I don't see what there is to discuss, Mr. Prefontaine. I explained our position to you a couple of weeks ago. You have accepted a rent payment from my client of $200. That creates a tenancy relationship between you and her. Although I agree with your statement that it is a tenancy-at-will, the law in Boston is clear— a tenancy-at-will in Boston may not be terminated by the landlord without good cause. Unfortunately for you, the fact that you want to sell the unit is not considered good cause. Now, if you wanted to move in to the unit, that would qualify, but we know you already own a condo in Brookline."

"I understand your position, Ms. Baskin. My attorney advises me that we would have a good case to evict your client, but he agrees that it would be time-consuming and expensive. What I would like to do is pay your client $5,000 in exchange for her vacating the apartment." She smiled to herself. She guessed that what his attorney had really told Pierre was that accepting that $200 check was the stupidest thing he could have done and that he was screwed. The pro-tenant judges sitting in Boston would have little sympathy for his position. By depositing the check that said "April rent" on it, he had in the eyes of the law accepted $200 as the agreed-upon rent. He could raise her rent once a year, but even then by no more than 10 percent. And as long as Charese paid him every month, he was stuck with her.

Shelby actually felt bad for Pierre, but that was life. She contemplated Pierre's offer in her mind. Five grand sounded like a good chunk of cash, but after paying a moving company and giving a new landlord a security deposit and first and last month's rent, there really would be nothing left over. And any new apartment would cost much more than $200 per month. Besides, she could tell Pierre was desperate, and she was confident he could not evict Charese. If $5,000 were on the table now, at least that much would be on the table later. "I'll communicate your offer to my client, Mr. Prefontaine, but I will also counsel her against accepting it. I'll get back to you if we're interested. Good-bye."

43

[May 22, 1990]

Roberge was surprised to hear his father's voice on the line—they barely spoke anymore, maybe only once or twice since the wedding. And not at all since the foreclosure of Roberge's condo. He figured it wasn't likely to be good news.

"Hi, Father. What's up?"

"Forget the bullshit, Roberge. What the fuck is this I hear about a movie with Mexican boys? You fucking pervert."

Roberge rarely heard his father swear, but he knew the swearing was the least of his problems now. Roberge's lawyer had relayed Shelby's message about the videotape, and he doubted Charese was bluffing. He had told his lawyer not to tell his father about it, but obviously, since Dear Old Dad was paying the legal bills now, it was unlikely they would keep him in the dark. He decided to keep his voice calm. "The tape did exist at one point. I thought it had been destroyed, but I don't think Charese is bluffing. If she says she has it, she probably does. I'm happy to talk to you about it, but only if we're going to have an adult conversation...."

"You listen to me you little piece of shit, and listen carefully. Don't you dare tell me what kind of conversation we're going to have! You're going to listen and I'm going to talk. And I'm going to talk clearly so you can understand. You can thank your mother for the fact that I didn't cut you off after the newspaper article. Not to mention taking a mortgage on that condo I gave you and then getting foreclosed on. But if this movie becomes public, I swear to God in Heaven you'll never see a penny of my money when I die. Not one penny. Now, I don't care how you do it, but you make sure that movie stays buried."

"I want it buried too! Just give me the money to settle the case." He had about $65,000 left over from the mortgage he took on his condo, but they had put that money in Megan's name to shield it from Charese, and Megan had made it clear that there was no way Charese was getting a penny of it. "Once we settle, she'll give up the video."

"You're such an idiot. Do you really think there's only one copy of this video? Give two hundred grand to that perversion now, and it'll just ask for more later. You have to deal with people like this forcefully, you gotta make them pay for fucking with you. I never should have let your mother name you after that interior decorator friend of hers."

Roberge started to respond, but his father spoke over him. "And one more thing you should know, you selfish little worm. Your mother and I are fighting like crazy to keep this little empire of ours afloat—this real estate crash is killing us. Banks are calling in loans, tenants are breaking leases, rents are nose-diving. Our best hope right now is to get the rent control laws repealed—that'll give us the extra income we need to ride this thing out. And I'm going to have to call in every favor I can to get the votes on the City Council I need. But if this movie comes out before the vote...."

Roberge was surprised—just last year his father had been named one of the fifty richest men in Massachusetts. Had the real estate market slumped that much? It would sure explain his father's fiery anger. "I understand Father. I'll try to...."

His father cut him off, and this time he spoke calmly, icily. "Don't try. Do it. I'm not kidding, Roberge. Do it. Any way you have to."

44

[May 23, 1990]

Shelby walked unannounced into Reese's office. The final exam period was over, and most of the students had made their pre-Memorial Day summer escape. Graduation was still a few days away, however, so there were still a few students hanging around. Shelby closed the door behind her—she hoped Reese didn't misinterpret her desire for privacy. She suppressed a shiver and sat down opposite him.

"Listen, Reese. This Charese thing has gone on long enough. I know you want to go to trial on this—it'll make for great publicity and further add to your glowing reputation as the Robin Hood of the legal community. But you're fucking with a human being, and it ends now. I have reason to believe that Krygier is going to be making another settlement offer. I expect you'll handle it correctly this time."

Reese was silent for a moment. Shelby had noticed that he had taken on an even more self-important air since embarrassing Krygier with the newspaper story. According to people Shelby knew, his stature in the tenant activists community had skyrocketed. He eyed Shelby with a half-smile, sucked the saliva off his lower lip, and pulled out his calendar book. "Now, Ms. Baskin, unless I am mistaken, today is May 24. And classes officially ended May 16, over one week ago. I don't believe you any longer have any say in this matter whatsoever. I will handle the matter in the manner I see fit." He sat back in his chair and folded his hands in his lap.

Shelby didn't respect him enough to be able to work up more than a mild anger. She stood up to leave. "All right, Reese, have it your way. But here's the deal. If that settlement offer is rejected without Charese's approval, she'll be filing this immediately." She dropped a copy of the Board of Bar Overseers complaint on Reese's desk, making sure he could read the caption on the legal document.

His cheeks and ears turned red, but he fought to keep his voice under control. "It's not even signed."

"Not yet. But it will be, if necessary."

"I wouldn't advise threatening me, Shelby. I have some powerful friends in this city."

"Well, you're going to need them. Because I also know how to use the press. And don't think Wesley Krygier wouldn't like to put the screws to you. Heck, he might even take out a full-page ad himself—I can picture it now, nothing but a copy of the Bar Overseers complaint, maybe page 3 of the Sunday *Globe*? I wonder how many friends you'd have then. They'd throw you away like the garbage you are."

Shelby turned and walked away. She opened the door and turned halfway back to address Reese. "Oh, and I'm sure that Mrs. Jeffries, poor soul, will enjoy reading about your sexual romps with Charese." Reese's lower lip dropped, a stream of drool threatening to escape onto his chin. "It's right there, in paragraph 7 of the complaint."

He jumped to his feet. "You know that's not true!"

Shelby smiled. "For Charese's sake, I sure hope not. She's suffered enough. But it's what she remembers, so who was I to tell her not to put it in the complaint?"

45

[May 24, 1990]

It was Thursday, May 24. Bid day. Howie had taken a week off from work, and he and Pierre had spent the last four days pouring through the Fenway Place books and touring the property with a building inspector. Felloff had been true to his word—he had given Pierre and Howie complete access to the property and to all the relevant financial information. More importantly, he had produced the promised "wart removers"—Pierre and Howie were comfortable that the rent control and oil contamination "problems" described to Pierre by Felloff's lawyer could easily be dealt with. Now it was time for Pierre and Howie to nail down the final bid figure and fax it to the RTC offices by 5:00.

"Look, Howie, there are three ways to analyze this. One way is to decide what we would pay if we had unlimited money. The second way is to make the decision based on what we can afford. And the third way is to try to predict how little we can spend and still win the bid."

Howie sat back in his chair. His hair and clothes were disheveled, and whatever tan he brought with him from California had disappeared under the gray skies of a New England spring. He really was, Pierre thought, the antithesis of the California cliché—chubby, frumpy, pasty. "All right, Pierre, let's go through each and see where the numbers fall. First, unlimited money—what would you pay?"

Pierre pulled out his notes. "Well, if you figure you can sell twenty units a year at a price of...."

Howie interrupted. "Wait, I don't want to make that assumption. I know the market isn't falling as fast as it did last fall and winter, but I'm not going to invest my money based on speculation that we'll be able to sell twenty units a year. Let's look at the worst case scenario—that we can't sell any units and have to just rent the units out for a few years until the market comes back."

Pierre sighed. This "sell now" versus "sell later" conflict was a recurring one between him and Howie, but at least Howie hadn't said he wouldn't sell the units now. He just wanted to analyze the deal based on the assumption that they would be unable to sell the units right away. Pierre couldn't really argue with that logic. "All right, let's look at the rental stream then. The gross potential rental income is about $1.9 million. Take off vacancy and expenses and you get a net of about half that—call it $900,000. What would you pay for that kind of income stream?"

"Last year, about ten million. And I would have done a deal like that if you hadn't stopped me, remember?"

Pierre nodded and smiled. He was glad Howie remembered, and it was generous of him to bring it up again. "By the way, did I tell you that somebody just bought that property for $1.4 million?"

"Wow, it was just about this time last year that I signed the P&S to pay $1.8 million. It must have been a hell of a year up here for you guys."

"Yeah, I'd say prices are down twenty percent across the board in the last year, and condos maybe thirty percent. But it seems now to have flattened out, finally."

"Well, thank God for you and Bruce Arrujo, or I'd be down four hundred grand."

"And we wouldn't be talking about bidding on this property. So back to my question: What would you pay for a $900,000 annual income stream?"

"Well, I've been spoiled a little the last few months with the properties you've been finding at auction. But I'd probably pay around $6.5 million. That's almost a fourteen percent annual return, not counting the tax benefits."

"But don't forget, they're giving you 90 percent financing here, so you might pay a little more."

"You're right. But we have to pay $400,000 to Felloff. Hold on." Pierre watched Howie punch numbers into a calculator. "So call it $6.7 million. If I had unlimited money."

Pierre nodded. "Good. Second scenario. What can we afford? Or more accurately, what can you afford?"

"I've got about $480,000 in my investment account. Plus I could come up with another eighty or ninety."

"And we need 10 percent down, plus we have to pay closing costs. Other expenses we can just fund out of the cash flow. So we can afford to pay up to $5.4 million, the way I figure it."

"Sounds about right. Now the tough one. How much will it take to win the bid?"

Pierre stood and began pacing. "Good question. Felloff says he's seen about a dozen people seriously looking at the deal. But remember, most of them are going to build in reserves for the oil contamination and the rent control. So let's work backwards. A really aggressive bidder would pay maybe $7.2 million— that's a ten percent discount off of the appraised value and he gets some good financing, plus he believes he can sell them off as condos in a few years for a big score. But, he has to take off a million for the oil clean-up, and who knows how much for the rent control."

"Well, if he really thinks it's rent controlled, he wouldn't pay much of anything for the project."

"You and I wouldn't, but some people think rent control might end soon. One of the big developers in town—a guy named Wesley Krygier—is trying to get it repealed. He's connected politically and I've heard he's got a decent chance now that rents are falling and there's really no housing shortage. So he might make a bid. Besides him, other people might just assume they can figure it out after they close if they spend enough money on legal fees. So somebody might take a shot."

"OK, take off maybe another million then?"

Pierre nodded. "At least. If the project really were rent controlled, it would be almost worthless."

"So now our competition's down to $5.2 million. Then we would win with a $5.4 million bid, as long as nobody does anything stupid."

Pierre was silent for a moment, then nodded his head a few times. "I'll tell you, Howie, this would be a great deal at anything less than six million. Really solid. That's still less than $25,000 per unit, and I bet these things are worth at least $50,000 in a few years. Remember, units like this were selling for almost a hundred two years ago. And if not, it's still a good deal as an apartment building."

Howie clapped his hands together. "Done. I agree. Five point four million it is. Oh, maybe we should add five thousand just in case there's a tie, right?"

"Hey, it's your five thousand." Pierre tried to sound cavalier about it, but he was desperate for five grand right now, and Howie was tossing it around like it was loose change. But Howie had already lent him $20,000, and Pierre had promised himself he wouldn't ask for more. Plus, he didn't want Howie to be concerned about his financial condition—surely at least one of Howie's sacred investment books warned of the dangers of entering into business deals with insolvent partners.

Pierre pulled the bidder's form out of a folder, and filled in the bid figure— $5,405,000.00. He signed the bid and walked over to the fax machine. It was on its way.

          *   *   *

Pierre was at his office by eight o'clock the next morning. He couldn't remember the last time he had left the house before Valerie was awake—normally mornings were their special time together. He would put Valerie in a jogging stroller and push her while he roller-bladed, or he would take her to the park to look at the dogs and ride the swings, or they would go out and stomp in the snow. The routine allowed Carla to shower and have some personal time before Pierre went into the office, and it was Pierre's favorite time of the day.

But today he wanted to make sure he didn't miss a call from the RTC. They had said they would try to make a decision before noon, but in any event not later than five o'clock. And Carla had promised she would bring Valerie over for a picnic lunch on the floor of Pierre's office. It would give Pierre a chance to see his little angel and, besides that, it would save Pierre from spending five bucks for a sandwich at the sub shop.

At ten past nine, the phone rang. Pierre grabbed it on the first ring. It was Howie. He sounded almost as nervous as Pierre. "Heard anything yet?"

"Not a word. What time's your flight?"

"Eleven. Trying to beat the holiday traffic. I was planning to bring you the deposit check on my way to the airport. Fifty grand, right?"

"Right."

"And I couldn't sleep last night, so I typed out the terms of our deal, just so there's no confusion."

"Good idea. Why don't you fax it to me so I can see it in writing. Then we can sign it when you get here. Hopefully it will mean something."

"I've got my fingers crossed. I'm faxing now, and I'll be there in half hour."

The deal Pierre and Howie had struck was simple, though a bit unorthodox. Whatever income the property generated was to be distributed in the following order: First, to pay the mortgage and other expenses. Second, to pay Felloff his consultant's fee. Third, to pay Howie back his $580,000 investment, plus twenty percent yearly interest. Above that, Pierre and Howie would split 80-20, with Pierre getting the lion's share. Pierre had wanted to take money earlier in the deal, but Howie had been insistent on making Pierre wait until the end. "Look, Pierre, you talked me into this deal because you said you could sell these things as condos and we wouldn't be stuck with an apartment building. If you're right, you make a huge profit—maybe two or three million. And that's fair because you'll be doing all the work and it's your deal. But if you're wrong, I'm protected because my money is safe and I know I get at least 20 percent interest. I'm sorry, but it's the only way I'll agree to do the deal." Pierre knew Howie had structured the deal based on a formula in some investment book, and though he would have liked a different structure, he couldn't really blame him for assuming a worst-case scenario and trying to protect his investment.

*   *   *

Howie had come and gone, and Carla and Valerie had come and gone, and still Pierre had heard nothing from the RTC. It was three o'clock, the city was emptying for the holiday weekend, and Pierre knew that every hour that passed lessened the likelihood that theirs had been the high bid. Should they have bid a little higher? Had Felloff hedged his bet and made a similar deal with other bidders? Had the RTC decided to reject all bids?

It had been a rare opportunity—a chance to purchase a multi-million dollar property at a steep discount. You only get a couple of chances like that in a lifetime, if at all. Blow it and the financial repercussions would likely be felt all the way into the next generation. If only that damn phone would ring.

At three fifteen, Pierre could hold it no longer and walked down the hall to the bathroom. He knew that, with his bladder full, it would take him almost a full minute to finish. It was the type of thing men kept track of when there was no sports page taped to the wall—in Pierre's case, he liked to count by naming a Boston sports hero whose number corresponded with the number of seconds elapsed. He had counted to 26—Wade Boggs—and was about to recite the name "Carlton Fisk" when he heard the phone ring. Pants still around his ankles, he waddled back to his office. He reached the phone on the fourth ring.

"Hello, hello."

"Mr. Prefontaine?"

"Yes, please hold on. Just one second." He puled up his pants—the office was technically open for business so he really couldn't stand there naked—then picked up the phone again. "Sorry about that. This is Pierre Prefontaine."

"Hi. This is Andrea Cameron calling from the RTC. Congratulations. Your bid is the high bid."

Pierre closed his eyes and silently pumped his fist into the air. He fought to remain calm. "Thank you. Thank you very much. What happens next?" It was a stupid question, but he needed time to think. Most of all he didn't want to seem overly excited—the easiest way for a buyer to kill a deal was to let the seller think the buyer would have paid more.

"Well, unfortunately, I need to ask you to bring your deposit check down this afternoon. Or you can wire it to me."

Wire it? I can't even maintain the minimum balance in my checking account. "No, I can bring you a check."

"I wish we could have given you more time, but we had to wait for approval from Washington. I'm in Lowell. Can you be here by five o'clock? They're pretty strict about locking the doors right at five. Government, you know."

Pierre looked at his watch. Lowell was due north, the same direction as thousands of Memorial Day travelers were heading. It would be tight in the traffic. "I'll give it a try. Please don't leave until I get there." He took the address, grabbed the check and his file, and ran to his car.

*   *   *

At seven minutes before five o'clock, Pierre pulled his two-year old Grand Am into a parking space in front of an old brick mill building in downtown Lowell. He ran into the building; the receptionist was gathering her things to leave.

"Andrea Cameron, please. I'm Pierre Prefontaine."

"Yes, sir, she's waiting for you. Second door on your right."

Pierre walked down the hall, took a deep breath, ran his hand through what was left of his hair, and knocked lightly against the half-open door.

"Come in." An attractive woman of about thirty greeted Pierre. "You must be Mr. Prefontaine. I appreciate your coming in on such short notice. Please have a seat. I'm Andrea Cameron."

Pierre shook her extended hand. "Thanks for waiting for me."

Andrea smiled and shrugged. "No big deal. I used to be a paralegal in a big law firm, so five o'clock seems early to me. But the stereotype is true—five o'clock comes, and this place clears out in a hurry. Including my boss, who's in charge of liquidating this asset." She paused, cocked her head. "Did we meet before?"

"I think so. I was in last week to review the files and sign some forms."

"Right. Actually, that's one of the things I wanted to talk to you about. Before we can accept your bid, I need to have you sign those forms again. Basically, they alert you to the fact that it's a federal crime to buy property from the RTC if you or any of the people in your ownership group are in default on any mortgages held by the RTC. You have to sign the forms under the penalties of perjury."

"Not a problem." The RTC was one of the few entities Pierre didn't owe money to. And he knew Howie was current on all his loans. Pierre took the documents and signed them. "And I suppose you want a check, too."

Andrea smiled. "Yeah. Make it out to Andrea Cameron."

"Too late. It's already made out to the RTC. But you could change your name."

"No thanks, I'm sort of attached to Andrea. But speaking of names, what's the name of the new owner of the property going to be?"

"Good question. Can I let you know? I want to talk to my lawyer first to figure this all out. We only have twenty days to close, right?"

"Right. And I'm afraid it'll be tough to get an extension. So June 15 is the closing deadline."

"And how does the financing work?"

"I assume you want the maximum?" Pierre nodded in response. "All right. It's pretty standard documentation—I can send the forms to your lawyer if you want."

"Great. We'll be using Bruce Arrujo, at Stoak, Puck & Beal."

46

[May 29, 1990]

Pierre had been in many downtown office buildings, but never as a client. And also never in the penthouse of the tallest building in the city. He couldn't help feeling a little pride at the thought of hiring the largest firm in the state to help him consummate a multi-million dollar real estate transaction. But he didn't get too carried away with himself—he knew that if push came to shove, he would have to ask Bruce to spot him five bucks for lunch.

Bruce personally came to the reception area to greet Pierre. "Pierre, great to see you again. And congratulations on your bid. The woman at the RTC already faxed me over the loan documents this morning. Come on in—I've reserved a conference room for us."

Bruce escorted Pierre into a plush conference room with views looking out over Boston Harbor. Everything in the room was either leather or cherry or oriental. The room had no smell, yet reeked of scotch and cigars and money. And it made Pierre feel important, as he knew it was designed to do.

"Pretty nice view, huh?"

"I can't imagine a better one."

"Actually, Mr. Puck's office is a corner office and he has these views, plus views to the north of the Charles River. But I guess this'll do."

They sat down, and Bruce took out a notepad. "Before we get into this new deal of yours, let me take care of some preliminaries. First of all, who's my client? You? Howie? Both?" Bruce smiled again. "And whoever it is, thanks for thinking of me. I really appreciate it."

"Well, Bruce, it really was an easy choice. You do real estate, and Howie was impressed you were able to get him out of that last deal. But to answer your question—I'm not really sure who your client is. Howie and I are doing this together. He's putting up the money, and I'm running the deal."

"It's just procedural stuff, but I need to know for two reasons. First, I need to know who to send the bill to. Also, we have to do what's called a 'conflicts check' before I can represent you to make sure there's no conflict of interest between you and some other client."

"Well, didn't you do a conflicts check for Howie already?"

"I did."

"So let's just make Howie the client for now. And he'll be paying the bills, so it makes sense."

"Good. So Howie's the client. Now, tell me about this deal."

Pierre gave Bruce an overview of the deal, omitting none of the details of Felloff's involvement. He wasn't sure he was allowed to tell Bruce the entire story under the terms of the confidentiality agreement that Felloff's attorney had drafted, but he figured he needed somebody to watch his backside.

The Felloff connection seemed to intrigue Bruce. "Pierre, I'm not sure I understand the Felloff part. Have you paid him already?"

"No. We only have to pay him if we close. Two hundred thousand a year for two years, paid monthly."

"Do you have a written agreement?" Pierre pulled a two-page document out of his briefcase and handed it to Bruce, who read it quickly. "I see one potential problem already. The agreement says you'll give him a second mortgage on the property, and the RTC loan documents specifically say you can't have any second mortgages."

"I doubt it will be a problem. He just wants to have some security to make sure we pay him. He said—and I think these are the right words—that he wanted some type of 'connection to the property itself'. You know, beyond his agreement with me."

"I understand. Hey, mind if I go make a copy of this for my files?"

"Go ahead."

*   *   *

Bruce's mind raced as he walked down the hall to the copy room. He could have called his secretary to make the copies, but he wanted a few minutes to think. Along with the loan documents, the woman at the RTC had faxed him a copy of the affidavit Pierre had signed stating that nobody in the ownership group had defaulted on any RTC loan. It obviously hadn't occurred to Pierre that somebody might view Felloff as part of the ownership group.

Bruce returned to the conference room. He spoke casually. "Well, maybe you could make Felloff a silent partner or something. That way he would have a connection to the property. Why don't you ask him if that would satisfy him."

"Good idea. Speaking of partnerships and trusts, how do you think Howie and I should structure this deal?" Pierre explained the business deal he and Howie had agreed upon.

"Well, it seems to me that one way to do this is to have a trust to hold title to the property. The beneficiary of the trust would be a partnership that you and Howie create that spells out your business arrangement. And you could make Felloff some kind of non-voting limited partner who has no powers or voice, so long as he's getting paid his consultant's fee."

Bruce could tell that it seemed complicated to Pierre. "Why do you need the trust at all if you have the partnership? Why not just have the partnership own the property?"

"Fair question. It's just easier to have a single trustee of a trust. Especially when you go to sell the units, it'll be a lot less paper work at the closings. Plus, with a trust nobody has to know who the real owners are."

"Could Howie and I both be trustees?"

"You'll need an odd number of trustees, usually either one or three."

"Would you do it?"

Bruce laughed to himself. *That would be too easy, and too obvious. Like a dentist copping a feel while his patient was awake.* "No. It should be one of you guys. Probably Howie since it's his money. When it gets time to start selling units, we can change it to you so we don't have to keep sending things out to Howie to sign."

"Sounds good. But back to the partnership. Can you draft an agreement for us?"

"Sure."

"Here's a summary of our deal." He handed Bruce the notes Howie had typed-up. "Basically, it's my responsibility to manage the deal and Howie's to fund it. But he's not obligated to put in any more money."

Bruce asked a few more questions, then put down his pen. "All right. I think I get the gist. I can put together a draft of the agreement, probably by tomorrow or the next day. Then I'll have a partner review it, and send it out to you guys for your review. I'll give you a call later this afternoon if I have any other questions."

"Actually, I'll be out. Here's my pager number if you need me. I can call you right back."

Bruce walked Pierre to the elevator, shook his hand, and said good-bye.

*   *   *

Pierre stepped out of the elevator and began the long walk to his car—he had parked almost a mile away to save on parking costs.

After about ten minutes, his beeper went off. He recognized Bruce's number, and stopped at a pizza parlor to use a pay phone.

"Hi, Bruce, I got your page."

"Yeah, Pierre, one thing I forgot to ask you. Is Howie going to be here for the closing? Because if he's not, I need to prepare a power-of-attorney document for him, and also make sure the RTC is okay with him not being here in person to sign everything."

"No, he'll be coming out for the closing."

"Good. Hey, I've got an auction in Brookline on that Monday, the eleventh, if you want to bring him. I haven't seen you at my last couple of auctions."

"Well, I've been busy with this RTC deal, plus I've got a big problem with another unit I bought at foreclosure. It's that renovated old church in the South End, Two Clarendon Street. I can't get rid of the tenant."

Bruce knew the building. "Why not?"

"I did a stupid thing—after the auction, I took a check from her for 200 bucks that said 'April rent' on it. Actually, you may have read about her, or his, case—she's the transvestite who's suing that real estate developer Krygier's son to try to get him to pay for her sex change operation. It was in the *Herald* about six months ago. Anyway, she has a lawyer from LAP who says that $200 is the rent and I'm stuck with it, and stuck with her as long as she keeps paying the $200 every month. Does that sound right?"

"I remember reading the story. I'm not an expert on rent control, but, yeah, you could be stuck with her, especially since it's a Boston property. The Boston tenant laws are pretty protective."

"Tell me about it. And the carrying costs are bleeding me to death—I'm down a couple of grand every month."

"Wow. That is a killer—death by a thousand small cuts."

Pierre didn't want Bruce to know that it would only take one or two more cuts to finish him off financially. "Yeah, that's about the size of it. And, speaking of death, that may be the only way I can get rid of the tenant." Pierre shook his head and laughed wryly. "At this point, it's my best option. What's the penalty for murder in Massachusetts, anyway?"

Bruce laughed politely. Pierre hoped he hadn't said too much—he didn't want Bruce to think he couldn't handle a simple tenant problem. "No death penalty, yet, Pierre. Just life in prison."

"Well, maybe it's worth it to get rid of her. Anyway, thanks again for your help."

"My pleasure. I'll start working on it right away."

Pierre walked for another few minutes, then reached his car in Chinatown. He drove down Tremont Street toward the South End. Another day spent driving instead of roller blading. He crossed over the Massachusetts Turnpike and continued south toward Roxbury. At Washington Street he turned right and continued until he saw the storefront he was looking for—Talanian's Pawn Shop. He parked in front, locked the doors, and went in. A pot-bellied man wearing a white T-shirt and blue workpants approached the counter from behind a plexiglass wall. Pierre could see that he also wore a black holster around his waist—well, not his waist exactly, but around the crotch area below his waist, his belly making it impossible to secure anything around the waistline.

"Whad'ya got?" The man was unshaven, and eyed Pierre aggressively.

Pierre took off his watch, a gift from Carla on their first anniversary. He would tell her he lost it. He slipped it under a cutout in the Plexiglas, like making a deposit at a bank. "It cost $1,400 new."

The man examined it. "I'll give you three hundred for it."

"That's it, huh?" Pierre had hoped for five hundred.

"Yup. Ten percent interest per month until you buy it back."

"I'll take it."

The man scribbled a claim check for Pierre, handed him fifteen twenties, and walked away. Pierre shuffled to his car and sat down, trying to collect his thoughts and regain his balance. He had loved that watch. He took a deep breath. From penthouse to pawnshop, all in one morning. If only he could get rid of that damn tenant.

*   *   *

Meanwhile, Bruce hung up from his phone call with Pierre, closed his door, and told his secretary to hold his calls. He turned his chair toward the window and looked out over the city. In the distance he could see Fenway Park, and knew that Fenway Place sat nearby. Bruce agreed with Pierre—the project was a sure thing. The market hadn't recovered yet, but at least it wasn't continuing its freefall. If the market just continued to tread water, Pierre should make over half a million. And even a mild recovery should give Pierre a million or two, maybe more.

Bruce stared out his window for another ten minutes, letting his brain race. He thought about Pierre, and about Charese, and about Gus. He thought about

Felloff, and about Fenway Place, and about the RTC. They were all pieces of a giant puzzle, random chunks of driftwood that had washed ashore on the beach that was Bruce's life. Could he fit them together to make a sailing ship?

47

[May 30, 1990]

Bruce turned the sleek Laser into the wind and released the main sheet, allowing the sail to flap impatiently in the wind. He had joined a sailing club on the Charles River, and tried to sail every evening after work. It wasn't the same as ocean sailing, but it was a decent substitute.

Bruce looked west. The sun was beginning to set in an orange glow over the Massachusetts Avenue bridge. Bruce closed his eyes and pictured himself as a sleek sailing ship, skimming across the surface of the ocean, his profile carved into the bow of the boat like some ancient Viking vessel of conquest. But he knew the vision wasn't entirely accurate. He knew, for better or for worse, that he was human, animate, alive. He could never be that sailboat, could never be merely a fusion of the strength of the land and the passion of the ocean. Because to be that and nothing more would be to ignore the third side of the human triangle—an ability to reason, and to do so in the context of a moral code.

A minor episode had recently reminded Bruce of this aspect of his personality. The *Globe*, in one of its many follow-up articles on the Gardner art theft, had interviewed a career art thief to gain his insight on the heist. The thief claimed that he and other art thieves all knew how easy it would be to rob the museum, but they had all passed on it because—at heart—they, too, were art lovers and wanted the paintings to be displayed in a public forum for all to see.

Bruce had laughed at the story—in all likelihood the real reason nobody had stolen the Gardner art was that the pieces were too famous to try to sell. If the "career art thief" interviewed in the story had been telling the truth, then he was pretty stupid. Which explained why he was sitting in jail giving interviews instead of lounging on a yacht somewhere in the Caribbean.

Even so, the article had stayed with Bruce for the past couple of weeks. It reminded him of the way he felt when, years earlier, he and Gus had spent a few weekends casing the Museum of Fine Arts for a possible hit. In the end, Bruce had rejected the attempt, telling Gus it was too well guarded. Bruce's real reasoning had been similar to that articulated by the thief in the *Globe* article, although it took him weeks of introspection and more than a couple of trips to the beach before he figured out why: Robbing the MFA was the wrong thing to do. Not 'wrong' merely because it was illegal or against some societal code of conduct, but 'wrong' in the sense that Bruce believed it to be not right. Based solely on his own moral compass. His intellect told him he could complete the theft with acceptable risk, his emotions told him he wanted the money the paintings would bring, yet his personal code of morality overruled both of them. The experience had actually surprised Bruce. But it had also empowered him, because it allowed him to self-righteously define himself: "I am not evil. I just subscribe to a different moral code than does the rest of society."

Of course, he then had to sit down and define this private code of morality of his. What in this code made it acceptable to steal paintings from private collections—such as the theft from the collection of the President of Harvard University—but not from museums? Was it because the Harvard President was such a bad guy? No, that wasn't it, because Bruce knew nothing at all about him other than his daily routine and the details of his security system. The answer, Bruce had finally concluded, was that his behavior toward a potential victim was determined by whether or not the victim had elected to enter into what Bruce now referred to as The Competition of the Marketplace.

For example, private art collectors had elected to compete with other collectors for the right not only to own rare works of art, but to sell them for profit someday. The collectors had chosen to enter The Competition of the Marketplace, and would therefore have to assume the risks of that decision. To Bruce, the rules of this competition—specifically, laws prohibiting theft—were no more than guideposts. If you broke the rules and were caught, you would suffer the proscribed punishment. But Bruce in no way saw these rules as a reflection of some greater morality. If you struck out in baseball, you were called out and went to the bench; if you got caught stealing art, you were found guilty and sent to jail. Each rule proscribed punishment for its violation, but one rule carried no more moral weight than the other. To put it simply: it was no more immoral to steal art than it was to strike out.

The museums, on the other hand, presumably did not have a profit motive, had not chosen to be competitors in the marketplace. They were like civilians in war—it was expected that you would maim or murder an enemy soldier, but civilians were supposed to be off-limits.

Under Bruce's moral code, Pierre Prefontaine and the firm's other clients, including Nickel Bank, had chosen to enter The Competition—or perhaps Battleground was a better word for it—of the Marketplace. They were therefore fair game for Bruce to defeat, all of them competitors in the contest of acquiring wealth. The bank, for example, was relying on a rule of the competition—a law—that mandated that an attorney owed a duty to act in his client's best interests. But they were relying on this rule to their detriment, like a man who left his keys in the car in reliance on the fact that auto theft was illegal, or even a man who left himself vulnerable to a knife in the back in reliance on the fact that murder was illegal. Bruce saw no moral distinction between whether he took the bank's money or the bank kept it; the only difference was that if he got caught taking it, he would be punished. Similarly, Pierre had joined with Felloff to gain an advantage over the other bidders. So Pierre relied on Bruce's kindness at his own risk—if he allowed Bruce to dupe him, well, that was his punishment for being a weak competitor. The competition really was simple: eat or be eaten; kill or be killed. And if Pierre or the bank or anyone else didn't like the ruthlessness of the game, they had a simple choice—don't play.

But despite his ruthlessness in The Competition of the Marketplace, Bruce clung to his moral compass as if it were a treasured miniature of a lost loved one. Someday, when he had accumulated sufficient wealth, he would retire—victoriously—from the competition, and marry and start a family. And at that time, he would need some core of morality, because he knew that only from that core could he hope to build a future of happiness and normalcy.

Bruce opened his eyes. The sun had now dipped completely below the horizon, and he knew that all boats were supposed to be back to the docks no later than sunset. He grabbed the main sheet, pushed the tiller away from himself, and expertly spun the boat about onto a homeward course. He was tied up at the dock in ten minutes.

He looked back at the small boat. He could never completely be the ruthless Viking ship of his imagination. His morality—perverse though it may be—precluded it.

He walked away from the boathouse, toward his apartment on Beacon Hill. He reflected again on Gus' theft at the Gardner. He had been angry about it because it put him at risk—if Gus were caught, would he try to cut a deal and rat on Bruce? But had it affected Bruce in other ways as well? It would be a good test for him, for his morality.

He jogged back to his apartment and quickly threw on a pair of jeans and a tennis shirt. His apartment was only a few miles from the Gardner, and Bruce navigated the distance quickly and parked. The museum closed in half an hour, but that still gave him time to pay his respects.

As he moved from room to room in the old mansion, he felt the sadness welling up inside him. The thieves had taken the paintings by cutting them from their frames; the museum responded by re-hanging the empty frames as a memorial to the loss. In front of each empty frame, Bruce stopped and pictured in his mind the missing work, most of which he knew intimately from his frequent childhood trips to the Gardner with his grandfather.

When he arrived at the spot where Rembrandt's "Storm on the Sea of Galilee" once hung, Grandpa's voice spoke to him. *You know, Brucie, this is Rembrandt's only seascape. Everything else he painted was land.* It was Grandpa's favorite, and Bruce felt the tears well up in his eyes.

The salty droplets made him smile—he had passed the test.

48

[June 4, 1990]

Five days later, the digital display on Bruce's phone indicated an incoming call from Mr. Puck. Puck had already authorized Bruce to send the partnership agreement to Pierre and Howie, so Bruce had no idea what Puck wanted to speak with him about today. Bruce had struggled with the decision to let Puck review the partnership agreement, but it had been unavoidable—firm policy was that no junior associate could forward documents to a client without a partner's review. Bruce could have given the agreement to a different partner, but everyone knew he was working mostly for Puck, and it would have raised eyebrows if he went behind Puck's back. Besides, another partner might have suggested changes to the format of the document, which was the last thing Bruce wanted. He had guessed—correctly, as it turned out—that Puck would simply grunt his approval and Bruce could send it on its way. He picked up the receiver on the third ring. "Hello."

"Mr. Arrujo. Come to my office."

Bruce strolled down the hallway to Puck's office. Jan was at her desk, but was on the phone and gave only a polite wave. He knocked on Puck's door, and stood and waited. After almost a full minute, Jan hung up the phone and motioned for Bruce to enter.

He opened the door, took two steps into the room, and froze. Puck was not alone—the two other partners on the firm's management committee were seated in wingchairs in front of Puck's desk.

Puck's voice boomed, freezing Bruce in mid-stride. "Pardon us, Mr. Arrujo. I do not recall telling you to come in." The two other senior partners turned and looked disdainfully at Bruce.

"I'm sorry sir. Jan told me to come in."

"Mr. Arrujo. Kindly remember that this is my office, not Ms. Fountain's. Now leave."

Bruce felt the blood rush to his face, fought back his anger, and turned and walked out. Jan was no longer seated at her desk. He wondered if he had been set up. He thought about going back to his office, then decided to wait it out. But he had a bad feeling about this.

Ten minutes later, Puck ushered the two other senior partners out of the office. Without looking at Bruce, he commanded, "Come in."

Puck sat down at his desk and glared at Bruce. He did not invite Bruce to sit. "Mr. Arrujo. I have just been discussing your situation with the other members of the firm's management committee. I will get right to it. Law enforcement personnel have—indirectly—contacted us. They believe you may have been involved in the recent theft at the Gardner Museum."

Bruce tried to remain impassive, but he noticed his toes had curled up inside his shoes, and he was having trouble getting enough oxygen into his lungs. "I don't know what to say, sir, other than to say that they are mistaken." It came out pretty calmly, Bruce noticed. Probably because it was true. But Bruce had found it difficult to speak.

Puck ignored him, which was fine with Bruce. He wanted Puck to do all the talking. "Our sources have also made us aware of past art thefts that you may have been involved in. Naturally, the firm's reputation is of paramount importance in these types of matters. Unfortunately, the firm's hands are tied at the moment. If we were to take steps against you, our source would be revealed, and therefore compromised. So we will do nothing at this time. But we will be watching you, Mr. Arrujo. Now leave my office."

Bruce thought about trying to defend himself, then thought better of it. He was having trouble breathing, never mind speaking coherently. He left Puck's office and walked straight to the elevator. He jogged the eight blocks to his Beacon Hill apartment; it was normally an easy run, but this time he had to stop twice to catch his breath. When he finally reached his apartment, he stepped out of his gray suite and threw on a pair of shorts and a T-shirt. Ten minutes later both his main sail and his lungs were filled with wind, and his small day-sailor was skimming across the surface of the Charles River, tacking its way into the breeze.

Bruce forced himself to concentrate on the sailing for a moment. The concept of tacking had always astonished him: the wind was blowing north to south, yet the boat was able to harness the wind's energy and sail almost exactly south to north. It was a fascinating accomplishment. And an apt metaphor for his present situation.

He let his thoughts run free. Had Gus tried to save his skin by giving the cops a false scent—Bruce's? Probably not, because anybody who knew of Bruce's history knew that he and Gus had been partners in crime ever since Bruce acted as the lookout while Gus stole hockey cards from the corner store in fourth grade.

So Gus could hardly escape scrutiny by having the police focus on Bruce. A more likely explanation was that the police were suspicious of Gus, and Bruce had become a suspect by association.

Bruce contemplated Gus' situation. Knowing Gus, he had figured out a way to deliver the paintings to the Columbian drug lord, even with the cops watching him; Gus was nothing if not resourceful. If that was the case, Gus and his partner owed Bruce a favor. A big one.

Bruce brought the boat about, and could now see the Boston skyline. The setting sun reflected off the westward facing windows of the office towers. He squinted into the glare, and his eye quickly settled on the top floors of the tallest office tower, the home of Stoak, Puck & Beal. It was clear now that his time at the firm was limited. He knew he would be cleared of any involvement in the Gardner theft, but his history had been revealed, and it would forever taint him both at the firm and in the close-knit and conservative Boston legal community. The firm would find an excuse to let him go in the next few months, he was sure, and that would be the end of his legal career in Boston.

But at least he had those few months—probably until the October performance reviews. If they were going to fire him, Puck would have done it already. But the firm was in an awkward position—Bruce had received glowing job performance reviews only a month earlier, and he was still one of the highest billing associates in the entire firm. The firm was already sensitive to its reputation as a sweatshop—it didn't want to add to it by firing a highly regarded associate for no apparent reason. And it would be too embarrassing for the firm to admit that one of its associates was an art thief. So, Bruce was reasonably certain that the firm would instead slowly build a case against him—orchestrate a client complaint, force a decrease in billable hours by withholding assignments, lay the blame for a lost case at the feet of Bruce's poor research skills. It was simply easier that way: pay him for a few months, then fire him based on a recent record of poor performance.

End of career. End of plan. End of dreams.

Damn. He had been so careful over the past five years, fought so hard to cover his tracks, worked so carefully to position himself for the big score. And now he was being brought down by something he didn't even do. *Thanks a lot, Gus. Thanks a whole fucking lot. And you're damn right you owe me one.*

The wind shifted as Bruce approached the Boston side of the river, and he let out the sail and skimmed along the shoreline, heading up-river toward the Massachusetts Avenue bridge. He couldn't see Fenway Place from the river, but he knew it was there, just beyond his reach behind the brownstones that lined the Back Bay streets. Bruce knew that in the first half of the century, before the highway system blocked the navigational routes, he could have veered off the Charles and onto the Muddy River, a small tributary that flowed through the Fenway section of the city. He could have sailed right up to the grounds of what was then the Gardner mansion, in fact. From that point, the only object that would have stood between Bruce and the Fenway Place buildings was the imposing structure of the Gardner itself.

Bruce leaned down to peak under the sail at the sun now almost completely set on the western horizon. It was almost dark. The wind had almost completely stilled itself. He knew he was almost out of time.

49

[June 7, 1996]

Reese was still steaming over his confrontation with Shelby-the-bitch, but he had also spent the last two weeks preparing for the phone call from Krygier's lawyers that Shelby had promised would be coming. But how did Shelby know they were going to make another settlement offer? The more he thought about it, the more he came to the same conclusion: Shelby must have spoken to them and threatened to expose more embarrassing information or material. When they called, he would make every effort to find out what it was.

But now, two weeks later, he was wondering if Shelby had miscalculated. Maybe Krygier's attorneys wouldn't call, or maybe they were communicating with Shelby directly. No, that didn't make sense—they knew she was off the case after graduation.

There was no need for further speculation. His secretary told him Krygier's attorney was on the line. Reese picked up.

"Reese Jeffries speaking." The attorneys exchanged pleasantries—Reese prided himself on always being polite and courteous.

"Reese, I just wanted to let you know that we're trying to put together a settlement offer, but we need more time. Can you give us a couple more weeks before doing anything?"

Doing anything? What more was there to do? Shelby must have threatened them with something. Reese needed more information. "Before I answer you, can you tell me what the delay is?"

"Well, the old man Krygier went ballistic when he found out about the video. He won't give Roberge a penny to settle. Roberge has some money, but not enough. So Roberge is trying to get the money from his mother. But that's creating quite a family tiff, if you know what I mean."

A video! He sucked in and swallowed. "Does the mother know about the video?"

"No. Roberge told his father about it, but not his mother. The one thing they agree on is that there's no reason the mother should know about the little Mexican boys."

Little Mexican boys! No wonder old man Krygier went ballistic. The fallout from the *Herald* story was just starting to fade away; the last thing he would want would be another dose of embarrassing publicity. "Well, I suppose we can give you another two weeks to get things straightened out." And to give me time to figure out how to get hold of that video. "Is that acceptable?"

"Yeah, that's fine. And I appreciate it. Talk to you in two weeks."

Reese stood up and paced around his cluttered office. He had to get his hands on that video. Krygier was wounded, but had survived the newspaper pictures and was still leading the fight to repeal rent control. But a video of his son with little boys would be fatal. He would be radioactive—politicians and business leaders alike would do whatever they could to distance themselves from him and his causes. Rent control would survive, and Reese would be a hero. Probably even get appointed to fill the next vacancy at the Housing Court. Judge Jeffries. Judge Reese Jeffries.

But before Reese could get too excited, he remembered the threats made by Shelby. He could defend himself against the charges that he failed to convey the settlement offer to Charese—it was just his word against hers. And even his peers that might not believe him would understand his actions: Sometimes it was necessary to sacrifice a few pawns in order to win a battle. He had simply sacrificed Charese's monetary interests in order to inflict serious damage upon the enemy Krygier. As an officer fighting the good fight, it was a perfectly justifiable decision, and his peers would understand it.

But the sexual charges were another thing entirely. The mere allegation of sexual misconduct would tarnish his reputation forever. And he had been so careful in cultivating his image as a progressive and sensitive "Man of the Eighties"; even his extra-marital affairs had been conducted in a manner so as to leave no ill feelings or bitterness—he couldn't think of a single woman who had been upset over the end of their affair. No, there were too many militant feminists in the circles he ran in to risk allegations of being a sexual predator. Not to mention what his wife would say, although he could always mollify her with some jewelry or something. And forget about becoming a judge.

Ideally, he could both expose the tape and silence Charese. That would be a home run. He had an idea and picked up the phone—it was worth a shot.

"Charese. Hi, this is Reese Jeffries, your lawyer."

"Oh, hello."

"Listen, I know that Shelby has convinced you that I'm a terrible person and all, but I'm still your lawyer, and I just heard from Roberge's lawyer a few minutes ago. I have some good news." He stopped there—he wanted Charese to take the affirmative step of asking him what it was.

Charese was silent for a few seconds. Finally, as Reese had expected, her hopes overcame her disdain. "What kind of good news?"

"They are preparing a settlement offer." He almost said "another settlement offer", but stopped himself. "And I think it should be a good one. But, they want me to assure them that I have the video."

Charese sounded surprised. "You know about the video?"

"Of course. Little Mexican boys and all. But they want to make sure I have the only copy before they settle the case. So can you bring it down to the office?"

"Listen, Mr. Lawyer. I carry that video with me at all times. There's only one copy, and if you think I'm giving it to you, you're crazy."

Boy, Shelby-the-bitch had really gotten to her. But at least now he knew where the video was. "Listen, about that Bar Overseers complaint...."

Reese heard the click of the phone being hung up.

*   *   *

Five minutes later, Shelby picked up the phone and called Reese.

"Nice try, Reesey-boy. Did you really think Charese would give you the video?"

"I really have nothing to say to you."

"Well, I have something to say to you. That little stunt of yours is going to cost you. I've been thinking—why can't we both settle the case and file the Bar Overseers complaint? It's not like we need your help anymore. Charese has the tape, not you. So maybe I'll just tell Charese to file the complaint and then we can go settle the case without you." Shelby could hear Reese's breathing get heavier, heard him swallow his saliva. She was just bluffing, but Reese didn't know that. Shelby realized that the last thing Charese needed was another long, drawn-out legal action where she would be under constant attack by Reese's high-priced lawyers.

"Wait, Shelby. That's not necessary. Let's talk about this some more."

Shelby quietly hung up the phone.

50

For the first time in his life, Roberge could not persuade his mother to help him out of a jam. She had always understood his sensitive nature, sided with him, protected him from his father. But this time, she was resolute. She would not disobey her husband. She would not give him the two hundred thousand dollars he needed to pay off Charese.

"I'm sorry, Roberge. You know I love you very much. But I have never seen your father so adamant—and he is a very adamant man, as you know. He says he will leave me if I give you the money, and I believe him. And Roberge, I love your father and don't want to lose him. This is your problem. You're just going to have to handle it without our help."

Roberge was torn. His father had always been stubborn and pig-headed, sometimes to his own detriment. If the video came out, it would damage the entire Krygier family, both financially and socially. Usually he and the other family members could count on his mother to counsel his father to be practical in these situations. But since she didn't know about the video, she was unaware of the risks to the family name and fortune. However, if Roberge told her about the video, he ran the risk of completely alienating her. And it was a substantial risk—he doubted his mother would have much tolerance for her son's sexual exploitation of little boys. She would probably still refuse to give him the money, and he would have alienated her for nothing. He went back to begging.

"But, Mother, I don't have the money to settle the case. You know that. I'm really in a bind here."

"Well, then, you may have to consider bankruptcy or something. I simply can't help you this time. Good-bye, dear."

Bankruptcy. If only it would solve my problem, Roberge thought. *But it won't help me keep my job, it won't prevent Megan from leaving me, and it won't prevent Father from writing me out of his will. I'd be bankrupt with no job, no wife, and no inheritance. Damn you, Charese. Damn the day you entered my life. Damn you to Hell.*

51

[June 13, 1990]

Bruce waited in his office for Pierre and Howie. It was still two days before the official closing date, but Bruce had finished the legal work early and the RTC was more than willing to accommodate an early closing.

Howie was flying in on the red-eye from San Diego. The plan was for Pierre to pick him up at the airport, come to Bruce's office to formalize the partnership details, then drive to the RTC offices in Lowell at one o'clock for the closing. Howie would then stick around on Thursday and Friday to help Pierre organize the management of the property.

Pierre and Howie arrived a little before ten. They met in the same conference room with the spectacular views of the city. Bruce doubted he would get many other chances to entertain clients in this room. "As you guys requested, I have prepared the partnership agreement for the deal. Most of it is just boilerplate language I took off of the generic agreement the firm uses. Of course, I tailored the business terms to reflect this particular deal. I sent the drafts to you a couple of weeks ago, and you've each had a chance to request changes and ask questions. Before I sent it to you, I had a senior partner in the firm—Mr. Puck—look the agreement over just to make sure I didn't miss anything. Before you sign it, are there any last questions?"

Howie and Pierre shook their heads. Bruce had drafted a lengthy and complex document that was, he knew, beyond either of their capacity to completely comprehend. But he also knew that the document accurately reflected their business arrangement and their deal with Felloff, who had agreed to accept a position as a silent limited partner as a means of securing his right to his consultant's fee.

Bruce continued. "Now, remember, the property will be owned by a trust, with Howie as the only trustee. So as far as the world knows, Howie is the owner. But the beneficiary of the trust is the partnership, which is comprised of Howie, Pierre and Sebastian Felloff, with Felloff's interest a silent one. The only people who will know the true owners are the three of us and Felloff. And the IRS— they know everything."

Howie chuckled at Bruce's comment; Bruce had noticed that, in Howie's world, there was always room for humor, no matter how serious the situation.

But Pierre was unusually quiet. Howie apparently also had noticed. "Hey, Pierre, what's wrong? We're about to do the biggest deal of our lives. You getting cold feet?"

Pierre forced a smile. "No, no, nothing like that. My stomach's just bothering me a little. I'll be right back."

*　　　　　*　　　　　*

Pierre slipped into a bathroom and splashed cold water on his face. His financial pressures were continuing to wear him down, and he was about to sign a document that required him to work almost full time on a project that wouldn't be paying him a penny's salary for almost a year. Sure, he might make a million dollars on the deal, but only if he didn't go bankrupt before the deal started paying off. The bank had begun to foreclose on his Brookline condo, and the leasing company had come and repossessed the telephone equipment and furniture in his real estate office. All that remained in the office was a single phone, an old desk and a couple of metal folding chairs. And to top it off, Valerie had a cough and fever. He and Carla hoped it was only a mild case of the flu, but they were holding off bringing her to the doctor because their insurance had lapsed. But every time Valerie had coughed, Pierre had been racked with guilt. If she wasn't better by tomorrow morning, he promised himself, they would take her to the doctor, cost be damned.

He took a deep breath, straightened his tie, and returned to the conference room.

*　　　　　*　　　　　*

Bruce eyed Pierre warily as he returned. It looked to Bruce like Pierre had spread himself a little—or a lot—too thin. He hoped it wouldn't interfere with Pierre's ability to manage the Fenway Place project.

Bruce handed copies of the partnership documents to Pierre and Howie and showed them where to sign. Felloff had already executed the documents.

They signed, and Bruce was signing next to their names as witness to their signatures when a knock on the door interrupted them. Bruce put down his pen and opened the door. It was Mr. Puck.

"I'm sorry to interrupt you, Mr. Arrujo. I was wondering how long you will be using this conference room." They were the first words Puck had spoken to

Bruce in the two weeks since Puck had confronted Bruce with the Gardner Museum matter.

Bruce smelled a rat—why didn't Puck simply send his secretary to ask? Puck smiled at Pierre and Howie, obviously waiting to be introduced. *Could that be it,* Bruce thought, *could he be trying to steal my clients? What a cheap old bastard!* Bruce laughed to himself, and performed the introductions. "Gentlemen, it is my pleasure to introduce you to Bertram Puck, Jr., one of the firm's senior partners. Mr. Puck, this is Pierre Prefontaine, and this is Howard Plansky. I am handling a closing for them—they were the successful bidders at an RTC auction. You may remember that you were kind enough to look over the partnership agreement I prepared for them. We were actually just leaving for the closing right now."

"Ah, a very opportunistic time to be investing in real estate. I commend you gentlemen, and wish you luck."

Puck bowed politely and left. Bruce had to admit to himself that the old man could actually be a bit engaging when there were clients around.

Bruce finished witnessing the documents, and gave a final copy of each to Pierre and Howie. "All right guys. Let's grab some lunch, and then go to beautiful downtown Lowell for a closing."

*   *   *

The closing went without a hitch, and by four o'clock Howie and Pierre were the official owners of a two hundred forty-five-unit condominium complex. Howie let out a whoop, stood up and high-fived Bruce and Pierre. "We did it, boys. Now how about going out for a little celebration? Dinner's on me."

Bruce politely declined. "Thanks for the offer, Howie, but I've got to get back to the office. I'm just a working stiff, unlike you real estate moguls."

Howie turned to Pierre. "How about you, partner?"

Pierre knew he had no right to be angry at Howie. But he couldn't help feeling resentment toward him as a result of the way they had structured the deal. Why couldn't Howie have agreed to let Pierre take a small percentage of the profits up front? That would have gone a long way toward solving Pierre's financial problems. "I think I'm going to pass, Howie. I've got a few things I need to take care of before the weekend, and I figure I'll spend all day tomorrow and Friday at the property getting things organized."

"Oh. All right."

Pierre could see Howie was hurt, and Pierre felt a bit guilty for it. Howie had been accommodating (if not exactly generous) in lending Pierre the twenty grand, and it wasn't Howie's fault Pierre was in trouble. But Pierre felt it would be best if he skipped the celebration dinner and focused on solving the Charese problem. He smiled at Howie and squeezed his shoulder. "Hey, partner, it's nothing personal. I've just got to deal with some things. Can I take a rain check on that dinner? Maybe after the weekend I'll feel more like celebrating."

Pigeon Pie

C H A P T E R

52

[June 14, 1990]

The next morning, Jan walked into Bruce's office, one hand behind her back. "I've got a surprise for you."

Bruce looked up and smiled. Her friendliness had continued, probably because she was unaware of his new status as the firm's resident art thief. "I bet you do."

"Are you a ball fan?"

"I've never heard it worded quite that way, but if you mean baseball, yes I am." Actually, he hated the game, but he was curious to see what Jan wanted. "Why do you ask?"

"Mr. Puck wanted to know if you want to use what's behind my back for Saturday night."

"Somehow I doubt that. But if he's offering me tickets to the Red Sox game, sounds great." *Actually, it sounds suspicious. Unless it's the firm's idea of a severance package.*

"Good guess." She spun around on one heel and presented a pair of tickets—held between index finger and thumb just above her right buttocks—to Bruce.

He laughed. "That's quite a pair. I just wonder if I'll find the seat comfortable."

Jan turned slowly back around, leaned over so that both of her breasts dangled in front of Bruce at eye level, and dropped the tickets on Bruce's desk. "Like you died and went to heaven."

"I'm sure you're right. But sometimes heaven has to wait." He smiled gently. "Now, I'd love the Sox tickets, but what's the catch?"

Jan sighed and stood up straight. "Well, can't blame a girl for trying. And you're right about a catch. They're the firm's seats—front row right next to the Red Sox dugout, and they're playing the Yankees—but Mr. Puck says you can only use them if you bring a client. He mentioned that Pierre Prefontaine guy you did a closing for."

Ah, the old Puck can smell new business. He must have noticed that I had cultivated Pierre into a promising new client. No doubt that Puck has already taken credit for him, since I met him at a Yankee Bank auction. Puck probably wants me to cement the firm's relationship with Pierre, so that when I get fired Pierre will still use the firm. Way to go Puck—stab me in the back and pick my pocket at the same time.

"Fine. I'll call him to see if he's available. If he's not, I'll bring the tickets back down to you."

"Why don't you come down and let me know either way?"

Bruce laughed. "I'll see you in an hour or so."

He thought about it for a few minutes. He was inclined to turn down the tickets for the simple reason that Puck wanted him to accept them. But that type of analysis was intellectually flawed. In truth, whatever Puck's motivations, Bruce found the offer of the tickets to be opportune for him as well. After all, the road to riches ran straight through Pierre's wallet. His now-empty wallet, ironically.

He dialed Pierre's pager number and waited for the return call.

*   *   *

"Front row next to the dugout? Against the Yankees?" Pierre's excitement quickly faded as he remembered he couldn't even afford to buy Bruce a hot dog and beer. But the seats were too good to pass up, and he was flattered Bruce had thought to invite him. Plus, he knew by then he would be sick of Howie, who wasn't scheduled to leave until Sunday night. And Carla had taken such a dislike to Howie and his crass sense of humor that she had made plans to take Valerie (whose fever had finally broken) for a visit to her parents for the weekend. He accepted Bruce's invitation.

"Great. I'll meet you at seven-thirty in front of the ticket office, all right?"

"See you there. And thanks, Bruce."

"Don't mention it."

53

[June 16, 1990]

Bruce grabbed a sailboat early, before the Saturday crowds had a chance to swarm to the sailing club, then came into the office to eat lunch at his desk. He looked at his "To do" list—he had nothing pressing, largely because he hadn't received a single new assignment since his meeting with Puck. No reason to get him involved in new cases if he was going to be fired soon. But he had fallen behind on his stack of newspapers. He made a point of reading the local papers every day, as well as trying to keep up with the Wall Street Journal on a regular basis. He pulled out a stack of newspapers and began leafing through them.

An article itemizing the huge claims currently being paid by Lloyd's of London caught his eye. He had never figured out whether Puck had any connection to the insurance company, but he knew that many other wealthy American Anglophiles had invested in Lloyd's. Actually, "invested" was the wrong word; rather, the investors, called "names", pledged their entire net worth to back any losses the company might suffer relating to a specific bundle of insurance policies. In exchange for this pledge, they received a percentage of the premiums paid under that bundle of policies. Historically, the investment had yielded high returns, except in those rare instances when a catastrophic event— such as a shipwreck—would totally wipe out the group of "names" backing that particular policy.

According to the news article, the current losses at Lloyd's stemmed not from a single, or even group of, catastrophic events, but from a fundamental miscalculation in the way the company evaluated the risks of insuring against pollution claims. Lloyd's had written policies that covered losses due to such things as asbestos exposure and environmental contamination, never expecting that the claims stemming from these policies would total in the billions of dollars. Now, Lloyd's was asking the "names" to write six- and even seven-figure checks to cover their share of the losses, which were continuing to mount.

Could Puck be one of the "names" affected?

Bruce looked at his watch. Seven o'clock. It was time to head over to Fenway Park to meet Pierre. He locked his office and, as usual, took the long way toward the elevator bank—he wanted as many partners as possible to see him in the office on a Saturday evening. As he passed Puck's office, he could see light escaping from under the closed door. He stopped and knocked.

"Yes, yes, just one moment please." Bruce heard the sound of fumbling. "Now you may enter."

Bruce opened the door and stood in the doorway. It surprised him to see Puck in a pair of khakis and a dark tennis shirt—Puck always wore a suit to the office. "Hello, Mr. Puck. I just wanted to thank you for the Red Sox tickets." He figured it was best to just try to act normally toward Puck. Plus, it was a good excuse to have a conversation with the old man—not that he was particularly easy to read.

Puck looked quickly at his watch. "Yes, Mr. Arrujo. And aren't you attending the ball game?"

"Yes, sir. I'm heading over there right now." Bruce noticed a small duffel bag in the corner and a set of car keys on Puck's desk. Was Puck going away for the night? Maybe even a love interest? He seemed a little nervous about something.

"I believe Mr. Prefontaine is joining you?"

"Yes, sir.

Puck nodded slightly, then dismissed Bruce with a wave toward the door.

*   *   *

Charese looked out the window of her condo—in the distance she could see the lights of Fenway Park.

She closed the shade. She, too, would have to play a little ball tonight if she hoped to pay the $200 she owed Pierre for rent. Pierre may have thought of the $200 as grossly inadequate, but to Charese it was $200 she didn't have and would have to go out and earn every month. She could earn it in one night, but it wasn't exactly easy work.

She slipped on fishnet stockings, red heels and a black halter-top and miniskirt. She glanced at the clock. Ten after ten. She looked at herself in the mirror—not bad, but only because she had caked her face in makeup to hide the bags under her eyes and the sallowness of her skin. She was glad summer was here—even her olive-tinted skin could use some sun. Especially because her facial hair had begun growing again. The first thing she would do if the lawsuit settled would be to re-fill her female hormone drug prescription. She might decide later to abandon the sex-change operation, but she wanted to at least wake up every morning and have the option to be a woman that day if she felt like it. A woman, that is, without whiskers.

She sighed, and let her dog out onto the deck for a little fresh air. It was Saturday night, her usual working night. She could wait until after midnight when some of the bars closed and hope for some drunk college guy. Or she could try her luck right now and try to find some older guy looking for a quickie before bedtime—maybe an out-of-town conventioneer leaving the theater, or a businessman taking a detour on his way home from the Red Sox game. Her experience had been that the college boys always wanted intercourse, which made for a rather awkward situation. But at least, if she could talk them into a blow job, they were quick. Some of the older guys required fifteen or twenty minutes of constant sucking and licking before coming, and then Charese had to rest her jaw for half an hour before looking for another customer. But they always paid her price, and never hassled her afterwards.

Either way, the heroin helped. It made the time pass in a warm, drowsy, dream-like way—it was as if she had checked out of her body for the night, but decided to hang around and watch to see what the new occupant would do with it. In the morning, of course, she would have to return to clean up the mess. But it was usually worth it.

She reached into her medicine cabinet and pulled out an old aspirin bottle. Inside were four or five gray chunks of heroin tar, each about the size of a raisin. Each cost Charese about forty dollars. Charese took one out and placed it on the cut-off bottom of an aluminum soda can. Using a syringe, she added a little water to the aluminum base, heated the base from beneath with a lighter, and stirred the chunk until it had dissolved in the water. She then took a cotton ball and ripped off an aspirin-sized piece and dropped it into the heroin solution. The cotton piece quickly became bloated. Using the syringe, she extracted the liquid heroin from the cotton, which served as a filter as the solution passed through it. After a few seconds, she had sucked the entirety of the solution into the syringe.

Holding the syringe so as not to spill the heroin solution, Charese took another cotton ball, dabbed it in alcohol, and rubbed clean the spot on the bend of her arm. She angled the needle so that it was almost parallel to her forearm, and slowly pushed the needle into her vein, careful not to push it all the way through and out the other side. Holding the syringe flat against her forearm so that she wouldn't jostle the needle loose, she depressed the plunger and forced the heroin solution into her vein. She injected about half the dosage, then waited a few minutes to make sure it wasn't a bad dose before completing the injection. The whole episode took less than ten minutes.

Almost immediately she could feel the drug coursing through her body like a cup of soup on a cold day, washing away her unhappiness, empowering her to face the world. She had become experienced enough with the drug to get just the right dosage—too large a dose and she would be too high to work effectively, too small a dose and it would wear off before she had completed her night's work. She looked out the window—it was a quiet, warm night. A good night to be outside, and she was feeling giddy, so why not go out and get it over with now? She threw on an old, oversized sun dress and a pair of sandals which she would wear on her walk to and from the Theater District—why should her neighbors see her leaving the building looking like a whore? Besides, she had been arrested twice already, so she wanted to keep a low profile as much as possible. So she wore the sundress and sandals until it was time to work, then she simply stuffed them into her oversized pocketbook.

The pocketbook—purple and gloriously gaudy—hung on a doorknob; she grabbed it and looked inside: lipstick, mouthwash, hairbrush, mace, keys. And videotape. She carried the video everywhere—she didn't trust Roberge enough to leave it in the apartment.

She rode the elevator to the first floor and left the building, then walked up Clarendon Street toward the Back Bay and cut right on Columbus Avenue. Three more blocks, and she was in the Theater District. The shows were just letting out, so she stepped out of her sun dress, stepped into her heels, and leaned up against a streetlight, one leg wrapped snakelike around the lightpole. Her legs were her best feature, and the pose had caused frequent traffic tie-ups and an occasional fender bender.

She kept one eye on the pedestrian traffic and one eye on the creeping line of cars exiting the parking lots. These were not great trolling conditions—too many people and too much congestion. Johns liked anonymity, and they didn't like to feel trapped—as if any of them would really try to make a run for it, dick flapping up against their thigh, if the cops showed up. Charese relaxed her pose. She would wait fifteen minutes for the crowds to thin. She slipped back into her sun dress and sandals and walked across the street to a convenience store for a cup of coffee and a corn muffin; she hadn't eaten dinner, and she knew her stomach, if empty, would react badly to the semen.

Twenty minutes later, the crowds still had not thinned. It was the first dry night after a period of rain, and people seemed content just strolling the streets.

Charese decided to walk back toward Arlington Street, where at least the pedestrian traffic would be thinner. She again removed her sun dress and sandals and began to walk, singing a Motown hit aloud, her hips swinging back and forth to the beat.

A gray Grand Am, which she had seen double-parked in front of the convenience store, pulled out into traffic and followed her. Charese noticed the car immediately, glanced inside. She couldn't see well, but it was a male driver and he was alone. So far, so good—she tried to avoid group situations. Maybe he had seen her before her coffee break and had been waiting for her. She smiled seductively and continued her walk, detouring around a traffic island so that the Grand Am could follow her in the one-way traffic pattern. They continued together for one long block and one short one, Charese walking slowly so the traffic-bound car could keep pace. Just past the entrance to Legal Sea Foods, the Grand Am's left blinker flashed red, and the man turned left on Arlington Street. He drove fifty feet up Arlington Street and swung into a narrow alley running behind a large stone building known as the Castle. The driver turned off his lights and waited.

Charese hesitated for a moment. The man was obviously expecting her to follow, but the Grand Am was parked in a darkened area in the shadows behind the building. The Castle, a former armory now used as a convention hall, was empty tonight, and there was no other activity in that area—it was a block comprised of smaller brick office buildings and now-empty parking lots.

She approached the car cautiously. It was a newer model, clean and in good shape. It gave her a bit of comfort, but, even in her drugged euphoria, she knew she was taking a huge risk every time she climbed into a stranger's car. The passenger side window was rolled down about three inches, but the car was dark. In the darkness she could see only the outline of the driver—baseball cap, beard and mustache, dark glasses. She spoke through the crack. "Hey, Baby, thought you could hide from me, driving down this alley?"

He spoke gruffly, in a gravely voice that sounded somehow unnatural to Charese. Maybe he was just nervous. "How much?"

"That depends. You a cop?" She wanted to get a better feel for the guy before agreeing to anything. One thing for sure, he didn't want her to get a good look at him.

"No. How 'bout you?"

Smart question, she thought. She laughed lightly. "No, honey. Just a working girl."

"How much?" he asked again.

"Seventy-five for a blow job. Best you ever had, too." He reached out and, with a gloved hand, handed her four twenties through the window. She stuck them in her bag. "Sorry, honey, I don't make change." She laughed alone at the joke.

"Get in, but leave the door open."

She opened the door, but the car remained dark—he must have turned off the dome light. She climbed in, hoping her eyes would adjust to the darkness. He had pushed his seat all the way back, and before she could even get a look at his face, he took her by the back of the neck and pushed her mouth down to his open fly. She noticed the smell of expensive cologne, which calmed her a bit— he was probably just a nervous, rich guy cheating on his frigid wife.

It surprised her to see a flaccid penis barely protruding through the opening in his khakis. Normally, by the time she got in the car, the john was already erect and quivering with excitement. *Damn*, she thought, *I hope this doesn't take too long.* "Hello, big boy. Come out and play." She bent over further, resting her right hand on the floor of the car and using her left hand to extract his penis. She opened her mouth and flicked the end of his penis two or three times with her tongue. It barely moved, and the john made no sound. Something was wrong here—nobody had ever reacted, or not reacted, that way.

It was her last thought. Suddenly her entire existence was reduced to a desperate struggle for air. Her mouth, her nose, even her eyes and fingers opened wide in an attempt to grab hold of a bit of life and feed it to her lungs. Gasping, clawing, wreathing. Then finally one final gurgle. Her last sensation was the taste of her own hot blood pulsating into her mouth as she bit through her tongue.

                    *   *   *

The john held the garrote tightly around her neck, slowly continuing to compress her windpipe with the steel-corded strangulation device. He was careful not to break her skin—the garrote was designed to kill bloodlessly by crushing the windpipe. Maintaining constant pressure on both ends of the cord with his left hand, he removed his right hand from the garrote and turned Charese's face upwards toward him and closed her mouth. He did not want her saliva—or, he saw with disgust, a part of her bleeding tongue—to spill out of her mouth and onto the car's upholstery.

He looked away from her anguished face, counted to thirty, and felt for a pulse. There was none. He took a deep breath, and released tension on the garrote, still using it like a puppeteer string to hold her head up above his lap. He swung her head back over her prone body, where it dangled awkwardly over her left shoulder like a fish on a hook, and reached his left hand under her buttocks and tried to slide her over onto the passenger side. She was caught on something. He looked down—the fingernails of her right hand were imbedded in the car's upholstery in what must have been a final claw against death.

He pried her fingers open, and now was able to slide her body over to the passenger side of the car. He looked around—there was nobody else in the alley. He pushed her head and upper body out the door, again careful that no bodily fluids dripped into the car. He walked around the car, tossed her crumpled torso out onto the pavement, and closed the door.

Crouching down, he removed the garrote from Charese's neck and stuck it into a plastic bag he took from his pocket. He walked back to the driver's side of the car, pulled the seat forward and turned the ignition key. The car started on the first try, and he shifted into reverse. He heard a slight thump as the right front tire rolled over Charese's body, felt the car settle a bit as her bone structure collapsed under the car's weight. He waited for the traffic to clear, then backed onto Arlington Street and drove away.

54

[June 18, 1990]

Shelby was still having trouble getting used to getting to work by nine o'clock, but it was her third week on the job and her internal clock, for years set to a student's semi-nocturnal schedule, was beginning to adapt to the business world's demands. Shelby was actually beginning to like it—imagine leaving work at five or six o'clock and having the whole evening to do what you want! No homework, no evening classes, no study groups. Just free time, to go to lectures, shows, sporting events, recitals. Or play tennis. Or just read. Or even watch television.

This free time was only temporary, unfortunately. In a couple of weeks, she would have to begin cramming for the bar exam, scheduled for the end of July. But her free evenings now gave her a taste of what life would be like after the bar exam, and it excited her.

For the umpteenth time, she congratulated herself on her decision to work for the District Attorney's office. Almost all of her classmates had elected to go into private practice. But Shelby had no desire to work eighty hours a week for some corporate law firm. Sure, she took less money to work in the public sector, but how much money did she need, anyway? She could afford a nice apartment outside Harvard Square, and she didn't really need a car. And she could always get a job in the private sector if she wanted—her experience at the DA's office would provide her with valuable courtroom skills that many of her classmates would never acquire. But most of all, her experience at the DA's office would tell her whether she really wanted to be a lawyer. It was where the action was, and she hoped that she would find that, for the most part, the system was staffed by decent, honest people working to ensure that the concept of justice was more than just an abstraction.

Shelby knew that if she left her apartment by 8:15, she would have time to take the subway downtown, grab a cup of coffee, and get to her desk by nine. And, if the subway was running efficiently, she would have time to get off one stop early and enjoy a half-mile walk to her office.

So she dressed quickly, threw an apple into her briefcase and scooped up the newspaper—she generally glanced at the front page before she left her apartment, but a thorough reading usually had to wait until the subway ride or lunch time. She cut across the Cambridge Common, stopping for a moment to pet a friendly dog, and entered the subway station. It always depressed her a bit to enter the gloom of the underground at the beginning of a bright summer day, but Boston drivers were particular about not sharing the roads with bicyclists, and it would take over an hour to walk to work. She wasn't prepared to get up that early, at least not yet.

The subway was too crowded even to open her newspaper, so Shelby contented herself with people watching. One of the reasons she preferred to live in Cambridge instead of the Back Bay or another Boston neighborhood was that Cambridge maintained at least some semblance of racial diversity. Boston, despite its history of abolitionism and liberalism, was a remarkably segregated city. But for a New York City girl, even the Cambridge crowd on the subway seemed disproportionately Caucasian. It was impossible to drive in Boston during rush hour, so how did the city's minority residents get to work, if not on the subway?

The train ran slowly this morning, so Shelby did not disembark at the Charles Street station and instead rode all the way to Park Street. The train stopped, and she ran up the stairs of the subway station. Forty-eight stairs later, she emerged into the daylight, mouth closed, and strolled toward the Government Center area and the Suffolk County DA's office.

The Consumer Fraud Division, where Shelby had been assigned, usually held weekly Monday morning staff meetings. Cases were assigned, workloads evaluated, experiences shared. Especially for the young attorneys, many of whom had never tried a case, it was an opportunity to pick the brains of the senior lawyers. This week, however, the meeting had been moved to Tuesday because one of the Division's attorneys had gotten married over the weekend in Maryland and many of the other attorneys were still making their way back to Boston from the wedding.

This was fine with Shelby. She and the other young ADAs—Assistant District Attorneys—had been encouraged to sit in on other Divisions' staff meetings during their first few months on the job; it was a way to give them a flavor of how exciting the ADA job could be once they moved beyond the junior level. Boredom had become a major problem for the DA's office—young, talented attorneys fresh out of law school expected to be prosecuting murder and drug cases within a few months. When they discovered they would have to first cut their teeth on misdemeanor cases, many of them turned an envious eye back toward the private sector. If they were going to be doing drudgework, why not

get paid the big bucks for it? The DA hoped to address this problem by expos-
ing his young attorneys as much as possible to the glamorous side of their career.

   Shelby decided to attend the Homicide Division's staff meeting. The serious-
ness of the crime meant that only the most senior and talented ADAs were
assigned to this division, and Shelby knew that many of the ADAs sitting in the
staff meeting that morning would someday become high-priced defense attorneys. It had been a quiet weekend—the only new case was a 'John Jane Doe',
an unidentified male dressed as a female, found strangled in an alley in the South
End. Believed to be a prostitute. Time of death: Saturday night, just before midnight. Shelby's mouth suddenly felt dry.

   The staff meeting adjourned, and Shelby rushed back to her office. Fighting
a rising sense of panic, she fumbled with her purse, found her address book, and
dialed Charese's phone number. Three rings, four rings, answering machine.
"Charese, pick up. This is Shelby Baskin. Please pick up, it's important."
Nothing. Charese was never out this early. Could she be in the shower? Shelby
forced herself to wait ten minutes, the second hand creeping its way around the
clock face, then dialed again. Again the machine. "Charese, are you there? Are
you there? Please answer...."

   Shelby put her head down on her desk and cried.

                 *   *   *

   Detective Dominic Mazzutti was kind enough not to ask Shelby to come to
the morgue to identify the body; the doorman at the condo complex was able to
do that. The detective, however, had come up to Shelby's office to question her,
and she readily agreed to tell him what she knew about Charese's life. Even
though she wasn't assigned to Homicide, she was hoping her relationship with
Charese would convince her superiors to allow her to assist in the case, and a lev-
elheaded performance in front of the lead detective might help her cause.

   The autopsy had revealed coffee in Charese's stomach, and the detective had
been lucky and found a convenience store clerk who remembered selling coffee
and a muffin to Charese at around eleven-thirty Saturday night. The clerk was
apparently the last person, other than the murderer, to see Charese alive that
night. Other than the coffee, and the heroin in her bloodstream, the forensic
people had discovered automobile carpet fibers under her fingernails and a tire
tread on her left arm. They were running this evidence through their computer
to try to make a specific automobile identification.

The detective had been inclined to treat the case as a random homicide—some wacko angry at the world, or some john pissed off when he found out Charese was really a guy. Shelby sensed that he had begun to change his mind as she answered his questions. "So, it sounds like Charese had at least a few enemies. Do you think any of them could have killed her?"

Shelby took a deep breath and tried to gain control of her emotions. She wanted to think clearly, logically. She wanted to be assigned to this case, and she knew the Division Chief would ask the detective about her state of mind. It would be unusual for such a young ADA to be assigned to a homicide, but Shelby hoped the Division Chief would realize that her relationship with Charese and her knowledge of Charese's enemies could be beneficial to the investigation. She tried to focus her thoughts, and struggled to fight back a sense of guilt—had she pushed too hard? Had she backed Reese or Roberge or Pierre so far into a corner that they reacted by murdering Charese?

Shelby shook the thoughts away, and tried to focus on the detective's question. Could one of them have killed her? It was one thing to describe for the detective the reasons why Pierre, Roberge and Reese might all want to see Charese dead. It was another thing entirely to reach the intellectual conclusion that one of them could have committed the murder. "I really don't know if one of them could have killed her. I know Reese fairly well, but I don't know the other two beyond a couple of phone conversations. The fact that the video is missing makes it hard to eliminate Reese or Roberge right now. Did you say you searched her apartment for the video?"

"My guys are over there right now. So far, no video. Would she have put it in a safe deposit box or something?"

"No, that wasn't her style. Besides, I'm pretty sure she kept it with her all the time. She was worried Roberge might be able to get the doorman to let him back into the apartment."

"Let's get back to the three potential suspects."

"All right. But all this is just between you and me, right?"

The detective nodded. "I'm just trying to get the lay of the land here. I'm not arresting anyone yet."

Shelby took another deep breath, fighting for some control. "Reese Jeffries is a world-class sleaze ball, and he definitely was worried Charese was going to report him to the Board of Bar Overseers, and maybe even blackmail him. And he was desperate to get the video, because he thought he could bring Krygier down with it. But I'm just not sure he has the balls to murder someone. Maybe he does, but he just strikes me as a bit of a wimp, you know?

"As for Roberge Krygier, from what I know he was pretty cold-hearted. Real spoiled rich boy. And he needed to shut Charese up to keep Daddy from cutting him off. So it could definitely be him.

"And Pierre Prefontaine, he actually seemed like a decent guy when I talked to him, and Charese said he was pleasant enough when they met. But he also seemed a bit desperate, and he was pretty exasperated by the fact he couldn't get her out of the condo. But he would have had no interest in the video, as far as I know. Or even knowledge of it."

"So if she had been killed and the murderer didn't take the video, that would point more toward Pierre Prefontaine in your mind, right?"

"Yeah, but the flip side of that isn't necessarily true: the fact that the video is missing doesn't necessarily eliminate Prefontaine as a suspect."

"I agree. And, of course, it still could be a random thing. But let's get back to the three musketeers here. Did any of them know her well enough to know her schedule? I mean, if it wasn't random, it stands to reason that the murderer was waiting for her."

"Let's see. I know that Saturday night was her regular night to work, as long as the weather was good, and that she liked to work the Theater District. I would guess that anybody who followed her for even a few weeks could have guessed that she'd be there on Saturday night. But I have a question for you. Why would she get in the car if she recognized the driver?"

"Well, we don't even know she actually got in the car."

"But you said there was automobile carpet fibers under her fingernails."

"Right." He smiled at her kindly, as if apologizing for having to test her. "So you tell me. Would she get in the car with any of them?"

Shelby thought for a moment. "Maybe Reese. She would never trust him, but he seems like such a wimp that my guess is that she wouldn't be very afraid of him. Maybe Roberge also. I mean, they were lovers for sixteen years; she might get in the car with him. As far as I know, he never beat her up or anything. As for Pierre Prefontaine, I don't know. I don't even know if she would recognize him. I think she only met him once, a couple of months ago."

"And, of course, the other two could have been wearing a disguise so she wouldn't have recognized them, either. The alley where they found the body was fairly dark."

"How about other evidence? You said they found coffee in her stomach and carpet fibers under her nails."

"Eighty bucks in her shoe—four twenties, probably from the john. But no prints."

"Anything else, like semen?"

He looked away from Shelby. "No, miss, they didn't find anything else in her stomach."

Shelby noticed the detective's discomfort, saw his face begin to blush. He was probably a few years older than her, and not bad looking in a boy-next-door kind of way. But a bit old-fashioned; he could talk freely about the death of a transvestite hooker but was discomforted by the mention of semen. Shelby actually didn't mind guys like that—they were better than the guys who cried at toilet paper commercials. But the last thing she felt like doing now was flirting, even if it might help her stay assigned to the case. "How about other bruises, like from a struggle?"

"No, nothing. My guess is that she was strangled while, um, performing a sexual act, and never had time to really put up a fight."

"So she gets in the car, starts performing, then gets strangled?"

"That's how I figure it. Maybe the guy's frustrated because he can't, um, ejaculate, or maybe he discovers she's a guy. Or, if it was a set-up, maybe it was just a way to get a clear shot at her throat. Whatever the case, I think the guy used some kind of rubber-coated metal cable. Something that wouldn't cut the skin, but would be strong enough to..." He could see Shelby didn't need to hear a step-by-step account of the murder. "... to cut off the air supply."

Shelby fought to get the image of Charese's face turning purple from strangulation out of her mind and to re-focus on the conversation. "Again, your scenario gets back to the conclusion that she didn't know her murderer. I mean, I can't picture her performing sex on Reese or Roberge or Pierre."

"Unless she didn't recognize them. Maybe he kept the car lights off or, again, wore a disguise. We're just guessing now—hopefully the computer will spit out a car ID based on the tire tracks and carpet fibers. In the meantime, I'm going to get started on seeing if any of these guys have an alibi."

"Detective, may I make a suggestion?"

"Sure."

"Since the papers haven't reported the identity of the murder victim yet, none of the suspects should know she's dead, right?"

"Right. Unless one of them killed her."

"Well, both Reese and Pierre Prefontaine are expecting me to call them today. And Roberge's lawyer is also expecting a call from me. Why don't I proceed as if nothing's happened, and see what each of their responses is? Maybe one of them will give himself away."

The detective was silent for a moment. She knew her request was unusual—she was wearing quite a few hats here. But she also knew her suggestion made sense, and there was no reason for any of the suspects to become suspicious if they received a call from her. "All right with me, so long as you clear it with Ms. Palmer." Jennifer Palmer was the senior ADA assigned to the case. She and Shelby had hit it off right from Shelby's first interview, and Shelby knew she had been lucky that Jennifer had drawn the case. "If she says okay, I'll wait until tomorrow to begin questioning the suspects."

"Great. And, Detective, thanks a lot."

"No problem. And please call me Dom."

*   *   *

Shelby closed the door and stared out the window. Just this morning, life had been so good. Now death had intruded again. This time, she knew she would have to ask herself some tough questions. Had she killed Charese? Had she, in her inexperience and naiveté, failed to understand what desperate men could do when they were backed into a corner? She had been dealing with Charese's problem like a chess match, positioning the pieces on the board so that her opponent—sometimes Reese, sometimes Roberge, sometimes Pierre—would be completely surrounded and would have no choice but to concede to her demands. Checkmate. But this was the real world, not some board game. Had one of the players, angered at the thought of losing, simply knocked the board over and jumped across the table to settle the competition with his fists? It sure looked that way.

She looked at her watch. Two o'clock. Some people were probably still eating lunch, yet she felt as if this day had already gone on for weeks. She went out to the vending machine and grabbed some peanut butter crackers and a Diet Coke; she didn't have much of an appetite, but she needed to be sharp if she was going to interview the three suspects. And she couldn't even do that until she sold the idea to Jennifer. She forced the crackers down and finished the soda, then went to the ladies' room to wash her face and brush the crackers out of her teeth. The cold water and the cool toothpaste refreshed her a bit, and she went to find the woman she hoped would be supervising her for the next few months.

Before she could even knock, Jennifer looked up at her and smiled. "Don't even bother coming in, Shelby. I just talked to Detective Mazzutti and he told me what you want to do. I think it's a good idea, definitely worth a shot. I've got a trial tomorrow, so I can't do it myself anyway. Why don't you work with Mazzutti on this for a couple of days, then we'll decide whether you can stay on the case, all right?"

Shelby marched back to her office.

She phoned Reese first. She decided to be aggressive, to taunt him. Maybe his male ego would betray him. "Hi, Reese. I haven't heard from you in a while. Where's Charese's money?"

"Who is this?"

Shelby knew Reese was just trying to buy some time—there was no doubt in his mind who she was. "This is Shelby Baskin."

"Oh, hello, Miss Baskin. For your information, Krygier's lawyer asked for a two-week extension. Which I gave him. I expect to hear from him this week, at which point I will call you. I don't believe we have anything else to discuss." And he hung up.

Shelby sat back and replayed the conversation in her mind. She could analyze the nuances of the conversation for hours, but in the end there was simply too little on which to base a conclusion. If Reese had killed her, or even knew she was dead, he hadn't revealed that knowledge in their conversation.

As for Gerard Krygier, she couldn't call him directly because he was represented by his father's attorney. And, based on what Reese had said, there was no use in calling the lawyer. The lawyer was supposed to be contacting Reese in a couple of days with a settlement offer, assuming by that point they hadn't learned of Charese's death. But it was doubtful the police could keep Charese's identity out of the papers that long, and Krygier would be stupid to make the offer once he found out Charese was dead.

That left Pierre. She dialed his number, and he answered on the third ring.

"Premier Properties. This is Pierre."

"Mr. Prefontaine, this is Shelby Baskin, Charese Galloway's attorney."

"Oh. Hi."

"I was wondering, is your offer to pay Charese to leave the apartment still open?"

Pierre paused before responding. Shelby guessed that her offer came as a bit of a surprise. "Well, sure, I guess so. The only thing is, it will take a few days to get the money together."

Was he stalling, knowing that in a few days it would be a moot point? "I see. And we would want $20,000, not $5,000." Shelby was just looking for reactions now, shooting in the dark.

Pierre again paused. "Listen, this is not a great time to talk, and I need to think about this a little. Can I call you back?"

Another meaningless response. "Sure." She gave Pierre her number and hung up.

Maybe she just wasn't very good at this type of investigative work. She had spoken to both Reese and Pierre and was no closer to knowing whether they had killed Charese than she was before. She would have to call Detective Mazzutti and tell him she had struck out. Maybe he would have better luck meeting them face to face.

55

[June 19, 1990]

The local newspapers identified the murder victim on Tuesday. The *Globe* buried the follow-up story in a small box in the Metro section, but the *Herald* liked the racy angle of it and featured it on page 3. The murder of a prostitute was, even in Boston, a fairly rare occurrence, and the tie-in with the Krygier family made it a natural story for the tabloid *Herald*. The paper devoted half a page to the story, and included the same picture of Charese and father and son Krygier that it had run the previous fall.

Shelby spoke to Detective Mazzutti later that morning. "Listen, Shelby." They had moved to a first-name basis. "I know you think it's sleazy for the *Herald* to use Charese's death to sell newspapers, but it's actually good that they ran the story and the picture. We need to find somebody who may have seen something that can help fill in the blanks here. The publicity will help us."

"I guess you're right. Have you talked to any of the suspects?"

"Yeah, I actually spoke to all three of the musketeers already this morning. Actually, maybe we should start calling them the three blind mice—none of them know anything. They all have what I would call 'soft' alibis. Prefontaine says he went to the Red Sox game, got stuck in traffic, then got home around half past midnight. Got a ticket stub and a mustard stain to prove it. One of his neighbors pulled into the parking lot with him and she confirms the twelve-thirty time. The alibi makes sense; there was a lot of traffic getting out of Fenway that night. But, he could have just as easily left Fenway and headed over to the Theater District—no traffic going that direction—in plenty of time to kill Charese at around midnight, which is when we think she died, ditched the murder weapon and gotten home by twelve-thirty. So who knows?

"As for Jeffries, he was at some fund-raiser downtown which ended at about eleven o'clock. Then he says he went home. Plenty of witnesses at the fund-raiser, but his wife was out of town visiting her parents, so who knows where he went after that? Could have gone home, could have visited a girlfriend, could have driven over to the Theater District to kill Charese.

"Young Krygier says his wife went to bed early because she wasn't feeling well, and he just stayed up watching TV. His wife confirms the story, but, you know, this is a woman who had no idea her husband was gay, so how sharp could

231

she be? He could have slipped out while she was sleeping. So, they all have stories, but nothing airtight like they were out of town or even at a party with lots of witnesses."

"So we're no closer than we were yesterday?"

"Actually, we did get one break. The forensic people cross-referenced the tire tracks with the carpet fibers and came up with a blue or gray Pontiac Grand Am, any of the last three model years. And according to the Department of Motor Vehicle records, Pierre Prefontaine owns a 1988 Grand Am. Gray."

Shelby banged her desk with her fist. "Shit. I really wouldn't have guessed him."

"Well, let's not jump to conclusions just yet. This definitely makes him the prime suspect, but there's a lot of blue and gray Grand Am's around. Over 1,500 registered in Massachusetts alone, according to the Motor Vehicle records. And a lot of them are owned by rental car companies, so that widens the possibilities even more."

Shelby was unimpressed. "Sure, fifteen hundred cars, but out of how many drivers? I mean, aren't there, like, six million people in Massachusetts? That's a lot of coincidence."

"I agree. But a jury's not going to convict a man just based on a car match, even a man with a motive. We need more."

*   *   *

Bruce thumbed back three weeks in his calendar, found the day Pierre had come to the office to discuss the Fenway Place deal. May 29. That was the same day Pierre had mentioned his problems with his tenant.

Bruce pre-dated the memo, and began typing on the keyboard:

To: File
From: Bruce Arrujo
Date: May 29, 1990
Re: Conversation with Pierre Prefontaine

> Earlier today I spoke by telephone with Pierre Prefontaine regarding a contemplated real estate purchase. (Our Client: Howard Plansky. Matter: Fenway Place Purchase.) During this conversation, Mr. Prefontaine mentioned to me that he was having problems with a tenant (by the name of "Charese") in a condominium unit he had recently purchased at a foreclosure sale at Two Clarendon

Street in Boston. The tenant was only paying rent of $200 per month and Mr. Prefontaine believed he could not evict her as long as she paid her rent. He stated that he was losing over two thousand dollars per month on the unit, and that this was causing him extreme financial hardship. He then made a comment to the effect that the only way to "get rid" of this tenant was to kill her. He stated that either he or the tenant would have to die since the financial drain was "killing" him. He then asked me what the penalty in Massachusetts was for murder.

I am writing this memo to memorialize my conversation with Mr. Prefontaine in the event of any future criminal activity involving Mr. Prefontaine or the tenant.

Bruce paused to pull out a paperback book containing the professional rules of conduct for Massachusetts lawyers from the bottom shelf of his bookcase. He dusted it off, found the section he was looking for, studied the rules for a few minutes, then continued on the memo.

Note: I have not notified the police of this matter because I do not feel that the comments made to me by Mr. Prefontaine were sufficient to give me "knowledge" of his "intention to commit a crime". I fear that Mr. Prefontaine may indeed commit a crime, but my fears are not the same as actual "knowledge". Absent such "knowledge", Disciplinary Rule 4-101(C)(3) does not allow me to violate the attorney-client privilege by reporting this conversation to the police.

He printed out a single copy of the memo and slid it in into the innermost pocket of his briefcase. From that same pocket, he removed the copy of the affidavit Pierre had signed—the one certifying that none of the members of the ownership group was in default on any RTC debts. He hid the affidavit in a legal ethics textbook on his bookshelf.

Bruce told his secretary he had an early lunch appointment, and jumped on the green line train heading out to Newton.

Thirty-five minutes later, he walked off the train and ducked into a public restroom. He took a fake mustache and beard and a pair of heavy-framed glasses from his briefcase and put them on. From his suitcoat pocket he pulled out a yarmulke, a Jewish skullcap, and bobby-pinned it to the hair on the top of his head. He looked in the mirror: his parents would still recognize him, but the disguise would probably fool a casual acquaintance. The disguise was sufficient for his purposes today.

Still carrying the briefcase, he walked to the Newton Police station and entered the front door. Five minutes later, he left the station and walked back to the green line train stop. He was empty-handed.

*   *   *

Shelby was just about ready to call it a day when her phone rang. It was Dominic.

"Hey, how'ya holding up?"

"Pretty good, as long as no one's actually expecting me to get any work done."

"Well, I just got an interesting phone call. Are you free for a few minutes?"

"Actually, I could really go for a drink. You want to meet me in Fanieul Hall?"

Shelby sensed that the offer surprised Dom, but he quickly accepted. She had begun to sense that he was interested in her, though still a bit intimidated. "Sure, I'm off duty now. How about Frog's Lane in twenty minutes? It's upstairs at the west end of the building. The bar should be quiet enough so we can talk."

Shelby had been there a few times. "Sounds good. See you in twenty."

*   *   *

Twenty minutes later, Shelby arrived to find Dom seated at the bar sipping a beer and nibbling at a plate of nachos. He stood when he saw her enter, and gestured for her to sit down. He started to get the bartender's attention, then stopped himself.

Shelby smiled to herself at his indecisiveness. It was as if he had to remind himself that this wasn't a date, it was a business meeting. So he should let her call the bartender herself. She ordered a dark rum on the rocks, asked for a stirring straw, then turned to Dom to explain. "I started drinking this when I was on vacation in Santo Domingo a few years ago. Sometimes it makes me feel like a pirate or something, but I really do like the taste."

Dom wasn't sure how he was supposed to respond. "You want some nachos?"

"Thanks." Shelby reached across and grabbed a couple. "So, what's this phone call about?"

"I was out all day, but when I got back at around four there was a message from a cop over in Newton. Tells me that some guy found a briefcase on the subway this afternoon. The guy turned it into the police because there was a memo in the briefcase about somebody possibly murdering someone named Charese, and he recognized the Charese name from this morning's newspaper article. The Newton cop faxed it over to me. Here it is."

He handed Shelby a single typewritten page on flimsy thermal fax paper. She flattened it out and read it to herself, stirring the ice cubes in her drink around in increasingly rapid rotations as she did so:

To: File
From: Bruce Arrujo
Date: May 29, 1990
Re: Conversation with Pierre Prefontaine

> Earlier today I spoke by telephone with Pierre Prefontaine regarding a contemplated real estate purchase. (Our Client: Howard Plansky. Matter: Fenway Place Purchase.) During this conversation, Mr. Prefontaine mentioned to me that he was having problems with a tenant (by the name of "Charese") in a condominium unit he had recently purchased at a foreclosure sale at Two Clarendon Street in Boston. The tenant was only paying rent of $200 per month and Mr. Prefontaine believed he could not evict her as long as she paid her rent. He stated that he was losing over two thousand dollars per month on the unit, and that this was causing him extreme financial hardship. He then made a comment to the effect that the only way to "get rid" of this tenant was to kill her. He stated that either he or the tenant would have to die since the financial drain was "killing" him. He then asked me what the penalty in Massachusetts was for murder.

> I am writing this memo to memorialize my conversation with Mr. Prefontaine in the event of any future criminal activity involving Mr. Prefontaine or the tenant.

> Note: I have not notified the police of this matter because I do not feel that the comments made to me by Mr. Prefontaine were sufficient to give me "knowledge" of his "intention to commit a crime". I fear that Mr. Prefontaine may indeed commit a crime, but my fears are not the same as actual "knowledge". Absent such "knowledge", Disciplinary Rule 4-101(C)(3) does not allow me to violate the attorney-client privilege by reporting this conversation to the police.

Shelby sat silently for a few seconds. She had stopped swirling, and was now chewing on her straw. She stopped when she noticed Dom looking at her mouth.

Finally she spoke. "Wow. This is pretty incriminating. I really didn't think Prefontaine was that desperate."

"Well, apparently this Arrujo guy did. He's at a big firm—Stoak, Puck & Beal. Even I've heard of them."

"Yeah. They're the biggest in town. So have you called this Arrujo guy?"

"That's what I wanted to talk to you about. Before I talk to him, what's my landscape like here? Can he even talk to us? Can we force him to?"

Shelby had just finished taking the required course in legal ethics, but some of the details were a bit fuzzy. It reminded her that she better pick up the pace on her bar exam studies—the test was in six weeks. "Good question. I think he's right in his memo—he can't violate the attorney-client privilege unless he knows his client is intending to commit a crime."

"But now that the crime is committed, can we make him testify?"

"I doubt it, as long as Prefontaine was his client. There are exceptions, but they have to do with the lawyer helping the client commit fraud."

"So you mean if Prefontaine committed fraud, we could force Arrujo to testify against him, but not for murder?"

"Yeah, something like that. Pretty screwy, huh?"

Dom nodded. "I'll say. What about just using the memo as evidence?"

"No. Same problem. We'd still need the attorney to authenticate it, and we can't compel him to testify. Plus, he wrote it a few days after their conversation, so it's probably hearsay. Bottom line is that the whole thing between Prefontaine and Arrujo was a confidential communication. Conversations between someone and his lawyer or his doctor or his clergyman are confidential and can't be used as evidence. So as long as Prefontaine was Arrujo's client at the time he made the incriminating statements, we can't get the evidence in front of the jury."

"Hey, wait a second." Dom reached across and grabbed the memo from Shelby and scanned it quickly. "This thing says that some guy named Plansky was the client, not Prefontaine. You said the privilege is only good if Prefontaine was Arrujo's client."

Shelby thought for a moment. Dom was pretty sharp. And he had been right when he said the publicity would help the case; better still, he hadn't gloated about it when he showed her the Arrujo memo. "Excellent point, Detective." She clinked her glass against his. "We may have to send you to law school. And guess what? It's up to the client to prove the existence of the attorney-client relationship. So we can at least force Prefontaine to prove he was Arrujo's client. But it's pretty easy to prove. So we're probably going to need other evidence, it seems to me."

"Yeah, I agree. Without the lawyer's testimony, all we really have is the car match. And that's not enough to convict. But it's definitely enough to get a search warrant to search his car and his clothes. Maybe get some more evidence."

"Sounds like a good idea. I'll clear it with Jennifer."

*　　　　　*　　　　　*

Pierre and Carla took a seat at a cozy table in a small Italian restaurant in the North End. They were celebrating.

As far as Carla knew, they were celebrating Pierre and Howie's purchase of the Fenway Place project. Pierre had spent the last few days at the complex, and he was more bullish on the project than ever. Felloff was being as cooperative as he had promised he would be, and already they had begun removing many of the warts on the project. Pierre was sure the deal would be a huge winner.

But, privately, Pierre was also celebrating Charese's death. As close as he and Carla were, he didn't feel he could openly rejoice over the death of another human being. Yesterday he had showed Carla the *Herald* article, trying to be as matter of fact about the situation as he could, reminding her that Charese's death would allow them to quickly flip the condo for a $35,000 profit. Less than the $60,000 profit he had originally hoped, but at least they would finally be able to get their heads above water.

Carla, too, seemed relieved that their financial pressures would soon be eased. But when the police detective had come to their home to question Pierre about the murder, Carla had, for a brief second, looked at Pierre a bit funny. And Pierre couldn't really blame Carla for wondering—he clearly had a motive to kill Charese. But he was confident there was nothing else to tie him to Charese's death.

"You know, Pierre, I can't get over this Charese murder. You know how I always say that you step in shit and come out smelling like a rose? Well, this was a huge mound of manure, but now Charese is dead and you end up smelling like a bordello." Carla stopped there—Pierre understood perfectly what had gone unsaid, and what still needed to be spoken.

Pierre took Carla's hand in both of his and looked her straight in the eye. "Honey, I understand why you might be worried, especially with the police coming to question us and all. But I can't believe they really think I'm a suspect. I mean, she was a hooker working the streets of a big city. Anybody could have killed her."

The waiter came and interrupted their conversation. Carla ordered her meal, then excused herself to visit the ladies' room.

*   *   *

Carla eyed herself in the mirror. She had been listening carefully to Pierre's words. Now she replayed them in her mind—he had never actually said he didn't kill Charese. But would an innocent man even bother to proclaim his innocence to his wife? Didn't it go without saying? And did she even want to press the issue? She had agreed to marry Pierre 'for better or for worse', and she still loved him deeply. Not to mention how close he and Valerie were. Should she ask him straight out if he had killed Charese? If he were innocent, the question would, understandably, offend him. And if he were guilty, he would either have to lie to her or admit to it. But if he admitted to it, could she stay married to a murderer? She took a deep breath, splashed some water on her face. He was a good man—a decent, loyal, kind, generous man.

She left the ladies' room and caught the eye of the waiter on the way back to the table. He scurried over. "Could we have a bottle of champagne, please? We're celebrating tonight."

56

[June 22, 1990]

Bruce was eating Friday night dinner at his desk, even though he had no work to do and many of his co-workers had already left for the weekend. But Bruce knew it was only a matter of time now. And when his pigeon came home to roost, he didn't want to be out at McDonald's stuffing his face.

The phone rang. "Bruce, thank God you're still there. This is Pierre Prefontaine. I've got a major problem."

You don't know the half of it, Pierre. "Calm down. What's wrong?"

"The cops are here, at my house. They've got a search warrant, and they're tearing up the place. They think I killed Charese last weekend."

Bruce sighed deeply, partly for effect and partly because he was nervous. He knew this was his best—and probably only—chance. "Listen, Pierre, I'll do whatever I can to help you. But I have no experience in criminal law, and this firm only does white collar stuff. But I know a guy who does a lot of criminal defense work who I think can help you. Do you want me to call him for you?"

"Yeah, please, Bruce."

"All right, I'm going to put you on hold while I try to catch him before he leaves for the weekend." Bruce put Pierre on hold, then looked down at the phone number scrawled onto the piece of paper in front of him. He dialed Mike Callahan's number. Callahan had successfully defended Bruce from the assault charges stemming from the beating Bruce had inflicted on the tenant activists six years earlier. At the time, Callahan was just a young lawyer from West Roxbury trying to make a name for himself. And he had taken a liking to Bruce—boys from West Roxbury saw nothing wrong with throwing a few punches to knock some sense into a bunch of Cambridge pinkos. Since then, Bruce had kept in touch with him—he was never sure when he might need a good criminal defense lawyer.

But Callahan was also a young lawyer with four older brothers and close to a dozen cousins and uncles in the law enforcement community. Just as he had gained experience in the court system, other Callahans had moved into increasing positions of prominence in various law enforcement arenas. Today, at the relatively young age of 34, he was known as one of the most effective members of the criminal bar. It wasn't so much that he possessed outstanding trial skills. It

239

was more that he was so well connected and well liked that it was rare that he couldn't cajole a benign plea bargain out of the DA's office. As a member of a police family, he bought into the assumption that his client was guilty; otherwise, why would the police have arrested him? From that common ground, it was simply a matter of persuading the overworked ADA to avoid the risk and expense of trial in exchange for a minimal sentence for his client. And if a case did go to trial, he didn't attempt to embarrass the police on the witness stand, didn't reveal prosecution misconduct or incompetence to the press, didn't create political brushfires by turning criminal trials into forums on racism or socio-economic injustices. He re-paid favors, with interest, didn't hold grudges, and was quick to buy a round of drinks or hand out a pair of Bruins tickets. He was the consummate dealmaker, in a city where nobody considered that moniker to be anything less than a badge of honor.

Bruce arranged for the defense attorney to come to his office, then picked up Pierre's line. "We got lucky, Pierre. I just caught him before he left the office. Can you come down here right now?"

"I think I should wait here until the cops leave. But I'll come right down after."

"Good. Why don't we say nine o'clock? And don't worry if you're going to be later than that. We'll wait for you."

"Thanks, Bruce. Thanks a lot."

*   *   *

It was almost ten o'clock before Pierre finally staggered off the elevator and into the reception area of Boston's largest law firm. He couldn't help remembering the pride that he had felt the last time that he had been here, preparing to close on a multi-million-dollar real estate purchase.

Bruce, who had been sitting on a couch in the reception area waiting for him, put down *Fortune* magazine and stood up to greet him. "We're going to beat this Pierre, don't worry." He clenched Pierre's hand firmly with his right hand and squeezed Pierre's shoulder with his left. "Mike Callahan is the criminal lawyer I was talking about. He's in the conference room now, reviewing the newspaper articles on Charese's death and calling around to his contacts in the police department to see what he can find out. Come on in and meet him, see if you like him."

Callahan was just hanging up the phone when Bruce and Pierre walked into the conference room. They shook hands, and Pierre couldn't help but wonder whether an experienced criminal lawyer like Callahan could tell if a man was innocent or guilty just by looking at him, the way an art expert can tell a masterpiece from an imitation with just a glance.

The three men sat down. Callahan looked to Bruce, deferring to him to lead the meeting.

Bruce turned to Pierre. "Listen, Pierre, there's something I have to tell you. I think it will explain why the police view you as the chief suspect. Remember when you first came here to go over the Fenway Place deal with me?" It was a rhetorical question, and Bruce didn't wait for a response. "After you left, I paged you and you called me back. I forget why—I had a question about something. Anyway, at the end of that phone call, you told me about the problems you were having getting rid of a tenant, and about how it was a major financial drain for you. And then you said something to the effect that maybe the only way to get rid of her was to kill her, and you asked me about the death penalty in Massachusetts."

Pierre felt his face begin to flush. Why was Bruce bringing this up now? "But I was only joking around. You knew that."

Bruce nodded. "You're right. I thought you were only kidding. I didn't know for sure, but that's what I thought. But then I couldn't get it out of my mind, that you might possibly have been serious. I mean, I hardly knew you then. So I typed up a memo to memorialize our conversation, and I was going to give it to the police. I mean, just in case you were serious, I didn't want to have it hanging over my head. And if you were only kidding, then what difference would the memo make, right? So I typed up the memo on the computer at work. But then I realized that I better check the attorney ethical rules—before I gave the memo to the police, I wanted to make sure it was allowed under the attorney-client confidentiality rules. And it turns out I wasn't allowed to tell the police, because I didn't *know* you were going to commit a crime, I only had suspicions. So I added a note to the memo explaining why I wasn't giving it to the police. Then I stuck the memo in my briefcase, and pretty much forgot about it."

Bruce paused here and picked up a pen. Holding it between his thumb and forefinger, he tapped it repeatedly on his yellow legal pad. He turned away from Pierre and focused on the pen. "And that's where I really fucked up, Pierre. Last week sometime, I lost my briefcase. I think I left it on the subway. Anyway, according to Mike's sources at the police department, somebody found it and turned it into the police. And they read the memo."

Pierre stood up and began pacing. The three men had been gathered at one end of the rectangular table, and Pierre was now walking in a U-shape, up one side of the table, around the end, down the other side, stop, back up the side, around the end, down the first side, stop, and then back up again.

Bruce waited a few seconds, allowing Pierre to digest the meaning of this revelation. "Anyway, Mike knows all about this already, and he's looked at it from a legal point of view."

Callahan took his cue. He spoke with a noticeable Boston accent, which Pierre guessed was an asset rather than a liability in a Boston courtroom. "There's actually a silver lining to this cloud, Pierre. The memo—along with some other things—definitely makes you the prime suspect, but the good news is that the DA can't use the memo as evidence since it's hearsay. And they can't compel Bruce to testify against you because you can assert the attorney-client privilege."

Pierre stopped pacing and leaned heavily onto the back of a chair. "That sounds like great news, not good. Right?"

Callahan responded. "Well, it's not that clear-cut. And before I even get to that, let me tell you what they've got on you so far, because it's more than just the memo. They've got motive: you couldn't get rid of her as a tenant, so why not knock her off? They've got opportunity: you said you were at the Sox game that night, right?"

"Yeah, with Bruce actually." Bruce nodded.

"And you've got a neighbor who saw you come home around 12:30. But the game ended in plenty of time for you to drive over to Arlington Street, kill Charese, and still get home by 12:30. So you really don't have an alibi."

"I was stuck in traffic, for God's sake."

Callahan smiled at Pierre comfortingly. "Look, Pierre, I don't doubt that, but it really is going to be next to impossible to prove. Unless you gave somebody the finger or something, and they remember you."

"No, nothing like that."

"So motive and opportunity are there. Plus they've got evidence."

"You mean the memo?"

"No, more than that. They took some tire prints off of Charese's arm and some carpet fibers out of her fingernails. They've identified the car she was killed in as a blue or gray Grand Am, 1988, '89 or '90."

Pierre felt the blood rush to his cheeks. He leaned over and pounded his fist against the table. "What is going on here? My car's gray. 1988 Grand Am. This is un-frigging-believable." Pierre took a deep breath, exhaled, and slumped into a chair.

"Yeah, I know. But that's all they have so far, unless they found anything at your apartment today, which they don't think they did. I don't think it's enough to convict on, without the memo or Bruce's testimony. So let's talk about that. First of all, the attorney-client privilege can only be used if you and Bruce had an attorney-client relationship at the time you guys had the conversation. According to Bruce, the client in the Fenway Place deal was actually Howard Plansky, not you."

"Yeah, but I'm part owner of the property with Howie."

"That's what Bruce told me, and that definitely helps us. The problem is, we'll have to prove you're a part owner."

"So why can't we just show the partnership agreement?"

Callahan turned to Bruce, who addressed Pierre. "We can, Pierre, but there's a problem with that, too. After you called tonight, I pulled out the Fenway Place file to get the partnership agreement out. I had some time to kill while we were waiting for you, so I was just looking through the rest of the file. Remember at the closing, I asked the woman from the RTC to send me copies of all the documents from this transaction so we could make a closing binder for you?" Pierre nodded. "Well, my secretary made a nice binder, all organized and indexed and everything. So I was looking through it tonight, and I found this."

Bruce handed both Callahan and Pierre a one-page typewritten document entitled *Bidder Affidavit*. Pierre looked at it, noticed his signature on the bottom, and looked back up to Bruce. "So?"

"Well, look at paragraph 4(b). It basically says that the bidder, under the pains and penalties of perjury, states that there will be nobody in the bidder's ownership group who is in default on any RTC mortgages. Now, I had no idea you had signed this affidavit; from the date at the bottom, it looks like you signed it when you submitted your bid. And you never gave me a copy. If I had known about it, I never would have set up the partnership to make Felloff one of the partners, since he is definitely in default on his RTC mortgage. But I never saw this document until tonight."

Pierre stared down at the paper, rubbing his forehead.

Callahan took over. "The problem, of course, is that if we show them the partnership agreement to prove you were a client of Bruce's, there also going to

see that this Felloff character is part of the ownership group and that you lied
on your affidavit."

"But I didn't know when I signed the affidavit that we were going to make
Felloff a silent partner." Pierre directed the statement to Callahan.

"I appreciate that, Pierre. And I agree that it's a valid distinction from an ethical point of view. But legally, it's irrelevant. You signed the affidavit. Then you
signed the partnership agreement, right above Felloff's signature. So you're
going to have trouble arguing you didn't know Felloff was part of the ownership group."

Pierre took a deep breath, slowly exhaled it through pursed lips. "So what? If
I can beat the murder charge, what do I care about the affidavit anyway? I mean,
what's the punishment for lying? It's not like anybody got hurt by it."

"It's not that clear-cut a choice. For one thing, they can use the fact you lied
on the affidavit as evidence that you aren't telling the truth when you say you didn't
kill Charese. But to answer your question, I heard of a guy in Texas who got two
to three years—I'll have to check to get the exact range for you. Plus, forfeiture
of the property you bid on."

Pierre swallowed. "Even so, compared to murder, that's nothing, right?" He
continued to direct his questions to Callahan. "And who's to say they'll even
make the connection between the affidavit and the partnership agreement?"

"Good point, they might miss it totally. It is sort of an obscure point. But let's
not get ahead of ourselves. First of all, the police aren't anywhere near finishing
their investigation. They may find more evidence. If they don't, my bet is that
they know they don't have enough to convict you on—all they would really have
is a car match, and a jury isn't going to convict on just that. But, from the guys
I talked to, they're pretty convinced you're the killer. They may agree to some
kind of plea bargain, but they'd rather try the case and lose than let you walk
away. Maybe the deal is that you plead guilty to defrauding the RTC, or maybe
it's just a straight plea on a reduced charge if they miss the RTC thing. But either
way, you might want to start getting used to the idea of some jail time."

Jail time. That was the second time somebody had mentioned it, and Pierre's
thoughts turned to Valerie. If he went a day without seeing her, he felt empty. A
weekend away was intolerable. How could he bear to miss months, or even years,
or her life? To become a stranger to his little, precious angel girl. Carla might
understand, but how do you explain to a toddler that Daddy was going away and
wasn't coming back until...until when? Until she was old enough to ride a bike?

To read? To drive? He slumped into a chair and turned his glistening eyes away from Bruce and Callahan. Finally, he spoke. "What if we took it to trial?"

"Well, I think your chances would be pretty good, as it stands now. But I'll be honest with you Pierre; it'll cost you a fortune. I charge two hundred fifty bucks an hour, and you're probably talking close to a thousand hours. More if there's an appeal. Not to mention other costs like expert witnesses and private detectives. So it could go as high as a half million dollars. And no guarantee you'll win. And then they still might come after you on the RTC thing, because they'll be pissed they lost."

Bruce spoke up. "You know what else, Pierre? Even if you're acquitted, just being tried for murder will taint you for a long time. I mean, who's going to choose to go alone with a suspected murderer into an apartment when there are dozens of other brokers around? Look, Pierre, I know the thought of jail time is scary, but if Mike can cut a deal for only short time and forfeiture of the property, that seems to be a better decision than risking a murder conviction. Not to mention the half million even if you're found innocent."

"How much time are we talking?"

"Is your record clean?"

"Yeah."

"Maybe six months, but that's just a guess. More if their case gets stronger."

Pierre tried to picture the scene. *Valerie, honey, Daddy has to go away for a little while. I'll be back after Christmas, when the snow starts to melt.*

But what was his other choice? *Valerie, honey, I'm sorry Sally's mommy won't let her come over to play, but you have to believe me when I tell you I would never try to hurt anyone, and I definitely wouldn't kill anyone.* Even if he were acquitted, the stigma of being arrested for murder would never fade. And it would attach to his children. No. He wouldn't make his children pay for his mistakes.

Pierre dropped his head onto the table, covered his face with his arms. There really was no choice. He would be miserable in jail, but at least they'd be able to lead a semi-normal life when he got out. But six months away from his precious girl was almost too much to bear.

57

[June 25, 1990]

Shelby arrived at her office Monday morning to find a message from Dominic Mazzutti on her desk. She reached over to pick up the phone and grimaced as her blouse rubbed against the back of her sunburned shoulder, courtesy of an unplanned nap on the beach in Newport, Rhode Island. She'd been having trouble sleeping since Charese's death, and the Margarita-induced nap had been refreshing, although irritating—in addition to the painful sunburn, she had been forced to repeatedly resist the efforts of another resident of the beach house to spread ointment onto her burned skin. Why was it that a weekend at the beach caused otherwise mature men to revert back to their frat boy days?

"Detective Dominic?" She surprised herself with the playfulness in her voice. She accepted the fact that men found her attractive, and was normally more careful about sending the wrong message. She quickly toned it down. "This is Shelby returning your call."

"Thanks for calling back, Shelby. I just wanted to update you. We found nothing at Prefontaine's house Friday night. We're sending some stuff over to the lab, but we're not hopeful it'll turn into anything. The car was clean, and so were his clothes. Either he was very careful, or he didn't do it."

"What's your gut tell you?"

"I'll be honest. Everyone thinks he's the guy, what with the memo and the car match and the motive. But it doesn't smell quite right to me for some reason. I mean, I watched the guy during the search on Friday, saw his wife and kid, saw where he lived. It's a lot to risk, and for what? So the guys having financial problems, but who doesn't, you know? It wouldn't surprise me if he did it, but I'm not sure, you know? What about you?"

"I don't know either. At first I didn't think he had it in him, but what do I know? It's not like I'm experienced in this kind of stuff. So I guess I defer to you. How about the other suspects?"

"Nothing new. We've checked the car rental companies—nothing to tie either Jeffries or Krygier to the Grand Am. But it's possible they rented the car under a false name; there were hundreds rented that weekend in the Boston area. We're showing pictures of Jeffries and Krygier to the rental company clerks, but so far no match. And no gray Grand Ams stolen that weekend, although it's also possible they "borrowed" a car for a few hours and returned it before the owner knew it had been taken. But neither of those guys seems to me like they would know how to hot-wire a car. I think if one of them did it, they paid a professional. We've got our sources checking that angle, too."

"Well, the video hasn't turned up yet, as far as I know. I least I haven't seen it on the evening news."

"Yeah. We went through her apartment; it wasn't there. By the way, what does this do to Charese's lawsuit?"

"It's pretty much over. Without her testimony, it'll be hard to prove her case. Plus, who really cares anymore? I had trouble even getting her sister to come up and claim the body and pack up her personal items. Personally, I'm not psyched about fighting for a big judgment that would just go to her family. They sound like real assholes."

"Speaking of assholes, have you spoken to Jeffries at all?"

Dom's comment surprised Shelby. Dom didn't really know Reese at all—did he respect Shelby enough to simply adopt her opinion? "No. Since he's a suspect I thought I should avoid him. Actually, Jennifer thought I should avoid him."

*　　　　　*　　　　　*

An hour later, Dom phoned back. "Hey, I just heard something. Prefontaine hired Mike Callahan to represent him."

"I don't recognize the name."

"You'll be hearing it a lot if you stay in the DA's office. He's one of the best at negotiating plea bargains, cutting deals, that kind of stuff. I mean, he's got cousins and brothers everywhere. And an uncle that's a lawyer in your office."

Great. Another lawyer taking advantage of the system. Anybody out there become a lawyer because they care about justice? "I don't know any Callahans working here."

"Not a Callahan. Reardon. Bobby Reardon's his mother's brother."

"Yeah. I know him. He's one of the senior guys in Homicide."

"Anyway, the thing about Callahan is that he almost always plea bargains. He hardly ever goes to trial, mostly because the guys that hire him are guilty and are just trying to cut the best deal they can. So I'm not sure why Prefontaine would hire him if he was innocent."

*　　　　　*　　　　　*

Pierre was just trying to stay in his normal routine, to just live his life. He had spent the weekend with Carla and Valerie—alternating between rejoicing in their company and spiraling into periods of depression. Through it all, Carla was a rock. "We'll get through this like we get through everything. This may go without saying, but in my heart I know you're innocent. I also know that innocent men don't normally go to jail in this country, especially middle class white men. The important thing is to keep living our lives."

And so on Monday morning, Pierre was in the office. There was plenty to keep him busy. First of all, Charese's death meant he could finally sell her apartment. The police lines were down, and he was meeting a painter at the apartment that afternoon—once it was painted, he would list it for sale. Hopefully, within a couple of months, he would have a $35,000 payday. Blood money or not, it would stabilize their finances for at least a few months. He would simply have to hold on until then.

In addition, there was plenty of work to do at Fenway Place. Pierre's goal was to have 95 percent of the apartments rented by September 1, and he felt the way to accomplish that was to invest some money into making the property more attractive to tenants. In a slumping economy, it was natural for landlords to cut back on repairs and maintenance of their properties. And Felloff had been no exception. The result was that vacancies had increased and rents had decreased.

But, unlike other landlords, Pierre and Howie had the luxury of having purchased the project at a price that allowed them to pour money back into the property. Pierre's theory was that people had to live somewhere, and a superior property would attract the best tenants at the highest rents. And Fenway Place, though a bit neglected, was a superior property; Felloff had thoroughly renovated it only three years earlier, and it offered many modern amenities that other apartment complexes did not.

In the two weeks since they had purchased the property, Pierre had used rental income from the project to paint the vacant apartments, sand and polish the hardwood floors, and install tasteful window blinds. He had also hired a landscaping company to keep the grounds neat and attractive, and had worked out a deal with the local cable TV company to provide basic cable services to all the tenants at the landlord's expense. And it seemed to be working. He had already rented a couple of apartments for July 1, normally a slow period in a college town like Boston. And he had gotten decent rents.

Pierre took out a calculator and worked through some rough calculations. If he could reach his goal of 95 percent occupancy, and if he continued to rent the apartments at the same price as the new tenants were paying.... Pierre punched more numbers, then allowed himself to smile for one of the first times since the police had knocked on his door. If things went as planned for the September 1 rental season, the property would be worth close to $8 million. That was a full fifty percent more than they had paid for it. Pierre calculated his share of the profits—$1.3 million.

Unless the RTC found out about the affidavit and made him forfeit it all.

58

[July 19, 1990]

"Hi, Mike. This is Bruce Arrujo. Have you heard anything?"

"Nothing earth-shattering. The police haven't come up with anything new. I think they're getting close to the point where they've got to make a decision."

"How strong do they think their case is?"

"Well, I sent over the partnership agreement to establish the attorney-client relationship, and they conceded that the privilege exists. So they know their case isn't great. My sense is that if they thought they had enough to get a conviction, they would have arrested Pierre already. It's been five weeks now since the murder. They don't like to make an arrest and then lose at trial—it's bad publicity for the DA, and he's got an election coming up. And it's not like there are crowds of people demanding justice for the victim in this case. So it looks pretty good."

"Did they pick up on the RTC fraud angle?"

"Not yet. I don't think they even know about the affidavit. I think what's happening is that I'm dealing with the state on the murder case, and all they care about is state law. It's really only the Feds who would care about the RTC fraud. The state people probably have never heard about this whole RTC bidding procedure, so it hasn't even occurred to them to look for the fraud. And the Feds aren't involved in the murder investigation, so they're not around to tell the state people what to look for. And I'm sure not gonna tell them. So, things are looking pretty good."

Bruce pounded his fist into his thigh. "Yeah, that's great news." Idiots. That's why they couldn't get jobs in the private sector.

*   *   *

Bruce dug through his Fenway Place file, searching for a name. There—Andrea Cameron. He walked to a pay phone on the street corner and dialed her number.

"RTC. Andrea Cameron speaking."

"Hi. I don't want to give you my name, but I think you should look into the Fenway Place auction. The guy who won the bid was in cahoots with the developer, Sebastian Felloff. The Suffolk County District Attorney's office has a copy of their partnership agreement."

CHAPTER

59

[August 6, 1990]

Jennifer Palmer had called a meeting for Monday afternoon to discuss the Charese murder case. In attendance were the Division Chief, Shelby and Dom Mazzutti.

Jennifer got right to the point. "Charese Galloway was murdered June 16. Today's August 6. It seems to me that this investigation has hit a dead-end. We've got a possible car match on Prefontaine, and we've even got motive and opportunity, but I don't think it's enough to get a conviction without the lawyer's memo. Everybody agree?"

Dom and the Chief nodded. Shelby appreciated that Jennifer waited for her nod before proceeding. "So it seems we have three choices left. One is that we can just keep digging for evidence and hope something comes up. Dom, where are you on new leads?"

Dom shifted uncomfortably. "Nowhere, unfortunately. We've checked the surveillance cameras in the office buildings and convenience stores to see if they picked-up the car. No luck. We've questioned every prostitute we can find to see if they saw anything. Nothing. We searched the neighborhood dumpsters and the ones near where Prefontaine lives. Lots of trash, but no evidence. We searched his house and car. Nothing. We've looked at the hired killer angle. None of our sources have heard anything. Something else may come up, but I have no idea what or when it might be."

"So if we find something new, it would just be dumb luck." She smiled at Dom as she said it, as if to make sure he didn't take it personally.

"Yeah."

"Thanks, Dom. So that's one choice—hope we get lucky. Second choice is to do nothing and just let Prefontaine walk. If we choose this we're making a tacit statement that we think he's innocent. Dom and Shelby, you guys know this case best. Dom, what's your gut tell you?"

"I think Prefontaine did it. At first I didn't think so, but then when I saw Arrujo's memo, I started to go back and forth. And when he hired Mike Callahan as his lawyer, that sealed it for me. The thing is, it just doesn't smell like a random homicide to me. And that leaves us with our three main suspects. It could be that either Jeffries or Krygier did it—or, more likely, hired someone to do it—

but I still put my money on Prefontaine. There are too many things that otherwise have to be chalked up to coincidence: the car match, him being downtown that night, his financial situation. Not to mention the lawyer's memo. It all seems to fit together. Unless someone was framing him."

"Like who?" Shelby knew that Jennifer would not let a statement like that go by unchallenged.

"Again, could be Jeffries or could be Krygier, although Jeffries seems less likely to me because the video hasn't turned up."

"Any evidence to support a frame-up theory?"

"No.

Shelby spoke up. "I'm not sure I buy the frame-up theory anyway. I mean, there's no way Krygier or Jeffries could have orchestrated the lawyer's memo, right? Or Pierre being downtown that night. Which, by the way, seems a little strange—why is Arrujo socializing with Prefontaine if he's worried Prefontaine might be planning a murder?"

Jennifer responded. "Well, we all know lawyers that would dine with the devil in exchange for a large retainer. I don't think there's anything to that. But I agree with you on the frame-up theory; I don't see any evidence for it. So, Shelby, bottom line—who do you think killed Charese? Dom's already given us his opinion."

Shelby had thought about little else over the past seven weeks. If Pierre was the killer, letting him go just because they couldn't put the Arrujo memo into evidence made her want to quit and go find a new career. The law was supposed to be a search for justice, not a contest between lawyers over who could find the most loopholes. How could she dishonor her family's death by devoting her life to a judicial system that let yet another killer go free on some technicality? She had not taken a job in the DA's office to be part of a system where rules were more important than truth.

Yet she wasn't convinced they had discovered the truth. Pierre could have committed the murder, but was she so certain of it that she was willing to send him to jail for the rest of his life? To destroy a family, much as hers had been destroyed? The words of one of her law professors kept coming back to her: *Our judicial system is based on the tenet that it is better to let ten guilty men go free than to put one innocent man in jail.*

She took a deep breath. "I'm sorry if this sounds like an over-analytical response, but this is where I am: My guess is that Pierre Prefontaine murdered Charese. But if I were on a jury and heard this evidence and had to decide if he was guilty beyond a reasonable doubt, I'd vote for acquittal."

Jennifer immediately tested Shelby. "Even if the lawyer's memo were part of that evidence?"

Shelby knew she couldn't back down. A man going free because of reasonable doubt was different than a guilty man going free because of a technicality. "Yeah, even with the memo as evidence, I think I'd still have too much doubt to vote for a conviction." She half-expected the ghosts of her family to pop into the room and condemn her, but the only voice she heard was Jennifer's.

"All right. I agree with Shelby—no jury would convict on this evidence, especially since we can't introduce the lawyer's memo. But both Dom and Shelby think he probably did it, so I'm not thrilled with the thought of just letting him walk if we can help it. That leaves us with our third choice—take our pound of flesh by nailing him on this bullshit little RTC fraud thing. It's not much, but he did lie when he signed the affidavit, and that's a federal crime. It's better than letting him walk, and maybe we get lucky and he blabs to his cellmate or something. Comments?"

The Division Chief spoke for the first time. "That's fine with the DA. He's not under any pressure to solve this case—most people have already forgotten about it. Plus he scores a few points with the Feds. So it's your call, Jennifer."

"Anybody else?" Shelby thought about speaking up. Wasn't putting someone in jail because of a technicality the same as keeping someone out because of one? But Jennifer's proposal to take a pound of flesh was something she hadn't yet had time to consider, and she knew that her thoughts were not well formed on the matter. She let the moment pass. "All right then. I'll contact Prefontaine's lawyer and offer him a deal." She looked back at Shelby. "But I'll make it clear to him that, if new evidence comes in, his client can still be prosecuted."

Shelby remained in her chair as Dom and the chief stood up to leave. She reviewed the meeting in her mind—had Jennifer orchestrated the whole thing? It made sense. The chief tells Jennifer to end the investigation and move on to other cases—the investigation has hit a dead end, the office is under-staffed, and the public doesn't care about a dead prostitute anyway. But Jennifer doesn't want to rule by fiat, so she calls the team together for a little strategy session. First she gets Dom to admit that the police have exhausted all leads. Then she gets Shelby to admit she wouldn't vote for conviction. Then, she "elicits" the chief's permission. Finally, just in case Shelby is having mixed feelings about letting Charese's killer walk, she agrees to push the RTC fraud thing and tells Shelby they can still prosecute for murder if they find new evidence.

Shelby realized she had a lot to learn.

60

[August 9, 1990]

Bruce looked at his calendar. August 9. One year ago today, he had been standing at a urinal trying to not splatter himself with urine when he heard Gus' voice through the door of a toilet stall. Now, it was Gus who had stepped in a huge pile of horse shit when he committed the Gardner heist, and it had splattered all over Bruce.

But the stench was beginning to dissipate. Slowly, Bruce was receiving new assignments. They were small, and it may have been nothing more than a function of half the lawyers taking August vacations and needing somebody to do their work while they were away, but Bruce was hopeful—even desperate—that he might last just a few more weeks. Things were on track, but he needed the firm as a base of operations. And to give him continued credibility with both Pierre and Howie. He wondered how much use for him either of them would have if they found out he had been fired.

Bruce, as he often did, looked out at the boats on the river. The cargo ship *Prefontaine* was a rich one, and he was on course to intercept it. But he knew his own ship was taking on water quickly. If he couldn't pirate the *Prefontaine* soon, it would be too late.

His secretary buzzed him. "Mr. Prefontaine is here. Attorney Callahan called to say he'd be right along."

Bruce went out to meet Pierre in the reception area and escorted him to a conference room.

Pierre sat down heavily. "Thanks for being a part of this meeting, Bruce. Mike says he's cut the best deal he can for me, and that I need to make a decision. I was hoping to get your input before I do."

"Of course, Pierre. Anything I can do to help. I still feel like this whole thing is my fault, because of the memo."

Pierre mustered up a response. "Hey, it's not your fault. It wasn't like you were trying to set me up or anything. And I appreciate you refusing to talk to the DA's office. Mike tells me it would have been worse for me if you had been cooperative."

"Hey, I'll do whatever I can to help you. I don't want to see you go to jail." That last part, at least, was true. Bruce was having trouble with the thought of Pierre rotting away in prison, even for a few months.

Callahan knocked softly and entered the room. "Sorry I'm late. All right. Here's what the DA's office will do. They can't agree to anything officially, but they've exhausted all of their leads and they're willing to close the investigation."

Pierre cut in. "What does that mean?"

"Basically, it means that nobody will be assigned to continue looking for evidence in the case. That's not to say that new evidence won't walk in the door, but the cops won't be out looking for it. The ADA—Jennifer Palmer is her name—will give me her word on that, and I'm comfortable telling you her word is solid. Now, this is different from a plea bargain. A plea bargain would protect you even if new evidence comes up."

"Why can't we do a plea bargain then?"

"Because, under the law, you can plea bargain a murder charge down to manslaughter, for example, but not down to something really minor like assault. And I don't think you're willing to plead guilty to manslaughter, right?"

"Right."

"But, they want something. Apparently one of the ADAs was friends with the victim, and she can't stomach just seeing Pierre walk. Bad luck for you that it had to get a little personal. So they want you to plead guilty to making false statements to the RTC. Now I don't know how they got clued-in to the whole RTC thing, but somehow they did. One year sentence, six months suspended, out in three or four months on good behavior. $10,000 fine. Plus forfeiture of your ownership interest in Fenway Place."

Pierre pounded the table. "Shit! The jail time's bad enough, but I knew that was coming. But couldn't you keep the forfeiture out of it? I've been working my ass off over there. I've got the place almost filled up for September 1."

"No, there's really no leeway there. The RTC has the final say on the settlement terms, and they can't just let you rub their face in it and then expect to keep the property. That's the type of bad publicity that ends up in hearings on Capital Hill just when the RTC is looking to increase its budget."

Bruce spoke up. "What's your interest worth over there, Pierre?"

"Just over a million, conservatively. Probably closer to two million by this time next year if things keep going smoothly."

Bruce feigned surprise. "That much?"

"Yeah, believe it or not. Remember, I get 80 percent of the back end of the deal. So if I can add a million dollars of value to the project, I get $800,000 of that. To add a million in value, I need to raise rents by $100,000 per year—that's how you figure the value of real estate, just multiply the yearly rents by ten. And to do that, I only need to raise rents about $40 per month on each unit. That's the great thing about real estate—if you own enough units, even a small rent increase can translate into millions of dollars. Then if I raise rents again $25 next year, plus decrease the vacancy rates.... Well, the numbers speak for themselves."

Callahan spoke. "Well, Pierre, we could take the false statement charges to trial. But if you lose, and the case is pretty strong against you, the sentencing guidelines for making a false statement to the RTC are tied to the amount of your profit. Using rough figures, they'll argue you bought a $8 million property for just over $5 million. The guidelines for that are 37 to 46 months in jail and a fine of between $7,500 and $75,000. Plus, you'd still have to forfeit the property. Not to mention that the murder investigation would be hanging over your head."

"Mike's right, Pierre. What they're offering sounds like a pretty good deal to me. Plus, it seems to me that if you're going to have to forfeit the property, you might as well do it now instead of putting any more work into it."

"Good point, since I don't get paid for the management. Will the forfeiture affect Howie at all?"

Callahan answered the question. "No. It's not a forfeiture of the property, just of your ownership interest in it."

"All right. I'll talk to Carla and give you a call tomorrow, Mike."

$$*\qquad\qquad*\qquad\qquad*$$

Pierre heard the sound of little feet running toward the door as he fumbled with his key in the lock. He opened the door slowly, careful not to swing it into a self-propelled, hug-seeking toddler. She was nineteen months old now—the plan was for her to have a sibling on the way by now, but the world hadn't exactly cooperated. Pierre took a deep breath and put on a happy face.

"Hi, my pumpkin angel." He scooped her up and fell backwards onto the ground, Valerie giggling on top of him. "You're such a big girl that you knocked Daddy right over."

Carla smiled at them and moved around Pierre to close the apartment door. She bent over and kissed him on the forehead, which Pierre had noticed had become an increasingly large target over the past year. It was the least of his problems, but he had a quarter inch sunburn strip where his previously hair-covered scalp now nakedly braved the sunshine. He looked up at Carla—she hadn't lost any hair, but there were a few gray highlights that weren't visible last summer.

She tried smiling casually, but he could see the concern in her eyes. "How did it go?" It was tough enough for him, but he knew it must be even tougher for Carla. She had to sit at home with a toddler and just wait for him to arrive home with more bad news. And although she had never said anything, he knew, in her most private thoughts, that she must have had at least a shadow of a doubt about his innocence. There were too many things pointing at Pierre, and Carla was too analytical, and the human brain simply too curious, for her not to wonder.

"Not great. The deal is three to four months in jail and forfeiture of my interest in Fenway Place. Plus a $10,000 fine. They'll close the murder investigation. But there's no guarantee they won't re-open it someday, although Callahan's pretty confident that won't happen unless they find important new evidence against me." Pierre paused to wipe some Valerie drool off his cheek with his shirttail. "Bruce and Callahan both think it's the best we can do."

Carla stared off into the distance, out the window, toward a young couple in the park pushing a baby stroller. "All right, let's put this whole thing behind us then. We can manage without you for a few months. What about the ten grand?"

"The closing's set for next week for the Clarendon Street condo. We should net about $40,000, so we'll be okay for a while."

"And after that?"

"Well, I think I'll try to do some more foreclosure deals. The one good thing that's come out of this is that Bruce has been right there for me. Maybe he can steer some more deals my way after I get out."

61

[August 10, 1990]

"Hi, Howie, this is Pierre."

"Hey, partner. Have you heard the one about the three priests and the nun?"

"No, but Howie I don't really feel like hearing it right now."

"Oh. All right."

"Sorry, but I've got some stuff to tell you about. Got a few minutes?"

"Sure."

Pierre summarized the case against him for Charese's murder. "So, the bottom line is that they don't think they can convict me, but they want to nail me on this RTC fraud thing. It's such a piddly little thing, I can't believe I'm going to jail over it."

Howie was silent. Pierre couldn't help but thinking that none of Howie's books told Howie what to do in the case of his partner being accused of murder. When he finally did speak, Pierre was a little surprised at the question. "Pierre, did you kill her?"

Nobody had actually asked Pierre that question. Not his lawyer, not Bruce, not even Carla. "No, Howie, of course I didn't. I went to the Red Sox game with Bruce Arrujo, then I got stuck in traffic driving home."

"All right. Fine. So what happens next?" Howie didn't really sound like someone who was without his doubts.

"Well, I'm going to accept this deal with the District Attorney. That means the RTC is going to auction off my ownership interest in Fenway Place."

"You mean I'm going to have some stranger as my partner, managing the project?"

Yeah, life is tough, Howie. I'm going to jail over a deal I did together with you, plus I lose my profit. And you're complaining about having to break in a new partner. "Unfortunately, yes. I'll stay on for another month to get the September transition complete. That's part of my deal with the RTC, plus I wouldn't leave you hanging like that." *Although it's tempting.* "Then, if the judge agrees, I start my sentence on September 15—I'm hoping to be out by Christmas. Anyway, they're going to hold the auction the middle of October, with a thirty-day closing. So you might want to get a property manager in there right away to work with me. He can manage the project after I leave and before your new partner takes over in November."

"What do you think it'll go for? Maybe I'll make a bid."

Nice guy. I just took one for the team, and now your main concern is whether you can take a bite out of my dead carcass. "Well, based on the new September rents, I figure my interest is worth about a million. But Bruce thinks that, since my interest is so convoluted and the deal is so complicated, there won't be much bidding. Basically, somebody would be buying the right to manage a huge project for no salary, and to wait for their profit until after you've been paid back your half million plus 20 percent profit. Even I wasn't thrilled with the arrangement at first, so you can imagine what some outside investor would think. Anyway, you should give Bruce a call to talk about it."

"Yeah, I will. And Pierre, tough break. I know how much this project meant to you."

How about an offer to throw me a few bucks for the time I spent getting the property running so well? "I'll tell you, Howie. It's not the project so much as not being home with my girl that has me really bummed out. I'm really worried she's going to forget me. You hear stories about guys going away in the army or something and they come back and the kids don't even know who they are."

"I hear you. But when you do get out, you're going to have to feed her. And Fenway Place would have kept you guys in caviar. I have to admit, you took the piece of cake with all the frosting when we split up this deal."

"Yeah, too bad I choked on it. Anyway, I've still got a couple of other properties with you, and they're doing well. We'll survive. By the way, Carla will take care of the other properties while I'm gone."

"Fine. She has my number if she needs me?"

"Yup." *And thanks for volunteering to take care of things while I'm gone.*

"All right. I'm going to call Bruce to see about bidding. I'll be talking to you soon."

Pierre took a deep breath and paused for a moment. They were supposed to be partners. So why was Pierre the only one taking the hit here? He wanted to tell Howie to go fuck himself—the only reason Pierre was the one who signed that affidavit was because Howie was in California at the time. But Pierre knew he needed to maintain his business relationship with Howie. He would be coming out of jail unemployed and a convicted felon—he wasn't in a position to be burning any bridges. He forced himself to end the conversation on a light tone.

"Oh, Howie, one more thing. Please, no jail jokes."

"Not even stuff about soap in the shower?"

"Especially that." Actually, Pierre wasn't too worried. He would be serving his time in a minimum-security federal prison, sometimes referred to as the Country Club. But just in case, he planned to spend the next month at the local martial arts studio; he used to be a brown belt in tae kwon do, but his skills had grown rusty since Valerie's birth.

"Oh, all right. But when you get out, you're fair game again."

*   *   *

Bruce recognized Howie's voice. "Shit, Bruce, what's going on up there with Pierre? I just got off the phone with him."

Bruce was wondering when Howie would call. "You know, Howie, I really can't talk about it too much. You understand that it's confidential because of the attorney-client relationship, right?"

"Yeah, I guess so. But what about this forfeiture thing?"

"Well, assuming it happens, the RTC will set up a sealed-bid auction for Pierre's interest in the Fenway Place partnership."

"Well, I'd like to bid. I don't want some stranger running this deal. Plus, it sounds like it might go cheap."

"I see your point, Howie, but I think you should be careful. So far the RTC has only gone after Pierre. But they could go after you, too, technically. I mean, you knew about the Felloff thing, right?"

"You're right. I hadn't thought about that. You mean my half million could be at risk?"

"Could be. If I were you, I'd just lay low and not do anything to get the RTC's attention. You didn't sign the affidavit like Pierre did, but they could try to go after you anyway since you're Pierre's partner.

"Good point, but let's get one thing clear: *I'm* not the one who strangled my tenant."

"Well, we don't know that Pierre did either, but that's not the point. The point is that the RTC is just one giant bureaucracy, and they care more about paper than they do about people, so to them this whole affidavit thing looks like a big deal."

Howie didn't respond for a few seconds. "So you think I shouldn't bid?"

"I wouldn't. They might think you were rubbing their face in it, you know? Or they might think you're just a straw for Pierre."

"Well, what happens if somebody else buys it?"

"Basically, they would step into Pierre's shoes. They would have to manage the project, and they could take Pierre's share of the profits."

"What if they fuck it up?"

"Good question. Under the terms of the partnership agreement, the manager is required to provide 'professional management services'—that includes giving you monthly reports and getting yearly audits. Besides, don't forget, it'll be in their interest to manage the property well, otherwise they don't make any money. But if they're incompetent or start stealing from you, we can go to court and try to get them replaced with a court-appointed receiver."

"That sounds like it might be a bit expensive."

"Yeah, you're right. Any fight you have with the new guy is going to be expensive. But do you mind if I make a general comment?"

"Shoot."

"It seems to me that you'll be better off if whoever buys Pierre's interest gets it really cheap. That way they won't have to steal from you to make a nice profit. My experience has been that even basically honest people do things like steal and cheat when they're desperate. But, when everyone's making lots of money, even scoundrels can get along okay."

Howie was silent. Bruce guessed he had never read such a theory in any of his books. "I can't argue with that at all. Got any ideas how to make sure it goes cheap?"

"Well, as a matter of fact, I do."

Howie laughed. "I thought you might."

"First of all, the RTC has asked Pierre for a rent roll so that bidders can evaluate the property. I know the rents are going up in September, so why not have Pierre send over the current rent roll as of today instead of waiting until they go up next month?"

"Good idea. And we're fixing up some of the apartments, so the vacancy rate looks really high this month. I'll tell Pierre to send the info over right away. Anything else?"

"Yeah. They've also asked Pierre for a general description of the property. I don't see why Pierre shouldn't also include information about the lawsuit brought by the adjoining property owners over the oil contamination."

"But we've settled that suit, right? Felloff took care of it."

"Actually, the final documents haven't been filed yet, so technically it's still a liability. To the tune of $1.6 million, if I remember correctly. In the interest of full disclosure, I think Pierre should mention it. Remember, our goal is to make it look like Pierre's profits from the deal are hit or miss so somebody can buy it cheap. I really do think that's your best protection against somebody ripping you off."

"Sounds good. In the meantime, I gotta get somebody over there so Pierre can teach them the ropes before he goes on his little mini-vacation. Do you know of anybody?"

"I'll check around."

62

[September 13, 1990]

"Come on Sweetheart, Daddy's going to bring you to bed now." Pierre scooped Valerie up off the couch. He could smell the baby shampoo on her wet hair as she wrapped her tiny arms tightly around his neck and nestled her cheek on his shoulder.

As he carried her into her room, she squirmed and reached for an object over Pierre's shoulder. "Go swimming."

Pierre turned and saw her bathing suit hanging from a hook on her door. He and Carla had taken Valerie to the ocean for the day, most of which they spent with Valerie on Pierre's shoulders as he waded into the water and then turned and ran before the breaking surf could touch Valerie's dangling toes. The sounds of her giggles still resonated, like the crashing surf, in his ears.

"I'm sorry, my girl, I can't take you swimming tomorrow. Daddy has to go away for a little while."

She leaned away from his shoulder to look into his eyes. She reached her arms out to him, as she would if she wanted him to lift her into his arms. "Va'rie come."

"I'm sorry, but I can't bring you with me, Sweetheart." Pierre lowered her slowly into her crib. Valerie's big green eyes looked up at him expectantly. "But Grandmother and Grandfather are going to come stay with you and Mommy for a little while. That'll be fun, right?"

Valerie thought about it for a moment, but didn't answer. Pierre tried to stifle a laugh—he was never thrilled to see Carla's parents either. "I bet they'll bring you presents, because you've been a good girl. But even if they don't bring presents, it will still be fun to play with them."

"Gama and Papa?" Valerie preferred Pierre's parents—for one thing, they actually got down on the floor and played with Valerie.

"They'll come visit also, and you and Mommy can go visit them too, but not tomorrow. Now, my big girl, Daddy won't be here when you wake up in the morning, or even the morning after that. I have to go to work. But I'll come home as soon as I can, okay?"

"Mama stay here?"

"Yes, Angel. Mommy will stay with you."

She pointed up at Pierre's eyes. "Wawa. Wawa."

Pierre wiped his eyes. "You're right, smart girl, there is water in Daddy's eyes. Daddy has a little boo-boo in his eyes."

She looked up at him, pensive, and reached up a pair of open hands toward his face. "Va'rie kiss boo-boo."

"Oh, thank you. I would love you to kiss my boo-boo." He pulled her face up to his and cradled her in his arms while she kissed his eye. Then he fluttered his eyelashes on her lips until she giggled, and lowered her back onto her sheets.

"Thank you for those wonderful kisses. Now it's time to go to sleep. Remember, Daddy loves you very much."

Valerie cuddled up with her doll, rolled onto her side and closed her eyes. Pierre waited fifteen minutes until she had fallen asleep, then kissed her gently on the cheek. He closed her door quietly, washed his face and blew his nose in the bathroom, and went to join Carla in the living room.

*   *   *

Carla poured a large glass of wine and waited on the couch for Pierre. "So, Honey, talk to me. What are you thinking?"

Pierre sat on the floor at Carla's feet. She stroked his hair gently as they took turns sipping from the glass. It was a custom borne of their early days together, when a single wineglass was the best Pierre's bachelor kitchen could provide. "Well, I'm trying to be optimistic. It's only three or four months, and it's not like it's hard time. Plenty of people go away for that long, even longer if there's a war or something. The worst part will be not seeing you and Valerie."

Carla laughed lightly. "Nice try, big shot. You can deal with not seeing me, it's Valerie that's breaking your heart."

Pierre wrapped his arm around her knee. "I have to admit you're right. I can talk to you on the phone, and you understand that four months isn't that long a time and that I'll be back. But will Val even remember me when I come back? It scares the hell out of me."

"It might take a few days, but I bet within a week things will be back to normal. We'll visit as much as we can, assuming you end up somewhere close by. Plus we have plenty of video of you, so I'll make sure she watches it a lot."

"Good idea."

"But when I asked what you were thinking, I meant are you mad or anything?"

"No, not really. I did sign the affidavit, so it's my own fault."

"Don't you feel like you got screwed by the system or anything?" Carla knew it was the type of question that would give Pierre a lot of trouble. In many ways, he was a critical and open-minded thinker. He questioned everything, saw both sides of an argument, was willing to change his mind in the face of strong persuasion. But when it came to his country, Pierre was blindly patriotic. It would simply never occur to him to question the behavior of the government. In Pierre's mind, the government was infallible, just like the Pope. It was a giant blind spot. Carla often wondered just what it was in the Catholic upbringing that allowed otherwise intelligent and critical thinkers to blindly accept the infallibility of their religious leaders. Whatever it was, in Pierre's case it had also blinded him to the faults of his government as well.

"Actually, the system worked pretty well. I mean, without the system, they could have used Bruce's memo against me and probably convicted me for murder. So in a way, I feel pretty lucky."

Carla was tempted to remind him that no innocent man should feel lucky to be going to jail, but on their last night together she didn't want it to sound as if she was questioning either his innocence or his country. "Well, I don't. It seems to me that if anybody messed up, it was Bruce, not you. He's the one who had the bright idea to make Felloff a partner, and he's the one who wrote that stupid memo. I mean, he's supposed to be protecting you, right?"

"Come on Carla, we've been through this all already. He didn't even know about me signing the affidavit, or else he wouldn't have suggested making Felloff a partner. And as for the memo, I can't really blame him. He's a young lawyer at a big firm; he was just covering his ass in case something happened."

"I still can't believe he wouldn't have known you were just joking around."

"Well, it was over the phone, so sometimes it's hard to tell. And he didn't really know me that well at the time. Besides, the bottom line on this whole thing is that my behavior wasn't exactly angelic. I did sign that affidavit."

"But you didn't know when you signed it that you were lying."

"That's just a technicality. When it comes right down to it, it was wrong for me and Howie to gain an advantage over the other bidders by teaming up with Felloff. It was an unfair advantage, and I deserved to be punished."

"Oh, Pierre, you drive me crazy with this Catholic guilt stuff! I love you dearly, but I'm not buying this 'Fallen Angel' crap. Everyone else is out there stealing and cheating, and you're condemning yourself because you cut a little corner. Well I, for one, have no problem with what you did. Nobody got hurt. Nobody suffered."

"Maybe you're right, Carla. I haven't quite figured it all out yet."

The two sat silently for a few minutes, sharing the single wineglass, thinking separate thoughts. Finally Pierre spoke. "You're comfortable lying to your parents?"

"Yeah, no problem. They firmly believe in telling lies to protect others from bad news, anyway. I told them you had to go away for business for a few days, and invited them up for a long weekend. After that, they wouldn't expect to see you until Thanksgiving anyway, and I'll just call them the day before and tell them you have the flu or something. It shouldn't be too tough to fool them; these are people who didn't know we lived together for a year before we got married."

"Thanks, I appreciate you not telling them."

"I understand. And I appreciate how much you want to win them over. And you are making some progress, believe it or not."

"Well, only because even they can't help but love their granddaughter."

"What's not to love?"

"Exactly."

"Want to make another one?"

"Right now?" Pierre spun around and looked up at Carla. She had shaken her hair down and unbuttoned the top button on her cotton blouse.

"Why not? We've finally got a few bucks in the bank. And if I'm going to be stuck here alone for months, I might as well be doing something productive. Besides, with you gone, I'll only have to take care of one kid, not two, so I'll have plenty of time and energy to nurture. And it'll be extra insurance against you falling in love with your cellmate."

"You are an incredible woman." Pierre pulled her down off the couch and buried his face in the warm, sweet nape of her neck.

Trouble at Sea

63

[October 23, 1990]

Bruce dialed a number in California. "Hi Howie, this is Bruce Arrujo." *And, much to my surprise, I'm still employed at Choke, Suck and Steal.*

"Hey, Bruce, how are things on the wrong coast?"

"Actually, Howie, if you're on the left coast, doesn't that make us the right coast?"

"Touché. What's up."

"Well, I went over to the RTC this morning to see what I could find out about the auction. You know bids are due tomorrow, right? October 24."

"Yeah, I knew it was sometime this week."

"Well, so far only five people have signed in to inspect the files. Some guy named Cathgart, from Texas. Two more from Boston that I've never heard of—Anthony Davis is one and Rosanne Luccia is the other. Ever heard of them?"

"No."

"I'll ask around. Also some Arab company out of New York; they had a lawyer from Springfield in reviewing the files for them. And finally some corporation out of the Netherlands Antilles—that's an island that rich investors use to set up shell corporations. It has good tax benefits and some strict privacy laws."

"Only five, huh? I know there were over twenty people registered to bid when Pierre and I bought the property back it in May."

"Yeah. At first I was a little surprised at how little advertising they did for this auction. I've seen one small ad in the *Globe* and one in the *Journal*. But then I started thinking about it. You've got some bureaucrat over at the RTC who was in charge of an auction a few months ago and the highest bid was $5.4 million, right? So now the same guy is in charge of an auction to sell the same property again, but this time only a minority ownership interest. And the winning bidder interest isn't entitled to a penny until $5.4 million has been repaid to the RTC and the other partners and until some guy named Howie Plansky has been paid 20% interest on his money. So how does this bureaucrat look if all of a sudden some cowboy comes in and pays big bucks for the minority interest? Do you think they congratulate him for a job well done? They might. But I bet our bureaucrat friend is far more worried that some citizen's group at the next set of hearings on Capitol Hill will ask why the RTC didn't get a higher price a few months ago for the whole property if a minority interest is worth so much more today. He's probably thinking that he won't get promoted no matter how much it sells for, but he might get fired if it looks like he messed-up on the first auction."

"Sounds like a good theory. I know that Andrea woman who was in charge of the closing was on the ball. Not bad looking, either. But she was just somebody's assistant. She didn't call the shots. So you could be right."

"Well, whatever the reason, there doesn't appear to be a lot of bidders. And it could go pretty cheap—all they've got in the file is the August rent roll, and it shows high vacancies and low rents. Plus, the oil contamination lawsuit stuff's in there."

"Damn. I wish I could bid."

"I know, but it really would be risky. You've heard the expression about bears, bulls and pigs?"

"You mean the one with the farmer's daughter?"

"No, Howie. I mean the one that goes: 'Bears make money, and bulls make money, and pigs get slaughtered.'"

Howie laughed loudly. "That's a good one. So you think I'm being a pig?"

"Well, I think you'd be taking an unnecessary risk by bidding. You've got yourself a nice profit already."

"Yeah. I guess you're right. You're the boss. I pay good money for your advice; I guess I should follow it."

"All right, then. If I hear anything about the bid tomorrow, I'll give you a call."

"Thanks for your help, Bruce."

"My pleasure."

Bruce hung up the phone and left the office. He told his secretary he was going for lunch, took the elevator to the ground floor of the high rise, and walked into the bank on the ground floor of the building.

He got in line behind a dozen other customers, most of them professionals with deposit slips in hand. *How many of these people have any clue how badly these banks are managed?* he wondered. He had just finished reading a book about Edward Ponzi, the infamous Bostonian after whom a whole category of investment scams was named. In the early 1920's, professionals and laborers alike had lined up—blocks at a time—to invest in Ponzi's company. Ponzi, of course, didn't really have a company at all. He simply took money from his new investors and used it to repay—with generous interest—his earlier investors. These investors spread the word about their profit, thereby attracting even more investors. Eventually, of course, the house of cards collapsed, but not before thousands of people had lost millions of dollars.

That old appraiser, Samuel Leumas, was right—many Massachusetts banks were little better than Ponzi's company. On paper, they were solvent, and even profitable. They had taken deposits at five percent and lent the money out at ten percent. Unfortunately, the loans were secured by apartment buildings and office towers and strip malls, properties that were worth far less today than they had been when the banks first made the loans. From the banks' point of view, however, to actually recognize this loss in value would be tantamount to a declaration of insolvency. So the banks had entered into a ritualistic dance with their borrowers in which the borrower agreed to repay the loan at a later date—with all accrued interest, of course—and the bank agreed to give them a "grace period" to allow the economy to "stabilize". It reminded Bruce of the way Soviet workers described their economic system: "We'll make believe we're working if you make believe you're paying us." The arrangement allowed both the bank and the borrower to delay the day of reckoning, but it did nothing to add to the underlying solvency of the banks. Yet depositors continued to line up and hand over their paychecks. And even if the federal government insured the deposits, it did so with the public's tax dollars.

Bruce reached the front of the line and handed over a twenty-dollar bill. "Could I have two rolls of quarters please?" He thanked the teller, left the building, and went into a movie theater down the street. He wanted some privacy to make a phone call, but didn't want to use his office phone. He figured a theater during the workday would afford some privacy.

He called the operator and asked her how much money a twenty minute phone call to Springfield would cost. He knew he would not be on the line for the full twenty minutes, but he did not want his Springfield lawyer to know he was calling from a pay phone so wanted to avoid the intrusion of a metallic voice requesting more money. He dialed the number and dumped a handful of quarters into the slot.

He adopted his accent. "Yes. I am the man Ahmed Bahery. Is the lawyer available for to speak with me?"

The attorney picked up a few seconds later. "Mr. Bahery, I've been expecting your call."

Bruce had sent a letter to the attorney a couple of weeks earlier, prepared by Bruce himself on his office computer one night. Bruce typed so many of his

documents himself that it no longer surprised the support staff and other attorneys to see him hard at work at his computer terminal.

The letter requested that the Springfield lawyer enter a bid of $182,230 on
behalf of Arab Acquisitions for Pierre Prefontaine's interest in the Fenway Place
property. It was all the money Bruce could scrounge together—profits from the
sale of the two condos he had bought and sold, money he had saved from his
salary, lines of credit he had been collecting over the past year, two month's
worth of bills that had gone unpaid, coins dug out from under the cushion of
his couch. It reminded him of playing Monopoly as a kid and using every last
dollar he could find to put up hotels on his properties.

He was fairly confident that the other bids would be far less than his, and he
had considered bidding less, but eventually rejected the idea. This was the score
he had been waiting for—a seven-figure profit, a completely hidden interest, an
untraceable path back to him. Not to mention the fact that, once he paid off
Howie, the rental income would pay him another $100,000-plus per year. No
wonder losing the property had upset Pierre so much. So why risk it all by trying to save a piddling $50,000 or so on the bid price? He would take his best
shot, and happily subsist on stale bread in a cold apartment for a few months if
his bid was successful.

"Yes, thank you. You have received my letter?" Bruce had actually driven to
New York state to mail the letter because he didn't want the Springfield attorney
to see a Boston postmark. With the letter, of course, he had enclosed a generous retainer check.

"Yes, and I have reviewed the files at the RTC offices for your bid, as you
requested."

"Good. And do you decide the asset is acceptable?" Bruce didn't give a damn
what the lawyer thought, but it concerned him that the RTC might be suspicious
if his trust purchased the asset without anyone even first reviewing the files. So
he sent the lawyer up to Lowell, and now had to listen to him babble about what
he found. Bruce asked a couple of obligatory questions, listened to the answers,
checked his watch to make sure they didn't go over the twenty-minute time limit,
then moved to conclude the conversation.

"Well, I think I am quite satisfied, and I thank you very much for your work.
Would you please to prepare the bid and send it to RTC?"

"Yes. I will use the same trust we've been using. And you still want to bid the
amount you put in your letter—$182,230?"

"Yes, that is the number I wish." Bruce thanked him and ended the call.

64

[October 24, 1990]

Bids were due by 5:00, and Andrea had told Bruce that she would be sticking around for at least another hour after that to field calls from curious bidders.

It was now fifteen minutes after five, and Bruce, in the last hour, had visited the men's room three times, gone for a walk around the block, and besieged his wastebasket with an aerial assault of crumpled-up paper basketballs.

Finally he could wait no longer. He phoned Andrea. She picked up on the fifth ring, just as Bruce had begun to wish her dead for lying to him about staying until six. "RTC, Andrea Cameron speaking."

Bruce quickly regained his composure. "Oh, yes, Ms. Cameron. This is Bruce Arrujo. I'm the attorney for Howie Plansky, and I met you yesterday at your office."

"Yes Mr. Arrujo, what can I do for you?"

"My client is curious to learn who his new partner is going to be. Understandably so. Can you tell me the results of the Fenway Place auction?"

"Of course. There were actually two bids within a thousand dollars of each other, and then everyone else was way behind."

Bruce shifted in his chair. He could feel a bead of sweat drip from his underarm and run down the side of his body. He began to speak, then remembered he had to first unclench his teeth. He coughed to cover up the grunt and tried again. "Really? Can you tell me who the high bidder was?"

"Yes. It was an offshore company, from the Netherlands Antilles, I believe. Collateral Acquisition Corporation. High bid of $183,000, even. Beat the second-highest bid by less than eight hundred bucks."

Andrea waited for a response. There was none.

"Mr. Arrujo? Are you there? Mr. Arrujo? Mr. Arrujo?"

Battle with a Pirate

65

[October 30, 1990]

Since his conversation with Andrea Cameron, Bruce had spent six days walking the rocky coastline of the North Shore. When walking didn't calm him, he ran on the deserted beaches until he collapsed from fatigue. He lived in his car, although he hadn't driven it since he arrived in Marblehead; on warmer nights, he slept on the beach—or, more accurately, napped between periods of staring at the stars—and awakened himself with a swim in the frigid waters. He didn't shave, and hadn't bothered to wash the salt water off his skin.

On his second day, a Thursday, he had walked to a convenience store to buy a toothbrush, some food and a bar of soap. He had also called his secretary—he told her he was in a Vermont hospital with a severe viral infection, and asked her to inform the firm's managing partner that he would be out of work for another few days. Otherwise, he had had no contact with another human being.

Mostly he watched the sailboats.

Not once did he see a boat capsize. Not once did he see a boat run aground. Not once did he see a crewmember fall overboard. Not once did he see even the most inexperienced captain, in the most unseaworthy boat, lose the battle to sail another day.

So how could he have so misjudged the winds and the currents and the tides and..., yes, most of all, his own sailing abilities? How could his plan—so carefully and methodically crafted, so thoroughly and painstakingly detailed—so suddenly fail in such a titanic fashion?

He ran through the Fenway Place auction again in his mind. He simply couldn't have miscalculated that badly. It just didn't make sense—there was no way that anyone else would value Pierre's interest so highly. In a booming market, there was always too much money chasing too few deals, and people would take silly risks and overpay for the privilege of sleeping with sugar plumbs dancing in their dreams. But money was tight now, especially for real estate people—most investors were just struggling to pay the mortgage. Anyone who did have a wad of cash had his choice of prime properties at huge discounts. So why buy a minority interest in a leveraged property with mediocre cash flow and oil contamination liability?

Why?

Adrift and alone, the question was the hunk of driftwood Bruce clung to, the one thing preventing Bruce from descending rock-like to the ocean depths. The answer wouldn't right his ship, but every ounce of his intellect demanded an explanation. It was traumatic enough to find himself shipwrecked, but it was paralyzing to not know what had caused the calamity. Whether swamped and splintered by a savage storm, or battered and broken by boulders lurking beneath blue-black waters, or made motionless by a morose and moody Mariah, the culprit was always visible, always apparent. This time, Bruce had been beaten up and busted open, yet he didn't know by what or by whom.

Bruce again turned his eyes toward the Atlantic, toward the sailboats skimming across the surface, sea spray splashing from beneath their bows. A particular boat caught his eye: three young women skillfully sailing a mid-size daysailor had drawn the attention of a group of young men racing through the harbor in a cigarette-style speedboat. Bruce watched as a couple of the guys raised beer bottles toward the women in salutation; the women ignored the gesture and angled away from the pursuing motor boat. The speed boaters apparently took this as a direct challenge to their manhood, and responded with a roar of engines and three bare asses. The women continued to ignore them, angling further away, but the speedboat easily flanked them and raced up alongside the sailboat. Bruce could hear their shouts over the motor boat's engine: "Show your tits. Show your tits."

Suddenly one of the men reached out, grabbed the railing of the sailboat, and pulled the two boats even closer together. He then flung himself over the railing and into the sailboat. Two of his friends quickly joined him, the three of them drunkenly staggered to their feet, and the remaining motorboys tossed them a few beers and raced off. The pirates had boarded.

Bruce turned away. The women, if they wanted, could probably just throw the guys overboard—the guys were drunk and not very big. More likely the women would just sail into the marina and call the harbormaster. Still, the pirates had ruined their sail.

Pirates had always been the scourge of the high seas. Ships could be durably built, mutinous crewmen disciplined, coastlines charted and mapped, bad weather—if not exactly predicted—skirted or ridden through by an experienced crew. But a pirate attack was unpredictable and usually lethal. No amount of planning or seamanship could prevent it, and few crews had the skill—or courage—to fight off the attackers. Indeed, sometimes the pirates attacked at night, slipping aboard under the cloak of darkness, their quarry oblivious to the danger that lay just beyond their own gunwale. Only after their ship was aflame, their on-duty crewmates dead, their treasures pillaged did the sleeping crewmen become belatedly aware of the peril to themselves and their vessel.

Bruce stood up and began slowly jogging along the shoreline. Pirate attacks. Sudden, unseen, unpredictable. A human variable capable of sabotaging even the most well planned and skillfully executed sailing voyage.

Bruce contemplated the unimaginable. Had he been stalked, raided and plundered by a predator even more skilled than he? Had the winning bid come not from some random real estate investor but from a cunning, calculating adversary?

Had he himself been the pigeon? Had he been so intent on the stalking that he had been blind to his own vulnerability?

Bruce increased his pace, his muscular legs now pounding the wet sand with rhythmic regularity, his toes curling into the sand at every impacting stride. He stopped briefly, vomited, snorted the vomit residue out his nostrils, then continued running. He forced himself to continue the analysis, to imagine himself as the unwitting foil.

He thought back over the past few months, trying to analyze the series of events. He was almost sure Pierre didn't commit the murder—he knew Pierre had only been kidding when he asked Bruce about the penalties for murder. So the fact that the killer's car matched Pierre's had been an incredibly lucky coincidence. As had the fact that Pierre happened to be at Fenway Park the night of the murder—Pierre's activities fit perfectly into a time-line supporting the theory that he was the murderer. Bruce couldn't have scripted the events better if he himself had been trying to frame Pierre.

What if someone had wanted to frame Pierre? What if the car match and Fenway Park were not merely coincidences? What if someone had simply learned what kind of car Pierre drove, rented an identical one, then stalked and killed Charese? And had done so at a time when he or she knew Pierre would be downtown and alone? Bruce cursed himself. How could he have accepted these coincidences as nothing more than lucky breaks? He had failed to examine them critically, failed until this moment to recognize how incredibly fortuitous the timing and circumstances of Charese's murder had been.

So who could have framed Pierre? Who else might have benefited from Charese's death?

Bruce stopped abruptly, and waded into the ocean again. He dove into a crashing wave, came out the other side, and began swimming parallel to the shoreline. He swam with his eyes closed, stroke after stroke, his internal compass guiding him. He tried to relax and clear his head—he sensed an understanding taking shape deep within his consciousness. He knew it was an understanding borne of instinct and intuition rather than of logic and analysis, and he knew it needed time to form itself, unimpeded by thought or reasoning. Stroke after stroke, he fought to resist the temptation to think, fought to keep his brain from interfering with the work of his gut. When the urge to think became too great, he held his breath underwater until his brain became totally consumed by his body's demand for oxygen.

Finally, exhausted, he dragged himself ashore. He knew that his intuition had unveiled the painful truth, and was waiting to share the information with his brain. Slowly, Bruce allowed his brain to lift the shrouds, to peek in, to see the face of his enemy.

He blinked the face away, then nodded in understanding. It was time for revenge.

66

[October 31, 1990]

Halloween. Bruce had been out of the office for almost a week. But it was time to return to the land of the living. It was time to put on his lawyer costume again.

He greeted his co-workers cheerfully, patiently answered their questions about his sickness. "Yeah, it was some rare virus. And of course I'm stuck in some country hospital up in Vermont. But they took good care of me. Matter of fact, I feel like a new person." They shook his hand, patted him on the back. Nobody bothered to ask why he was in Vermont on a Wednesday night. By nine-thirty, it was as if he had never left.

He went into his office and closed the door. His enemy had beaten him, beaten him out of a couple of million dollars. But he had survived. And his enemy had lost a crucial tactical advantage—Bruce had figured out the identity of his adversary.

But Bruce was realistic. He was fighting a defensive battle now. Success would be defined as denying his enemy the fruits of its victory. Anything more would be an added bonus.

He ignored his stack of phone messages and mail—he would deal with those later. He picked up the phone and called Andrea Cameron at the RTC.

"Hi, Andrea, this is Bruce Arrujo. Could you tell me if the successful bidder has closed yet on the Fenway Place sale?"

"As a matter of fact, they're closing tomorrow."

"Who's 'they'?"

"Good question. Some offshore corporation."

"Do you know who's representing them?"

"Actually, I don't. The whole thing's sort of weird. It's like they want to remain completely anonymous—the only person I ever talk to is the property manager they've hired to run the project. I've never even gotten a call from their lawyer."

"Could you give me the property manager's name? My client, Howard Plansky, just wants to touch base and see what's going on."

"Of course." Andrea gave Bruce the name of one of the large residential property management firms in the city. Bruce thanked her and hung up.

It was almost ten o'clock now. Bruce called Howie at home, knowing it was not yet seven in California. Howie answered on the third ring; Bruce could hear the sleep in his voice. "Hi, Howie, this is Bruce Arrujo. Sorry to call so early. Hope I didn't interrupt anything interesting."

"Jesus Christ Bruce, where have you been? I've been calling you for a week; you're secretary told me you were in the hospital up in Vermont or something. And no, you didn't interrupt anything."

"Good. Well, I'm back at my desk now. What were you trying to reach me for?"

"What's going on with Fenway Place? I talked to that RTC woman, and she said they were closing this week."

"Have you heard from anybody?"

"Yeah, some property management company called me, looking for the vacancy decontrol certificates. I guess we have the only copies. Beacon Management was their name. Ever heard of them?

"Sure. It's one of the biggest in the city. High fees, but they're honest and competent, from what I hear. So I don't think you have to worry about them ripping you off. Did you send them the certificates?" *Please say no.*

"No, I wanted to check with you first. Do you think I should? You know, without them, the whole property's not worth snot."

"Well, I think you just answered your own question. Don't forget, you still have a huge stake in this project, so you don't want it to go back into rent control. Besides, you're going to have to live with these guys as your partner, so it might be a good peace offering if you sent the certificates over."

"That was my feeling, but I wanted to talk to you first. I think Pierre left them in the safe deposit box. Carla has the key."

"You know what? I was going to call her anyway. Why don't I just arrange to have them sent over to Beacon Management?"

"Sounds good."

Bruce thought for a moment, then dialed Pierre's home number. Carla answered on the fourth ring. "Hi, Carla, this is Bruce Arrujo. I hope I didn't catch you at a bad time."

"No, not at all, Bruce. Just feeding Valerie. What can I do for you?"

"Well, first of all, I just wanted to check in and see how things are. See if there's anything I can do for you."

There was a slight pause before she responded. Bruce half-expected an answer like: "You've done enough already." Instead, he got: "That's nice of you to ask, Bruce, but we're all set. We've been spending a lot of time with Pierre's parents—they live in the area."

"How's Pierre doing?"

"All right, I guess. Actually, he's pretty depressed. And a little bitter. We're hoping he's home by Christmas, but it may not be until January or February."

"That really is just around the corner. So keep hanging in there."

"Thanks."

"While I've got you on the phone, do you by chance have the vacancy decontrol certificates for Fenway Place? They're the ones issued by the Boston Rent Equity Board that prove the units aren't under rent control. Howie thinks Pierre left them in the safe deposit box."

"Yeah, I know what you're talking about. Howie's right—I'm pretty sure Pierre put them in the safe deposit box before he…left."

"That would make sense. He probably got them from Felloff, and they're the only set of originals."

"Do you need them?"

"Well, Howie thinks—and I agree—that the new property manager should have them. Especially since there's only one set. The Rent Equity Board will do anything they can to make life miserable for landlords. Their latest thing is that they won't accept copies of the certificates as proof that the apartments aren't under rent control. They'll only take originals or certified copies of the originals. They say there's too much risk of forgery."

"Yeah, Pierre was telling me about that. That was one of the reasons he needed Felloff's help when he and Howie first made their bid. All the back-up documentation had disappeared from City Hall, so without the actual certificates, the property could be thrown back into rent control. He said that then it would be almost worthless."

Exactly. "So would you mind if I swing by and grab them? I wouldn't ask you to come all the way downtown, and I don't want to trust them to a delivery service."

"Sure. How does tomorrow afternoon sound, around four o'clock? That'll give me all day today and most of tomorrow to get over to the bank and get them."

"Perfect. Thanks, Carla."

"No problem. See you tomorrow."

Bruce put the phone down, stood up and stretched. He would spend another eight or nine hours opening mail, returning phone calls, and meeting with other lawyers at the firm that had worked on his cases in his absence. But his work for the day was done.

*   *   *

Bruce left the office at seven o'clock, grabbed a sandwich on his way home, then began preparations for the evening. As a child, Halloween had always been his favorite day of the year. No chance that his parents would forget it, like they sometimes did his birthday. No reason to jealously eye his brother's Christmas presents. Halloween evened the playing field: in their masks, all children were treated equally.

As a teenager, too old to trick or treat, he had begun a yearly tradition of putting on a Werewolf mask and, alone, prowling the streets—jumping out from behind bushes to scare people, howling to the moon in front of churches, flying off of sidewalks and onto the hoods of stopped cars.

Gus—who never passed on an opportunity to make insights into Bruce's psyche—once observed that Bruce enjoyed Halloween so much because it was the one day during the year when Bruce could take his mask *off*. Bruce remembered Gus' words: "Most of us are just people 364 days a year who get to dress up and act like monsters on the 365th day. You're the opposite. You're a monster who has to dress up and act like a human being for 364 days. Finally, on Halloween, you get to let your real self out."

Bruce always thought Gus was overstating it a bit. But, at this very moment in his life, he needed to be the monster that would not die, a creature that could survive a mortal wound and return to avenge that attack.

He would hunt down his enemy, haunt him like the ghouls and demons of a feverish nightmare.

67

Bruce arrived in front of Pierre's condominium building a few minutes before four o'clock, as he and Carla had arranged. He rang the bell and identified himself, and Carla buzzed the front door open.

He walked up one flight of stairs; she had opened the front door to the unit and was waiting for him. Even holding another man's baby, Carla was an alluring woman, and Bruce had to force his brain to stop remembering that her husband had been in jail for the last couple of months. "Hi Carla. And that must be Valerie; she's a beautiful little girl."

"Thanks, Bruce. Honey, this is Mr. Bruce. Can you say hi?" Valerie buried her face in her mother's shoulder. "Sweetheart, what's wrong? Can't you just say hi?" Valerie shook her head side-to-side, her little blond curls bobbing with every shake.

Bruce filled the awkward silence. "That's okay. It's probably good that she's a bit afraid of strangers."

"Actually, she generally likes strangers." Carla lifted her eyes from Valerie and looked at Bruce, deep into his eyes. The three of them were still standing at the front door of the apartment.

Bruce chuckled lightly, knowing it sounded forced. "Well, you know what they say: Kids and dogs are the best judges of character."

Carla laughed politely, started to turn away from Bruce to re-enter the apartment, then stopped. "I'm really sorry, Bruce, but I just didn't have a chance to get to the bank today. There was a huge line at the grocery store, then Valerie got fussy.... I think trick-or-treating last night wore her out. I tried calling your office, but you had already left. Could you come back tomorrow? I promise I'll have the certificates for you then."

Bruce felt his hand clench into a fist, and stuffed it into his pocket before Carla could see it. "Yeah, sure, whatever. After lunch okay, say two o'clock?"

"Perfect."

"See you then. Bye Valerie." Bruce tried to wave to Valerie, but Carla had already closed the door.

*   *   *

Bruce took the subway back to Pierre and Carla's apartment the next after-noon. He went into the foyer area, started to ring the bell, and saw a package propped up against the side wall with his name on it. He bent over and picked up a large brown envelope, with a note taped to the front. He read it: *Bruce—I had to run out for a few minutes. Sorry I missed you.—Carla.*

He opened the package—inside he found a stack of vacancy decontrol cer-tificates for Fenway Place. He thumbed through them; it looked like all 245 cer-tificates were there. *Thank you, Carla. I doubted you for a moment there.*

Bruce looked at his watch—barely two o'clock. He put the package into his briefcase, made sure the case was locked, and jogged two blocks to the main street. He quickly flagged a taxi. "City Hall please. Boston, not Brookline. Right in Government Center."

Fifteen minutes later, Bruce hopped out of the cab and onto the brick sur-face of City Hall Plaza. The autumn wind whipped across the barren plaza, and Bruce blew on his fingers to keep them warm. He remembered how he had wel-comed the cold the previous winter at the Marlborough Street foreclosure sale, how the other bidders had suffered as Bruce had used the cold as a weapon against them. The stakes were much lower then.

He entered City Hall and took the elevator to the seventh floor. Bruce went down one hallway, then another, before he finally found the Rent Equity Board at the end of a third. *Even finding these maggots is impossible, never mind dealing with them.* Bruce took a deep breath to calm himself—these were the same people who had killed his grandfather.

He found a clerk sitting behind a desk, waited for the man to look up from his newspaper. The clerk weighed close to four hundred pounds, and even the act of lifting his head seemed to tire him. "May I help you?", he wheezed at Bruce. Bruce could see the residue of lunch wedged between the man's teeth. *These people truly are parasites.*

"Yes. I would like to make certified copies of these documents." A certified copy was simply a copy of a document that included a certification—usually in the form of a governmental seal or a stamp—that the document was an accu-rate copy of the original. Bruce held up the decontrol certificates. "There are 245 vacancy decontrol certificates in here. I would like certified copies of all 245."

The clerk dropped his head back down and paused, as if re-marshaling his strength for more conversation. After a few seconds, he looked back up at Bruce. "Costs a dollar a page. We only take cash."

Bruce opened up his wallet—he had $40. "Can you start making the copies while I go to the bank?"

The clerk shook his head slowly from side to side, then rested for a moment. "Sorry. I have to have the money first. Told the same thing to a lady yesterday, and she had a crying baby with her. But it's our policy."

Bruce was tempted to grab the clerk by his jowls and twist his head off. *I don't give a damn what happened yesterday, you fat pig.* He fought again to stay calm, not wanting to make a scene that would cause the clerk to remember him. "I understand. I'll be back in ten minutes. You'll still be here?" It was Friday, and Bruce didn't want to wait until after the weekend to complete this task.

The clerk looked around the room, skeptical that there could be anything that could induce him to lift himself from his chair. "I'll be here."

Ten minutes later, Bruce handed over $245 and a stack of decontrol certificates. The clerk reached out slowly to take them, rotated himself in his chair, and put the cash and the documents on a shelf behind him. He rang a bell, rotated back around, took a deep breath and dropped his chin back onto his chest. Apparently another clerk, on the other side of the shelf, had responsibility for actually making the certified copies. Or maybe there were two other clerks—one to make the copies, and another to certify them.

Bruce decided it would be best if he just left the room. He waited in the hallway with a magazine.

*   *   *

An hour later, Bruce was on his way home with 245 originals and 245 certified copies. It wasn't even four o'clock. He would return to the office later, but for his next task he didn't want to risk being interrupted.

He turned left off Cambridge Street and walked up Beacon Hill along one of the side streets on the eastern face of the Hill. These streets were comprised almost entirely of nineteenth century rowhouses, usually brick or brownstone. Bruce's apartment was a small one—one room plus a bathroom—on the fifth floor of a brick rowhouse located near the foot of the Hill. Real estate agents liked to refer to these top-floor apartments as "penthouse" units, but anybody who knew anything about Victorian-era architecture knew that the upper floors of these buildings were actually the least desirable ones. The buildings were originally built for single family occupancy, with the ground floor used for cooking and cleaning, the parlor level for entertaining, and the upper floors for sleeping quarters for the family and servants. Since the second floor was where the master bedrooms were located, this floor—like the parlor level—was ornately constructed and detailed. The third floor housed the children and was less ornate. The top floor, however, housed the servants—the ceilings on this floor were low, there were no decorative moldings or carvings, the windows were small, and instead of mantled fireplaces small coal stoves heated the rooms. Not to mention the four flights of stairs.

But Bruce's penthouse apartment was moderately priced, and it offered Bruce the convenience of being located less than a five minute walk from both his office building downtown and the sailing club on the Charles River. And it had a door that Bruce could secure from the inside with a thick deadbolt.

Bruce swept aside the clutter on the apartment's only table—an old farmer's table he inherited from his grandfather—and took the original vacancy decontrol certificates out of his briefcase. He left the certified copies in the case. He made sure the table was clean, then placed the stack of certificates in front of him. He examined them closely—he knew what he wanted to do, he just didn't know how to do it.

The certificates were one-page documents consisting primarily of pre-printed form language attesting to the fact that the Board had conducted a hearing and had determined that the apartment unit had been found to have been voluntarily vacated by the tenant and was therefore now "decontrolled"—that is, no longer under rent control. At the top of the form there was a blank spot for the building address and apartment number to be inserted; at the bottom was a blank for the date to be inserted and blank lines for the signatures of the Board members who had officiated at the hearing.

Bruce thumbed through the stack of certificates. He noticed that all but twenty or thirty of them were dated the same date, April 28, 1986. This was not uncommon—typically a developer would purchase a building with many rent control tenants and "buy out" the tenants by paying them ten or even twenty thousand dollars. The developer would then file decontrol applications for these units and for any other units that had been vacated voluntarily in the previous few years. Since the landlord could charge market rent on the newly decontrolled units prior to obtaining the decontrol certificates as long as he put the rents into an escrow account, often these decontrol applications were filed in bulk and were handled together at a single hearing to save time and money on attorney's fees.

Bruce also noticed that, while the signatures of the Board members were made by blue signature stamps, the date had been written in by hand on each certificate. The person who had performed this task—Bruce could not help but picturing the hulking, wheezing clerk hunched over a stack of certificates—had apparently quickly grown impatient with the drudgery, because the "6" in "1986" was penned in such a way that the tail was not fully looped. That is, the bottom part of the "6" looked somewhat like the bottom part of a "C".

That was it then. The certificates were dated in blue ink, so Bruce pulled a blue Bic pen from his briefcase. He didn't actually care if the ink matched exactly, but he tested the Bic on some scrap paper to make sure the colors were not dissimilar. He then took the certificates and, one by one, added an elliptical line, joining the semi-looped portion of the bottom of the "6" with the point at the top of the "6". The effect was to turn the "6" into a "0", so that the date read "1980" instead of "1986". After completing a dozen or so, Bruce stopped and inspected his work. At a casual glance, the change went unnoticed. But on close examination, especially with a magnifying glass, it was apparent that somebody had tampered with the documents.

Bruce completed the alterations on the documents, put the documents in his briefcase, and looked at his watch. Almost 5:30. He called information, requested the number for Beacon Management, and phoned their offices. "Yes, how late do you stay open in the evening?"

"Somebody will be here at least until six o'clock, sir."

"And what is your address?"

The woman gave Bruce an address on Boylston Street, in the Back Bay. A fifteen-minute walk for Bruce. Plus five more to stop at the copy center around the corner to make copies of the altered certificates.

Bruce re-opened his briefcase and found a letter he had typed earlier in the day at his office. It was a cover letter from him addressed to Beacon Management, enclosing the Fenway Place vacancy decontrol certificates they had requested from Howie Plansky. Bruce took the letter, placed it on top of the stack of the altered original certificates, put everything into a large brown envelope, grabbed his jacket and went out to make a delivery.

68

[November 5, 1990]

Bruce knew that the altered vacancy decontrol certificates were like a cannon pointed directly at the ship of the owner of the Fenway Place project. Now all he needed was somebody to light the fuse.

He spent a few hours in the office Monday morning, then at around lunch time walked over the to Suffolk County Courthouse. Using an alias, he requested the entire file for Civil Case Number 89-1962, *Charese Galloway v. Roberge Krygier*. Somewhere in the hundreds of pages of court pleadings, he hoped he would glean a piece of information that would lead him to his fuse-lighter.

He began by making a list of the players in this almost comically tragic case. Under each name, he left three or four lines of blank space. His goal today was to fill these spaces with information about each of the players: Who were they, and why were they involved in the case? What did they hope to accomplish? What were they afraid of? In short, what were their hot buttons, and how could Bruce push them?

He started with the key players. Even though Charese was dead, he began the exercise with her. She was easy. She wanted revenge against Roberge, and she wanted money. She may also have been trying to re-claim some self-esteem. All of these would have been easy buttons to push. Except she was now dead.

He moved on to Roberge. Bottom line for him: he just wanted to go on as if the whole Charese chapter of his life had never occurred. He initially had simply ignored the complaint, and it looked to Bruce as if he might have continued to ignore it had a team of high-priced lawyers not suddenly appeared on his behalf. And even they were probably hired by his father. Bruce guessed that Roberge would have been happy to write a check to be rid of the whole sordid mess, especially since the check would be drawn on Daddy's bank account. He looked to Bruce like a classic rich boy who never developed the skills necessary to function in society. Now that Charese was dead, Roberge was probably praying that the case died with her. Obvious buttons to push: make noise about resurrecting the case; cause Daddy to cut him off; threaten to disturb whatever heterosexual bliss existed in his young marriage.

Bruce already knew a lot about Wesley Krygier, just from reading the papers. Bruce could see his silent hand in the hardball tactics Roberge's lawyers were playing. But Bruce could also see the desperation of a proud man trying to maintain and preserve the dignity of his family name. Bruce smiled to himself as he read through Roberge's attorneys' repeated requests—all of which were denied—that the court take steps to make the proceedings confidential. For Wesley Krygier, this case wasn't about winning or losing, it was about publicity. If his son lost the case, it might cost a few hundred grand. But the publicity could cost the family both its name and its fortune. So, Bruce wondered, why hadn't Krygier simply settled the case?

The answer, Bruce concluded, had more to do with issues of rent control than with the particulars of the Charese-Roberge love affair. Bruce had never met Reese Jeffries, but he felt that he knew him intimately. He was the young activist poring over the Cambridge rent control ordinance while eating cold Chinese food, the pony-tailed heckler chanting "Slumlord" at Grandpa, the sanctimonious rent board member whose jaw had shattered beneath Bruce's flying fist. Jeffries was all of those things, and Bruce—never having met him—hated him with a fiery passion. Bruce rubbed his eyes, tried to clear his head. *Don't jump to conclusions. This is too important.* He re-read Jeffries' arguments in opposition to Roberge's request that the proceedings be kept confidential. The arguments were passionate, almost venomous. Why should Jeffries care so much? The chances of victory for Charese would be largely unaffected by the court's decision on keeping the proceedings confidential. So why bother submitting a thirty-five page legal brief on the issue? Bruce knew the answer: for Jeffries, this case wasn't about Charese at all. Rather, it was about an opportunity to deal a serious blow to one of Boston's largest landlords and the man who posed a serious threat to the continued existence of rent control in the city. And Charese's death had taken that opportunity away, since her case had died with her. So Jeffries' button was obvious, bright red and smack in the middle of his forehead: give him another shot at Krygier.

Shelby Baskin. Bruce actually recognized her name—they had been at Harvard Law School at the same time. He made a note to check his yearbook later. He reviewed the pleadings—some were signed by both her and Jeffries, while others, such as the ones relating to the confidentiality issues, were signed by Jeffries only. Bruce pulled out the ones signed by her; he knew these were the ones she had drafted. He re-read them. The early pleadings, such as the original complaint, were well written and compelling, though not particularly passionate. As the case progressed, however, Bruce noticed that Shelby's writing became more forceful, more urgent. The last filing, only weeks before Charese's death, was almost desperate in its tone:

> *"... It is imperative that this Court put an immediate and final end to the Defendant's delay tactics in this case. The Defendant has on three different occasions in this action requested extensions to discovery deadlines; on one occasion, the stated ground for this extension was to allow Defendant and his wife to travel to the Cayman Islands for a two week vacation. But while Defendant is sipping pina coladas on the beach and working on his tan, Plaintiff is scrounging for food and wrapping herself in blankets to keep warm because she cannot afford her heating bills. Counsel for Plaintiff has personally witnessed a marked and frightening deterioration in Plaintiff's health during the pendency of this action, and said Counsel hereby implores this Court to heed the maxim that 'Justice delayed is justice denied' and to take immediate steps to prevent further delays in this case...."*

Bruce re-read the section, again comparing it to Shelby's earlier writing style. No doubt about it: Shelby had personalized this case; her client had become more to her than just a client. And now her client was dead. Did she believe Pierre was the killer? If not, Bruce was sure Shelby would jump at the opportunity to help find Charese's real killer. Hopefully, she had stayed in the Boston area after graduation.

Bruce returned the pleadings to the clerk. It had been a successful few hours—the players in this case all seemed to have complex agendas and motivations that transcended the facts and the issues of the legal action itself. There were plenty of buttons to push. Hopefully Bruce could push them in such a way as to trigger the gun pointed at the head of his enemy.

*   *   *

Bruce returned to his office and pulled out his Harvard Law School yearbook. Shelby Baskin was in the class behind Bruce, so she would not be pictured individually in his yearbook. But she would likely be pictured in some group picture of a club or other activity. He thumbed through the pages, quickly skimming the names beneath the group pictures. There. He found her name, beneath a picture of the *Harvard Law Journal* staff. He lifted his eyes to the picture, counted four faces in from the left in the front row. *So you're Shelby Baskin.* He felt his skin tingle, then closed his eyes and remembered:

It was near the end of his second year in law school, sometime late in the spring of 1988. The winter had been a harsh one, but it had turned suddenly, and a warm spring rain was falling. It was late at night—maybe one in the morning—when he finally left the library. He began to jog slowly toward his apartment, at first indifferent to the puddles, then playfully splashing his way through them.

In the faint light of the city, he saw that the Cambridge Common had become a giant mud puddle, and he ran for it. He stopped to take off his jacket, draped it and his book bag over a branch, and sprinted toward an open area. Two long strides into the mud, then he launched himself headfirst into a full body slide. The water was warm, and the mud soft. Bruce slid forty, maybe fifty, feet, before he came to a stop. Then he stood up and did it again. And a third time. He had now traveled to the far side of the clearing and was about to turn around and body surf his way back to his belongings when he heard a young woman's voice. She was just ahead of him, running toward a swing set. Her head was turned as she spoke, but Bruce could not see her companion.

"Come on, just one swing." Her voice floated to him in the nighttime air.

"Not me. I'm not putting this umbrella down—what if I catch a cold right before finals?"

"Okay, have it your way. But I feel like swinging in the rain. Get it? 'Swinging in the rain'?" The woman skipped over to a swing and began to swing. She sang: "I'm swinging in the rain, just swinging in the rain. What a glorious feeling, I'm happy again, I'm laughing again...."

Bruce could see her face as she swung in and out of the shadows cast by a nearby streetlight—a beautiful, confident, joyous face. Eyes glistening through the raindrops. Loose hair rising and falling as she fell and rose. Droplets of water running down her cheeks, joining her mouth in delighted song. A vision from a song his grandfather used to sing about enchanting mermaids.

Sensing his darkened, muddy presence, she turned her face toward him. Their eyes met, and she smiled through her song to him, urging him to continue his frolic, to share with her in the pure joy of living. He returned her smile, held her eyes for one, two, three swings, then broke away and ran. He dove, landed and slid, then twisted himself onto his back and slid even further, laughter and muddy water in his wake. He strained, unsuccessfully, to see her through the spray, but the night air transmitted her own sweet laugh across the watery clearing to him.

He stood up to slide his way back to her, then heard a distant voice. The male voice. "Come on, please, I'm getting soaked. Let's go home. We still might be able

*to catch the end of Letterman." In the distance he could see a figure, holding an
umbrella, moving toward the swing set. He watched as she hesitantly brought her
swinging to a stop and walked slowly to meet her companion. They began walking
away, his arm around her waist and his umbrella over her head.*

*In mid-stride she suddenly stopped, stepped out from underneath his shelter and
turned. Bruce watched her search for his dark figure. Her eyes flashed as they settled on him, and Bruce squinted—it was as if her eyes had captured all the world's
light and somehow reflected it back directly into his darkness. He held her gaze for
a few seconds, then her companion turned to retrieve her and guide her home, and
she was gone.*

He had looked for her around campus and in Harvard Square for the next
few weeks, but he never saw her again. Until the picture in the yearbook in front
of him.

He sat for a moment and reflected on his discovery. How much of life was
fated, and how much just coincidence? With a flick of his neck, he shook the
question away—he had work to do; answers to philosophical questions would
have to wait for a more leisurely time in his life. But, he had to admit, the yearbook discovery had put a smile on his face for the first time in a month.

He picked up his phone and called the Harvard alumni office. They had
hounded him for money since graduation—he had no doubt they did the same
to every alumnus, and would know exactly where Shelby Baskin was living and
working.

He was right, and the news was good: Suffolk County District Attorney's
Office. This was a huge bonus for Bruce—not only was she still in Boston, but
she was working in the very office that was in charge of the murder investigation.

Maybe he could do more than just deny his enemy his profit. Maybe he could,
subtly, point the DA's office to the real killer. A lucky break. It was about time.

*   *   *

Bruce left the office at 4:30 and jogged home. He threw on a pair of blue
jeans, a T-shirt and an old leather jacket, and continued jogging toward the LAP
offices.

He arrived at 4:50, just as the receptionist was gathering her things to leave for the day. He eyed her quickly—she wore plain clothes, making no attempt to distract from an equally plain face. He mustered his best smile. "Oh, I'm sorry, are you closing up? I heard there was a tenant rally coming up, and I wanted to get some information."

She looked him up and down, smiled back. "Yeah, here's a flyer. Thursday night at City Hall. The City Council is considering rolling back rent control, so we need a big turnout."

"Great stuff. I'll be there. Anything I can bring?"

"Friends, as many as you can."

"Actually, a buddy of mine is the one who told me about it. He's friends with a lawyer named Reese, I think—does that sound right?"

"Yeah, Reese Jeffries, he's one of our senior attorneys. He'll be there Thursday, running the show."

Bruce smiled. "I thought the President of the City Council ran the show."

The receptionist shook her head and smiled back. "Not in Reese's mind."

69

[November 8, 1990]

Three times over the past two days Bruce had been tempted to dial the District Attorney's office and ask for Shelby Baskin, only to talk himself out of it. She—or more accurately, the enchanted she of Bruce's memory—was becoming a bit of a distraction to him, and he wanted to make contact with her as soon as possible so that he could replace the almost surreal quality of their first encounter with something a bit more mundane. But he also realized that, for tactical reasons, he should first wait until after his encounter with Reese Jeffries. After all, with Shelby's help, there was a slight chance he would be able to put his enemy in jail. But with Jeffries' assistance, he could almost surely deny his enemy his profit, and maybe recapture it himself. So first things first.

The tenant rally that night was being held outside City Hall at five o'clock. Jeffries wasn't stupid—the City Council didn't meet until 7:30, but a five o'clock rally would be sure to provide lively footage for the six o'clock news.

Bruce again left work early, went home to change out of his lawyer uniform, then walked down to City Hall. He was forty-five minutes early, but he wanted the chance to observe Jeffries during the set-up period of the rally. It was then, absent the scrutiny of the press and hidden from sight from his unwashed followers, that Jeffries would be at his least staged. At some point during the evening Bruce planned to make contact with him, and he hoped to gain some insights into the man before that encounter.

What Bruce knew about him so far came from what he had gleaned from the pleadings in Charese's lawsuit, and from deductions Bruce had made based on Jeffries' academic and professional background published in a directory of Massachusetts lawyers. From the pleadings Bruce had concluded that Jeffries' primary objective was to champion the cause of tenants' rights. This conclusion was consistent with Jeffries' academic and professional history—Middlebury College in the late 1960's, with a major in sociology; two years off, probably to travel the country by van and protest the war; law degree from NYU; and a series of professional affiliations with non-profit organizations focusing on the liberal cause *du jour*: first human rights, then nuclear disarmament, then homelessness. Poster boy for the left. Trusted Lapdog of the liberals.

Now that Bruce watched him in person, he was a bit surprised to see a man who looked like he was organizing a political convention rather than an outdoor rally. Law students ran to fetch him coffee, assistants dabbed the sweat away from his face, activists dutifully assumed the positions he assigned to them and held their signs aloft. Bruce had assumed Jeffries would be just an older version of a Sixties flower child—sort of like Jerry Garcia in a blue suit, still intent on changing the world. But Jeffries seemed too comfortable to be a true radical. It was as if he was not so much interested in provoking changes in society, but rather in ensuring that his would be the loudest voice in the fight for these changes. He would never admit to no longer being a radical, yet he appeared perfectly comfortable in his role as emperor of the opposition to the establishment. The issues were not important; what was important was that Reese Jeffries was the top dog in fighting on the anti-establishment side of them, then could go home to his house in the suburbs.

Bruce watched him closely, watched his eyes. They usually gave a man away, especially a man who didn't know he was being watched. There it was. A quick wink directed toward one of the young female lawyers. And there. A step closer—within the range of intimacy—to the woman applying powder to his face. So maybe that was the key. Maybe here was a weakness Bruce could use to his advantage.

Bruce turned toward the young lawyer who had been the lucky recipient of the Jeffries wink. It had seemed to Bruce that she had been lukewarm to the flirtation. Maybe she had no desire to see the emperor in no clothes. Or maybe she had seen it already, and had been unimpressed.

"Hi, my name's Bruce. Is there anything I can do to help?"

"Actually, yes. I need somebody to read this to me." She spoke quickly, impatiently. She stuffed a three-page document in Bruce's hand. "It's the latest draft of the proposed ordinance filed by the landlord assholes. I need to see what they've changed from the previous draft. Read it out loud while I compare it to the older version."

"I think I can handle that."

"Good boy. Now read." She looked up and flashed a quick smile. "My name's Laura, by the way."

As Bruce read, she lit a cigarette, her eyes never leaving the page. Occasionally she would reach down and swig from a bottle of Diet Coke, but mostly she just puffed and read. Bruce could see that her teeth had yellowed a bit from the cigarettes, but otherwise she was fairly attractive—long curly hair, green eyes, the hint of full breasts beneath her baggy sweater.

She cut him off. "Stop. Read that again." As he did, she made notes on her text. "Go on."

They continued in this manner for ten minutes, until he had completed the text. "And they lived happily ever after."

She gave him a sardonic smile. "Thanks, asshole."

"Anytime. Any changes?"

"A couple. Nothing major. Who are you, anyway? I've never seen you before."

"Name's Bruce Arrujo. I'm actually a lawyer at Stoak, Puck & Beal."

She arched an eyebrow. "You mean 'Choke, Suck and Steal'? That explains your fluency with words like 'heretofore'."

"That's us. I work on the Steal side of the firm. Sometimes the Choke side."

"Oh. That's too bad. Well, what are you doing here?"

"I left the office early, jumped into a phone booth to change, and here I am. Ready to help make the world safe for tenants again. Just don't tell any of the partners at my firm that I'm here. They probably think this is some kind of Communist insurrection or something."

"Don't worry. You're secret's safe with me, *comrade*."

"How about you?"

"I'm on staff at LAP. Known to you big-firm types as a Lapdog. I usually do consumer protection stuff, but we're all helping out on this rent control fight."

Bruce could tell he had sparked her interest a bit, and knew it was time now to leave. He would come back to her later. "Well, let me know if there's anything else I can do. Nice meeting you." He shook her hand firmly, like he would a man's, smiled, then turned and waded back into the crowd of gathering rally participants.

The rally began a few minutes later, with Reese orchestrating the event for the television cameras. Bruce did his best to cheer and jeer, as directed, along with the other activists, trying to put out of his mind that these were the same people who had heckled his grandfather to his grave. Another minute or two and Bruce was sure he was going to pummel a fellow demonstrator who had eaten too much garlic for lunch, but then the cameras stopped, which also signaled the end of the demonstrating, and everyone watched quietly as Reese was interviewed by the television news reporters.

"Let me be clear about this. If rent control is terminated in Boston, thousands of tenants—including the elderly and the handicapped—will be forced to live on the streets of this city. And for what? I'll tell you for what—so that millionaire landlords living on estates in Dover can afford to re-stock their wine cellars and trout ponds. Since when do we in this country rob from the poor to give to the rich?" One of the LAP staff members cued the crowd, and it again cheered zestfully.

Bruce smiled. He knew the Dover millionaire was a reference to Wesley Krygier—he was glad that Jeffries still had Krygier in his cross hairs. It would make his job a bit easier.

After the last of the interviews were complete, Reese moved away from the reporters and re-joined the other LAP staff. Bruce caught Laura's eye, smiled, and walked over toward her. Reese was nearby, close enough to hear. "I know you think I'm a capitalist pig, but would you allow me to buy you a drink anyway? You know, use the product of some poor laborer's sweat to indulge my idle follies."

She looked up at him, a bit surprised. He noticed that she recovered quickly. "Sure. I'll be with you in five, although I'm not sure I like you referring to me as a folly."

"Great." Bruce then quickly turned and introduced himself to Reese, who had overheard his invitation to Laura and was eyeing him jealously. "Hi, I'm Bruce Arrujo." He reached out and shook Reese's hand, using two of his own. He made sure to speak loudly enough so that the other staff members could hear. "I thought that last interview was fabulous, Mr. Jeffries. I have a lot of respect for what you do."

"Well, uh, thank you."

Bruce knew his metamorphosis from romantic rival to reverent supplicator would throw Reese off-balance. He pressed on. "I'm an associate at Stoak, Puck & Beal, and I don't have much free time, but I'd really like to help out if I can—you know, volunteer work, whatever you need."

Reese puffed out his chest a bit, nodded. He was still leader of the pack, top dog.

"As a matter of fact, I invited Laura out for a drink to talk to her about what I could do to help. I'd be honored if you would join us. If you have time, that is, sir." Normally the "sir" would have been a bit much, but this guy seemed to eat it up.

Reese considered the invitation—Bruce guessed he normally didn't waste his time socializing with young male lawyers. But Reese might figure it wouldn't hurt to have Laura see the young buck fawning all over him. "All right, perhaps one drink, then."

Bruce beamed. "That's great. Just great. Thank you. I'll grab Laura, and we can go."

Bruce could see that Laura was surprised to see Reese joining them. He noticed that she was even more surprised at how obsequious Bruce was acting toward him. She eyed him questioningly: Are you the same guy who was so sarcastically self-assured just an hour ago?

One drink led to two, then to dinner. Most of the conversation was spent with Reese—and, to a lesser extent, Laura—regaling Bruce with war stories from the long-running battle between tenants and landlords. Bruce was attentive enough to keep Laura interested—and even flirtatious, to the extent he could be without appearing to be a threat to Reese—but spent most of his time playing rapt audience to Reese's soliloquy. Finally, over after-dinner drinks, he made his play.

"Hey, Mr. Jeffries—oh, I'm sorry, Reese—was that a true story about some millionaire in Dover stocking his wine cellar?"

"Oh yeah, he's one of our worst enemies. Wesley Krygier is his name—one of the biggest landlords in the city, and also the leader of the fight to repeal rent control. We almost ruined him last year, but he was able to survive, unfortunately."

"Oh, I remember. Is that the guy whose son was involved with a transvestite or something?"

Laura spoke. "That's the one. Reese was nice enough to send some pictures to the *Herald*. You may have seen them."

Reese seemed oblivious to Laura's sarcasm. "Yeah. I really thought that humiliating him would put an end to this little rent control crusade of his. But it actually just made the motherfucker even more desperate. He practically owns the City Council now, all the money he's given them over the past year. What we really need to do is to break him financially—see, the City Council doesn't care how much money he gave them in the past, they just care about what he can give them in the future. If they think the gravy train is slowing down, they'll abandon ship no matter how much he gave them over the years. Then he'll be lucky if he gets a single vote on this rent control repeal. But until then, he just might be able to pull it off."

Bruce was quiet for a moment, swirling the ice cubes around in his drink. He interpreted Reese's mixing of his train and ship metaphors as a sign the wine was doing its job. Bruce spoke softly, intently. "You know, I said earlier that I wanted to help. I may have some information that would be helpful against Krygier."

Laura eyed him suspiciously, Reese eagerly. Bruce addressed Laura first. "I see the way you're looking at me, Laura, and you're right to be a little suspicious. I had an ulterior motive when I invited the two of you out tonight—I wanted to make sure I could trust you enough to tell you what I'm about to tell you."

Bruce paused, took a deep swig from his drink, then continued. "You two are both lawyers, so you know that what I'm about to tell you is a violation of any number of ethical rules. But I feel strongly that there are issues and matters in play here that take precedence over our ethical rules. So here goes:

"A couple of days ago, a new matter came into our office, and I was asked to work on it. I'll skip the irrelevant details, but basically a client of ours bought an apartment complex in Boston known as Fenway Place. He bought it from the RTC at one of their auctions. The problem the client was having was that the vacancy decontrol certificates that he has for the property have been altered. The client noticed the alterations immediately, and wanted our legal opinion as to whether or not the certificates would be considered valid in their altered state. Unfortunately for the client, there are no other copies of the certificates, and the back-up documentation has been lost by the Rent Equity Board."

Bruce took another large sip, then continued. "Well, our conclusion was that they probably were not valid." He looked at Reese. "I don't need to explain this to you, since you're the expert in this area, but there is a presumption under the law that rent control exists; the burden is on the landlord to prove otherwise. The alteration to the certificates makes that proof difficult if not impossible." Bruce looked to Reese for affirmation, which was given in the form of a sage nod. "Well, I didn't think much of it until I asked who to bill my time to. The partner told me the name of the client was some offshore corporation, but the client billing identification number he gave me was the same number he had given me for another matter I had worked on just a couple of days earlier. For Wesley Krygier. I double-checked it, and I'm sure." There was no way that Reese or Laura could know that Krygier was not one of the firm's clients.

Laura grasped the ramifications right away. "You mean you think that Krygier bought a whole complex that he thought was decontrolled but it's actually rent controlled?"

"I don't just think it, I'm almost positive of it."

"How many units?"

"About 250 all together. Maybe 225 of the certificates have been altered."

"Holy shit!"

Reese was only a few seconds behind Laura. "You mean Krygier has 225 units that he's charging market rent for and they're actually rent controlled?"

"Exactly. I can't help you anymore than I have, because, quite frankly, I don't want to get disbarred. But it seems to me that it would be easy enough to independently verify what I've told you and you can just leave me out of it."

Laura jumped in. "Of course. It's simple. Just have one of Krygier's tenants challenge the rent. Krygier produces the certificate, then we challenge its authenticity. Then we bring a class action on behalf of all the tenants, challenging all the certificates. Plus we ask for back rent, tripled."

Bruce noticed a little spittle forming on Reese's lower lip. "It's perfect, absolutely perfect. Too good to be true. We'll have the rents rolled-back within six weeks—what a Christmas present for the tenants! I'm sure I can convince the City Council to wait until the first of the year to put the rent control repeal question to vote—they don't want to look like Scrooges, after all. And by the first of the year, Krygier will be on the hook for...let's see—225 tenants, overcharged by, say, $400 per month, average of two years each...two million dollars in back rent. Two million dollars! Which he won't pay, of course. But then the City Councilors will know the gravy train ride is over, and we win. Too good to be true!"

Bruce lifted his drink in salutation. *Too good indeed, you schmuck.*

*   *   *

[November 15, 1990]

Bruce waited a full week, then called Laura at the LAP office from the lobby pay phone. Her tone was polite, but distant—she had probably deduced that Bruce's interest in her had been less than sincere, and her ego was still having a little trouble getting over it. But Bruce figured she couldn't help but recognize the value of the gift Bruce had given them. Intellectually, at least, she would understood that a bruised ego was a small price to pay to save rent control.

"As a matter of fact, Bruce, we filed an action yesterday in the Housing Court. I expect the landlord will come running in with a vacancy decontrol certificate right away—that's what they would do if they didn't doubt the certificate's authenticity, so that's probably what they'll do this time as well. In their mind, to do anything else would just make us suspicious."

"Sounds logical."

"And Reese has already started to draft the class action suit, so that we can file it as soon as we show this first certificate is invalid. We've got him by the balls, and he doesn't even know it."

"Well, my guess is he'll know it when you start squeezing."

"Damn right. I haven't cut my fingernails in weeks."

Bruce laughed. "Ow. Well, thanks for the update. And Laura, I really am sorry that I wasn't completely straight with you last week. Maybe give me another chance someday, after this whole thing blows over?"

Laura made him wait a second for her answer. "Maybe."

70

[December 4, 1990]

The message light on Bruce's home answering machine was flashing. He dropped his overcoat and briefcase, then tapped the play button.

"Hey Bruce, it's Laura over at LAP. Give me a call when you get a chance. I'll be at the office late tonight."

He had given his home number to Laura and Reese and told them to leave messages if they needed him. It was safer for him, and was consistent with the double agent image he was trying to project. He called her back.

"Just wanted to let you know there's a hearing tomorrow afternoon over at the Housing Court." Bruce already knew—he had been checking the court's docket daily to monitor the progress of the case. He was a little surprised he hadn't received a panicked call from Howie—his December 1 check would now be four days late. "We've asked for an injunction to prevent the landlord from collecting market rents until he produces valid decontrol certificates."

"What do you think your chances are?"

"Well, pretty good, actually. The judge ruled in our favor last week on the single tenant case we brought, so we're optimistic. By the way, I was surprised that your firm wasn't representing the landlord."

"Yeah, me too. I was half expecting to be asked to work on the case against you guys, but for some reason the client used a different firm. Maybe they didn't like our conclusion that the certificates were invalid. Anyway, mind if I show up at the hearing?"

"Not at all. Two o'clock, courtroom 3, Old Courthouse. See you there."

*   *   *

[December 5, 1990]

Bruce took a seat in the back of the courtroom, midway between an open window and a steaming radiator. He listened as a number of minor landlord-tenant disputes were resolved. Then the clerk called the Fenway Place case.

As the party requesting the injunction from the court, Reese spoke first. "Your honor, you may remember that we were in front of you just last week on a matter involving the very same facts and issues that are in front of this court today. Basically, this case involves approximately 225 vacancy decontrol certificates relating to the Fenway Place Condominium complex. Each of these certificates has been altered, the most apparent alteration being a rather obvious change in the date of the certificate from the year '1986' to the year '1980'. As we set forth in our legal brief, we believe that this alteration invalidates the certificates. Since the landlord in this case has no other evidence that the units have been decontrolled, and since the law is well-established that the burden rests with the landlord to prove that the units are not under rent control, we feel that this court must, as a matter of law, immediately enter an order enjoining and restraining the landlord from collecting any rents for these units in excess of the rent control rents. In addition, we would ask that—given the uncertain state of the current real estate market, and the fact that this particular landlord is an off-shore corporation with no other assets in the United States—given these factors, we are requesting that this court grant a three million dollar attachment on this property as security for recovery by the tenants of the estimated rent overcharges at this property over the past several years."

The attorney for the landlord stood to respond, but the judge motioned him to sit down. "Mr. Jeffries, how are you so certain that this alteration from the year '1986' to '1980' was an alteration at all, as opposed to, say, a clerk correcting some innocent ministerial error?"

"Fair question, your Honor. And the answer is simple. If you notice, these certificates are signed by three Rent Equity Board Members—Ramon Cordero, Anthony Testa and Eleanor Oldham. We have checked the public records, and neither Mr. Cordero nor Ms. Oldham was members of the Rent Board in 1980. All three, of course, were members in 1986. What we believe happened here, your Honor, is that a prior landlord altered these certificates to the earlier 1980 date to avoid paying rent overcharge rebates to tenants. For example, a tenant arguing overcharges for, say, 1984 or 1985 would be entitled to rebates under a scenario where the vacancy decontrol certificates were issued in 1986, but would not be so entitled under a scenario where the certificates were issued in 1980."

"So you believe the certificates were altered by a prior owner of the property?"

"It's really the only plausible explanation, your Honor. Not only would a prior owner have cause to do so, but who else could possibly have had an opportunity to make the alterations? Presumably, custody of the certificates has always been with the owner of the property."

The judge nodded, then turned to the attorney for the landlord. "Counselor?"

"Your Honor, allow me to begin by emphasizing that nobody—including opposing counsel in this case—is accusing my client of altering these certificates."

The judge nodded. "Very well, counselor, though I don't see how that helps your client very much. You do concede, I take it, that the certificates have been altered?"

"It does appears that way, your Honor."

"Well, it seems to be that I have no choice but to rule the certificates invalid on their face. It is well-established law that an altered document of this type is of no force or effect. Now, my conclusion might be different if your client had any other documentation that could substantiate the validity of the certificates. Perhaps copies that are un-altered, or minutes from the Board's meetings?"

"My client has been looking, your Honor, but so far we have been unable to find any substantiating documentation."

"Well, then, I have no choice but to grant the request for injunctive relief. As of today, your client is permanently enjoined and restrained from collecting any rents in excess of the rent-controlled rents for all 225 units. I will leave this matter open and will entertain a motion from you to lift this injunction in the event you are able to submit documentation that somehow re-authenticates the vacancy decontrol certificates. So ordered."

Jeffries stood to speak. "Your Honor, what about our request for an attachment on the property?"

The judge turned toward the attorney for the landlord. "Is it true that your client is an offshore corporation with no other assets in this country?"

"Um, that is correct, your Honor."

Jeffries jumped up again. "And the problem, your Honor, is that they refuse to identify the person or persons who are the principal shareholders of the corporation."

The judge turned back toward the attorney for the landlord and waited for a response. "That is true, your Honor. My client at this time does not wish to disclose the identity of its principals." Laura turned in her chair and winked at Bruce, then lifted her fingers to display her long fingernails. He winked back.

"Well, it seems that if your client is unwilling to disclose such information, I have no choice but to grant the attachment on the property. Otherwise, how else could the plaintiffs satisfy any judgment that they might eventually obtain?

Request for attachment in the amount of three million dollars approved. Next case."

Bruce slid down the aisle seat and waited as Reese and Laura gathered their things. He smiled at Laura as she approached, and she leaned over to whisper in his ear. "How about a late lunch?" The strong smell of hair conditioner overpowered the faint smells of coffee and cigarettes on her breath.

"Sounds good."

"Let me lose Reese first. Meet me in the lobby in fifteen minutes."

Bruce knew that Laura had more than lunch in mind, and she made little effort to disguise her desires. She ordered a pina colada from the bar, gave Bruce a naughty look. "Ever seen this trick before?"

"What trick?"

Laura took the cherry out of her drink, pulled off the stem, and popped the stem into her mouth. A few seconds later, she removed the stem and placed it gently into Bruce's hand. She had knotted it with her tongue.

Bruce had been expecting Laura's invitation. Normally he would reject her advances, but he had recently become increasingly distracted by his memory of Shelby Baskin. Perhaps, he had decided, he needed to relieve some sexual tension. And he sensed that Laura would be content with a casual fling. "Wow. My next life I want to come back as a cherry stem."

Laura smiled, and called for the waiter. "We've changed our mind about lunch. Could you bring the check please?"

She turned to Bruce, handed him a roll. "Here, eat this. You need to keep up your strength."

*   *   *

Laura's bed was tucked into an alcove of her modest apartment. A lacy curtain separated the sleeping area from the living space. She threw her coat onto the couch, looked at Bruce, and cocked her head toward the bed.

He smiled and removed his jacket. She approached him, tilted her head up to him, and pulled his lips onto her mouth. She opened her mouth and probed his teeth and gums with her tongue, the pina colada now masking the taste of coffee and cigarettes. Lips still locked onto his, she backed him toward the alcove, flicked the curtain aside, and eased him over the footboard and onto the mattress. Bruce opened his eyes to see a silky canopy, illuminated by the late afternoon sun, draped over the four posters of the bed. There was a subtle scent of lavender in the room, and it made Bruce realize that it had been many years since he had shared a woman's bed.

She stood in front of him, unbuttoned her blouse, and let it drop to the floor. He could see her hardened nipples protruding through her bra, and he reached up and flicked the front clasp. The bra fell to the floor.

"Not bad. Let's see what else you can do." Her voice had turned throaty. Two large, firm white breasts rose up and down in concert with her breathing.

Bruce, now sitting on the foot of the bed, reached both hands around her buttocks and pulled Laura closer to him. He took her left breast in his mouth and flicked his tongue at her nipple. She moaned, and he could hear her heart begin to race.

Laura reached down, felt his erect penis through his pants, and hummed her approval. She lifted his chin from her bosom and again thrust her tongue deep into his mouth, one hand continuing to caress his penis through the cloth of his pants. They were both panting now, and Bruce could feel their mixed saliva beginning to seep onto his cheeks and chin.

She pulled her mouth away and began nibbling on his ear. "Lie down."

He obeyed, and she stepped out of her skirt and kicked it onto the floor. She was now wearing only panties, a garter belt and a pair of long stockings. Bruce doubted that the garter belt was part of her normal daily wardrobe—she had obviously anticipated their little romp. She quickly yanked the stockings off and tossed them onto the bed, rubbed at his genitals again, then walked around the side of the bed and gently took his left arm and raised it over his head. She kissed him quickly and smiled, then wrapped one of the stockings around his wrist, knotted it, and secured it to a bedpost. She climbed onto him, kissed him yet again, then rolled off him to the other side of the bed. She bound his other wrist to its bedpost, and panted into his ear. "Welcome to my web, said the spider to the fly."

Bruce closed his eyes, and Laura unbuckled his belt and removed his pants and boxers. She flicked at him with her tongue, then raised her head and dangled her silky hair onto his genitals. She slowly moved her head up and down, then side to side, causing her curls to caress and slither over his penis. At the same time, she gently blew her warm breath onto him. Bruce smiled to himself: hot air and soft tendrils—it was like the drying cycle of an automatic car wash. Then he arched his back and enjoyed the sensation.

After a few minutes, Laura lowered her head and enveloped Bruce into her mouth. Bruce lifted his head to watch her, then felt the pressure building in his loins, sensed the imminence of his explosion.

He lay back and closed his eyes, trying to abandon himself to the moment. But his brain refused to disengage. He would erupt into her mouth, then…what? Kiss her? Cuddle with her? Make love to her? Play Scrabble? Not likely. Once he came, he would roll away from her, make a few minutes of small talk, then slip out the door, mumbling some excuse or another. And she would feel used, cheated, humiliated. Which would normally be okay, but not this time—he might still need Laura in his battle against his enemy. No, this dalliance had been a careless and undisciplined choice on his part.

But he was here now, and he couldn't very well get up and walk away. At the least, he had to satisfy her sexually before he left, which was probably all she wanted anyway. He opened his eyes, saw Laura's knee only a foot or so from his mouth. He twisted toward it, nibbled it gently. She shifted toward him, and he nibbled and sucked his way up her thigh. He reached her panties, then slid his tongue under the elastic. He could smell her smell through the fine weaves of cotton—a gamy combination of sweat, sex and diaphragm gel.

Bruce's slow journey up her thigh had caused Laura to lose her rhythm, and Bruce knew he was no longer in danger of imminent eruption. With his teeth, he began tugging at her panties, until Laura reached down with one hand and shoved them down to her knees. She rolled herself onto him, her thighs straddling his face. She made a valiant effort to continue stimulating him, but her new position made it uncomfortable to do so, so she abandoned herself to his efforts.

Just as Bruce's lips and tongue began to numb from contact with the diaphragm gel, Laura began panting. Bruce increased his pace to match hers, until suddenly she sat straight up, arched her back, and convulsed in spasms of ecstasy.

"Oh, yes, that was wonderful. Now come inside me."

She looked to make sure he was still erect, then mounted him. She gasped as he slid deep into her, and she leaned down and engaged him in another open-mouthed kiss. Then she sat up and rode him, her pelvic muscles contracting around him as she moved. One of his hands came free, and he used it to squeeze and knead her breasts. They continued this way for a few minutes, then she unbound his other wrist and rolled him on top of her.

Bruce buried his head in her neck, closed his eyes, tried not to think about Shelby. Laura was spirited and talented, but he was getting bored. More to the point, he just didn't want her drooling into his mouth anymore. He knew it was time to reach orgasm, wash his face, and go home.

He thrust himself into her, back and forth, concentrating on the sensations in his loins. Laura moaned, her hands on his buttocks, unsuccessfully trying to slow the pace of his thrusts. He felt himself grow, and this time he did not try to hold back the eruptive, violent torrent building inside him.

C H A P T E R

71

[December 6, 1990]

Bruce knew now that it was just a matter of time before he had a second shot at Fenway Place. The decision by the court invalidating the decontrol certificates essentially made a ten million dollar property virtually worthless—with the income limited to the rent control rents, there was no way the property could support the mortgage payments. Bruce knew that the property currently had a rental stream of $160,000 per month, expenses of $70,000, and mortgage payments of $55,000. The new rental restrictions would reduce the income stream to approximately $60,000, which wasn't even enough to pay the expenses of the property, much less the mortgage. With a monthly shortfall of $65,000, Bruce had no doubt that his enemy would simply stop paying the mortgage to the RTC. The RTC would foreclose, and potential bidders would be faced with a building with fixed expenses of $70,000 per month and court-ordered maximum rents of only $60,000 per month. Somebody might pay a couple of million in hopes of eventually buying the tenants off, but it would go for far less than even the $5.4 million Pierre and Howie had bid for it last spring.

The question, of course, was where would Bruce get two or three million to outbid the other vultures at the RTC foreclosure? The RTC—once burned but never shy with taxpayers' money—would probably again offer 90 percent financing to the successful bidder, so Bruce would need approximately $300,000 to close on a $3 million purchase. He had already been able to scrape together $180,000 for last month's auction. He could save an additional $10,000 before the closing, and could grab another $10,000 by cheating on his taxes and claiming a refund. He would later amend his return and correct it before the IRS caught him, and happily pay whatever penalties and interest they would assess him. He also figured he could start collecting rents before he even closed on the purchase of the property—the RTC wouldn't bother doing so, and his enemy would no longer have ownership rights as of the day of the foreclosure auction. So he could likely just step into the vacuum and collect the rents; he had seen it happen many times before. So that would be another $60,000, which meant he would only be, at the most, $40,000 short. If he couldn't secure a few more lines of credit, he'd just have to go to a loan shark and pay the juice for a few months.

Even if they charged him 100 percent per month, it would be short money if it enabled him to buy a $10 million property for $3 million.

Bruce leaned back in his chair and looked out the window—there were a few scullers rowing on the Charles River, but otherwise the boating season had ended. He thought back to his meeting with Puck—five months had passed, and nothing had ever come of it. No follow up meetings. No police investigations. And no firing. Bruce shrugged his shoulders—they would either fire him or they wouldn't, and there wasn't anything he could do about it either way. Not that it mattered much anyway; within a couple of months, he would either be the successful bidder at the Fenway Place auction, or not. In either case, it would be time to leave the firm.

So it looked like he had denied his enemy his booty. And he might soon reclaim the treasure for himself. But there was one more unfinished piece of business. And after that, maybe even some pleasure.

He left his office and took the elevator to the lobby of the building. He put eight quarters into a pay phone and dialed the District Attorney's Office. "Shelby Baskin, please." He heard Shelby's voice. "Ms. Baskin, my name is Bruce Arrujo. I'm an attorney at Stoak, Puck & Beal. I was wondering if you had a few moments to discuss the Charese Galloway murder case with me." He rubbed his hand on his pant leg to dry it off.

There was a pause before Shelby responded. "Mr. Arrujo, I'm not sure how to respond. If this involves your client, Mr. Prefontaine, I think you should be speaking with the lead prosecutor in this case...."

"Actually, it doesn't really involve Mr. Prefontaine, except to the extent his name would be cleared once and for all if you found the real killer."

"I'm not sure I understand where you're going with this. In fact, how did you even get my name? I'm not the prosecutor of record in this case."

"I'm sorry, I'm not being very clear." Bruce took a deep breath, let it out slowly into the mouthpiece, then continued. "As you might imagine, I feel pretty badly about what happened to Pierre Prefontaine. I mean, basically, it was my stupid memo that really made him a suspect in the case."

"That and other things."

"Well, the memo definitely played a part in it. And now I go to bed every night knowing that some little girl is not getting tucked in by her daddy because I was trying to cover my ass with a stupid memo. And I know Pierre Prefontaine did not kill Charese Galloway. So I went back and researched every thing I could find about this case—that's how I found your name, in the civil action pleadings.

I was going to call you just to ask some questions about Charese's lawsuit against Krygier, then I found out you were at the DA's office. So I figured you'd be a good person to talk to about this."

"All right. I'm listening."

"Well, there may be an angle to this murder that nobody else has looked at. Actually, that's presumptuous of me—you may be looking at it already, but I would sure sleep better knowing it was being investigated. So can you spare a few minutes to meet with me?"

"Can't you tell me over the phone?"

Bruce had debated this issue in his mind a number of times: Would it be better to meet with her face to face before or after he explained his murder theory to her? He knew that when he did meet with her, there was a good chance she would recognize him as her rainy night companion-in-frolic. Even if she didn't, it wasn't the type of thing he could just bring up casually in conversation a few weeks later: "By the way, you look a lot like a mermaid I met one rainy night." So the question was, would the revelation have a positive or negative effect on her inclination to subscribe to his theory of Charese's murder? It was a tough call, but he concluded—or maybe hoped was a better word—that she was likely to react positively to the revelation, which would cause her to also react positively to his theory. "I'd really rather not discuss it over the phone, if you don't mind. I'd be happy to come over to your office, if that's convenient."

"Well, okay, I guess. I'm free later this afternoon, say three o'clock?"

"Perfect. I'll see you then."

Bruce spent the next four hours pacing around his office, just waiting for the time to pass until his meeting with Shelby. It was the type of behavior his Grandpa had always scorned: *Why do you want to wish the time away? Why? Do you think you can ever get it back? Do you throw money into the ocean? Once it's gone, it's gone for good. So never wish it away—relax, if you want, or read a book, or just sleep, but do something that gives you some benefit or pleasure. Otherwise you'll wake up one day an old man, and realize you wished away your whole life.* But this time, despite Grandpa's words, Bruce just wanted to snap his fingers and move four hours into the future.

Finally it was 2:30, and Bruce walked to the bathroom. He washed his face, brushed his teeth, dabbed his underarms with a moist paper towel, and changed into a clean shirt. He looked at himself in the mirror, saw the combination of hope and concern in his own face, and laughed. It had been a long time since he felt nervous about meeting a girl. Maybe he should just wet his hair and cover himself with mud.

*   *   *

Bruce stood up as he saw Shelby approaching from down the hall. She was more rigid and controlled than the night he first saw her, but there was no doubt about it—same faultless features, same dark hair, same turquoise eyes. And same grace. She moved as if she were weightless, as if the air surrounding her buoyed her, cushioning and softening each of her movements. He turned away from her before she spotted him. He wanted to observe her reaction close-up when she first saw his face, though he realized she may not even recognize him.

When she had glided to about ten feet away, he stood and turned toward her. Her eyes locked onto his, then her face relaxed into a smile. "I figured someday I'd run into you again. But I thought it'd be at a water slide or something."

She recognized him. He fought for a light response. "Wouldn't catch me at one of those places—not enough mud. How about you? Did you catch Letterman that night?"

Bruce could see a cloud pass over Shelby's face. She answered softly. "Actually, no. I had some bad news waiting for me when I got home that night." Bruce waited as she studied his face; he could see she was trying to decide how much to confide in him.

They stood looking at each other for a few seconds, then Shelby spoke. "Come on down to my office. We can talk there." She reached out, took him gently by the elbow, and guided him down the hall.

They walked down the corridor in silence, each using the time to try to gain control of his or her emotions. Bruce sensed that they both understood that there was really nothing more to be said about the rainy night frolic, and by the time they sat down they had each concluded that it would be best to ease into their exploration of each other through a discussion of Charese's murder. Hardly the normal small talk of a first date, but better than an immediate leap to the surreal intensity of their first encounter.

"So what's your theory about Charese's murder?"

Bruce struggled to focus his thoughts, but he was having trouble taking his eyes off Shelby. Her eyes, especially—green and wet and blue and soft and large and sad and strong and kind. Not that the rest of her face would sully a canvas.

He fumbled in his briefcase for some notes he had made. He didn't usually rely on notes, but he didn't trust himself to keep separate in his head what he knew about Charese's death because he was Pierre's concerned attorney on the one hand and what he had figured out because he had been Pierre's blundering predator on the other. This was a fine line he was walking—it would be simple to reveal to Shelby the identify of Charese's killer, but to do so would require him to reveal his role in setting Pierre up for a sting. On the other hand, he had to give Shelby enough information so that she would agree to pursue the investigation and could discover the killer on her own.

He took a deep breath. "First of all, I know I'm totally out of my league here. I have no experience in criminal investigations, and I haven't been privy to your investigation. But I do know Pierre Prefontaine pretty well, so I think I bring a fresh perspective to this case."

"I see your point, but I don't see how your knowing Pierre will help in finding Charese's killer. It may somehow prove Pierre is innocent, which I admit is a laudable goal in and of itself, but it doesn't really help solve the crime."

"That's what I thought at first—I kept asking myself, Who would benefit from Charese's death? But, other than the obvious choice—the Krygiers—I didn't know enough about the case to answer that question. Besides, I assume you guys already had taken a careful look at the Krygiers, and couldn't find any evidence. So I decided to work from the assumption that Pierre was innocent and might have been framed. Then the question became: Who would benefit from Pierre becoming a suspect in the murder?"

"Okay. That's a valid inquiry."

"Well, at first, I couldn't think of anybody. It's not like I'm that close to Pierre or anything. But something happened recently that might be worth looking into. The RTC auctioned off Pierre's interest in a property in the Fenway area called Fenway Place."

"I know. That was part of his deal with the federal government."

"Right. Well, some offshore corporation was the high bidder. And from what I can tell, they got quite a deal. Pierre thinks his interest in the property is worth at least a million, maybe two, and it sold for only $180,000. So somebody made a killing. And that somebody is trying to remain anonymous by hiding behind an offshore corporation."

"Let me get this straight: You think somebody killed Charese just to frame Pierre so that they could get a great deal on Pierre's property at an auction? I'll be honest. It seems a bit far-fetched to me."

Bruce nodded. *Actually, what really happened is that somebody killed Charese because they knew I would frame Pierre so that I could buy his property, and then they outbid me on it. And you're right, it does seem far-fetched. Which is why it's so brilliant. But I can't tell you any of this, because you'd put me in jail. So I need you to find the killer yourself, without any help from me.* "You're right, it does seem far-fetched. But what if that person were planning to kill Charese anyway and then saw the opportunity to frame Pierre for the murder?"

Shelby responded. "That brings us back to the Krygiers, father and/or son. They could have killed Charese and framed Pierre for the murder. It wouldn't take much for them to learn that Pierre was having trouble getting Charese to leave the apartment. Plus they know a lot of people in the real estate community—they could have figured out that Pierre was hurting financially. That holds water."

The phone rang and interrupted them. Shelby picked it up. "Oh, hi, Dom."

Bruce was content to take the opportunity just to observe her—to watch her think, to note her mannerisms, to follow the lines of her shape, to memorize her features. How could someone have such light-colored eyes and such dark-colored hair? Her features looked almost Scandinavian, though he noticed that a Jewish star dangled from a thin gold chain around her neck.

He barely heard her words: "Bruce, could you excuse me for a minute?" Bruce nodded and stepped out of the room.

*   *   *

Shelby waited until he closed the door, then summarized Bruce's theory of the case to the detective. Then she continued. "But, Dom, I think his theory holds water not just for the Krygiers. Why couldn't it also apply to Reese Jeffries? He kills Charese so she won't file the complaint against him, and frames Pierre for it. Reese takes the video, but can't use it right away because he can't explain how he got hold of it. But then, after Pierre takes the fall for the murder, Reese makes up some story about the video arriving in the mail anonymously, then nails Krygier with it. End of Krygier, end of rent control repeal. Reese the hero."

"It's worth thinking about. Why don't you call me later after you've finished meeting with Bruce? See what else he's got."

"Okay. Talk you to later, Dom."

Shelby hung up the phone and tapped a pen against her desk blotter, gazing at a spot on the wall. She was having a little trouble focusing.

When she had returned to her apartment that rainy night to watch Letterman, there had been a message from the police on her answering machine—her brother and parents had been killed in a car accident in Connecticut. In the shock of their deaths, she had totally forgotten her nighttime encounter with the tall, playful stranger in the park. Months later, however, while she was walking through that same park in a rainstorm, the memory had burst into her consciousness. It had remained there, almost hauntingly, since. She didn't believe in ghosts, and the concept of heaven was not really part of her Jewish faith, but she had continued to wrestle with the thought that the spirit of her family, before ascending to heaven, had joined her in the rainy park for one last merry romp. And she had gone home to watch TV with Barry instead.

She dabbed at her eyes, not sure if the tears were for her or her parents or even for Charese, and called to Bruce.

"All right, sorry for the interruption. So continue on your theory of how the Krygiers, or somebody else, framed Pierre."

"Right. So the Krygiers rent a car that matches Pierre's, and they kill Charese. Or they hire somebody to do it, whatever. They make sure to leave tire tracks and carpet fibers at the crime scene which point to Pierre, and sure enough, the police match the crime car to Pierre's Grand Am. Little did the Krygiers know that they'd get so much help from a paranoid young memo-writing lawyer, but hey, sometimes it's better to be lucky than good. So Pierre goes from a possible suspect to the primary one."

"It's a decent theory, Bruce, but we have no evidence, as you pointed out."

"I agree. But take it one step further. Obviously, the Krygiers watch carefully to see what happens to Pierre, right? They've got their little spies around and, well, the next thing they know, not only have they successfully focused the police's attention on Pierre, but also as an added bonus, the RTC has decided to auction off Pierre's interest in Fenway Place. Most people don't really pay attention to the auction, but the Krygiers know all about the property because they know all about Pierre, and they know the property's a gold mine. Wouldn't that just be frosting on the cake, especially for a family that is in a bit of trouble financially?"

Shelby picked up the train of thought. "But they don't want to have anyone to have any reason whatsoever to connect them with Pierre, so they set up an offshore corporation to make the purchase. So Charese is dead, plus they've turned $180,000 into a million-plus. And Pierre takes the fall."

Bruce smiled, nodded. "Exactly. So my theory is to just follow the money. Find out who's behind that offshore corporation. If I'm right, it'll lead you right to the killer."

Shelby was quiet for a moment while she pondered Bruce's theory.

She interrupted his thoughts. "All right. I'll talk to the ADA. It's worth a shot, at least. But you know I'm not going to be able to keep you informed on the details of the investigation, right?"

"Of course. And thanks, Shelby. I appreciate you taking it to the ADA." He turned and looked out the window, then smiled back at her. "Now, unless my brain has tricked my eyes into seeing what it wants them to see, I think it's raining, and it's not that cold out. Care to go for a walk?"

She grinned and jumped out of her chair. "You got it. But I better not see you opening an umbrella, or you'll be walking alone."

*   *   *

They walked together for over an hour, cutting through the Common and the Public Garden to Commonwealth Avenue, then along Commonwealth for eight blocks to the western edge of the Back Bay. At Massachusetts Avenue, they turned right toward the Charles River, and followed the bike paths on the Charles back toward the financial district of the city. Once in a while, their elbows touched lightly, and Shelby was contenct to continue in that manner for a few seconds.

The conversation flowed effortlessly, but not into areas one would expect from two young lawyers who had shared a common law school experience. They spoke not once of law school, or of work, or even of Charese's murder case. Instead, like their feet, the conversation simply meandered along.

"I have a theory. Ready to hear it?"

Shelby laughed lightly, then licked a raindrop off her upper lip. "Do I have a choice?"

"Not really. Here it is: *For every proverb known to man, there is an equal and opposite anti-proverb.* For example, take the proverb, 'Look before you leap.'"

"All right, I've taken it."

Bruce looked sideways at her. "Please, there's no room in this theory for sarcasm; this is important stuff."

"Oh. Sorry."

"Anyway, the equal and opposite anti-proverb is, 'He who hesitates is lost.' See what I mean? It's the opposite of 'Look before you leap', yet both of them are spoken like the gospel. And here's another: You've heard, 'Absence makes the heart grow fonder'?"

"Once or twice."

"Well, what about the opposite, 'Out of sight, out of mind'? See what I mean? Try it out, give me a proverb."

"All right. Try this: 'A penny saved is a penny earned.'"

"Hold on a second." They walked in silence as Bruce thought. "Got it. 'Don't be penny wise and pound foolish.'"

"Good job. I have another one. 'Don't put off until tomorrow what you can do today.'"

Bruce answered quickly. "Simple. 'There's a sucker born every day.'"

"What?!"

"Just kidding. How about, 'Good things come to those who wait.'"

Shelby nodded, then thought for a moment. "Okay, and I'll counter your opposite and raise it: 'The early bird catches the worm' is the anti-proverb of 'Good things come to those who wait.'"

"Excellent. And the anti-proverb of, 'The early bird catches the worm' is, 'You are what you eat.'"

Shelby burst out in laughter again. "You're cheating. That's not an opposite, that's a commentary."

"Well, maybe you're right. I have one for you though. Ready?"

"Okay."

Bruce stopped, and turned toward Shelby. He took a deep breath. "How about this one: 'Love at first sight.'"

She looked deep into his dark eyes, tried to reconcile the complexities with which they spoke to her. She felt a tingling in her limbs. Who was this man, who had haunted her past and had now dropped into her present? And why did he seem to travel with death— first her parents, then Charese—as his companion? "I can't use, 'Look before you leap' again, can I?"

Bruce answered softly. "Sorry, no."

"All right. Then I guess my opposite would have to be, 'Fools rush in where angels fear to tread.' But I don't subscribe to that one. Put me down as a 'Nothing ventured, nothing gained' type of girl."

"I was hoping you'd say that." Bruce leaned down and kissed her gently on the cheek, lingered there for a few seconds. "And thanks for not choosing, 'Love is blind' as your opposite of 'Love is at first sight.' I'm not sure my ego could have taken it."

She smiled into his eyes. "Somehow, I doubt that your ego could easily be damaged." She linked her arm in his, took a deep breath. "Come on. We've been under this tree for too long, and I'm starting to dry off, God forbid."

They ambled along together in the twilight as the rain fell around them. Bruce broke the silence, speaking more to himself than to Shelby. "'Behind every rain cloud lies a silver lining.'"

72

[December 21, 1990]

Two weeks later, Bruce sat on the floor in the vestibule of Shelby's Cambridge apartment building, content to read a magazine and wait. It was past ten o'clock, and Shelby had warned him that she would have trouble leaving her office Christmas party much before ten or ten-thirty.

He, on the other hand, had been one of the few attorneys to stay past eight o'clock at his firm's party earlier that evening. Actually, "party" would be the wrong word to describe the staid and proper buffet dinner his firm had provided its employees; the appropriate word was probably "function". No alcohol, and the only music was provided by an elderly woman from the accounting department tapping out Christmas tunes on an organ. Holiday bonuses—in the amount, as always, of one week's pay—were distributed, a toast was made, and dinner was served and consumed. Then the herd rushed for the exits. A group of support staffers planned to re-congregate at a dance club, but word had filtered down earlier in the week that the firm partners felt it inappropriate for any of the attorneys to attend this "after hours" event. After all, God help the firm if, in an alcohol-induced haze, one of the attorneys actually mated with a support staffer and, gasp, inter-bred.

Bruce put down his magazine. In some ways, he envied Shelby's job situation. She seemed to have genuine affection for her workmates, and there was little of the politics and competition that pervaded the atmosphere at Stoak, Puck & Beal. He doubted that he would find in any of her co-workers that rare combination of ocean and continent, but there was something to be said for a group of people—some sea-based, some land-based—working together in a cooperative venture. They didn't exactly morph into a majestic sailing ship, but collectively they could at least experience the satisfaction of lounging on the beach together.

Not that he was complaining about his choice of workplace—he had chosen his firm based largely on its less than congenial environment. It was just that he was ready to put this whole chapter of his life behind him. He had only known Shelby for two weeks, and the experience had been a complete revelation to him. He had, quite simply, never known what it was like to be in love. It wasn't as though he was intoxicated by it to the point of irrationality—he was still intent on denying his enemy his treasure and claiming it as his own. But he'd found contentment with Shelby that he'd never known before. Even better than contentment, he'd found peace. He could simply be himself with her, and she accepted it. No deception, no airs, no games. Except, of course, that he was in the midst of a deception and lie that, unavoidably, required that she be one of the persons he deceived and lied to. He knew he could never explore the possibility of building a life with her until he had moved beyond that lie.

A car door slammed outside on the street, interrupting his thoughts. He heard Shelby's voice thanking the cab driver, and stood up to greet her. She ran up the stairs, broke into a smile when she saw him standing in the foyer holding the door for her. She paused on the top stair, looked up into the sky, and yelled, "Thank you, Santa, for my Adonis present." She lowered her voice and smiled at Bruce. "I may even think about converting. I like this Christmas stuff. But aren't you supposed to be wrapped in green and red paper or something?"

He leaned over and kissed her on her mouth. They held the kiss for a few seconds, then embraced. He felt a pang of guilt, tried to shake it off. "I see you're in quite a good mood."

"Even better seeing you here. I was worried you wouldn't wait."

Bruce chuckled. "Yeah, right. I bet you were real worried."

She grinned back at him. "Well, maybe not so much. Oh, I forgot." She reached into her purse, pulled out a strand of mistletoe, held it over his head. Slowly she lifted her mouth to his, her free hand resting gently on his cheek. Finally they separated, and she rested her head on his shoulder and spoke into his ear. "I've been feasting all night, and nothing has been nearly as delicious as that."

He didn't know what to say, so he just smiled and kissed her hair. And again tried to shake off the guilt.

She squeezed his hand and led him upstairs. He lit the fire, while she microwaved a couple of mugs of apple cider mixed with rum and cinnamon. She put on some light jazz, and cuddled up against him on the couch.

After a few seconds of silence, she spoke. "You know, Bruce, you never talk about your job. Which, by the way, is great—I know a lot of couples who are lawyers and all they do is talk about the law. But you totally avoid the subject."

Bruce felt his face begin to flush. "Well, it's really pretty boring. Besides, I don't think I'm going to be at the firm much longer. My plan from the beginning was to only stay a year or two. But I guess I don't talk about it because my work's not something I'm particularly proud of. I don't really feel like I do any-thing worthwhile. Other than write stupid memos that put my clients in jail."

"He's getting out in a few weeks, you know."

"Yeah. Thank God. He didn't deserve to be there at all."

Shelby started to respond, then caught herself. "I'm sorry, but you know I can't talk about this." Bruce nodded. "Anyway, it's a little bit sad, what you said about not liking your job." Bruce remembered how she had told him of being critical of Barry for his zealous representation of unworthy clients and causes. Bruce, it seemed was the opposite extreme.

He turned his entire body and looked at her. His eyes were dark and intent. "It's a *lot* sad. And I do understand that it's no way to go through life. I wish I liked my job as much as you do."

"Well, I have my moments. In fact, I almost decided to drop out of law school after the guy who killed my family was acquitted. But I see a lot of cases come through the office, and, for the most part, the system does a pretty good job of handing out justice. The problem, I think, is with the lawyers themselves, not with the system. Nobody seems to remember that we're supposed to be offi-cers of the court; there are lines we're not supposed to cross in representing our clients. And we're not supposed to have a hidden agenda that we promote over the interests of our clients."

Bruce didn't respond, and Shelby gently shifted the conversation. "Well, what would you do if you had the choice? Say somebody handed you a million dollars."

Which, he realized, was more than just an academic question. And one that he had been contemplating a lot recently. "In the summer I would sail. Probably buy an old wooden schooner and take out charter groups for weekends to help pay the expenses. In the winter, I think it would be fun to procure art for a muse-um. You know—travel the world, go to auctions, meet some of the new artists."

"Wow. I guess you've thought about this a little."

Bruce smiled sheepishly. "Yeah, a little." He paused, looked into the fire. "But for now, there's not a single place in the world that I'd rather be than right here with you."

They made love—for the first time—in front of the fireplace. It was slow and gentle and delicious, and Bruce held her tightly as she fell asleep in his arms. They had rolled onto the hearth during their lovemaking, and Bruce stroked her hair and stared over his knees into the nearby fire. He didn't want to wake Shelby by shifting away, but he could feel the flames nipping at his curled up legs, and he hoped he wouldn't get burned.

*   *   *

Shelby woke up the next morning to find that Bruce had already run out for some groceries. He served fresh fruit and pancakes to Shelby in bed. For dessert, they made love again.

Shelby rolled onto one elbow, her free hand playing with Bruce's hair. She eyed him mischievously.

"Uh oh, I don't like that look. What's on your mind, Shelby?"

"Promise you won't laugh?"

"All right."

"Well, every time I make love to a guy, I wonder if he thinks of baseball players."

"What are you talking about?"

"Haven't you ever heard that Woody Allen skit?" She switched to a New York accent. "When making love, in an effort to prolong the moment of ecstasy, I think of…baseball players."

"No, never heard it."

"Well, it's hysterical. He goes into a whole thing where he describes a game between the Giants and some other team. Thinking about the game distracts him enough so that he can delay his orgasm. So he starts with the first batter, who singles to right or something. Then the next batter, and so on. His whole point is that he can't allow himself to have an orgasm until the inning is over. Then, with two outs, in the middle of a Giants' rally, he announces he's pinch hitting for McCovey. It's a classic line."

Bruce looked puzzled. "I don't get it."

"Well, why would you pinch hit for Willie McCovey if you're trying to prolong the inning?"

Bruce shrugged. "I'm not following you."

Shelby caught herself—it was the first time since her parents died that a conversation about baseball hadn't conjured up numbingly depressing memories of sitting on her father's lap on a Saturday afternoon at Yankee Stadium. Maybe time was beginning to heal her. Or maybe it was Bruce. She smiled at her lover, punched him playfully. "You know, Willie McCovey. He was the Giants' best hitter. Hall of Famer."

"Oh. Never heard of him. I'm not much of a baseball fan."

"Really?"

"Actually, I can't stand the game. It's incredibly boring."

The Spoils

73

[February 27, 1991]

"I'm sorry. I just have a lot of work to do.

"All right. I'm a big boy—I can eat lunch alone. Hopefully I'll see you tomorrow at the auction. Bye Shelbs."

"Bye."

Bruce took a deep breath, then sighed, trying to remove the ache he felt in his chest. He knew a guy in college who had a theory that he called the "Six Week Rule", which basically stated that, after dating for six weeks, both parties had to make a conscious decision either to commit to a long-term relationship or to walk away. Had Shelby reached that point, and decided to punt? They had just spent an idyllic weekend together skiing in New Hampshire, complete with a horse-drawn sleigh ride and champagne in an outdoor hot tub. But for the three days since they had returned, she had been distant and reserved.

He knew she sensed he hadn't completely opened himself up to her, that there were parts of both his past and his present that he hadn't shared. But he also knew that to reveal his past and present to her would be to forfeit their future together. From the first day he had walked into her office, he had lied to her. She would never be able to accept that. But he was desperate not to lose her. She was the calm port in a stormy sea, and he was exhausted from his journey.

Bruce was aware that the possible loss of Shelby threatened to send him spiraling into a deep depression, and that it couldn't be happening at a worse time. The RTC had moved with private sector-like speed to bring Fenway Place to auction—perhaps the fact that it was the third time they were auctioning the same property had something to do with their efficiency. In any event, the auction was scheduled for the next day, at two o'clock in the afternoon. As a result, Bruce's emotions were flapping like a loose sail in a heavy wind, from adrenalized excitement about the auction to morose trepidation about Shelby.

Bruce knew that these emotions were incompatible, like two weather fronts set to meet. He had to keep them separated. If they collided, the resulting storm would swamp him, just as he was preparing to raid his enemy's ship, deal him a fatal blow, and hopefully make off with the treasure.

He looked at his watch. Just past noon. At least there was something this afternoon to focus his mind on—the court had scheduled an emergency hear-

ing on his enemy's request to postpone the foreclosure auction pending final res-
olution of the rent control dispute. The court would almost surely deny the
motion; absent some showing of wrongdoing on the part of the mortgage holder, there was no defense to not paying the mortgage. And there was no evidence
that the mortgage holder had been the cause of the vacancy decontrol fiasco.
Bruce, more than anyone, knew that to be true.

He pulled out his list of things to do prior to the auction. He had contacted
the Springfield lawyer and made arrangements—including sending him the
$50,000 deposit check—for him to drive in from Springfield to the auction and
to bid up to $3 million on behalf of Arab Acquisitions. He had spoken with
Reese Jeffries, and they had agreed that it would be a good idea to have somebody from his office attend the auction and hand out copies of the court's order
imposing rent control on the property; that way, Bruce wouldn't run the risk of
some bidder being ignorant of the rent control situation and out-bidding him.
And—in a gesture of paramount respect for his enemy—he had checked his
safe deposit box to make sure that the unaltered vacancy decontrol certificates
hadn't somehow disappeared.

One last thing to do. Howie would think it was strange if he didn't check in,
and there was no reason to raise anyone's suspicions. He dialed the phone.

"Howie Plansky here."

"Hi Howie, it's Bruce Arrujo."

"Oh, how you doing, Bruce? Any more bad news for me?"

"No. Just wanted to see if you wanted me to go to that hearing today. You
know, your partner is trying to get the foreclosure auction postponed."

"Yeah, I know. You might as well go. But I think my real estate days are over.
First Pierre murdered his tenant and went to jail. Then this deal blew up in my
face. And now my so-called partner's wasting what little money we have left running into court every week."

Bruce had noticed that Howie was really the only one who spoke of Pierre
as if it were a given that he had killed Charese. "Yeah, I'm sure it hasn't been
much fun. I'll give you a call after the hearing."

Bruce hung up the phone and looked at his watch. He had time for a quick
sandwich on the way to the hearing. And he preferred to be a few minutes late,
anyway; that way, he wouldn't have to make awkward small talk with Laura.

*   *   *

[February 28, 1991]

Bruce tried Shelby one last time before leaving his office.

"I'm sorry, Mr. Arrujo, but Ms. Baskin is in a meeting right now. But she did want me to tell you that she'd see you at the auction."

"Thank you." Well, at least she was coming to the auction. Of course, she had professional reasons for being there as well, although she had been dogmatic in her refusal to discuss the investigation with Bruce in any way. In fact, he had no clue as to whether the DA's office was close to making an arrest, or if they had followed the breadcrumbs Bruce had laid out to the point of even focusing on his enemy as a suspect.

Bruce looked out his window—a clear day, so the RTC officials traveling to Boston for the auction should have no problems getting to town. Bruce had heard a story where an auction had to be postponed, at a cost to the taxpayers of almost $20,000 in re-advertising expenses and attorney fees, simply because the RTC employee in charge of the foreclosure got a flat tire on the way to the auction.

With that story in mind, Bruce had instructed the Springfield attorney to arrive in Boston first thing in the morning to do a title search on the property; that way, even if he had a breakdown or minor accident, he would still have time to get to the auction by two o'clock. And at 11:30, Bruce actually telephoned the Registry of Deeds and paged the attorney, just to make sure he had made it to town. When the attorney answered the page, Bruce simply hung up.

There was still an hour to go before the auction. The court, at yesterday's hearing, had denied his enemy's request to postpone the auction, and Bruce smiled as he imagined the sense of loss his foe must be feeling now that he knew he would be losing his treasure. Bruce's sense of triumph was diminished, however, by the fact that his adversary did not yet know that Bruce had been the rock upon which his ship had shattered. And that Bruce's hands would soon be the ones in which his treasure rested. Perhaps, after the auction, Bruce would indulge in a little self-gratification and regale his enemy with some tales of the sea.

Bruce grabbed his jacket, scarf and gloves, took a final look at his "To do" list, and strolled down the hall to the elevator. He felt the adrenaline pumping through his system, so he broke into a slow jog when he reached the street. He needed to burn some energy—it would be of no use to him today. Today he was merely an observer. He had caused today's events, and in many ways could predict them, but he no longer could control them. He had built the bomb and then lit the fuse, trained the dog and then unleashed it, pointed the ship and then set it adrift. But today would be what today would be.

Bruce jogged slowly through the Common, then westward on Boylston Street for two or three miles, oblivious to the chafing caused by his wing tips rubbing against the back of his heels. Just past Fenway Park, he ducked into a fast food restaurant bathroom and washed his face, dried his armpits, and straightened his tie.

He walked the final two blocks to Fenway Place. Unlike the last RTC auctions when the agency utilized a sealed-bid format to sell first the Fenway Place mortgage and then Pierre's interest in the property, this auction was an actual foreclosure sale of the property and was required under Massachusetts law to be held in an "open cry" format at the property. The auction wouldn't begin for another twenty minutes, but there was already a crowd of about fifteen or twenty people milling about on the sidewalk in front of the main entrance to the complex. He nodded to Reese Jeffries, who was diligently handing out copies of the court order placing the property under rent control. He spotted the Springfield attorney; Bruce had never met him in person, but his face was familiar to Bruce from his late-night television commercials. Many of the other faces were familiar to Bruce as well, from foreclosures he had conducted. He moved through the crowd, exchanging pleasantries.

From what he could tell, only three people, in addition to the Springfield attorney, were carrying bidder registration folders, meaning the others were merely spectators. So far, so good—the fewer the number of bidders, the better. It only took one idiot bidding like a drunken sailor to ruin Bruce's plans.

The crowd was predominantly male and, almost in unison, heads turned toward the figure of an attractive woman approaching the group. She looked vaguely familiar to Bruce, but a brimmed hat, scarf and sunglasses hid her features, and he couldn't quite place her.

She slipped past him and approached the auctioneer. Bruce watched, saw her register to bid. Who was she?

A gentle tap on his shoulder interrupted his thoughts. He sensed Shelby more than saw or heard or smelled her. "Hi, Bruce." Her eyes were bloodshot, her expression somber. She was with two other people, a woman in a blue suit who looked to be in her mid-forties, and a muscular man who, though in street clothes, made no attempt to hide the fact that he was a cop. They broke away from Shelby and moved toward the auctioneer.

"Hi, Shelbs. You look upset. What's wrong?"

Her eyes, pained and angry, bore into him. "Everything."

Bruce stared back at her intently, then followed her eyes as they broke from his and looked over to the auctioneer. The auctioneer was pointing out the Springfield attorney to Shelby's two companions. Bruce spun his head back to Shelby. *What the fuck?!*

She had watched him, seen his reaction to the auctioneer identifying the Springfield attorney. A tear rolled down her porcelain cheek, then she spoke. "I was hoping I was wrong."

He looked back toward the Springfield attorney, saw Shelby's companion handing him an official-looking set of papers. "What are you talking about. What's going on?"

"Please, no more lies. We know all about Arab Acquisitions and your whole sick, evil plan. Your attorney friend won't be bidding today—he's just been served with an injunction. Arab Acquisitions and its agents are barred from bidding. At least I can take a little joy in that. You killed my friend, and you framed an innocent man, and you used me in the worst way, but at least you won't walk away with this property today." Her eyes fired in rage, the normally blue-green color now the blue-black of a twilight storm. "So fuck you, you murdering scumbag."

"Wait, Shelby, wait." He grabbed at her as she started to turn away. She shook his arm away. The cop took a threatening step toward Bruce, patted the gun on his hip. "Please, just listen for a minute. You're right about me framing Pierre, but I didn't kill Charese, and God knows I didn't use you, Shelby. I love you. Please listen to me."

She turned back to study him. For the first time, he wanted her to see him totally unmasked, to sense his vulnerability. He was finally telling the truth, for all it mattered. He pleaded with her with his eyes. But her voice was ice. "I'm listening. But I want the whole story, all the details. Start at the beginning. And no bullshit."

Bruce took a deep breath. "All right, you probably figured a lot of this out already, but here goes:

"As soon as Pierre came to me with the Fenway Place deal, I was trying to figure out a way to take it from him. When he first submitted his bid to the RTC, he had to sign the affidavit that attested that nobody in the ownership group was in default on any RTC loans. But he never gave me a copy of it, so I acted like I didn't know anything about it. But the woman at the RTC had faxed it to me, so I actually did know about it. So when it came time to structure Pierre's deal with Felloff, I made Felloff a silent partner. I didn't know how I was going to light the fuse, but I knew I had planted a little bomb in the deal that eventually I might be able to set off." In the background, the auctioneer was asking for opening bids.

Bruce continued. "Well, when Charese was found murdered, and I learned that Pierre was a suspect, well, it was almost too good to be true. As it turns out, it *was* too good to be true, but I'll get to that later. So I drafted that memo about Pierre talking about murdering Charese, then conveniently lost my briefcase, with the memo in it. Then I dressed up in disguise and turned the briefcase in to the police, knowing you guys would eventually get the memo. Of course I knew that Pierre was only kidding when he talked about killing Charese, but it was a perfect opportunity to keep him as the focus of the investigation."

Shelby interrupted him, in a low voice. "You were willing to let him go to jail for the rest of his life?"

Bruce thought for a moment, then shrugged meekly. "Well, I knew you wouldn't be able to convict him, because the memo was covered by the attorney-client privilege. That was the beauty of the memo—it made Pierre the prime suspect, but you couldn't use it as evidence against him."

"We couldn't use it against him once you established that Pierre was your client, you mean."

Bruce nodded. The bidding had started—the attractive woman who had looked familiar to him was bidding, as were a couple of others. "Exactly. And the only way to prove that Pierre was my client was to show you the partnership agreement, which listed him as a partner in the Fenway Place deal. That made him my client."

"And the partnership agreement listed Felloff as part of the ownership group."

"Right. And I was counting on somebody in your office to pick up on that. But nobody did."

"So let me guess—you called in an anonymous tip to the RTC. Mr. Good Citizen."

Bruce nodded, ignored the sarcasm. "I figured you guys would be thrilled to be able to put Pierre away, at least for a little while. I mean, here was a guy that you were almost sure killed Charese, and he was likely going to walk on a technicality. With my anonymous tip about the affidavit, at least you could make him serve a little time."

"Well, you'll be pleased to know that your little puppets did just as you thought they would."

"Anyway, to answer your original question, I was pretty sure Pierre wouldn't be spending the rest of his life in jail. I knew that you really didn't have much other evidence against him, so it seemed like he could beat a murder rap, if it came to that. But I knew it wouldn't get that far."

"Let me guess again—it was your idea to hire Mike Callahan as Pierre's attorney."

"Yeah. My goal was to get Pierre to agree to a forfeiture of the Fenway Place property in exchange for the DA dropping the murder charge. Callahan was the natural choice for putting that kind of deal together."

"So then you could go buy Pierre's interest at the forfeiture auction."

The bidding was now between the familiar-looking attractive woman and the RTC, and had moved to the $600,000 range. All of the other bidders had dropped out. "Right. But somebody outbid me. And that somebody is the murderer. That's why I told you to follow the money."

"That's right, you did tell me that, and that's why I did. You know what we found? We found that the winning bidder was some offshore corporation represented by a big New York law firm, and we couldn't even begin to penetrate its shell without probable cause to get a subpoena. But your theory seemed like a good one, so we decided to check out the other bidders. I mean, under your theory it stood to reason that the murderer would make a bid, but there was no guarantee he would win. So Dom"—Shelby nodded at the cop—"kept on digging. And you know what else he found? He found that some company named Arab Acquisitions was the second highest bidder, and that Arab Acquisitions also happened to be the high bidder at a couple of other foreclosure auctions. And at both of those auctions, you were the attorney. And it struck me: the name Bruce Arrujo keeps popping up in this case. Like a weed. And that triggered something in my mind. Why did you go to that baseball game with Pierre? You told me you hated baseball, and you also told me you never planned to stay at your firm for more than a year or two. So why cultivate Pierre as a client? Some people might do it just to be friendly, but that didn't sound like you either—I mean, you never went out of your way to socialize with him before. It just didn't add up, unless you had another reason."

Bruce nodded. It was always the stupid little details. That was the problem with intimacy—if he had reached orgasm sooner, Shelby never would have brought up the whole Woody Allen baseball skit, and she never would have known he hated baseball.

Shelby continued. "So, under your theory, I just kept following the money. If my suspicions were right, it would make sense that Arab Acquisitions would be here to bid today. So I watched carefully for your reaction when we served that injunction on the Springfield attorney. I'll tell you—the whole thing was almost worth it, just to see the look of horror on your face."

They stared at each other, neither speaking. The auctioneer broke the silence. "Sold! $640,000, to the young lady."

Bruce blanched. Shelby smiled broadly. "There's that look again. She got quite a good deal, huh? Recognize the winning bidder?"

Bruce turned to study the bidder again. As he did so, she met his glance. She smiled at him coldly, then removed her sunglasses, her hat, her scarf. Bruce gasped. "Carla!" She winked at him, turned away.

Shelby chuckled. "Oh, I forgot that part of the story. When I became suspicious of you, I went to visit Carla. She's the one who really had her doubts about you. Told me her kid wouldn't go near you. When I told her about the auction, and how the vacancy decontrol certificates had been altered, she just started laughing. She said she knew you were up to something, but she didn't know what. But she's no dummy, and she knew how important those certificates were to the property, so she went down to the Rent Equity Board and made certified copies of the certificates before she gave them to you. And now she owns the building—$640,000, and free from rent control. She might even be able to pay cash for it, given that it seems to me she and Pierre have quite a good case for malpractice against Stoak, Puck and Beal."

Bruce braced himself against a tree, fought to regain his composure. He had lost the treasure. And he had lost Shelby. As for his enemy, he—like Bruce—had had suffered grave losses; neither could yet declare victory over the other.

He looked back into the eyes of the woman he loved. "You've got everything right, except one thing. There's another player in this whole thing, and he's the killer, not me."

Shelby eyes softened, but only slightly. "I'd like to believe—at least—that you're not a murderer. I'm still listening."

*   *   *

An hour later, Bruce stepped into the lobby of his office building. He stopped, and looked out onto the street. He spoke in a normal voice: "Testing, one, two, three." Dom, sitting with Shelby and Jennifer Palmer in the unmarked police car, gave him the thumbs up sign. Bruce nodded, walked toward the elevator bank.

He pushed the 57 button, as he had hundreds of times before. It was late in the afternoon, and he was alone on his journey skyward. The doors opened, and Bruce smiled a greeting at the receptionist. "Do you know if Mr. Puck is in?"

"Um, yes, Bruce, I believe he's in his office."

"Thanks." Bruce walked down the hall, turned into a conference room facing the front of the building. He peered down to the street below; the car containing Shelby and Dom was barely visible. "Testing again, one, two, three." The passenger side door swung open in response.

Puck's office was just around the corner. Bruce didn't bother knocking. Puck's back was to him, looking out the window. "Puck, you son of a bitch."

Puck responded without even turning fully around. "Ah, Mr. Arrujo. So nice to see you. Have you fully recovered from your illness?" Bruce and Puck had communicated only by voicemail and memos since Bruce's return from his week on the beach.

"Fuck off. You know damn well I wasn't sick."

"Well, I knew you didn't have a viral infection. But I didn't for a moment doubt that you were feeling a bit under the weather."

Actually, Puck didn't look too good himself, like he hadn't slept or bathed in days. The smell of decay permeated the room, and Bruce noticed a feverish—almost yellowing—intensity in Puck's ice-gray eyes. "You're lucky I don't put you under the weather."

"Now, now, no reason for threats. I've been expecting you, and I have my little friend, Walther, here with me," Puck paused momentarily and patted his breast pocket, "just in case this little visit is anything other than a social call." Puck sat at his desk, motioned for Bruce to sit down opposite him. As Bruce sat, Puck reached under his desk and pushed a button—Bruce heard the door lock behind him. He hadn't planned on that.

Bruce felt his right hand curl into a fist, shoved it under his thigh. "Actually, this is a social call. I just wanted to tell you some good news: I purchased a nice condominium complex today. Got it cheap, too. Everyone else thought it was rent controlled, but I knew better."

Puck glared at Bruce, the partner's hands folded in a prayer-like fashion in front of his chest. The bright light of understanding swept across Puck's face, and Bruce saw Puck's pupils shrink to the size of ballpoints in response. Puck nodded slowly, bared his teeth in smile. "That would make sense. I had a feeling you might be behind that whole vacancy decontrol debacle." Bruce was a bit disappointed—Puck seemed almost resigned to the loss of his treasure. "I'm surprised you had the guts to pull it off. Or the brains to figure it out. You were sorely lacking in both when it came time to kill that transvestite."

Bruce had to admit that Puck was right. It had simply never occurred to him to kill Charese. And he doubted he could have done it anyway. "So you did it for me. You killed Charese Galloway. Strangled her."

Puck shrugged, then stood up and began pacing behind his desk. He held his chin high, the normally bowed neck now ramrod straight. "I will admit that his—or is it 'her', or even 'its'?—death was fortuitous." He glared again at Bruce, laughed derisively. "Poor boy. Poor simple boy. You had done all the hard work already. The whole thing about putting Felloff in as a partner when you knew Prefontaine had signed that affidavit was pure brilliance. Even I was impressed by that. And Prefontaine's joke to you about wanting to kill his tenant; well, it was just too perfect. You had set up the sting perfectly; all you needed to do was trigger it. But you had absolutely no idea how to separate that fool from his money."

"Let's talk about fools for a second. If you hadn't been so cheap, I never would have figured out you were the high bidder. But instead of outbidding me at the auction by, say, $25,000, you cut it so close that it couldn't pass as just a coincidence." Puck nodded slightly in concession to Bruce's point. "I knew then that someone must have accessed my computer records and learned what I was bidding. But you're right. I did have Prefontaine set up. And I was trying to figure out a way to get the RTC to make him forfeit his interest so I could buy it."

"Of course you were, dear boy."

"But there were other ways to do it without killing someone."

"Perhaps there were, but you apparently couldn't figure out what they were. Besides, none of them would have been nearly as effective as the murder. After all, absent the murder, the authorities wouldn't have given a damn about the affidavit; they only cared about it because they thought Prefontaine was a killer. Not to mention that, absent the murder, Prefontaine would have fought the forfeiture, and probably won. He only agreed to accept it as a way out of the murder charge."

Bruce had to admit Puck was right. Prior to the murder, he had been trying to come up with a way to ensnare Pierre with the false affidavit, but it was such a minor, technical violation of the law that he knew he wouldn't be able to get the authorities excited about it. He had thought a little publicity might force the authorities' hands, but that had been a dead end as well. Even Bailey, the coffee-drinking reporter, had shown no interest in the story.

Puck continued. "You see, you had put the noose around dear Mr. Prefontaine's neck. All you needed to do was kick the chair out from underneath him. Unfortunately—or fortunately, depending on one's feelings in these matters—the chair that needed to be kicked in this case was that transvestite."

"So you committed murder for a million bucks. To pay Lloyd's of London."

Puck smiled sadly. "I believe, Mr. Arrujo, that the correct figure would have ended up being north of two million. And, touché, I do owe a good chunk of that to Lloyd's of London—a debt, by the way, which they will now never collect upon." He bared his yellowing teeth to Bruce. "But come, come, let's not be so self-righteous. I believe there was a man sitting in jail these past few months—a father of a young child, no less—because you decided to make him a sacrificial lamb in your worship of the Almighty Dollar."

"That may be, but I didn't kill anybody."

Puck leaned his head back and roared in laughter, his Adam's apple bobbing like a buoy in a storm. "Ah, Mr. Arrujo, are you still rationalizing your life in that way?" Puck altered his voice, speaking in a mocking squeak. "It's okay for me to lie and steal, but I firmly draw the line at murder."

Bruce again balled his hand in a fist, again caught himself. He had won, not Puck. But why did it seem that Puck had gained control of the situation? Why was he acting so carefree? "Something like that."

"Well, you're still young. There's still time for you yet."

"Time for what?" Bruce didn't want to ask, but couldn't help himself.

"Time to slide a little further down that slippery slope. You remember the slippery slope, don't you Mr. Arrujo? The one they taught you about in law school? You know, if you make one exception to the rule, you will inevitably make others? Of course you do. Do you really think there is an ethical distinction between theft and murder? Can you really justify one and condemn the other? I mean, Mr. Arrujo, let's be honest. It's not like you're Robin Hood, stealing from the rich to give to the poor."

Bruce could not think of a response, so he looked away and remained silent. He had no desire to defend his code of morality to Puck, especially with Shelby listening on a speaker in the car on the street below.

"There, there, Mr. Arrujo. Don't despair. You're still young; you have time to grow. With a lot of hard work, you could become a killer someday yourself. 'In for a dime, in for a dollar,' as they say."

Bruce wanted to change the subject. He had come to clear himself from suspicion of murder, not engage Puck in some philosophical discussion about degrees of immorality. "So I figure I know the ending—you killed Charese, probably in some rental car that matches Pierre's. And you did it at the time you knew Pierre would be on his way home from Fenway Park." He paused here—hadn't Jan mentioned that Puck had an expertise in forensic evidence? "And you purposely left tire tracks and carpet fibers, knowing they would lead the police to Pierre." He paused here and looked at Puck.

"You don't expect me to actually confess to that, do you?"

"Whatever. And you somehow knew that I would take it the rest of the way, somehow complete the frame-up of Pierre and cause the forfeiture."

"I had much confidence in you, dear boy. I may have dealt you a stacked hand, but you played the cards beautifully. It was a fine line you walked—you had to give the police enough so they believed Pierre was the killer, but not enough so they could get a conviction. To be honest, I didn't know how you were going to pull it off. And then I saw the attorney-client privilege memo!" Puck paused and clapped once, loudly. "Nicely done, young man. But, then again, that's why we at Stoak, Puck & Beal hire only the finest young legal minds. The finest."

"Speaking of which, I don't know the beginning of the story. How long were you on to me?"

Puck put his forefinger over his lips in a mock pensive stance. Bruce was having a little trouble accepting that the theatrical, garrulous man sitting across from him was the same stooped, crotchety senior partner at Boston's largest law firm. "Let's see. How long have I been on to you? When was your first interview?"

"My first interview?!" Bruce cursed himself for showing his surprise.

"Poor, poor boy. Do you actually think I didn't know about you and your sordid past from the beginning? A firm like ours has many friends in the law enforcement community; it's a simple matter to cross check all applicants through their computers. And since I'm the firm's computer expert, I get first look—and in your case, the only look—at the data. Your name came up with bells and whistles, quick as you could say 'Bob's your uncle'. Why do you think I hired you?"

Bruce again was caught off-guard by Puck's disclosure. He was not used to playing the fool. He shrugged his shoulders in response to Puck's question.

"Because I needed a stalking-horse. I am, or I was, a man of not insignificant wealth. Unfortunately, a number of years ago I made what I thought was a safe investment of $250,000 in a Lloyd's of London insurance syndication. Well, between asbestos litigation and oil spills and natural disasters, I found myself on the hook for close to $3 million. As you may know, as a Lloyd's Name, one's liability to contribute to damage claims is unlimited."

Puck looked up to see Bruce smiling at him. Bruce couldn't resist. "I'm terribly sorry to hear that."

Puck grinned, almost as if he were pleased to see Bruce putting up a bit of a fight. "Well, such is life, dear boy. Sometimes our treasure-laden ships run aground. As, I'm sure, you know." Puck looked expectantly at Bruce for a response, but Bruce remained silent. "And it can be especially disappointing when the ship is so close to shore."

Bruce allowed himself a barbed response. "Unless the ship's insured. Then some crusty old Anglophile has to write you a big check."

Puck banged his desk with the palm of his hand. "Good retort, dear boy. Fine repartee." Puck looked across at Bruce expectantly, hoping for another thrust. Seeing none was coming, he shrugged and continued. "Well, anyway, I was able to pay off my Lloyd's debt, but only by borrowing and leveraging. This was a short-term solution, but I couldn't keep it up indefinitely. I was beginning to think that bankruptcy would be my only option, but a declaration of bankruptcy would have been such an unpleasant and dishonorable way to end an otherwise distinguished legal career. When you came along, I took the chance that you might help me solve my little problem. The worst that could have happened was that you had truly reformed yourself and would be a good little worker bee for us. As it turned out, you were my knight on a black horse."

"How did you know what I would do?"

"No, no, dear boy. I had no idea what you would do. But I figured you were up to something, and if I kept a close watch on you, I might profit from your mischievous little activities. So I gave you a wide berth and a free hand."

"That's why you let me handle the Nickel Bank foreclosures."

"That, and I made sure the other partners didn't put demands on your time. And I let you score a few minor hits. The cellular phone bidder at the

Marlborough Street auction was a fine play, by the way. But a quick check of the firm's cellular phone records showed that no call had been placed from that phone that day. And that fictitious lead poisoning letter from the tenant, that was also a nice touch. I had a nice laugh the night I accessed it from your computer files. Overall, I was very impressed by your little scams. I hoped they would give you the confidence to try something bigger."

Puck paused here to see if Bruce had any reaction, but Bruce continued to remain silent, refusing to give the old man the satisfaction of complimenting him on his sleuthing abilities.

"And, of course, you did try something bigger. And I almost missed it! I could tell you were positioning poor Mr. Prefontaine for something—the deal he made on Fenway Place was too good to pass up—but I couldn't figure out your angle. There was nothing in your computer records or your phone calls that gave me a clue. So I dug a little deeper, and started looking through the fax room files at all of the incoming faxes addressed to you over the previous few months." He smiled at Bruce. "Did you know that the firm makes a copy of every incoming fax before delivering it to the addressee? On my orders, of course. Well, that's where I found a copy of that wonderful little affidavit Mr. Prefontaine signed. So nice of that helpful lady at the RTC to fax it to you."

Bruce shook his head. Who knew that the firm kept copies of all incoming faxes? He knew that the firm logged both incoming and outgoing faxes, but he thought it was just for billing purposes. Paranoid bastards.

Puck continued. "Once I found that, it was clear what you were doing. Again, I tip my hat to you. It was wonderfully subtle the way you convinced all the parties that the best way to structure the deal was to make Felloff a silent partner. That phone call where you told Prefontaine the 'bad news'—that he couldn't give Felloff a second mortgage—was a classic. Well done, my boy."

So, as he suspected, Puck had been listening to his calls as well as accessing his computer. That's why he had switched to the lobby pay phones. What an idiot he had been to assume his phone and computer were private. But he was still unsure about one thing. "Let me guess. You made up that stuff about the FBI suspecting me in the Gardner theft. The other senior partners had no idea what was going on."

Puck nodded vigorously, grinning. "Exactly! I was trying to add to your sense of desperation. I thought if you expected you were to be fired, it might spur you into killing that dragqueen. But, alas, you disappointed me, so I had to...make other arrangements. But now you tell me—if you suspected me of the murder, why did you not simply tell the authorities?"

"Well, first of all, I didn't have any evidence. Plus, I knew you were tight with the law enforcement people. But mostly, I figured that if I ratted you, you would know exactly what happened and would tell the cops about my little scams. We were like the U.S. and Russia—we each had nuclear weapons pointed right at the other. If either fired, it would have been mutually assured destruction—you would have just ratted back on me. Then we would both be in jail. So, to continue the analogy, I had to beat you economically, not militarily. So I concentrated on getting the property back. And I had a good ally in the LAP people. Especially when I told them that the true owner of the property was Wesley Krygier."

Puck clapped his hands together in glee. "So that's why those rent control do-gooders were so tenacious in their attacks on me! I'm aware of Mr. Jeffries' personal animosity toward Mr. Krygier." He dropped his voice into a conspiratorial tone. "By the way, dear boy, whatever our differences, I think we can agree that Mr. Jeffries really is a twit."

Bruce nodded. "No argument from me on that one. I gave him your scent, and like the dumb Lapdog he is, he chased you down."

"Yes, he did. And he never figured out you had given him a false scent. He refused to negotiate with us. Then we tried every legal maneuver we could think of, but the judges in this state are just so damn liberal! A bunch of Socialists, is what they are. So again, nicely played." Puck put his hands to his side and bowed to Bruce.

When Puck raised his head, Bruce noticed a film of drool had formed on his chin. It continued to spread as he spoke. "But, to get back to your Cold War analogy, it should be noted that I still have my armaments, Mr. Arrujo." With a flourish, he withdrew the revolver from his pocket and did a little pirouette, the gun serving as a hat above his head. "I'm a madman with my finger on the button, as it were."

Bruce tensed, felt the sweat dripping off his armpits. He was seated in a small, locked room alone with a crazy old man who had just suffered a multi-million dollar loss. Bruce had caused that loss, the old man had a gun, and the old man had killed before. Bruce considered a leap across the desk.

Puck sensed his thoughts, reacted immediately. He leveled the gun at Bruce's chest. "Don't even think about it, Mr. Arrujo! Don't even so much as think about getting out of that chair." Bruce settled back in—he needed some kind of weapon himself. He took inventory of the room. Nothing visible.

He tried to buy some time. Maybe Dom had figured out what was happening and had made a mad dash for the elevator. Or, more likely, Dom had figured it out, decided Bruce would get what was coming to him, and opted to stay in the car to console Shelby. "You've got a gun aimed at my head." *Now you have no choice, Dom. Run for the damn elevator. Then kick the door down and save my butt.* "I'm not really in a position to argue with you."

Puck cackled. "No, I suppose you're not. All our scheming and planning, and it all comes down to who's holding the gun."

Bruce noticed a dark shadow pass over Puck's face, saw the pupils of his yellowing eyes widen, heard his breathing begin to labor. He sensed that Puck had made a decision, was about to implement it. The gun began to flutter in Puck's hand.

Bruce spun quickly in his chair, searching for something he could use as a weapon.

He saw an umbrella, an older style with a pointed metal end. He lunged for it, then heard Puck's cold voice: "Good-bye, dear boy."

Bruce heard the shot, closed his eyes, slumped down into his chair. He felt the splatter of warm, sticky blood on his cheek and on the back of his neck.

He waited for his body to cry out in pain, waited to feel the sensation of tumbling out of his chair and onto the floor, waited for his world to go black. He commanded himself to hold his bowels—he did not want Shelby to find him that way, on the floor, soiled.

Another second passed, and still he felt nothing. Slowly he reached his quivering hand to his face, opened his eyes and took a tentative breath of gunpowdered air. His lungs filled like a billowing sail.

He straightened himself in the chair and wiped the spray of Puck's blood and brain matter from his cheek. He was alive, and his enemy was dead, but Bruce felt no joy in it.

CHAPTER

74

Bruce spent the next couple of days at the DA's office, helping the authorities reconstruct the crime. They had promised him immunity from prosecution for his little scams, so he was willing to cooperate. He was also hoping he might see Shelby.

Finally, at the end of the second day of questioning, Jennifer Palmer addressed him. "You're free to go, Mr. Arrujo. Personally, if I never see you again, it will be too soon." Bruce wasn't sure if her animosity stemmed from her friendship with Shelby or from her resentment at being duped by Bruce into believing Pierre killed Charese. Probably both. "But stay here for a minute—Shelby Baskin wants to speak with you."

She left, and a few minutes later Shelby glided into the room. She looked tired and sad, but, as always, carried herself with a regal elegance. They looked at each other for a few seconds, then he spoke. "You may not want to hear this, but the loss of you is far more significant to me than the loss of Fenway Place."

She shook her head dismissively. "That's a crock, Bruce. You had the chance to come clean with me weeks before the auction. But you kept right on lying to me."

Bruce lowered his head. "I felt like I had to finish what I had started. But let's face it, Shelby—you never would have been able to love me if you knew the truth about what I had done. My only chance to keep you was to get past the auction, put my lies behind us, then try to build a life with you in the future."

"I don't know if that's true or not, Bruce, and it's not really relevant anymore." She rubbed the back of her hand across the corner of her eye. "But I've been thinking about this a lot the past couple of days. I realize now that when I called you a 'murdering scumbag', I was wrong."

Bruce straightened in his chair, searched her face for a hint that she might consider forgiving him.

Shelby continued, her blue-green eyes filling with tears. She spoke quietly, but firmly. "You told me once that you saw yourself as a sailboat, a combination of both the power and passion of the sea and the strength and stability of the land. I guess that's one way to look at it. But it strikes me another way. When I think of the way you try to live your life as some kind of combination of sea and land,

I don't think of a sailboat at all. I think of the sea and land combining to make mud. Your life isn't some graceful clipper ship, Bruce. It's mud. Dirty, useless, clingy, amorphous mud. Your face was covered with it the night I met you, and your soul is covered with it still."

Bruce lowered his eyes. Shelby, for the first time, raised her voice. "No, Bruce, look at me! Look into my eyes. I want you to feel what I say, not just hear the words. Maybe, just maybe, you can change. I know now that you didn't kill Charese. So, like I said, you're not a murdering scumbag. But you are a scumbag just the same. And I think you only have one choice—go buy that boat that you've always wanted, and sail far, far away. Look into yourself. Way down deep. Maybe there's something worth saving under the layers of mud. If not, don't ever come back. Because you're not meant to live with other human beings the way you are now."

He focused on a spot deep within the oceans of Shelby's salty eyes. The sea was wise in these matters, and the sea spoke the truth. Bruce straightened himself to accept its verdict: exile, but with the possibility of redemption. He nodded, and walked slowly toward the door.

He took one step into the hallway, then turned and looked once more into Shelby's eyes. "Please wait for me."

9 781583 486238